Monte Rio

A Novel by

Mark Joseph

Black Rose Writing | Texas

ISBN: 978-1-68433-142-0
PUBLISHED BY BLACK ROSE WRITING
www.blackrosewriting.com

Printed in the United States of America
Suggested Retail Price (SRP) $20.95

Monte Rio is printed in Giorgia

Monte Rio

Weaving spiders, come not here.
William Shakespeare
A Midsummer Night's Dream

Motto of the Bohemian Club

July 2009

Preface

Eleven miles inland from the Pacific Ocean and five miles downstream from Guerneville on the Russian River, the tiny hamlet of Monte Rio, California, pop. 1152, breathes a seedy air of decay. Once a prosperous logging town, Monte Rio lost its original purpose long ago when the coast redwoods were clear-cut to build San Francisco, seventy-five miles away. The town, which occupies both sides of the Russian River, now consists of a grocery store, a gas station, a trio of small riverfront resorts, a graceful old steel and concrete bridge over the Russian River, a quaint Quonset hut movie theater and cafe, an upscale deli, a few small restaurants along River Road, and one hard-core, shot-and-a-beer country saloon, the Pink Elephant.

While Monte Rio slowly declined over a century and a half into a pocket of genteel, rural eccentricity, 2700 acres of prime, old-growth redwood forest right next door to the little town were transformed into the legendary Bohemian Grove, the private campground of San Francisco's Bohemian Club, a veritable bastion of global power and privilege.

For most of the year, Monte Rio and the Bohemians ignore one another. From time to time a fancy car races across the Monte Rio bridge and disappears up Old Bohemian Highway in a cloud of high-octane dust. Bohemians aren't just one percenters. They are the top one percent of the top one percent, while most of the good people of Monte Rio occupy the other end of the spectrum. Sometimes a Boho stops at Pickett's Country Store and Delicatessen for a case of wine, but there is little interaction between the denizens of the Grove and the genuine country bohemians who inhabit Monte Rio.

There is little that is bohemian about the Bohemian Club, a wood-paneled gentlemen's club that occupies an immaculate, six-story, ivy-covered red brick building in downtown San Francisco. The name itself is misleading, the outermost layer of deception that veils Bohemians from the rest of the world. Most Bohos are fabulously rich, and Boho power is real. The membership includes two thousand of America's wealthiest men and their political friends: the Bushes, the Bechtels, the Fords, the Reagans, the CEOs of dozens of major corporations, senators, governors, and every Republican president of the United States from Calvin Coolidge to George W. Bush. A fair number of accomplished, like-minded artists, writers, musicians, and show business stars lend a certain pizzazz to an institution that, in spirit, is the opposite of a stuffy, old-world, London club. The primary goal of most Bohemians at the Grove is entertainment, no matter how exotic or expensive.

Every July since 1878 the Bohemians and their guests have gathered at the Grove for a seventeen-day mid-summer encampment, a conclave Herbert Hoover once described as "the greatest men's party on earth." During the encampment Bohos live in 120 camps with names like "Hillbillies" and "Ye Olde Owls" scattered among the serene hills and ravines of the heavily wooded grounds in beautiful Sonoma County. Most campsites are clusters of sturdy canvas and wood, old-school military tents, although a few camps boast glorious lodges designed by famous architects. Almost every camp has a valet or chef who caters to the members every whim.

Inside the Grove Bohemians do whatever they please – eat like Henry VIII, drink like Winston Churchill, shoot clay pigeons, act in a play, and generally behave like the rowdy fraternity boys many of them once were. A Boho can get drunk, walk around naked and piss in the woods, and no one cares. He can grill a prime steak over an open fire and shoot the breeze with a former president of the United States, and that's big fun. He can sing in a chorus with a Saudi prince or play poker with the governor of Arizona. And for every interaction among the prominent men at the Bohemian Grove, there is always a reaction among a multitude of conspiracy theorists who believe that what goes on inside the Grove is the work of a devil-worshipping blood cult, or worse.

Rarely does anything happen in the Grove that directly affects the citizens of Monte Rio. Nevertheless, the annual arrival of the Bohemians is a modest boon to local business. Many locals find work in the Grove as tram drivers and security guards, and thousands of

Grove employees patronize the bars and restaurants in town. The Bohos themselves pretty much stay inside the Grove. After all, that's why they assemble every year in their posh summer camp. Nevertheless, during the encampment, at any given hour, a handful of Bohemians will find reasons to visit the local towns of Guerneville, Occidental, Rio Nido, Forestville, Santa Rosa, and sometimes even Monte Rio itself. Bohos have been known to stash mistresses and boyfriends in vacation homes up and down the Russian River. In the twenty-first century this practice has become considerably less conspicuous since much of what was once illegal or considered immoral is now merely inconvenient. Nonetheless, some Bohemians still patronize local casinos and bordellos just as their great-grandfathers visited Santa Rosa's speakeasies during Prohibition.

During the encampment, the Bohemians take their privacy for granted. Security is simply part of the Grove ambiance, just like the giant redwoods, the fine food, the elegant wines and great music. The club itself employs a thousand guards, the Blue Blazers, and every July a swarm of government agencies surrounds the Grove with a thick blanket of high-tech protection. The Secret Service, the FBI, and the NSA form the center of a security web that extends to the California Highway Patrol and the Sonoma County Sheriff's Department. In some years, the main concern of all these agencies is the horde of protestors who from time to time descend upon the Main Gate on Opening Day, demonstrating against the one percent, the rich and powerful, the Establishment. The protests inevitably end well before sundown, usually without incident or arrest. The security apparatus then busies itself with checking Bohemians and their guests in and out the Main Gate, patrolling the perimeter of the 2700 acre enclave, and chasing down the deer that constantly activate the motion-detectors and infrared sensors that trigger automated alarms.

The Bohemians are surrounded by a dense forest of huge trees, thousands of guards and policemen, and every electronic security device yet invented. They feel safe and secure without really thinking about it. No one could possibly threaten the Bohemian Grove.

After all, who would dare?

1

It was great sport, spying on the Bohemians, a grand entertainment for The Russian River Society of Pirates and Thieves. "What good is life if it ain't fun?" Butler Rhodes shouted at least once a day to anyone within earshot. "Lord knows, in times like this we need all the fun we can get."

Since the Bohos cherished their privacy more than anything, penetrating the secrecy that surrounded the encampment was a tremendous source of satisfaction. If only they knew the things we could tell, hahaha. These captains of the universe think their shit don't stink, but guess what?

The Pirates had no intention of crashing the party by sneaking inside the Grove as waiters or cooks and secretly filming Bohemian rituals. They had no ax to grind, no agenda to promote, and no desire to sell their discoveries to the tabloids or post them on the Internet. It so happened that the Bohos showed up in their back yard every summer and presented the opportunity for some serious fun. The goal was not to reveal to the world that the Bohos conspired to loot and pillage vast tracts of the planet. Two thousand enormously rich capitalists did that every day without congregating in Monte Rio. No, the annual exercise of observing and recording Boho shenanigans was designed to test the Pirates' wits against the multitude of government agencies whose publicly funded duty was to protect the privacy of the Bohemian Grove. Like the National Security Agency, the Pirates spied with technical means: the most powerful radios, computers, lenses and microphones that money could buy – because they could.

A few locals knew more or less what the Pirates were up to. Marty the bartender at the Pink Elephant and General Pickett over at Pickett's Country Store and Delicatessen were aware of the Pirates, and Old Man Richardson and Deputy Alice guessed why Butler Rhodes and his roguish pals were always running around like demons during the encampment, but they didn't care enough to inquire too deeply.

After all, the Russian River Society of Pirates and Thieves was a small group of harmless goofballs in a town notorious for eccentric citizens.

.   .   .   .   .

As the sun peeked over the lush Sonoma hills to illuminate vast vineyards of pinot noir and sauvignon blanc, Opening Day of the summer encampment at the Bohemian Grove commenced with the thunder of massed motorcycles. The blast of dozens of Harley-Davidsons rumbling in unison just after dawn gave Monte Rio a wake-up call that seemed as though the Hells Angels instead of the Bohemian Club had chosen this rustic spot for a summer run.

Phillip Mercier knew what it was. Looking down on River Road from his kitchen porch, he could see dozens of flashing red and blue lights zooming past as a huge posse of California Highway Patrol motorcycle cops headed toward the bridge over the river, their assignment that day to serve as the Bohemians' first line of defense against the crowds of demonstrators who would arrive later in the morning by the busload from San Francisco and Berkeley.

The game was on. Opening Day had arrived.

A high school math teacher by trade, and at thirty the youngest member of the Society of Pirates and Thieves, Phillip fished a phone from his bathrobe pocket and called Jeremy Steadman, the Pirates' radio geek.

Before Phillip could say "Hi," Jeremy blurted, "I got 'em. It's biker cop heaven."

"They just passed by here. Must be sixty, at least."

"Yeah," Jeremy said, sipping a cup of double-pow espresso, his own blend. "They're going to the Pink Elephant for coffee."

Jeremy was an electronics maven whose year-round avocation was eavesdropping on government communications that were transmitted by radio. Bald, bearded, sixty years old and at least eighty pounds overweight, Jeremy always dressed in gigantic bib overalls and Birkenstock sandals. For several years Jeremy had arranged his annual vacation from his job as produce manager of the Guerneville Safeway to coincide with the summer encampment at the Bohemian Grove. Every July Jeremy engaged the Bohemian defenses with a formidable arsenal of radio receivers, scanners, computers, and finely tuned antennas.

Headset on, hunkered down in his little old house on top of Starrett's Hill across the river from Phillip's place, Jeremy sat in an ergonomic wheeled chair and faced a silvery radio console with twelve wide-band, computer-controlled receivers. This morning he had his choice of the California Highway Patrol, the FBI, the Secret Service, Homeland Security Special Ops, the U.S. Diplomatic Security Service, the California Army National Guard, the United States Air Force, the Sonoma County Sheriff's Department, and three crystal clear channels used by the Blue Blazers, the Bohemian Grove's private security service.

"What're the cops talking about?" Phillip asked.

"The Highway Patrol guys," Jeremy replied, "are laughing about how much overtime they're making."

Phillip stepped off the porch and shuffled across his scruffy, desolate back yard to the rotting fence where he could see a segment of the bridge over the river. The motorcycles were filing across two by two, their pipes reverberating all the way to the sea.

Just then, as the first streaks of daylight began to brighten the Russian River Valley, the roar of motorcycles was replaced by the hiccup of helicopter rotors.

Whop-whop-whop-whop-whop.

．　．　．　．　．

The helicopter awakened Butler Rhodes just after dawn. Groggy, his mouth sticky and dry, he listened to the twin rotors and knew it was a big Chinook from the Army National Guard battalion in Santa Rosa.

Whop-whop-whop-whop-whop.

His wife Maggie woke up and mumbled, "What's that?"

"Go back to sleep, babe."

"Is that a helicopter?"

"It's Opening Day, babe."

Fiery, red-headed, fifty years old to Butler's seventy, Maggie sat up in bed and frowned.

"Don't 'babe' me, Butler. You said you weren't going to do this anymore."

"I lied. It's too much fun."

Grizzled, tough as cheap jerky, Butler grabbed his jeans and a shirt and padded out of the bedroom, through the kitchen where he picked up his phone, and marched across the back yard littered with rusted metal fauna to a big, corrugated steel barn, his sculpture studio. His current projects lay in jigs on giant tables, or were partially assembled on the cement floor. An almost finished stainless steel and copper owl was center stage on a palette.

Butler's black Labrador Jojo ran in, tail wagging madly, and hunkered down at his master's feet.

Butler struggled into his pants, scratched his dog's head, and punched Jeremy's number into the phone.

"Hang on," Jeremy said to Phillip. "Butler's trying to call."

"You hear that big Chinook?" Butler asked.

"How could I miss it," Jeremy snapped. "He's right over my house."

"You listening to the pilot?" Butler asked.

"Of course."

"What's he saying?"

"He's talking to the AWACS plane from Travis Air Force Base that's always up there. AWACS, you know, the Always Wherever

Assholes Congregate plane. Whatever, the chopper is making a delivery to the Grove, and the AWACS is telling him it's clear."

Butler smiled. He loved Jeremy, champion nerd, radio ace non pareil. Jeremy could listen to just about anybody – the military, the cops, even his neighbors on their phones, which he usually declined to do.

"Here, I'll patch you guys in."

Whop-whop-whop-whop-whop.

"We're giving him the scenic tour," the helicopter pilot said into his microphone.

"Roger that," said the voice 30,000 feet above him, the radar chief on the AWACS plane. "You're clear."

"That's the Russian River, Mr. Secretary," the helicopter pilot said to the man sitting beside him in the co-pilot's seat.

"Call me Don," said a squeaky voice. "Is this how you navigate in Iraq, by following the rivers?"

"Yes, sir, but no one's shooting at us here."

A panorama of Sonoma County spread out below the big helicopter transport. Behind them lay the rolling hills of the Coast Range and mile upon mile of wine country vineyards. Ahead, the dark green river curved through the valley whose slopes were dotted with giant redwood trees. The chopper stayed right over the channel and hovered directly above the Monte Rio bridge.

"To get to the Grove you have to turn off River Road, cross this old bridge and go up Bohemian Avenue. About a mile up that steep hill you'll come the Main Gate. See all those motorcycles?"

"I see 'em."

"Cops."

"Uh huh," Don said.

"Who do you think that is?" Phillip asked.

"Five bucks says it's Donald Rumsfeld," Jeremy said. "His plane landed at Santa Rosa about forty-five minutes ago."

"You been up all night, Jeremy?" Butler asked.

"Oh yeah."

Phillip asked, "Anybody heard from Albert?"

"Not yet," Jeremy said. "I'll give him a call and get his fat ass out of bed."

"Ah, let him sleep," Butler said. "Besides, those motorcycles are going to be three blocks from his house in two minutes."

.   .   .   .   .

Albert Flowers, Ph.D., looked like Forest Whitaker for whom he was often mistaken, and he was the only Pirate who was not a native of Sonoma County. African-American, Albert was originally from Oakland, and more recently Stanford University and Silicon Valley where he'd made his fortune designing integrated circuits for network router switches.

Albert had arrived in Monte Rio ten years earlier with a cheerful disposition, a safe deposit box full of patents, an outlandish canary yellow 1989 Lamborghini LM002 SUV, and eight million dollars. Money and talent had made Albert a free man, and at forty he decided to move to the country. Driving along River Road one day, he stopped to take a leak beside a redwood tree, looked up, and realized in a moment of hilarious epiphany that he was in the one place that suited his proportions. Those trees were big. A one-time offensive tackle at Stanford, Albert, too, was big. His next stop was a real estate agency.

"What's your favorite book?" Albert had asked the real estate agent whose name was Susan Epstein. Susan was zaftig, Jewish, and from New York.

"Is this a test?"

"Yes."

"What do you want me to say? My favorite book is maybe *The Cat in the Hat*, or maybe *Goodbye, Columbus*. What's your favorite book, wise guy?"

"*Huckleberry Finn*."

"Black guys aren't supposed to like that book."

Albert smiled and unleashed the infectious and uproarious laugh that the good people of Monte Rio heard for the first time. Dogs lay down in the street and pricked up their ears. Toddlers giggled, their moms smiled, and Susan fell in love. Albert bought the third house he saw that day and paid one million seven hundred fifty thousand dollars cash for a tidy box on stilts on a quarter-acre of riverfront property near the end of River Boulevard.

"Who are the neighbors?" he inquired.

"Well, you have a young lady on the west side, Joanna Bucateli, who likes to sunbathe nude. I'm sure you'll find that amusing," Susan said. "And the house on the east side is a second home owned by a businessman from San Francisco who also owns a small vineyard on the other side of the hill. Mario Silva is his name, and he's a very nice man, very quiet, and he's not around much. I sold him his house about fifteen years ago. You couldn't have better neighbors, a naked lady and a guy who usually isn't there. And on the other side of Silva is the Bohemian Grove."

"The what?"

"The Bohos. Don't worry. They're good neighbors."

Six days later Susan moved in and a year after that they were married. Albert was content. He never washed the Lamborghini. If he weren't African-American, some folks might have thought he was a Boho, but of course, as Albert learned, eight million wasn't nearly enough.

.   .   .   .   .

Susan heard the motorcycles first.

"What the fuck is that?" she shrieked.

"It's Opening Day," Albert replied with a huge grin.

"Jesus fucking Christ. I forgot. I suppose you're going to spend all day at Pickett's with your buddies."

"Yup."

"You're going to get in trouble doing this, Albert. Why do you want to screw around with these people?"

"Because I can. Because I spent eighty thousand dollars buying Jeremy radios and computers so he can. Because I don't like rich Republicans. And mostly because it's a huge kick in the ass."

"You came up here to Monte Rio to get away from all those assholes. Jesus," Susan said, pouting as she tied the belt on her bathrobe.

Albert shrugged. "That was before I knew they came up here, too."

"Well, remember what happened last year."

"What about it?"

"You and Butler followed some Senator or whatever he was to a gay bathhouse in Guerneville," she said, working herself into a snit, "and got into a fight with his bodyguard."

Albert chuckled.

"A grown man, *Doctor* Albert Flowers, fighting in a back alley like a street punk."

"Sometimes a man's gotta do what a man's gotta do," Albert pronounced, laughing out loud. "It was great."

His phone rang as he headed for the shower. "Yeah!" he shouted into the phone. "Twenty minutes."

2

"This place is a God dammed *loony bin!*"

At ten o'clock in the morning this malediction erupted from the brightly lit interior of Pickett's Country Store and Delicatessen, followed by a screen door squeaking open and banging shut and then the heavy clump of boots across the porch. With a hollow metallic clank, Butler drop-kicked an empty Rainier Ale can toward the parking lot. Tracing a graceful arc across the blue sky and green trees, the can appeared to pause mid-trajectory, as though deciding whether to continue into orbit or return to earth. By the time it landed between Butler's vintage 1954 Ford pickup and Albert's Lamborghini SUV, Butler was lighting a Camel and muttering, "I swear, the Bohos show up and the world turns upside down. Just look at it. Jee-zus," he swore, waving his arms in a broad gesture that took in all of Monte Rio on both sides of the river, the regiment of CHP motorcycles in front of the Pink Elephant, the river with the redwood forest rising like an army of gigantic green soldiers from the far bank, and the writhing mass of anti-Bohemian demonstrators who were generating a bizarre political circus in the municipal parking lot across the street from Pickett's.

Butler was dressed for town in snakeskin boots, faded Levis, hand-tooled belt, maroon satin shirt with mother-of-pearl snaps, and a Mexican straw cowboy hat, attire selected to complement long, gray hair, droopy mustache, and ruby studs, four in his left ear, three in the right. He stepped off the porch and marched resolutely toward his compadres who were sitting at a picnic table under a sprawling fig tree. The table overflowed with beer bottles and cans that weighted down a red and white checkered tablecloth.

"Any place you're at is a loony bin, Butler," Jeremy remarked, blinking several times behind a pair of thick, rose-tinted lenses and tugging at the cabled earphones that connected his head to a computer-controlled radio receiver. The pockets in his overalls brimmed with antennas and electronic boxes.

"And calling this place a loony bin is like noticing a lot of trees in the woods," Albert said from behind a high-end, professional-grade, digital video camera, shaking his big, moon-shaped head – the dark side of the moon, he liked to say – and laughing his big Santa Claus laugh that flowed past the picnic tables, across the steaming highway crowded with Bohemian limousines and Russian River tourists, and over the heads of the banner-waving demonstrators.

Albert's hair was speckled gray, his eyes and mouth permanently wrinkled with a mischievous grin, and he always wore outrageously colorful Samoan shirts because they fit, just like his big Italian truck. Puffing a fat stogie and pointing the camera at Butler, he added, "I'm sure *The New York Times* would agree with you, Butler, but it's *our* loony bin."

Butler flopped on a redwood picnic bench, jammed his elbows into the tablecloth and scrutinized the parade of summer traffic on the slow-moving highway – summer tourists in SUVs, minivans packed with gawking families, pickups with Mexican farm workers piled in the back, and an amazing number of limos, Bentleys, Ferraris, and Aston Martins delivering Bohemians to the Grove.

"I wish that was true," Butler exclaimed, raising his voice. "But it's not, it's theirs." He gestured toward the highway. "Money rules, bud. The Bohos own half the fucking world and have their eyes on the other half, including the little piece that's yours and mine. We live by their say-so. It's because of them that General Pickett raises his prices through the roof."

"You're not thinking of joining the protestors and making an ass out of yourself, are you?" Albert asked.

The sound of a speaker's voice drifted up from the demonstration, the words distorted by the breeze but amplified by Jeremy's improvised, fiber-optic, parabolic microphone.

"These are the people behind every man-made catastrophe. These are the warmongers, the polluters, the deniers of climate change, the direct cause of climate change, the –" shouted the speaker of the moment, her words reduced to gibberish by the wind.

Having transported hundreds of demonstrators seventy-five miles from the San Francisco Bay Area, a herd of buses was parked beside a temporary stage. Between the buses and the crowd, dedicated activists behind a row of card tables distributed pamphlets, sold bumper stickers and solicited signatures for petitions.

Compared to the manifest might of the Bohemians, as evidenced by the constant flow of exotic and expensive cars and the brigade of motorcycle cops, the ragtag, scraggly, placard-carrying demonstrators were a swarm of small fleas on a very large dog.

Gazing toward the tattered collection of hipsters and progressives who were cheering the impassioned speaker, Butler bellowed, "These people think the rich getting richer and the poor getting poorer is news. They think their pathetic demonstration will make CNN and somebody will listen. Ha! Do you see any TV cameras today? No, 'cause these knuckleheads do this every year and nothin' happens. Nothin'! Maybe if they charged the gates and got a few of themselves massacred, that might make headlines, but that won't happen, either. No blood, no glory. They're as out of touch as the Bohos, and just as full of shit. And they're another reason why this is a loony bin."

"Oh, man," Albert said soothingly. "Relax. Enjoy the show."

"Instead of spying on these fucks and playing games, I'd like...I'd like...oh, hell, I don't know. You'd think the A-rabs would know about the Bohos. That would be serious."

"I'm sure they do," Phillip said. "The Bushes have Saudi royals in there every year."

Intense, wearing a San Francisco Giants baseball cap mounted backwards over his buzz-cut, Phillip was entering the license plate numbers of cars on the highway into a laptop, never taking his eye from the powerful telescope mounted on a squat tripod in front of him.

In the municipal parking lot, the noisy and energetic demonstrators were preparing to march across the bridge. At the stop sign next to the parking lot, a black Lincoln limo hesitated, then turned left and swiftly crossed the bridge. Butler followed the car by sighting down his arm to his thumb and forefinger which he pointed like a gun.

"Bang," he whispered.

Once upon a time Butler had spent twenty-six months in Vietnam and had come home with a healthy respect for armed citizens and an outlaw taste for dope, but that had been almost fifty years ago.

"Butler?" Jeremy asked tentatively.

"What!?"

"You all right?"

"I'd like to nail one of those sons of bitches, y'know? Catch him with his pants down in a whorehouse screwing a teenybopper. But what the hell, he'd buy his way out of it."

"Been there, done that," Albert snorted.

A pair of crows swooped out of the eucalyptus and caw-cawed into the fig tree. Butler picked up a stone and heaved it at the birds.

"How many so far, Phillip?" Albert asked.

"Over two hundred, about two-fifty-two. Most of these guys come in rented limos from the airport. Not much data there."

"We can listen to the limo drivers and their dispatchers," Jeremy said. "If we're so inclined."

"Whoop dee do," Butler mocked. "Limos, hot shit."

Spying on the Bohos had originally been Jeremy's idea. One day five years earlier, while monitoring federal frequencies a week before the Bohemian encampment, he'd noticed a surge of radio traffic from the Secret Service. He soon found himself listening to a host of federal and state security traffic. When Jeremy invited his pals to listen in, Albert promptly took him to a gray-market, underground, radio and communications dealer in San Jose, bought him whatever he wanted, then hooked up Phillip with his encryption software friends in Silicon Valley, and the Russian River Society of Pirates and Thieves was born.

"Anybody wanna listen to the FBI?" Jeremy asked. "They have three or four guys mixed in with the protesters. They're having problems with their equipment, so they're on a clear DEA frequency. One of their vehicles is real close, near the bridge. Unit Seven."

"This is Unit Seven approaching the intersection..."

"Fuck the FBI," Butler said.

"Okay, how about the CHP?"

"Forget it, Jeremy," Butler hissed. "You're the cop freak, not me."

"The demonstrators will start across the bridge pretty soon," Albert said. "That might be interesting."

"Nah," Butler said. "They're pussies."

As Phillip continued to record license plates, Albert picked up the thread of an old discussion with the math teacher, interrupted by Butler, on the subject of Noam Chomsky, a favorite quotation machine among the demonstrators.

"Chomsky is one of those people about whom everyone has an opinion," Albert said, "but few have actually read his work."

"Like James Joyce," Phillip said.

"Yeah, like Joyce," Albert agreed.

"Have you read Joyce?" Phillip asked. "Did you read *Ulysses* cover to cover?"

"Uh, yes, actually," Albert declared with a smirk. "*Finnegan's Wake*, as well. Did you?"

"No," Phillip admitted. "I haven't read Chomsky, either."

Listening with a twisted look on his thin face, Butler twitched his bushy gray-blond mustache and said, "You guys are full of shit. Noam Chomsky is full of shit. James Joyce is full of shit. The twentieth century is dead. Let it rest in peace. And so far the twenty-first doesn't show much promise."

"Why is James Joyce full of shit, Butler?" Phillip asked. "That's kind of off the wall."

From inside the store General Pickett was eavesdropping on the discussion through a microphone planted in the fig tree, and he suddenly wanted to know why James Joyce, a holy icon of English literature, was full of shit.

He was eavesdropping for no nefarious purpose but because he was interested in the discussion which had actually been going on for days. When the last customer exited the store, the general took off his apron and went out on the porch.

The Pirates knew the tree was bugged. Jeremy had suggested to General Pickett that he install a microphone and speaker in the tree so customers could order sandwiches and beer without troubling to go inside, but only the regulars knew it was there.

"Butler!" General Pickett shouted from the porch, "answer the question!"

The general's real name was Nguyen Van Duang, formerly Lieutenant General Nguyen Van Duang, Army of the Republic of Vietnam, and he'd exited Saigon when it was still Saigon and the exiting was good. After a successful run as a restaurateur in San Francisco, he'd purchased the store across the street from the Rio Theater from old Mr. Pickett in 2001. Butler had immediately recognized Van Duang, having met him in Saigon, and had named him General Pickett. A history buff, the General kept a copy of *Pickett's Charge* under the counter for semi-literate smart alecks who mentioned the Battle of Gettysburg.

Before Butler could articulate a response, a white Sonoma County Sheriff's Department cruiser crunched onto the gravel lot and Deputy Alice got out, slammed the door and glared across the street at the demonstrators.

Thick, shaped like a banana squash, a stone butch dyke with a pretty wife named Betty, Deputy Alice walked over to the fig tree, took off her cop hat, wiped her brow with her forearm and scowled at the demonstrators, the river, the bridge, and funky old downtown Monte Rio in the distance.

Without preamble she launched into a complaint against her boss, Sheriff Hix.

"I can't fuckin' believe it," she announced, "I got the fuckin' Bohos coming in, I got protestors, I got to liaison with the CHP and all this federal alphabet soup, and at the same time I got redneck wife beaters and homesick Mexicans with knives. It's gonna be a big crop this year, a humongous grape harvest, and that means lots and lots of Mexicans. And you know what's on Sheriff Hix's mind? Not the Bohos or the protestors or Homeland Security or our very own homegrown wackos. Ha! Hix is after the mythical giant pot farm that's supposed to be up the river somewhere around Healdsburg. That's what's on the sheriff's mind today. Maryjewanna. Pot. Weed. La mota loca. Christ. I can't fuckin' believe it."

When she finished, Butler asked, "Does he want to bust the farm or make them pay taxes?"

"Don't be cynical, Butler," Jeremy snapped. "Everybody knows you and Amory Hix don't get along."

"And you guys think this place isn't a loony bin?" Butler said with an easy chuckle.

A noise erupted from the other side of the river, the rumble of sixty Harley-Davidson motorcycle engines. The chrome posse of CHP biker cops roared up Bohemian Avenue to protect the Bohos from the demonstrators who were starting across the bridge.

"Oh, Christ," said Deputy Alice. "I'm stuck on this side."

"Don't they have a permit to march?" Jeremy asked.

"Yeah, they have a permit," the deputy sneered. "Even the Bohos can't stop that."

"Want a beer, Alice?" Butler asked.

"I'm gonna get me a Coke," the deputy said, heading for the store. "Or whatever he has in there that's cold."

Traffic began to back up at the stop sign in front of the Rio Theater as Bohos and their drivers suddenly found their route across the bridge obstructed by three hundred marching, chanting demonstrators. Three limos and a Bentley pulled into Pickett's parking lot. The limo drivers got out of their cars, leaving their engines running to operate the air-conditioning for their passengers, and convened on the gravel, shaking their heads and pointing at the bridge before resignation set in. After conferring with their passengers, the drivers went into the store.

"I know one of those guys," Phillip said. "Bobby MacIntyre. I've had both his kids in my Advanced Placement class."

Emerging with bags and bottles, the drivers delivered the packages to their charges who remained cloistered behind smoked glass.

Phillip hollered, "Hey, Bobby!"

"Mr. Mercier, son of a gun," said the liveried and sweating limo driver as he walked over to the picnic table. "How are ya?"

"I'm just fine. Bobby. Tell me about your kids."

"They're great, just great. Cathy has one more year at UCLA, and George joined the Navy and now he's a corpsman with the Marines. He seen some shit, I can tell you."

"I believe it. Wow," Phillip said. "Bobby, these are my friends Albert, Jeremy, and Butler. Gents, this is Bobby MacIntyre, proprietor of the world-famous Zinfandel Limousines. Who do you have in there, Bobby?"

"Oh, man, this is my fourth trip today. Man's name is Hoff. A.J. Hoff, and he's pretty pissed off at the protestors."

Deputy Alice came out of the store with a Dr. Brown's Cola in one hand and her cop radio in the other, holding it to her ear. The rear door of Bobby's car flew open and Mr. A.J. Hoff made a beeline for Alice's uniform and immediately began to berate her with a red face and manic gestures toward the demonstrators. Albert pointed his camera in their direction and pushed the record button.

"Uh oh," Bobby groaned.

"Don't worry," Butler said. "She can handle it."

They watched the deputy walk away from the outraged Bohemian, shaking her head and still listening to her radio. Wild-eyed, the Boho got back in the limo and slammed the door.

"You can take him around the back way," Phillip said. "Go back up the river to the Guerneville Bridge and follow the signs to Occidental Road. You'll come around on the Old Bohemian Highway. Maybe he'll give you a nice tip."

"Hey, thanks. Good idea."

Bobby hustled back to his limo, told the other drivers what he was going to do, then peeled out, followed by the other limos and the Bentley. Deputy Alice climbed into her Ford Crown Vic Police Interceptor, nudged across the highway through the jammed-up demonstrators, and took up a position near the buses.

The demonstrators began to chant, "No war! No way! Bring our soldiers home today!"

3

In the middle of all the commotion, a twenty-year-old, beat-up, faded red Chevy Suburban rumbled into the lot and stopped next to Albert's Lamborghini and Butler's pickup. The Pirates could see a pair of unusual radio antennas on the roof and two guys sitting in the front seats, the driver talking into a microphone while his passenger looked at the screen on his phone.

The Suburban's doors creaked open and a beer can and Burger King wrapper fell out the driver's side. The driver and his passenger glanced at the fellows under the fig tree, and they all stared at one another for a few seconds. The Pirates took note of the driver whose naturally blond hair was formed into dreadlocks. He wore a battered old Willie Nelson hat, silvered sun glasses, red neckerchief, denim jacket with no sleeves over a black t-shirt, filthy jeans, motorcycle boots and tattoos down both exposed arms to his knuckles. In contrast, his companion was a tall, conventionally coiffed blond white man in a light yellow windbreaker, plaid shirt, pressed chinos and shiny ankle boots.

"These are not Bohos," Phillip announced.

"You're a fucking genius," Butler declared. "They're not fishermen, either."

"If they go into Pickett's, they won't buy a danged thing," Albert declared with authority. "Five bucks says they won't drop a dime."

"They're cops," Jeremy said. "I think these are the guys I was listening to a few minutes ago. DEA or maybe FBI. Unit Seven."

"They don't look like government men," General Pickett said

through the speaker in the fig tree. "Too many tattoos."

"Feds," Jeremy repeated. "Take my word for it. And remember, George Schultz had a tattoo, and he was a Boho."

"Howdy," said the dread head, walking toward the picnic table.

"Good afternoon," Albert replied.

"Nice truck," the man said, waving toward Butler's Ford. "Is it yours?"

"Yes, thank you," Butler answered, determined to be polite.

"Store open?" asked the straight one.

"Most definitely," Albert replied. "If you're hungry, General Pickett makes a mighty fine sandwich. I recommend the pâté de campagne and a glass of Heitz cabernet."

"The what?" the man asked, blinking his eyes.

"The General will take care of you. Don't worry."

"Hey, Paulie," the tattooed one said. "Grab some beer."

The screen door banged, and the speaker in the fig tree reported the conversation inside the store.

They heard Paul say, "Hi, there. Got any chips? Potato chips?"

"Right behind you, sir," said the General.

"What's this?" Paul asked.

"Maui Wowee potato chips. The finest in the world, sir. From the Hawaiian isles."

"Eight dollars a bag?"

"Quality, sir, is worth the price."

Albert laughed and even Jeremy took off his earphones to listen. The dreadheaded freak gazed thoughtfully at the speaker in the tree.

Then they heard another customer's voice say, "They told us there'd be a demonstration today, and they said if we got stuck to come in here."

His friend replied, "This is an amazing place, isn't it? My God, he has a '98 Bonneau Chateauneuf de Pape. I wonder how much he has."

During the winter General Pickett's prices were reasonable and the fare less exotic, but in the summer the prices went up with the heat, culminating with the arrival of the Bohemians. Some locals and enlightened river tourists appreciated the General's gastronomic delights, but drop-ins often shrieked and giggled, expressing outrage and astonishment. Many were shocked into deep silence. The pretzels came from Pennsylvania, the pâté from Lyon, and the salami from Tuscany. General Pickett had Dr. Brown's Cola Drink, Cola Marimba from Jamaica, Kola Real from Peru, Boylan's from Brooklyn, but stocked no Coke, no Pepsi. He had 87 fancy, artisanal domestic and imported beers but no Bud or Miller Lite on the shelves, although he kept a few cases in the back for his regulars.

"How about a sandwich?" Paul asked the general, his voice uncertain. "Can I get a sandwich?"

"Of course. What would you like?"

"Man outside said try the I dunno what it was."

"The African-American gentleman?"

"Yeah."

"He's partial to the pâté."

"What's that?"

"In this case, pig's liver, a distant cousin of liverwurst."

"How much is that?"

"Fourteen ninety-five."

"For a sandwich? Whoa, Jack, wait a minute. Somethin' ain't right here, know what I mean?"

"I'm afraid not, sir. I don't know what you mean."

"Don't you have any, you know, regular food?"

"Perhaps you should try the Safeway in Guerneville, sir," said the general with an audible smile. "They may be able to accommodate your needs."

Paul settled on a Granola bar and six-pack of Corona Extra.

"Eight thirty-eight, plus tax," said the general.

Outside, Butler and Albert were in stitches, laughing and high fiving.

"You lose, Albert," Butler claimed. "Gimme five bucks. He bought some beer."

"Your friend seems unacquainted with local customs," Albert said to the Suburban driver, pulling out his wallet, extracting a five dollar bill, and giving it to Butler.

"I should've warned him," said the man with dreadlocks. "Look here, you fellas seem to have a lot of gear set up here."

"We're recording the demonstration for posterity," Albert said.

"You seem to be recording more than that. That's a wide-band receiver."

"Yeah," Jeremy said. "Lots of radio traffic out here today."

"And that's an unusual parabolic microphone," the dreadhead added.

"All the better to hear you with," Albert said with a smart-aleck smirk.

Butler moved close to the guy and said, "Do I know you? I seen you around town."

"Teddy Swan," the man said, introducing himself with a big grin. "Sometimes I go to the Pink Elephant for a beer."

"Yeah. That's right. That's where I seen you. I'm Butler Rhodes." They shook hands.

"Pleased to meet ya, Butler," Teddy said as his partner walked up.

The straight one asked, "You guys want a beer?"

Teddy said, "Butler, this is Paul, Paul Kruger, fresh from the wilds of Dearborn, Michigan. Paul, meet Butler Rhodes."

"Find what you needed inside?" Butler asked.

Paul laughed. "I don't know what that was in there. Holy Toledo!"

The screen door banged and two Bohos walked out, one carrying a case of wine which he stashed in the trunk of a Maserati Quattroporte. Phillip dutifully noted the license plate.

Across the street the first cadres of demonstrators reached the far side of the bridge and began to pass through the police motorcycles lining both side of Bohemian Avenue.

No war! No way! Bring our soldiers home today!

"Hey!" Jeremy cried, his eyes lit up with an aficionado's passion, "You guys wanna listen to the FBI? There's a bunch of 'em mixed in with the protestors."

Teddy looked at Paul, who nodded, and then Teddy said quietly but emphatically, "We *are* the FBI."

Teddy puffed up his chest a little and looked Jeremy and Albert and Butler each in the eye and from his hip pocket produced his FBI credentials, a gold badge and photo identity card. He smiled. Jeremy froze and began to pale, and Albert rolled back his eyes and started thinking about his lawyer in San Francisco.

"Can you turn off the microphone in the tree?" Teddy asked.

When nobody moved, Teddy reached up into the branches, found the mike and yanked out the wires.

"Sorry," he said. "Maybe we can fix it later."

Butler looked at Jeremy and Albert and they all looked at Phillip who was busy with his telescope and laptop and hadn't heard Teddy's declaration or seen his badge.

"Got one," Phillip announced. "Another Boho driving his own car, a Lincoln Navigator registered to William P. Anthony of Danville, California. Mr. Anthony, let's see, oh my goodness, is the Chairman of Shield Oil. Mr. Big Oil in person."

"Phillip," Albert said sharply.

"What?"

"*Phillip*," Albert shouted.

"What? Jesus. They're all stuck in traffic and I can read the plates."

Albert walked over, bent his face to Phillip's ear, pointed at Teddy and Paul and said, "These guys are from the FBI. The FBI, Phillip!"

Phillip jerked his head away from his telescope, clutched his laptop, blinked several times, then slowly turned his baseball cap around, bill forward, and sat up straight the way he would in a meeting with his school principal. The FBI? Ye gods. One wrong word and his teaching credential, his job, his life would be over. The idea of the Pirates was to spy on the Feds, not the other way around. Suddenly, the cozy little world of Monte Rio was screeching sideways, and Phillip felt as though his entire existence was going to crash down on his head in a matter of seconds.

Jeremy looked as though he'd been blanched by the sun and turned to stone. Like most radio geeks, he was more than a little paranoid and his worst fears had just been realized. They knew all about him! They had a file! A dossier! He was terrified.

With his hands spinning a little abracadabra flourish, Teddy declared, "And you gentlemen are the Russian River Society of Pirates and Spies."

Albert was checking his attorney's number on his phone. "Thieves," he corrected Teddy. "Russian River Society of Pirates and *Thieves.*"

"You know who we are," Butler muttered with a nod.

"Yes," Teddy acknowledged.

Butler stroked his mustache, lit a Camel, and looked ruefully at the sky. "And what we do."

"Right," Teddy said.

"So, are you gonna bust us?"

"For what? Snooping? Eavesdropping? No. Radio intercepts are not illegal, unless you listen to cell phones. Do you?"

When they didn't answer Teddy said, "I bet you have StingRays, though, don't you," and when Jeremy and Phillip continued their silence, he said, "No, gentlemen, I am not going to haul you off to the Sonoma County jail, although certain people would love for me to do just that. No. I'm going to hire you as consultants to the federal government."

There was a long pause, then Albert laughed his big laugh and blurted, "You gotta be kidding."

Teddy laughed with him. "Now, listen, there are some very important people who want you to cool your heels. They want you to pack up your gear and go away. And Butler, I know all about you and Sheriff Hix and your feud that goes back to high school. I know you're a Vietnam vet, and you, Albert, I know about your patents and your Lamborghini. I know all about all of you. Phillip, Jeremy, you, too."

Teddy had their full attention now. Paul popped open a beer and smiled at Albert.

"Nice shirt," he said. "Hawaiian, right?"

No war! No way! Bring our soldiers home today!

The demonstrators picked up the volume, and the traffic on the highway seemed to thicken under a cloud of smog, polluting the clear blue Sonoma sky.

Butler puffed his Camel and wagged his bushy eyebrows up and down at his fellow Pirates. "I told you this was a loony bin."

"Look," Teddy said. "There are people who don't like what you do, and they want you to cease and desist. One is a United States senator, and he has a lot of friends who can make your lives unspeakably miserable."

"Wiggens!" Albert blurted.

Teddy went on, "Let's just say that this year it's not in your interest to follow any Bohemians when they leave the Grove, especially Bohemians protected by the Secret Service. I don't care if some fucking senator is a screaming faggot any more than you do, but that's life on the big federal train."

"Wiggens isn't the only one," Albert said. "There's lots."

"Damn it, Albert," Teddy said sharply. "I know that, but I don't want you following these assholes on their midnight escapades and scuffling with federal agents like last year. You don't want to go to jail, and I don't want to put you there."

"Wiggens is the one who should be in jail," Albert said smugly, his big shoulders set in a posture of self-righteousness.

"Paul and I don't like the Bohos any more than you do," Teddy said earnestly, "but our job is to protect them. The thing is, see, you guys have what we don't, an overall picture of the situation around the Grove. With your gear, you can see our weaknesses, and we're going to write a report showing how vulnerable the Bohemians really are, not to mention how fucked up our inter-agency communications really are."

Teddy took a deep breath and said, "In other words, maybe you can protect the Bohemian Grove better than we can."

"Do you really believe that?" Butler squawked, incredulous.

"I don't know yet," Teddy answered. "But maybe. It's possible."

"Protect them from what?" Butler asked.

"Who knows?" Teddy replied. "It's a big, fat, juicy, soft target."

Butler smiled. "So it is, so it is," he said. "And you're not going to fuck with us?" he asked, mighty skeptical.

"That's not our intention."

"Does your boss know about this?" Albert asked.

"Oh, yeah," Teddy said. "Me and Paulie, we're not cowboys. We're not DEA. Our supervisor is Special Agent in Charge Carter McGee at the FBI office in Santa Rosa. Want his number? And beyond that the Sonoma County Counter-Terrorism Joint Task Force that's run by the Secret Service. You can call them, too, if you want. The guy's name is Raul Rodriguez and he's in the Grove."

Butler asked, "What do you think, Albert?"

Albert grinned and laughed his big laugh again, scratched the back of his neck and said, "It looks like we're caught with our pants down and our dicks hanging out, Butler. I think our little game has a new twist, so why not? What's to lose?"

"Jeremy," Butler said. "You with the program?"

Jeremy took a long time to answer. If he said no, every scenario he could think of ended with him in jail, or in the hospital with a heart attack, or something too awful to imagine. And if he said yes, it was inevitable that these two FBI agents would be in his house, sitting at his console, getting their greasy fingers all over his gear and discovering his bag of tricks. Did he take two weeks off from Safeway to play footsie with – he still couldn't quite accept it – the FBI? This was more than an invasion of privacy; this was a total demolition of privacy. On the other hand, if they really wanted his help to straighten out their communications mess, maybe they would show him some of their tricks.

"Hey, Jeremy!" Butler insisted. "Albert's right. We're caught. We're had. Our little game with the Bohos is over. Now we play the FBI game, all right? I can see inside your head, Jeremy. I can see all your crazy paranoid wheels spinning. Forget it, man. You've been listening to other people for years with your fancy radios, and now, the big wheel of karma has spun around. You can dig it. You take a little, then give a little back. Say yes!"

"What exactly do you want us to do?" Phillip asked.

"To start with, what you've always done – what you're doing now," Teddy said, "but a little more discreetly, if you please."

"You sure you want to sit around and watch us watch them for two weeks?" Jeremy said, dubious.

Teddy nodded vigorously and said, "What we really want is for you to help us make the Grove as secure as it can be."

"I don't see how that's possible," Butler said. "And why should we care about a bunch of zillionaires?"

"Because if anything happens to them, it's going to affect you and your town, that's why. Whether you like them or not, you're stuck with them."

Butler considered this cockeyed logic for a few seconds and asked again, "You're not going to fuck with us? You're not going to shut Jeremy down and confiscate his gear?"

"No," Teddy said. "You do what you've done for years, except you don't follow them around."

"But that's the fun part," Butler exclaimed, shaking his head.

Teddy folded his arms across his chest. "Sorry, but that's the way it is. Maybe you can help us pull off a few tricks of our own. That might be fun."

"Well, if it isn't gonna cost anything, okay. Why not?" Albert said.

The last of the demonstrators finally cleared the bridge and turned up Bohemian Avenue toward the main gate, impeding the traffic heading for the Grove.

"What's happening?" Teddy asked Jeremy who had never stopped listening to the speaker in his near-field receiver.

"Nothin'," Jeremy said. "Nothin' ever happens on Opening Day. There's at least four sheriff deputies up there just outside the gate, and all those CHP cops. The protestors whoop and holler for a while and then go home. All they ever get out of this is a bad case of poison oak."

Jeremy turned up the volume and Teddy heard a jumble of cop talk, all jargon and ten-codes.

"Who is this?" he asked.

"Sheriff's Department." Jeremy pushed a button, changing the channel, and said, "And this is the Highway Patrol."

"So Jeremy," Teddy asked, "are you going to co-operate?"

"What if I say no?"

"Then I call the NSA," Teddy replied instantly. "Would you rather deal with them?"

"Actually, the truth is," Jeremy squinted several times behind his rose-colored glasses, looking from Teddy to Paul and back to Teddy, "I like spooks. I'd like nothing more than a visit from the National Security Agency because we speak the same language. I could probably learn something from them, like for instance the other day I was reading..."

Bang! Butler slammed his beer bottle on the table, startling everyone, and shouted, "Jeremy! Just say yes!"

4

The last of the demonstrators crossed the bridge and headed east up the hill toward the main gate to the Bohemian Grove, and traffic was finally flowing slowly but steadily into downtown Monte Rio when Teddy shooed Jeremy and Phillip into his Suburban.

"Please don't puke in my truck," Teddy said to Phillip who looked like he was going to do just that.

"What I want to know," Jeremy said from the back seat, "is how you found us."

Teddy grinned into the mirror and said, "Wiggens. We've been tracking you since the incident in Guerneville last year."

"That was Butler's bullshit," Jeremy said. "Him and Albert."

"We know," Teddy said.

Butler left his truck in Pickett's parking lot and climbed into the back seat of Albert's dirty yellow SUV. Paul was in the front passenger's seat, plugging in an earpiece and calling Teddy on his phone as the small caravan pulled into the traffic.

"I think I better go up to the gate and get acquainted," Paul said to Teddy by phone. "And check out the demonstrators while I'm at it. I'll catch up with you later."

"Good idea," Teddy agreed. "They aren't gonna like you up there. They won't let you in."

"Let me out on the other side of the bridge," Paul said to Albert. "How far is it up to the gate?"

Scrunching up his expressive face into the epitome of disdain, Butler snorted and chuckled and said, "About a mile and a half, but you're wasting your time."

"We have seventeen days," Paul replied calmly as they reached downtown Monte Rio. In front of them, Teddy turned to the right, toward Starrett's Hill while the demonstrators went left up Bohemian Avenue.

"Stop here, please."

Albert braked and Paul got out, ran across the road and joined the last of the demonstrators starting the steep climb up to the Main Gate.

"Do you believe these guys?" Albert vented when he was alone in the car with Butler. "A white FBI agent in dreads, of all things, and another one who looks like an ad for Banana Republic."

"I'm not sure yet," Butler said. "I don't know what they really want."

"Should we call the FBI in Santa Rosa and make inquiries?" Albert asked.

"Are you nuts? Why go looking for more trouble?" Butler snapped.

"Just askin'."

"They can't do nothin' to me and you, Albert, but they surely can fuck with Phillip and Jeremy, so let's not provoke them."

They could see Teddy's truck disappear around a bend ahead of them.

"Well, you were right about one thing," Albert said. "This indeed is a fucking loony bin and we've been called out by the loonies. We'd better get on up the hill and see what the FBI is gonna do when that dude sees Jeremy's radio shack."

. . . . .

Covered with vines and faded red paint, Jeremy's little house sat high on the hill overlooking the river, the bridge, and downtown Monte Rio. A small greenhouse filled the back yard, but the only things Jeremy nurtured under its translucent plastic panels were radio antennas. The panels let radio waves in and kept airborne and satellite cameras out.

Guarding the premises, a four-foot-wide stainless steel tarantula fashioned by Butler crouched at the base of a giant redwood.

The instant Teddy turned into the driveway, lights began flashing in the driveway and The Who's *Won't Get Fooled Again* rumbled out of loudspeakers in the vines.

"Do your neighbors ever complain?" Teddy asked.

"They know I don't like surprises," Jeremy said tersely, pulling an infrared remote from his overalls. "And neither do they."

Jeremy got out of the truck, shut off the music and lights, leaned back in the truck window and asked Phillip, "Are you okay?"

Pale and sweating, Phillip said, "No. I think I'm gonna be sick. I wanna go home."

Teddy turned around in the front seat and told him, "You can stash your weed later, Phillip. I'm not gonna bust you for pot, so stop worrying about it. Besides, it's legal if you have a California medical marijuana card, and I'm sure you do, like everyone else. Light up now if you like. Medicate yourself. I don't give a shit."

Albert and Butler pulled in behind Teddy's truck and got out. Jeremy dredged a huge bunch of keys from his overalls, unlocked three locks on his front door, stepped inside and shut off two alarm systems. The house smelled musty in spite of filtered air-conditioning that kept the air clean and the radio gear cool.

Jeremy's listening post filled most of his small living room with computers and high-tech radio equipment arrayed in a horseshoe around a central console. The automated system was scanning thousands of frequencies and logging signals even in Jeremy's absence. Six flat screen monitors and dozens of blinking LCD displays gave the place the eerie atmosphere of a war room.

"Holy moley," Teddy said. "Where'd you get all this stuff?"

"Albert bought most of it in San Jose, but a lot comes from eBay," Jeremy answered. "Some is government surplus off the shelf, and some custom-built. It's a game of cat and mouse. The government — you, Special Agent Swan — knows people like me exist, so when you change frequencies and encryption systems and tweak this and that, then we have to play catch-up, so we build what we need."

"And the software?"

"I wrote some," Phillip volunteered. "Albert and his friends in Palo Alto helped a lot."

Albert and Butler came inside and stood awkwardly around in Jeremy's tiny living room which was not designed for guests. Huddled together, the Pirates and the FBI crowded toward Jeremy's radio console.

"So let's check it out," Teddy said.

Jeremy slipped on his headset and sat down at his console.

"Okay," he said, turning up a small speaker. "This is Grove security Channel One. They have three channels in the 400 megahertz range, but most of the traffic is right here."

"Cola Five," said a voice though the speaker. "Chickpea is through the gate and heading west on the Avenue."

"Cola One. Check, Cola Five. I'll call the Sheriff and let him know."

The loudspeakers cackled and buzzed and the entire console seemed to come alive.

"Cola Five is the Grove security shack at the Main Gate," Jeremy said, "And Cola One is the Grove dispatcher in the main security administration building. What this means is Chickpea is going out the gate, and to inform the sheriff's deputies right there at the gate, the guard shack has to call the sheriff's department dispatch office in Santa Rosa on the phone."

Jeremy tapped on his keyboard and "Chickpea" popped up on the main monitor, followed by a series of numbered notes.

"Yes, sir. Hello, Mr. Secretary," Jeremy said to Teddy. "Chickpea is in fact the Secretary of Energy of the United States of America, his very own self. Hello, Chickpea! Welcome back to Monte Rio."

"The truth isn't out there," Jeremy liked to say, waving at the universe and imitating the X-files. "It's right here, it's everywhere, and all you have to do is tune in."

He turned to Teddy and Paul and explained, "Last year Chickpea, this sterling example of public service, visited Mary's Russian River Massage Parlor and Escort Service six times. Do you find that interesting? Looks like he's at it again. Five will get you ten that's where he's heading. Since you don't want us to follow him, we may never know. You know, the Secret Service really should change its code words."

"The Grove security guys are talking in the clear," Teddy said. "That's not so bright."

"Yeah," Jeremy said with a grin. "Grove security has a fancy new digital system, high-end, very expensive, but the encryption system is too difficult to use, so they talk in the clear because they're lazy. Then the sheriff and the Secret Service get in on the act, and I can listen to them, too. It's not a mystery. Let's check in on the sheriff's department."

The edgy voice of a female dispatcher scratched through the speakers, "Unit 42, this is dispatch, do you need an ambulance?"

"That's a negative. We're under control here."

Jeremy said, "That's Alice, our favorite deputy."

"She a local?" Teddy asked.

"Oh, yeah. Alice grew up here in lesbian heaven and never left."

Opposite the radio console, most of the wall was covered by a very large map composed of satellite photos of the Bohemian Grove and surrounding communities. The map revealed the huge parking lots and central structures of the Grove, all 120 campsites, the roads, security bunkers, lakes and ponds, main lodges and administration buildings, dining areas, and outdoor theaters. The map was dotted with dozens of multicolored pins that represented the Bohos and the various agencies, their operatives and charges. Reds were Bohos, blues were Grove security, white was the Secret Service, and black was the National Security Agency. During each listening session the Pirates moved the pins around, often making guesses as to the locations of their targets.

Hastily, Phillip scribbled "Chickpea" on a tiny flag and stuck the red pin on Fourth Street in Guerneville.

"Jesus," Teddy said, walking over and studying the map. "Satellite?"

"Your basic Google map of the Grove is very low resolution, on purpose, and you can't see shit," Jeremy said. "But foreign satellites have no restrictions and no blackouts, if you know how to find them and access their data."

Teddy said, "So you know where every one of these guys is all the time."

"No," Jeremy said. "We guess a lot, and we never have all of them. They move around inside the Grove all the time, and are identified in person over the radio, along with their camps. When there's a lot of radio activity around Hillbillies Camp, for example, we know that very important persons are there. Like presidents and kings."

"We try to be thorough," Phillip said, "but it's unbelievably boring, listening to the radios and sticking pins in the map. You sure you want to sit here for two weeks and watch us track these guys all over creation?"

"You don't seem to mind putting in the time," Teddy said.

"Shouldn't you be catching bank robbers, or whatever it is the FBI does?" Phillip whined. "You sure don't look like any FBI guy I ever heard of."

"You had me pegged though, didn't you, Jeremy." It was not a question.

"You're Unit Seven," Jeremy replied. "It wasn't difficult."

"I wasn't trying to hide," Teddy said. "I knew you'd be listening."

"You couldn't hide if you wanted to," Jeremy said. "One of your FBI repeaters is down, and your guys haven't fixed it yet so for the last three days all FBI radio traffic from the Santa Rosa field office has been carried on two non-encrypted DEA frequencies."

"So you know about that," Teddy said.

"Of course," Jeremy snorted.

At that moment one of the speakers buzzed with a new sequence of voices.

"Unit One, clear."

"Unit Two, clear."

"Unit Three, clear."

"Unit Four, clear."

"See what I mean?" Jeremy said. "Those are your Special Agents in among the demonstrators."

Teddy speed dialed his phone.

"Paulie?"

"Yeah man."

"Everything cool?"

"Way cool. Lots of pretty women out here taking a hike through the woods."

Teddy ended the call, stood up and contemplated the large, elaborate map, then asked, "Do you guys think anybody else does what you do?"

"What? Track the Bohos? I don't know, but I'd be surprised," Jeremy answered. "They'd have to have as much money as Albert."

"And the inclination," Teddy added. "You guys do it for kicks. Why would anyone else go to all this trouble?"

"Kidnappers," Albert answered emphatically. "That's what all the security is for. Kidnappers. That's what I would do if I was a bad guy, kidnap one of the sons of bitches while he was out getting laid."

"Right!" Phillip said.

"No," Jeremy said. "You want to do a snatch, you do it at the airport in Santa Rosa. You turn up as a limo driver or something like that."

"You've thought about this?" Teddy asked.

"Sure," they all said together.

"How about an assassination. Have you thought about that?"

"That's Butler's department," Jeremy said. "He was in Vietnam."

"Hmmm," Teddy mused. "What's your part in all this, Butler?"

Butler placed one of his hands on his hip and used the other to point to his friends, like a rock star introducing the members of the band.

"Albert pays for everything," Butler said, gesturing toward the money man who smiled and saluted. Then Butler turned toward Jeremy at his console: "Jeremy finds the Bohos with his radios," and finally Butler indicated Phillip who was pale and sweating but sitting with his laptop in a folding chair next to Jeremy, "Phillip identifies them with his computers and very expensive data bases, and I follow them around on their escapades."

"And take pictures," Teddy said.

"So what? I take a lot of pictures, with a real camera, by the way, not a phone."

"What do you have against the Bohos?" Teddy asked.

"Nothing," Butler replied with a smile. "Who could possibly have anything against a bunch of billionaires?" Butler let the words hang in the air for a moment, then added, "But now, Mr. FBI, you say I can't chase them around any more. Okay! Far be it from me to mess with the Eff Bee Eye! So, Jeremy, you know Albert and me are not gonna sit here all day and listen to cops. No way. Teddy, as we say here in West County: Dude! Adios! Hasta la vista! Maybe I'll see you around the Pink Elephant. Let's go, Albert. Vámanos!"

And with that, Butler and Albert walked out, got into Albert's yellow Lambo and motored back across the bridge to Pickett's parking lot and Butler's pickup.

The lot was full and the line to the deli counter was out the door.

"I'm gonna get a sandwich," Albert said, getting in line. "You hungry?"

"Nah, I got a piece I gotta finish," Butler said with a wave, getting into his old Ford. "Gotta pay the bills. See ya later, alligator."

5

The most spirited and fit anti-Bohemians charged up Bohemian Avenue with banners and irrepressible zeal. Paul could hear them chanting in the distance – No more blood for oil! No more blood for oil! – as he trudged along with the last echelon of stragglers whose desire to protest was being eroded by the hill. Some gave up and turned back, while others took pictures and texted their friends about their adventure.

Every fifty feet along the road a CHP officer in helmet and flak jacket stood near his motorcycle, arms folded, pistol, nightstick and flashlight arranged for intimidation, silvered sunglasses reflecting the passing throngs. When Bohos came up the road, their cars moving at a walking pace through the crowd, the heavy police presence convinced the demonstrators to let the vehicles pass without beating on their roofs.

Paul easily picked out three of the four FBI Special Agents dispersed among the crowd – wrong shoes, wrong haircuts, visible earpieces, and that special arrogance that announced, "I'm a G-man!" He figured he looked equally charming, but it had never been his desire to go undercover and dress the part, like Teddy Swan. Geez, that guy! Teddy was crazy but maybe the most effective federal agent Paul had ever known. He and Teddy had worked together in a counter-terrorism unit in Fresno, and they had worked a few Super Bowls and other special events, but he hadn't seen Teddy for three years until two days ago.

One day last week Paul was in Detroit receiving his certificate in

Arabic language studies, and the next day he was told to report to the FBI field office in Santa Rosa, Sonoma County, California. When he showed up in the office of Special Agent in Charge Carter McGee, he was summarily assigned to the Bohemian Grove detail and reunited with Teddy Swan.

The Bureau works in mysterious ways, Paul thought as he walked through the northern California woods. He'd spent two years learning Arabic, becoming a specialist, and now his expertise was being put to brilliant use here among the redwoods.

"Why am I here?" he'd demanded of Teddy the day before yesterday in a Santa Rosa Denny's. "Why the fuck am I here? I expected to be assigned to an embassy somewhere in the Middle East."

"They said you were available, between assignments, so I asked for you, Paulie, because I know you, and because you're not a fucking moron," Teddy had answered. "I tell you, man, the joint task force assigned to the Bohemian Grove is a bunch of federal idiots in cheap suits, dark glasses and black Suburbans. And the locals are worse. The sheriff is a harebrained lunatic, and Grove Security has a thousand guys in blue blazers, but the Secret Service really runs the show inside the Grove. That means the Bureau is outside. That's our jurisdiction, everything surrounding the Grove, but the point is, inside the Grove and outside, all these agencies, including the Bureau, believe throwing their weight around will scare off any bad guys. Ain't gonna happen."

Paul had asked, "Got a whiff of any bad guys?"

"Not yet," Teddy had replied. "I've been here six weeks and I haven't seen jihadis parading through downtown Monte Rio with a black ISIS flag. But they're here, Paulie. They have to be here because it's too big a target for them not to be here. But Arabs are your thing, and that's a bonus, but you know me. I'm always on the look-out for our own home grown types. And that brings us to the Russian River Society of Pirates and Spies."

"The what?"

"Now listen," and Teddy had explained to Paul about these four guys in Monte Rio who made a game of spying on the Bohos every summer. "The Pirates have pissed off a lot of people, the Chief Justice of the State of Nevada, the Chairman of Wells Fargo Bank, United States senators, people like that. Last year this Senator Wiggens from Florida..."

Paul had interrupted, saying, "That far right Christian lunatic from Sarasota?"

"Yeah, him," Teddy had nodded enthusiastically, "except he's a closet fag, thank you very much. So one night last year Wiggens leaves the Grove to go to this gay bath house in Guerneville in his fly yellow Corvette, and the Pirates follow the Corvette and Grove Security follows the Pirates and the Secret Service follows Grove Security, and when Butler Rhodes starts taking pictures, there's a little tussle. Albert Flowers smacks one of the Blue Blazers and he's out for the count. No arrests, and since the Secret Service took the flash memory card out of Butler's camera, no pictures, either, but a few scrapes and bruises. So this year the Secret Service wants the Pirates to stop following Bohos around to bathhouses or whorehouses or crack houses or any other kind of houses."

"So let the Secret Service do their own dirty work," Paul said. "We're not federal errand boys, for chrissake."

"No. Listen! The Pirates are going to be our best friends. The best way to deal with people like this is to co-opt them," Teddy said. "Carter McGee figured it out. He wants to straighten out this communication mess and make the Bohemian Grove as secure as it's supposed to be, the way all these fucking idiots think it is, but it isn't, and we need the Pirates to do it. And — here's the thing, Paulie, if the bad guys are Muslim terrorists, they will use radios and phones, and a foreign language, maybe Arabic, maybe, who knows? Chechen or Farsi. If Jeremy can find them in the radiosphere, maybe you and I can find them in Monte Rio."

"Good luck, Teddy," Paul said. "This is fear-mongering, paranoid bullshit."

"Well," Teddy shrugged and grinned, "if nothin' happens, you get two weeks vacation in the redwoods on the Russian River, then maybe you go to Egypt. That ain't too bad."

There had to be more to it than that, Paul thought. Teddy had been undercover in Sonoma County for six weeks and blended right in, which explained the dreadlocks and the tattoos. That's how he found the Pirates in the first place, but there had to be more to it than just a communications mess.

Paul arrived at the crest of the hill. At the end of Bohemian Avenue, the Main Gate to the Grove was blocked by four white sheriff's department cruisers, one of which moved aside to let Boho cars pass, then moved back into place, securing the gate. Fifty feet from the police cars, two hundred impassioned demonstrators chanted, "No more blood for oil. No more blood for oil."

The deputies looked uncomfortably hot in their riot gear, but they were trained to ignore the taunts and jeers. The demonstrators were as disciplined as the cops, and everyone understood the rules. So long as no one started throwing rocks and bottles, no heads were going to be broken. Paul realized he was standing in the middle of a bizarre ritual in which everyone played a role, and that pissed him off. No anarchist crazies. No suicide bombers. No agents provocateurs. No threat to the Bohemians at all. He was wasting his time, just as Butler said he would.

He flashed his bureau creds at the deputies and approached the small, wooden pedestrian gate next to the heavy, welded iron gate over the road. Just beyond the smaller gate, the door to an old redwood guard shack opened, and four burly Grove security guards in blue blazers, gray slacks and clear plastic earpieces moved to bar his passage.

"FBI," he said, showing his badge and photo ID.

One of the guards bent over to inspect Paul's credentials. "Let me check, Special Agent Kruger," he said courteously, stepping back through the gate and inside the shack to pick up a hand-held radio.

Ho ho. Hey hey. Bring our soldiers home today.

Paul stood quietly by and watched a limousine draw near the gate. One of the sheriff's Crown Vics moved aside, and the big Lincoln pulled forward. Exceedingly polite, one of the guards stood by one of the rear passenger's windows and checked the member's Bohemian

Club ID and formal numbered invitation, then announced his arrival by head-set radio, giving the Boho's name and invitation number to the Blue Blazer command post on the far side of the vast parking lot, two hundred yards away. Seconds later, the command post cleared the arrival, the iron bars of the gate swung noiselessly aside and the car rolled through and into the lot. No one checked the driver.

Paul picked out two cameras trained on the gate, and two more high in the trees aimed at the road. The guards, he noted, were unarmed, and no weapons were visible inside the shack. They could see anyone approaching but could never stop anyone determined to crash the gate.

"Special Agent Kruger, wait here a moment, please."

"Thank you."

Two more cars passed through before Paul noticed a golf cart buzzing through the parking lot toward the guard shack. When it stopped near Paul, a stout but vigorous middle-aged man with marine-cut silver hair, sunglasses, and a perfectly tailored sky blue blazer hopped out.

"Special Agent Kruger? I'm John O'Shea," he announced to Paul with the air of a man used to command. "Chief of Grove Security. I thought you might be the one with the hair."

"That's my partner," Paul said, instantly annoyed.

"That guy, good lord..." O'Shea's voice trailed away, dripping with contempt.

"I'm not here to discuss Special Agent Swan," Paul said. "Since we're going to be working together on the Joint Task Force, I thought I'd introduce myself to you and the Secret Service."

"I appreciate that, Agent Kruger, but as you can see, it's Opening Day and we're very, very busy." O'Shea crossed his arms and spread his feet in a posture of defiance. "And I'm sure the Secret Service is equally busy. No one informed me that you were coming, but if you want to come inside the Grove, have your superior Special Agent in Charge Carter McGee contact my office, and we'll see what we can do."

With a nod of O'Shea's head, all the Blue Blazers turned and glared at Paul.

Paul looked at O'Shea and his coterie of upscale thugs, then turned around and looked at the deputy sheriffs and CHP motorcycle cops who were watching, and finally at the protestors who were oblivious to everything except their cause.

Ho ho. Hey hey. Bring our soldiers home today.

Then he texted Teddy: You were right. They won't let me in.

. . . . .

Paul walked back down the hill to the center of town, then up Starrett's Hill until he recognized the cars. From the porch he heard the crisp crackle of radio chatter, static punctuated by ten codes and cop talk.

Inside the radio room the lights were dimmed, the shades drawn, the small space crammed with folding chairs. By the time Paul arrived, Albert and Butler were long gone. Phillip had raced home on Jeremy's bicycle, buried his stash of weed in the back yard, taken a shower, swallowed a bottle of Pepto-Bismol, and then returned.

Jeremy was listening as the Blue Blazers checked in each Bohemian Club member and guest by radio at the gate, identifying him by name, membership number and the name of his camp, providing a wealth of information about hundreds of individuals who would be shocked to know what was being said about them on the air and in the clear.

While Jeremy listened to the Blue Blazers, Phillip was monitoring a number of federal frequencies, including the Secret Service and the FBI. Teddy and Paul administered the map, inserting and moving colored pins that tracked the Bohemians' movements, and incidentally becoming familiar with the geography of the Bohemian Grove and the surrounding area.

The radios clicked and chirped; the voices droned with bureaucratic tedium, the argot and slang endless and repetitive.

"Copy, Unit Five?"

"I copy, Control."

By one o'clock in the afternoon of Opening Day, Friday, 467

Bohemians had checked in at the Main Gate, and 467 pins were stuck into the big map. Five had gone back out the gate and two were being trailed by the Secret Service.

They listened as Deputy Alice resolved two more domestic disputes, one of which resulted in the arrest of Maynard P. Stow. Maynard had delivered one swift jab and knocked his wife Gracie out cold. Maynard was drunk and feeling remorseful. Deputy Alice got the cuffs on him, put him in the back seat of her car, called the paramedics and waited for them to collect Gracie, equally drunk and snoring through her broken nose. Three hours later, after hauling Maynard to the county jail in Santa Rosa, Alice came back to Monte Rio in a bad mood and cited two limo drivers for speeding.

Around three in the afternoon the last demonstrators shuffled back to their buses, having accomplished little but nonetheless assured of their righteousness. The CHP biker cops saddled up and zoomed off, leaving Monte Rio with one last chorus of blazing exhaust.

Teddy and Paul went into Jeremy's back yard next to the greenhouse to watch the motorcycles cross the bridge and disappear up River Road. All around them the sun beat down on the magnificent redwood forest. The river curled away to the sea, and Monte Rio was at peace.

"They're here somewhere, Paulie," Teddy said, "We just have to find them. I need to pick Butler's brain."

Late in the afternoon, three government executive jets checked in with the high-flying AWACS watchdog before landing at Santa Rosa. When their passengers arrived at the Grove an hour after touchdown, Phillip stuck three flags on the big map: "Four-Eyes," a former Vice-President of the United States, "Brass Balls," the junior United States Senator from Arizona, and "Sodapop," the Republican whip in the United States House of Representatives. Jeremy tracked them all by listening to the Blue Blazers, the Secret Service, the United States Air Force, and, once, the Diplomatic Security Service.

The smoke of wood fires drifted through the trees and over the river, and weekend traffic creaked up and down River Road. Sun-baked tourists paddled rented canoes along the river, and a lone fly fisherman cast his line under the bridge. At dusk the marquee lights flashed on above the Quonset hut Rio Theater, announcing that another Star Wars episode would ignite a galaxy far, far away at 7:30 and 10:00 PM. The air turned to silk and smelled of embers and pine. Soon it would be Friday night, and Monte Rio was starting to get a buzz on.

After spending an entire afternoon in Jeremy's radio room, Teddy and Paul were beginning to wonder if they could do this for another sixteen days. Like any communications stake out, it was excruciatingly tedious and boring.

By evening Monte Rio had resumed its existence as a forgotten old logging town, except for the stretch Lincolns and Cadillacs parked near the Pink Elephant. The drivers, not the Bohos, were enjoying a cold one before they made one last trip back to the airport.

At nine o'clock, just after dark, Teddy left Jeremy's, drove through town and out the Old Bohemian Highway toward Occidental. Two miles from Monte Rio he pulled off the road and parked in the shadows two hundred yards from the entrance to Butler's long driveway.

He checked in with Paul and settled down to wait.

6

The music in the studio was turned up loud, and Butler danced while he worked, humming and singing and bopping his head to Joe Cocker's *She Came in through the Bathroom Window*. The corrugated steel walls reeked of hot metal and sweat.

Bang! He smacked the glowing red steel with his hammer. Bang bang bang! All energy, all manpower, Butler forced his will upon the hot, pliant metal, shaping a bird's wing one feather at a time.

"Oh yeah!" he shouted, sweat glistening on his powerful chest. "Aw right!"

He was fabricating an owl, and the image of the bird had been captured in the dark with a digitally enhanced, exceedingly fast night vision camera, a lucky shot but there she was, swooping down, claws extended, snatching her prey. He glanced at a big black-and-white print of the photo as he worked, reaching for the finest nuance of life and death on the forest floor. The bird killed for food, unlike humans who slaughtered for religion or greed. The bird had no ideology, as far as he could tell, and never took more than she needed, never imposed injustice. Alas, the squirrel paid the price for being too bold or too slow. Perhaps one day the gene pool would concoct a squirrel that could fight back and kill and eat the owl. Why not? If human beings could turn the planet into a psycho ward, who knew what Mother Nature could do.

At nine o'clock, when it was well and truly dark, he turned off the music, shut down the welding torch and stepped back from the almost finished stainless steel and copper owl. A fierce predator with wings spread wide and talons extended, the three-foot high sculpture had been commissioned by a San Francisco banker for his garden in Pacific Heights. Twelve grand, Butler thought, not bad for a metalsmith and nothing for a rich guy. The bird still needed a wing, and the squirrel lacked forelegs and a tail, but the piece would be ready by Wednesday.

Over the years he'd made all kinds of birds, hummingbirds and hawks, flamingos, storks, parrots and emus, but this customer wanted an owl. Although it hadn't been mentioned during the negotiation, the owl is the symbol of the Bohemian Club and Butler's patron was probably a Bohemian. So it goes. If the Boho really liked the owl, maybe his friends would want one, too. He could do a whole series of owls, big ones, little ones, ferocious ones, any kind but wise.

Taking off his leather apron, Butler stepped through the open roll-up doorway and breathed in the night air seasoned with a touch of salt from the Pacific. This was his little piece of the woods, Maggie's Farm, four acres of scrub oak, manzanita and a few redwoods, a house he'd built with his own hands, and a metalworking business he ran with those same hands. As far as Butler was concerned, this was paradise, living with Maggie in the boonies two hours from San Francisco, with two satellite dishes on the roof and a microwave station on Black Cat Mountain to connect them to the big, bad world.

Butler and Maggie lived off the grid. The house and welding studio were powered by solar panels and windmills backed by two diesel marine generators, a self-sufficient energy plant that Butler considered a symbol of his life. A welder by trade, a genius with a torch, he fabricated metal gates and fancy doors as well as wildlife, and his work was on display in back yards, public parks and winery grounds along the entire length of the Russian River. He didn't care if they called him a craftsman or an artist or any other goddamed thing. He was a man, by God, an entrepreneur, and proud that local folks considered him an all-American hero when they weren't looking at him as a prized eccentric.

Left over from the Fourth of July, Old Glory still drooped from the flagpole between the windmills. He mostly flew the Bear Flag of the California Republic, and sometimes the Skull and Crossbones or Don't Tread on Me, depending on his mood. Once a year he ran up a ragged and torn banner of the People's Democratic Republic of Vietnam, a war trophy.

He admired the Stars and Stripes but didn't salute. Stretching, he jogged a few steps in place and decided to go for a run. He went back inside and shuffled around the studio, shutting down his welding equipment, turning off lights, checking the power levels in the batteries, and then changing into a custom-made, camouflage-print ninja suit. He grabbed his back pack full of cameras, pulled open the screen door to the house and hollered up the stairs, "Maggie! I'm goin' out. See ya later."

Just as he slammed the door to his truck, Maggie flew down the stairs and across the driveway to thrust a plastic baggie full of meat scraps through the window of the pickup.

"Here," she said. "If you're goin' where I think you're goin', give these to Old Man Richardson's dogs. Maybe you can keep them quiet."

"Damned if I'll stop and give him a chance to come out of his house with a shotgun," Butler scoffed, shoving the doggy bag back into her hands.

"You be careful," she said gently, her pretty face lined with concern. She knew her husband was a wild man, but he'd come home one way or another every night for seventeen years.

"Aw, Maggie, I just take pictures up there. You know."

As he drove down the long driveway, the flickering reflection of the computer screen in her home office window bounced in his rearview mirror. She'll be up half the night, he thought. Better not come home drunk.

· · · · ·

Teddy waited for Butler's old pickup to turn out of the driveway and head south, then he pulled out and followed. There were only three ungated roads in the next five miles that led off to the left, toward the Grove, and Butler turned into the second, Old Man Richardson's Road. The headlights climbed the hill and disappeared. Teddy waited two minutes and followed through the dark woods.

Suddenly a house on the right erupted with lights, and three excited, barking Rottweilers yowled at his Suburban. A half mile farther on he came upon Butler's empty pickup.

The trees were huge, the woods dark and deep, and Teddy knew he had no chance of finding Butler in the forest. That was all right. He didn't need to. He drove back down the hill, setting off the dogs again, and headed back to Monte Rio. He'd wait for Butler in the Pink Elephant.

. . . . .

The instant Butler turned off his motor he heard the engine behind him. He slipped into the trees, and a minute later Teddy's Suburban pulled up next to his truck. Teddy got out, walked a few yards into the woods, took a leak, got back into his truck and drove back down the hill.

He's only doing his job, Butler thought. He's just not very good at it.

Guided by shadows and the feel of forest detritus beneath his feet, Butler followed a deer path, moving swiftly through the redwoods with only his eyes and nose exposed by his ninja suit. Drinking in the rich scent of ferns and moist decay, he loved the monster trees, these giant symbols of something much older than civilization, and relished his ability to slink undetected beneath the canopy of three hundred foot towers.

Three minutes after leaving his truck, he reached Fat Freddie, a gigantic tree whose trunk was more than twelve feet in diameter. He'd never brought anyone to Fat Freddie, not Maggie, not the Pirates, not anyone.

He pushed a button on an infrared remote to start an electric winch, and one hundred fifty feet of rope and a sling dropped down to the ground. He grasped a knot in the rope, slipped into the sling, pushed the button, and rose up to his blind.

The night was cool with a slight mist from the Pacific drifting through the branches. Butler lay flat on a redwood platform a hundred fifty feet in the air and listened to the wind and the faint sounds of vehicles on the distant highways. Below, the forest stepped down a gentle slope toward the bottom of the ravine where a hard-packed dirt track wide enough for a Hummer cut through the trees. The road followed a fence, overgrown and disguised with vines, and beyond the fence lay a virgin forest of first-growth trees that had never suffered a logger's ax: the Bohemian Grove that stretched for more than two miles north to the river. He couldn't see much. The camps were in the ravines set well back from the perimeter, and all he usually saw were Blue Blazer security patrols in Hummer H2s and an occasional night hiker, perhaps the Secretary of State in Bermuda shorts, toting a thermos of martinis.

He watched the road through a fast 400 millimeter lens on his Nikon. After observing this part of the Grove for many years, he had a fair idea of security procedures. The Blue Blazers manned the South Gate to the Grove, about four hundred yards east along the perimeter road. Pairs of unarmed guards drove Hummers around this section of the perimeter every fifteen minutes. With a small wide-band receiver modified by Jeremy, he could listen to them talking on Grove Channel Two, but they usually didn't have much to say. What would he have to say if his job was to drive around in the woods all night just in case a roaring drunk Chief Justice of the California Supreme Court wandered into his sector and stubbed his toe?

After a few minutes a Hummer came along, eastbound, windows open, Huey Lewis and the News blaring *The Heart of Rock and Roll* into the night from the truck's CD player and speakers on the roof. The guy riding shotgun was smoking a cigar, creating a flare in the center of the light-sensitive image in the Nikon viewfinder. Butler tracked the vehicle until it reached a clearing on the south side of the road, Mario Silva's five-acre vineyard, where, eighty years ago, one of the Grove's neighbors had whacked down the redwoods and planted vines. He could see the rows of pinot noir grapes and the log bunkhouse where Silva stashed his farm workers a few days every year.

Fifteen minutes later the Hummer chugged along the road in the opposite direction and stopped at the vineyard. As Butler watched, the driver in a Bohemian blue blazer got out to stretch, walked into the vines and peed.

For the next thirty minutes, he observed the patrols driving the perimeter road twice more. Between Hummer spottings he listened to Bohemian security recite their radio mantras.

"Five Seven, report."

"Five Seven, all secure here."

"Five Eight, report."

"Five Eight, all secure here."

"Five Nine to control. I got a deer in here, a nice four-point buck. Anybody want him?"

"Copy that, Five Nine. That's affirmative. Ye Olde Owls say they'll take some venison."

"Roger that, control. Okey dokey. Ye Olde Owls."

Butler expected the flare from a rifle to temporarily blind his night vision, but he neither saw the flare nor heard the report from the sound-suppressed rifle. A moment later he heard, "Five Nine to control. Ye Olde Owls, you say?"

"That's right. Take it to the kitchen at the Dining Circle and they'll dress it out. I'll call the Owls' camp valet to collect it, and I'll send someone to cover your post, Five Nine. Wait for him."

"Five Nine, roger that. Stupid fucking deer."

Was it deer season? No. Did the Bohos and their guards have deer tags? Butler didn't give a damn, but it was one more proof that inside the Grove the Bohos were a law unto themselves. Ye Olde Owls were big oil, and maybe there were Gulf royals in there. Could Muslims eat venison? He didn't know.

Not a bad night in his blind, a little action, more than most nights. Butler lowered himself down to the ground, waited for the battery-powered electric motor to winch the rope back up, then jogged over the ridge to his truck. He guided his pickup back down the hill past Barney Richardson's house, provoking the old man's dogs again, and turned onto the Old Bohemian Highway. He thought he'd go have a few beers at the Pink Elephant and see what surprises the night had yet to yield.

7

Butler parked his truck a block from the Pink Elephant and ambled down the street toward the saloon. At midnight the limousines were gone, replaced by dusty pickups and a Friday night crowd that spilled out of the bar and into the street where people could smoke. A rowdy redneck cowboy punker band cranked up heavy metal country music that might never be heard in Texas, but the thumping beat, vicious guitar riffs and bawdy lyrics fired up the tattooed and pierced West County freaks, old hippies, crazed teenagers, Guerneville gays, lost tourists, and perhaps, he thought, even a Fed or two.

Before he got inside, he heard someone shout, "Butler!"

A white sheriff's cruiser pulled around the corner and stopped. Deputy Alice leaned out the window, elbows on the sill and chin on her fists, shaking her head and looking annoyed.

"Hey, Alice, having a busy night? You must be workin' a double shift."

"God dammit, Butler, I just had another complaint about you."

"Ah, shit."

"Old Man Richardson said you were on his road again tonight, stirring up his dogs. I see you're wearing your sneak-around-the-woods costume. What the hell were you doing up there?"

Butler looked down toward his feet and noticed several distinctive elongated, chevron-shaped redwood needles clinging to his camouflage clothing. There was no point in claiming innocence.

"Just takin' a hike."

Alice launched into a speech he'd heard more than once. "I told

Richardson that Butler Rhodes has been the same since he was eight years old, that he don't mean no harm and never hurt nobody. And Richardson said, 'Well, you tell him to stop driving up my private road and upsetting my dogs,' so that's what I'm telling you, Butler. Don't be a problem."

"I didn't do nothin' to Richardson or his dogs. Shit, Alice."

"Butler, he called and complained. That's a private road, and you know how it is."

"Damn straight I know how it is. Mrs. Moriarty complains, too. She's complained about the noise from the Pink Elephant every night for twenty-three years."

"Just watch it, dude."

"Aw, c'mon, Alice," Butler said with a smile and a wink. "Find Hix's pot farm yet?"

Deputy Alice squared her trooper's hat, and the patrol car slowly drifted away.

Butler shouted after her, "Heard you went up to the Stow place today. Everybody okay?"

"Yeah," she hollered back, "but I had to lock Maynard up."

Butler put on a pair of black plastic sunglasses and pushed into the bar. At the sight of a rough-hewn man in full-blown camouflage gear, the tourists froze, unsure if a terrorist or militia crazy had entered their midst. Their eyes followed as he strode purposefully through the crowd, past Albert and Teddy at the table reserved for the Pirates, to the bar where a Bud was open and ready.

He took a long, soulful swig.

"Ahhhh, yeah! How ya doin', Marty?" he asked the buffed up bartender whose black t-shirt announced: The Pink Elephant. Quality Bullshit and Redneck Booze.

"Busy, dude."

"That's what I like to hear."

"Who's the rastaman with Albert?" the bartender asked, tilting his head toward Special Agent Swan. "I seen him in here before."

"That's our new pal Teddy. Treat him right."

"Gotcha."

Butler laid a ten spot on the bar, took the rest of his beer and sat down with Teddy and Albert.

"Evenin', gents."

"Deputy Alice was in here looking for you," Albert said.

"She found me. Where's Jeremy?"

"He crashed," Teddy said. "He finally admitted that he hadn't slept in three days."

"Who's manning the fort?"

"Phillip and Paul."

Butler drank some beer and looked around the crowded bar. Then he glanced sideways at Teddy and said, "I guess you spent all day at Jeremy's Boho Central. Live up to your expectations?"

"It was quite an education," Teddy said. "Albert here spent his money well. It's all first class, but I was hoping to eavesdrop on the Bohos conspiring to rule the world."

"They already rule the world," Albert said. "They don't need to conspire."

Butler asked, "How many so far?"

"About eleven hundred," Albert said, checking a laptop. "They're still coming in, and a lot more will come in tomorrow."

"Any Boho doofusses running around outside?" Butler asked with mild interest.

"Oh, yeah. Some of 'em can't wait."

"Chickpea again?"

"Yeah, him, and we got Zip, Looper, Legacy, and Marlboro Man," Albert said, reading from his computer. "I think Teddy is amazed at how indiscreet these people are. Aren't you, Teddy?"

"Not really," Teddy said. "They have money and power, but they're still just guys with dicks and dinosaur brains."

Butler asked, "Any of 'em in here?"

"Naw."

"Who is?"

Albert looked around the crowded bar. "The guy in the green sport coat is Department of State Security, and the three ridiculous fake hippies in tie-dyes are Teddy's colleagues from the FBI. See, they're trying not to look at us. Doesn't that embarrass you, Agent Swan?"

Teddy laughed. "Yeah, but what the hell. All these guys will be gone tonight. They only showed up for the demonstration. Your tax dollars at work."

"You been out doing your thing?" Albert asked Butler.

"Yup."

"See anything?"

When Butler merely shrugged, Teddy asked. "Just what is your thing, Butler?"

"I run in the woods. Good exercise."

"Just run?"

"Yeah."

"Where?"

"In the woods. You know, lots of big ol' trees."

Albert suddenly fell asleep, slumped gently against Teddy's shoulder and quietly began to snore.

"So, who is Old Man Richardson?" Teddy asked, shifting a little so Albert wouldn't fall face first onto the table.

Butler wobbled his head, dancing to an interior tune, and answered, "Just an old fart who lives out in the boonies."

"Near the Grove? Look, Butler, don't be cagey, okay? Don't play games with me."

Butler poured more beer into his gullet, waved two fingers at Marty the bartender, took off his sunglasses and looked the FBI man squarely in the eye. "I go out at night with night-vision gear and take pictures of wildlife."

"Near the Grove?"

"Sometimes."

Teddy waited, and finally Butler said, "Tonight I heard Boho security kill a deer inside the perimeter. I don't think they bother with deer tags in there, let alone a game warden. Hell's bells, it ain't even deer season yet." He grinned at Teddy and gestured toward Albert.

"Albert is a morning person," Butler said, tilting his head to the east, "But over there, they never sleep in the Grove. They party around the clock, those boys."

Teddy gestured to take in the entire, noisy, rowdy saloon and said, "So does everybody else in Monte Rio."

"Yeah," Butler said with a laconic sigh. "It's Friday night, it's hot, and people get thirsty. They're not all going to sit at home and watch a PBS special on starving war orphans in Syria, or post their insipid little lives on Facebook and YouTube. The folks who come in here are willing to have their eardrums damaged just to get laid. Wouldn't you?"

Marty arrived with two beers.

"I'll get this," Teddy said, whipping out a twenty.

The band started up again, drowning out all conversation and jolting Albert awake. "Oh, man," Albert said. "I haven't been around so much federal government since the last time I got audited by the IRS."

They drank and listened to the punk cowboys torture the key of B flat.

She ain't my honey,
She took my money,
And left me with Tina and you.

"This is too much," Albert exclaimed. "I gotta get outta here."

Teddy and Butler grabbed their beers and followed Albert through the crowd and into the street. It was a little quieter outside, but not much. The scent of sinsemilla wafted from a group of teenagers hanging out on the sidewalk. A girl laughed. The band shifted into high gear.

"You're right, Butler," Albert said. "This is a loony bin. I'm calling it a night."

"Hey, maybe we'll go fishin' tomorrow," Butler said. "You and Susan and me and Maggie."

"Call me in the morning," Albert said as he limped toward his Lamborghini.

"He played football, right?" Teddy said.

"Yeah, Stanford," Butler answered. "Offensive lineman. He was drafted by the Cleveland Browns and wrecked his knee the first day in training camp, so he took his football money and went back to Stanford for his doctorate."

Albert pulled a remote from his pocket and hit the wrong button. All the lights on the dirty yellow SUV began to flash and the alarm went off.

Butler laughed. Albert kept hitting buttons until the lights and alarm shut down, then he got into the exotic yellow truck and drove away.

Butler started walking up the street in the direction of his pickup and Teddy stayed with him.

"He did all right for himself anyway, it seems," Teddy said.

"No shit," Butler laughed again. "How much do you know about us?"

"I've seen your military records, Butler."

"That was a lifetime ago."

"Do you own a rifle?"

Butler stopped in the middle of the street to wave at a pretty middle-aged woman passing by on the sidewalk – Hi Butler, Hi Marie – and folded his arms. Did this strange FBI guy know about his blind in Fat Freddie? Did the Feds think he'd drag a rifle up there and start taking potshots at the Bohemian Grove?

"Sure," he said. "I live in the woods. Everybody has a gun. Second amendment and all that."

"Do you shoot?"

"Only with a camera. Why?"

"I had quite a discussion with Jeremy and Phillip today about all the bad things that might happen to the Bohos. You know, kidnapping, assassination, stuff like that."

"So?"

"I'd like to hear your thoughts on the subject, from a military point of view."

"Why would I have a military point of view?"

"You were a specialist, Butler, a sniper. You had fifty-one kills. Do your friends know that?"

"I don't talk about it."

"I don't blame you. Not at all, but the thing is, you have, or used to have, skills that make your opinion valuable."

"You mean, how would I kill a Boho if that's what I wanted to do?"

"Yeah, something like that."

"Teddy, I'm a lot older than you. The last time I put crosshairs on a human being was before you were born."

"Indulge me. Expand my education."

"Were you in the service?"

"No. My partner Paul Kruger was in the Navy."

"You know anything about tactics?"

"Just what they teach us at the Academy."

"That's not military."

"That's why I'm asking you, Butler."

"Okay," Butler scuffed at the asphalt with his boot and lit a Camel. "To start with, you're not going to get inside the Grove, and you're not going to get a shot at the campgrounds from anywhere outside because you can't see anything, so forget that. As I'm sure you learned from Jeremy and Phillip, if you didn't already know, the main concern of all the security people is when one of these guys leaves the Grove for a little fun outside. They don't allow women inside during the encampment, y'know, and these are people who can buy the most expensive pussy in the world, so when they drive out the gate, anything that can go wrong, will go wrong. An accident, a car crash, a pissed-off whore, and it's all happened before. So all this security is here to prevent a scandal, nothing more, nothing less. If you want to kill a guy, you wait until he leaves, and get him on the Monte Rio bridge, or maybe even blow the bridge."

"Interesting idea."

"Has anybody checked out the bridge for explosives?" Butler asked.

"Probably not."

"There's a million ways to kill one guy," Butler continued, "but that can happen anywhere, so why do it here? It makes no sense. I mean, you're after one guy, and you know he's going to come here, you get him on the highway or at the Santa Rosa airport. No professional will take on all this security if he doesn't have to, and he doesn't."

"That's what Jeremy says."

"Because he's right."

"So you don't feel like there's a threat?" Teddy insisted.

"No," Butler said, throwing up his hands "The only danger to a Boho around here is himself, drunk and crazy fools that they are."

"What about a terrorist attack?" Teddy asked.

"A what?"

"You know. Muslim fanatics, Islamic militants, jihadists, Al-Qaida, ISIS."

Butler laughed and blew smoke at the almost full moon.

"You've thought about it though, haven't you?" Teddy insisted. "The thing is, the Grove is a perfect target for a terrorist attack, all these movers and shakers in one spot."

"You think so, hey?"

"Oh, yeah. You shoot your way in there, kill as many Bohos as you can, and then blow yourself up and collect your reward in Paradise, ninety-seven virgins or whatever it is."

"Maybe," Butler said, "but if there were bad guys out there, Jeremy would hear 'em, and he doesn't."

"Maybe, maybe not. They'd use cell phones."

"Sure, but if suddenly there was a rash of cellphone conversations in Arabic from Sonoma County, the NSA would know and you guys here on the ground would be all over it."

"You think the NSA is that good?"

"You tell me, bud. You're the federal agent. Besides, maybe they don't speak Arabic. Maybe they speak English. Maybe they'd be smart and use no electronic communications at all," Butler became insistent. "No, man, if there were A-rabs here, we'd see 'em. They'd be obvious."

"Maybe they aren't here in Monte Rio," Teddy said. "Maybe they're in Santa Rosa or San Francisco and won't show up until they attack."

"Are you really worried about this? Are you serious?" Butler asked. "The Golden Gate Bridge is a target, not the Grove."

"Everybody thinks like you, Butler, that Middle Eastern types would be spotted right away. Think like that and you're complacent and you're gonna get hit. Maybe they're not Arabs at all. Maybe it's Timothy McVeigh and his pals."

"That's just paranoid bullshit, Teddy."

"Maybe, but I have to cover all the bases, Butler. It's my job to be paranoid. I have to be thorough and check out everything and everyone."

"Including me. Us. The Pirates."

"Yeah, Butler. You, too."

Butler took a deep breath and listened to the wind blowing high up in the trees. He thought about how the wind pushes a bullet a few inches off center.

Anticipating the answer, he asked quietly, "What are you, man? Some kind of terrorism specialist?"

"Yes. Paul and I both are in the bureau counterterrorism section."

"I shoulda figured. Okay."

"And we take this very seriously," Teddy added, "because somebody has to. How do you think I convinced the Bureau to let me look the way I do? If you're going to go undercover, you have to go all the way. I shouldn't be saying this to you."

They reached Butler's pickup, and Butler climbed into the back and sat down on a bench he'd built into the bed. He looked into his beer and drank a little. Wiping foam from his mustache, he said, "There's never even been even the hint of an attack on the Bohemian Grove. Jesus, who could do it? First you have to know the Bohemian Grove exists, what it is, who it is, and where it is. It's too subtle a concept for terrorists who want to make a big splash. And even if you wanted to attack the Bohemian Grove, how do you do it? The Bohos have over a thousand guards in there, so you have to find a way to overpower the guards and get in. How do you do that? Helicopters? Well, you've got three-hundred-foot trees between you and your targets, and wind, so what you do is land your chopper in a clearing or even the heliport they have in there and twenty guys jump out and start shooting up the place. Well, okay, where do you get a helicopter that will carry twenty people and a pilot? Steal one from the Army National Guard? Don't you think Grove security has thought about it? What would you do if you were them? I'd have radar. I'd have a plane in the air at all times, which I know they do. I'd have a few Stingers on hand to shoot down any aircraft that came too close, even a drone. I'd have air defense pretty well covered. Remember, cost is no obstacle to these boys. Same thing goes for trying to attack from the river. As far as I know, they have guys in blinds who watch every foot of that river every minute twenty-four seven. Jesus. Like I said, the Golden Gate Bridge is a target, not the Bohemian Grove."

"Are you through?"

"No. I'm just getting warmed up," Butler said, polishing off his beer and standing up. "But what's the point? You're the anti-terrorist guy. You tell me. Don't you think you're wasting your time hanging around Monte Rio? We have plenty of crackpot radicals, but nobody's gonna start a revolution in West Sonoma County by attacking the Bohemian Grove. You know what Bohos are really afraid of?" he asked.

"What? Drones?" Teddy said.

"No. AIDS," Butler claimed. "That's what closed all the whorehouses that used to be here."

"Yeah," Teddy said with a little laugh. "I suppose you're right about that." He paused for a second then asked, "What kind of rifle do you own, Butler?"

Butler sucked in air between his teeth, looked long and hard at Teddy and said, "A Sharps .52 caliber, New Model 1859. And no, I don't have a Remington M24."

"Can I see it?"

"The Sharps? Sure. When?"

"Now."

"Now? You wanna come out to Maggie's Farm now? It's one in the morning."

"Yeah," Teddy said. "I do."

Butler chuckled and said, "You don't want to give me time to get rid of my machine gun?"

Teddy smirked and said, "I told you it's my job to be paranoid."

8

The sound of two trucks rolling down the gravel driveway woke up Maggie who came downstairs in her bathrobe and stood scowling inside the screen door. Jojo pushed through and ran to his master, panting with happiness.

"What's going on?" Maggie demanded.

"Maggie, this is Teddy Swan. Teddy, this is Maggie, my wife."

"Sorry to disturb you, ma'am," Teddy said, taking off his hat.

"We'll be in the studio, babe. Go back to sleep."

"You drunk?"

"Not yet."

Maggie pushed open the screen door and said, "Fat old Alice was out here asking about you, and Barney Richardson called and gave me a ration of shit. I told you to take those meat scraps up there."

Butler grinned, saying, "I saw Alice downtown. No big thing."

"I'll remember that when Amory Hix throws your ass in jail."

Maggie closed the door and tromped upstairs. Moths fluttered in the porch light. The moon hung in the sky like a lemon pie. Jojo stuck his nose in Teddy's crotch, then looked up and wagged his tail.

"Jojo thinks you're okay," Butler said. "That's a good sign. You married?"

"No. Used to be."

"On the job stress?"

"Yeah, something like that."

Butler led Teddy into the big corrugated-metal barn of a sculpture studio and started turning on lights.

"Wow," Teddy exclaimed, taking in all the welding equipment, sheet metal benders, drill presses, lathes and metal body parts for a half dozen unfinished animals. "You use all this stuff?"

"Naw," Butler said. "I just keep it around to impress yokels like you."

"That works."

"Let me show you something," Butler said, taking his camera out of his backpack. "This is the latest Nikon DX with a 400 millimeter lens and an AstroScope." Butler turned on a computer and the photo of the owl popped up on the big monitor.

"Wow," Teddy said "That's a hell of a camera rig. It's what, twenty, twenty-five grand?"

"That's the ballpark, yeah."

"That's all you shoot? The camera?"

"If you want to see my weapons stash, it's over here."

Butler went to the back of the cavernous space, jerked a canvas tarp off a row of steel cabinets, spun the combination on a lock and pulled out a well-oiled Civil War era Sharps infantry rifle with double set triggers and pellet primer system. He opened the breech with the lever-action trigger guard, peered into the chamber to make sure it wasn't loaded, closed the breech, and handed it to Teddy.

"Union sharpshooters could pick off a Confederate soldier at a thousand yards, maybe more," Butler said with a big smile. "Single shot. Have to reload every time with linen cartridges, but that's how many a Johnny Reb bit the dust."

"I know," Teddy said, hefting the heavy rifle and sighting down the long barrel. "Berdan's Sharpshooters. Ever fire it?"

"Every year on the Fourth of July. Once in a while at the range."

Teddy hefted the Sharps admiringly and said, "This is a famous gun, Butler, the world's first sniper rifle."

"Some people would argue that, but, yeah."

"Are you any good with it?"

Butler smiled and nodded modestly. "Oh, yeah."

Teddy gave back the rifle and asked, "Any other guns?"

"Only the machine gun."

"The what?"

Butler reached into the cabinet and pulled out a dirty, rusted World War Two German Wehrmacht machine pistol, an evil, snub-nosed mankiller that weighed almost as much as the Sharps.

"It's a Schmeisser," Butler explained. "My dad brought it back from North Africa in 1943. It has nine inches of lead in the barrel, and you can see that somebody took a sledge hammer to the firing mechanism. It doesn't work. It's legal."

"Das MP40 machinenpistole," Teddy declared in mock German.

"You know your guns."

"Comes with the territory," Teddy said. "A decent gunsmith could make this thing work."

"I suppose so. Not interested."

Teddy peered into the empty cabinet and asked, "That's it? That's all the guns, just two antiques?"

"Unless you're packing, and I expect you are, there are no more firearms around here. You want to search the rest of the studio? The house? I'll open every damned cabinet if you want."

"No." Teddy shook his head.

"I told you the only thing I shoot anymore is a camera. That's the truth. Want a beer?" Butler asked, wiping the guns with an oily rag, putting them away and locking the cabinet.

"Sure."

Butler crossed the studio to a small lounge area near the big roll-up doors, opened a small fridge, pulled out two Buds and handed one to his guest.

"Have a seat," he said, flopping down on a dilapidated old couch.

Teddy looked around the studio and noticed the almost finished owl with a squirrel in her claws.

"You're making an owl," he observed, reaching out and touching a steel wing. "You know the owl is the symbol of the Bohemian Club."

"Yeah, I'm making it for a Boho, as it turns out. Is that what they call irony?"

"Are you really interested in them, the Bohos?" Teddy asked.

"No," Butler replied. "Spying on the Bohos is Jeremy's thing. He's a radio freak, and he gets off on listening to all the shit he listens to. For me, it's fun for a couple of days, but I don't take off two weeks to play Boho games. Hell, no. Phillip, he's a teacher and he gets the summer off anyway, and Albert, well, he's just a rich, fat fuck who either goes fishing or sits in his house designing micro chips when he feels like it. Sometimes I think they're just star struck, y'know? The Secretary of Defense, Oooooo. The Governor, Oooooo. The chairman of Wells Fargo Bank, Oooooo. And sometimes even the Prez. Wow! Not me, man. Bohos make good clients, not that I've ever had more than three or four. Come to think of it, one was a big pain in the ass, but so what?"

From where they were sitting they could see the moon and the windmills and the flagpole with Old Glory hanging limp in the still air.

"You fly the colors," Teddy observed.

"Sometimes," Butler acknowledged. "We have a Fourth of July party every year, make speeches, get drunk, shoot off a lot of firecrackers and the Sharps. I just haven't taken it down yet."

They sat quietly for a minute or two, and Teddy finally asked, "What do you think the Bohos are doing right now?"

Butler laughed, "Who cares? Same thing we're doin', drinkin' and shootin' the shit. The world always has rich guys, powerful guys, Teddy, guys who call the shots and make the rules. I don't care. They're probably drinking more expensive booze than we are. No Bud for them. They probably have cases of some damn fool wine from Pickett's."

Teddy chortled, "That place is a hoot – Pickett's."

"Yeah, you tell me this, since you know so much. Do you know who the general is?"

"No," Teddy said.

"If you want a military opinion, ask him, Lieutenant General Nguyen Van Duang, Army of the Republic of Viet Nam. He had the honor of watching the French lose at Dien Bien Phu and the Americans lose at Khe Sanh. He's an expert on how to lose to an undermanned, underarmed opponent."

Butler lit a Camel, leaned forward with his elbows on his knees and said, "Look, Teddy, you know all about me and my friends, and I'm even telling you more, but I don't know a damned thing about you. What does your mother think of your tattoos?"

"My mom in Baltimore?" Teddy laughed. "She hates them. So does my boss, Special Agent in Charge Carter McGee in Santa Rosa. You don't believe I'm for real, do you?"

"I'm getting there, man." Butler leaned back, thinking: I've had enough to drink to really shoot off my mouth, so he said, "I just don't know what you really want, Teddy. I'm beginning to think you may be an okay guy, but I don't trust the government, and I don't mind telling that to the FBI. I don't know, man, but when the government walks into my house – that's you, amigo – I'm a little suspicious."

"I'm not after you," Teddy said. "I don't care what you think about the government. All I care about is the Grove and what could happen. I have a bad feeling, Butler. I don't know why and I can't explain it, but I've been here six weeks, and I've learned that the Bohemian Grove is an incredibly rich target and nobody cares. All those security guys in there, they're just putting in their time. All I want from you is to keep your eyes and ears open, because nobody else is awake. Does that make any sense?"

"I don't know. Maybe. I just don't feel like there's a threat."

"Most people seem to think what you think, Butler, that it would be impossible to attack. You're right, they have air defense and river patrols, and Grove security has a big arsenal but it's so locked up they'd never get at it in time." Teddy swallowed a big gulp of beer, then went on, "What I'd like to do tomorrow is go out on the river and see what the Grove looks like from there. I hear they have a beach."

"The Bohemian Beach," Butler said. "Yeah, they have a little river beach with a bar."

"Where can I rent a boat?" Teddy asked.

Before Butler could answer, his phone rang. He picked it up, looked at it and answered, "Phillip? What's up?"

"Butler," Phillip said breathlessly, "I'm at Jeremy's, listening to the Sheriff's Department. I think the sheriff..."

Suddenly, the night was lit up by blue and red lights flashing through the trees. Jojo ran out of the studio, barking barking barking, the lights came on in the house, and three sheriff's department police cars roared up the driveway, headlights on bright, spotlights aimed at the open studio door, dome lights recreating the Fourth of July.

"I'll call you back," Butler said into the phone and hung up.

Sheriff Amory Hix, all six-foot-eight of him, jumped out of the lead car, stuck a bullhorn in front of his face and bellowed, "Butler Rhodes!"

"What the fuck?" Butler exclaimed, walking into the open doorway and shielding his eyes against the lights.

Jojo charged across the driveway and hunkered down in front of the sheriff, growling and barking fiercely.

"Put your hands on your head and get down on your knees!" Hix ordered.

Butler dropped to his knees just as Teddy appeared in the spotlight.

"You, too! Whoever you are!"

Hix unholstered his service revolver and approached the two men on their knees in the gravel driveway.

Jojo was ready to attack, and the sheriff swung his gun around at the dog.

"Hey!" Butler yelled, "Jojo, down!" and the lab backed away, growling. "Leave my dog alone, Amory!"

"Twice in one night is too much, Butler. I don't know what you have in the woods up behind Richardson's house, but two complaints in one night is too much."

"Officer..." Teddy said.

"Shut up, asshole."

"Officer..."

"I said shut the fuck up."

"Federal Agent. FBI," Teddy shouted, his voice seething.

Hix jerked away from Butler and bent over, his face an inch from Teddy's and hissed, "What did you say?"

"I'm going to reach inside my vest and show you my creds."

Teddy slowly produced his badge and ID. Hix took Teddy's open wallet, inspecting it as if it were a hot charcoal briquette.

"Okay," he said. "What are you doing here?"

"Can I stand up?" Teddy asked. "And would you please put your cannon away?"

Hix jammed his gun into its holster and broke into a sweat.

"The question is, what are you doing here?" Teddy said, on his feet and dusting off his filthy jeans.

"I'm here to arrest Butler Rhodes for trespassing."

"For driving up Barney Richardson's road?"

"That's right."

"That was me on that road," Teddy said. "Can I see your warrant?"

"I don't have a goddam warrant. I have a complaint."

"Do you need six officers, three cars and the sheriff in person to serve a complaint? What kind of department are you running?"

Amory Hix was not accustomed to anyone challenging his authority, but he wore an American flag lapel pin, the Stars and Stripes were sewn onto the sleeves of his uniform, and the same patriotic symbol was painted on all the cars in his department. Flummoxed, he took a step back.

"Butler," Teddy commanded. "Stand up."

If looks were swords, Hix and Butler would have dueled there and then with lethal forged steel.

"Well, that's all I need, the fucking FBI running around the woods and stirring up the natives," Hix screeched. "Why wasn't I informed?"

"Need to know, Sheriff," Teddy said. "Need to know. I'm with the Joint Counter-Terrorism Task Force, same as you, and your record of cooperation with the Task Force is not exactly double A plus. Obviously, you have more pressing concerns than protecting our distinguished guests in the Bohemian Grove. Mr. Rhodes here, on the other hand, is co-operating one hundred percent. Now," and Teddy continued, "Barney Richardson's property is adjacent to the Grove's southern perimeter. I was up there tonight, and for the next two weeks I'll be all around the Grove on all sides. If you have any more complaints, I suggest you call my superior in Santa Rosa. I'm sure you know Carter McGee very well, Sheriff. But if I were you, I'd concentrate on protecting citizens from the real criminal activity in your jurisdiction. Are we on the same page yet?"

Hix was fuming, barely able to contain his rage and frustration. His deputies were watching with feigned shock and concern, not quite sure what was happening just out of earshot but sensing that their rampaging chief was getting his comeuppance. The long-haired freak was Somebody, probably a Fed. There were a lot of them around right now.

Butler's phone rang again, and he let it ring. Maggie came out of the house and marched across the driveway like a trooper. Furious, she shouted, "Goddammit, Butler, I told you you were gonna get in trouble if you kept going up there. Look at this! Look at this! What are all these cops doing here?"

"Easy, babe. It's okay. I think they'll be leaving soon."

Teddy walked the sheriff back to his car, opened the door and held it open, saying quietly, "Are you investigating Butler for anything else, Sheriff?"

"No."

"You sure? Don't you two have a history?"

Hix was smart enough not to lie. He slid into the driver's seat, looked up at Teddy through the window and said. "I'm a professional. I don't let personal stuff interfere with doing my job."

Teddy smiled and said, "I can see that clear as day."

The deputies all got back into their cars, shut off the flashing lights and followed the sheriff down the drive. The three cars turned onto the highway and hustled away.

Maggie's Farm was suddenly quiet. Crickets chirped, insects buzzed and a lone car passed by on the highway.

"I thought he was gonna kill my dog," Butler said.

"That's a good boy, Jojo," Teddy said and bent down to give the lab a scratch behind his ears.

"Hey, man," Butler said. "I saw you behind me on Richardson's Road."

"I'm not surprised. I told you I have to be thorough."

"You want another beer?"

Teddy asked, "You want to tell me where you go up that road and into the woods?"

"Nope."

"Well then, thanks for the Bud," Teddy said. "I gotta get some sleep. Maybe we'll get a boat and go out on the river tomorrow. G'night, Maggie. See ya, Butler."

Teddy got into his Suburban and his tail lights receded down the drive.

Maggie wrapped her arms around her husband. "Come to bed," she said. "I know what you need right now."

As they walked arm in arm to the house, she asked, "Who in the world is that guy?"

"If I didn't know any better," Butler said, "I'd say he's the Lone Ranger."

9

The rustic, isolated camp where Mario Silva, Albert's neighbor in Monte Rio, trained his jihadis, was fifty miles north of Ciudad del Este, Paraguay, near the Brazilian border.

The plan was to strike at night and so they practiced in the dark. It was midnight when Silva started the Hummer, turned on the lights and drove slowly along the dirt road through the forest. To his left, a high hedge concealed a chain-link fence topped with razor wire, and behind the fence, his two minders, Coco and Simón, simulated the guards who patrolled the heavily wooded knoll of the Bohemian Grove. A hundred meters deeper into the woods, over a ridge, the terrain spilled down a ravine dotted with six simulated Bohemian camps: Ye Olde Owls, Burnside, Windwalkers, Dogtown, Woodland Hills, and Dixie, configured as closely as possible to the Southland area of the Grove. The native South American cedars, beeches, and timbos weren't redwoods, but they were big.

Since the Blue Blazers who patrolled the Bohemian Grove perimeter in Hummers often played loud music, Silva turned on a CD and the Talking Heads' *Burning Down the House* blared into the Paraguayan night. The attack had two phases: the stealthy approach to the security bunker just inside the South Gate, and the assault on the designated camps. Silva didn't want any surprises before they got to the gate. After that, everything would be a surprise, and, he sincerely hoped, training and faith would carry the night.

In his experience, training had had erratic results, but faith worked wonders. For almost thirty years the suicide bombers he trained had always gone to Paradise.

As the Hummer approached a clearing with a simulated vineyard on the right, Silva waved to the Lebanese-Paraguayans and Palestinian-Argentineans pretending to be Mexicans. They wore white soccer jerseys with large red numbers, and he always called them by their numbers. He knew their names, their Arabic names and the Spanish names that would be in their passports, and every detail of their lives – he had had to assess their commitment to Holy War – but once a young man was selected as a candidate for martyrdom, he became a number.

Number Six moved in front of the Hummer, forcing Silva to stop. Number Two, a dark twenty-year-old in jeans, huaraches and a red and white jersey approached the driver's side and said, *"Hola. ¿Qué tal?"*

In an instant the two vineyard workers were menacing him with sound-suppressed Uzis.

Very good, he thought.

Firing pins snapped into empty chambers. Click click.

"Okay," he said. "I'm dead. Who is going to drive?"

"Me," said Number Two. All the young men had tried to impress him with their driving skills, but only three of the fifteen could actually maneuver the Hummer more than ten meters without mishap.

"Then do it."

When Number Two hesitated, Silva snapped, "I'm dead. I'm not going to get out of the car for your convenience."

"Sorry, Ali."

"Don't call me Ali. Never! I am Silva, Señor Silva. And don't say you're sorry. Lay your hands on me and drag me out of the damned car!"

Allowing himself to be pulled from the driver's seat, Silva snatched the keys, rolled onto the ground and waited while Number Two fumbled, trying to start the Hummer. Finally, the young man banged his hands on the steering wheel and cursed, *"Chraa!"*

Silva shook his head in disgust. "Speak Spanish! From now until you are greeted by the Prophet, blessèd be his name, no Arabic! *Por Diós, hable español.*"

"*Sí, Señor Silva. Cómo no.*"

"If I hear one word of Arabic on the other side, I'll send you to the next world myself."

"*Sí, maestro, sí, sí. Lo siento.*"

"Stand up straight! Act like a soldier of God."

The young man squared his shoulders and looked into the deep brown eyes of Ali al-Saif, Ali the Sword, one of the most famous terrorists in the world, the man he was supposed to call Silva. To Number Two, who had arrived in Paraguay at the age of five from a Palestinian refugee camp in Lebanon, Ali al-Saif was the face of justice. All his life he'd been taught to seek revenge for the loss of the family home in Haifa, long before he was born. Ali was giving him a chance to avenge his family's honor. Number Two was more than willing to die for Ali, for Islam, and for Palestine.

Silva surrendered the keys, and a moment later the Hummer continued down the road. The music still blared, and that was good. Silva trotted after it, thinking that when the time came, if it came, he would have to do the driving. The boys didn't know it, but this exercise could be their final dress rehearsal. Opening Day of the Bohemian Grove encampment six thousand miles north in California was taking place at this very moment.

Hands on hips, he watched his jihadis overwhelm the improvised security bunker. Click click click click down go the guards. Pom pom pom the communications console is destroyed. Quickly up the hill with night-vision goggles and click click click away with the security patrols. Then over the ridge to the camps, but before the young men in soccer jerseys and goggles could begin their attack, Silva blew a whistle and brought the exercise to a halt.

"That's it," he shouted. "Back to camp. Let's go."

"But Señor Silva, we want to practice with live ammunition."

"No. Not tonight. Coco! Simón! Check their weapons. Make sure they're clean."

He didn't want an accident. Only six of the fifteen could be trusted to handle Uzis. He could train his jihadis to become human bombs, but most could never be turned into soldiers. In any case, it was a bad idea to let suicide bombers rehearse their deaths too often.

He looked up into the sky and almost prayed. He knew the Holy Quran by heart and carried the wounds of a battle-scarred mujahadeen in his left leg. His young jihadis worshipped him, would die for him, but when he looked into the southern sky he saw only stars and unfamiliar southern hemisphere stars at that. He saw the infinity of the universe and thought of Albert Einstein, not the Prophet Mohammad, not Allah.

As he did on his prayer rug five times a day, on this night he looked into the sky and silently recited from the speeches of Vladimir Lenin, "Give me just one generation of youth, and I shall transform the whole world."

As he was climbing into the Hummer for the ride back to camp, his cell phone rang.

"Mañana por la mañana," said a voice he recognized. "Tomorrow in the morning."

He turned off the phone, glanced back at the sky and whispered, "Thank you, Brother Vlad."

. . . . .

The little shopping arcade in Ciudad del Este was busy at seven in the morning but the teahouse was almost empty when a man with a full blond beard and mirrored sunglasses suddenly appeared at the bar.

"Sala'am," he said politely to the startled barman. "I'm here to see Señor Antón."

"And you are?"

"Silva."

The Lebanese-Argentine barman had been told to listen for a Mexican accent when the expected guest spoke Spanish, and an Aleppo accent when the language was Arabic, but he couldn't tell one inflection from another. He glanced nervously toward the lone Russian bodyguard at the rear table who hesitated and finally nodded.

"In back," the barman said, gesturing with his head toward the rear.

Silva stared at the thin bodyguard who was sweating inside a cheap black suit, apparently worn to attract maximum attention. Flies buzzed under the ineffective fan, and noise from the arcade filtered through the nicotine-stained windows.

The bodyguard moved to stand up, flexing his fingers as he prepared to search the visitor.

"It's all right, Mikhail," boomed a Russian baritone from behind a flimsy curtain. "Let him pass."

Silva pushed through the curtain and into the presence of sixty-year-old Antón Cosmovitch Valisnikov, his 320 pounds immaculately tailored in white linen and ensconced in a wicker booth. A fine Panama hat, a pair of tall glasses, a bottle of Stoli and a bowl of mangoes and bananas were close at hand on the cracked tabletop.

"Mario Silva! Good to see you, my boy. Still a master practitioner of disguise, I see," he declared in English. "Very good, very good. It's been too long, but I must say, when we actually meet, it's always in the most fascinating places. Ciudad del Este. My God."

"Good to see you too, Antón, especially if you're the bearer of good news."

"Drink?" Antón raised the bottle of vodka.

"No, thanks. Tea."

Antón shouted in Russian for Mikhail to bring tea, and Silva slipped into the booth, saying with a laugh, "You get fatter every time I see you, and you still dress like you're living in a black and white movie."

"I see your powers of observation haven't diminished," Antón remarked with a rubbery frown. His wet, black eyes followed the younger, much slimmer man as Silva systematically scanned the room, checking off each doorway and shadowy corner. He noticed that Silva had made no noise when he moved. Nikes on his feet, hands loose and calloused on the edges, at least one firearm concealed somewhere on his person. He wore jeans and a photographer's vest with many zippered pockets. To complete the illusion a Nikon hung around his neck.

The bodyguard appeared with a glass of tea and retreated to the front. Silva bent over, sniffed the glass and left it untouched. He grinned and asked the fat man, "How do you like Paraguay?"

"Funny you should ask," Antón replied, licking his lips. "In the old days I would have been thrilled. Look at this bustling arcade brimming with commerce. Half the signs are in Arabic and you can buy a computer or a Kalashnikov within a few steps of where we're sitting. It's a bloody smuggler's paradise, the wild wild South, hey? This place ranks with Peshawar as a mecca – can I say mecca? – of free trade and lawless enterprise. No wonder so many Lebanese settle here. Magnificent, but I'm too old for this kind of entertainment, and definitely too rotund. In short, with the vast knowledge I have garnered in my –" he looked at his Rolex "– three hours in this landlocked nation, I can tell you without equivocation that this is one of the most spectacularly stinking shitholes on an increasingly decadent planet. The food is truly awful, and I won't eat anything except the fresh fruit I brought across the border. I can't wait to get back into my air-conditioned Mercedes and zoom across the river into Brazil. I hate fucking Paraguay. Does that answer your question?"

"You're a snob, old man, but you always were," Silva said, trying to cover his anxiety with a laugh. "You've taken the trouble to get here, so there must be a reason."

Antón placed an elbow on the table, leaned his head on his fist and said officiously, "You've been here a month."

"Yes."

"And how is the training going?"

"Very well, excellent in fact. We run through the jungle, shoot up some trees, play fútbol, and pray five times a day. In the morning we study the Quran."

"Do you trust them, your men?" the Russian asked.

"What kind of a question is that, Antón? Trust them? Of course not. They're boys. They have the bodies of men but the minds of children, and to them, I am the voice of Allah. To me, they are numbers One through Fifteen. They're as ready as they'll ever be." He paused and leaned across the table. "Are you going to screw around with me, you fat Russian pig, or tell me thumbs up or thumbs down?"

"I wanted to do this when you first proposed it – what? Twenty years ago?" Antón said.

"Twenty-four," Silva snapped. "You imperious prick. You're impossible."

"It would have been beautiful, a Soviet coup. Two thousand absurdly rich Americans in one place at the same time and boom! Take that, you capitalist pigs! An absolute decapitation. But those were the old days, the Cold War, and it never happened. Now, we are the capitalist pigs, or the wild boars, if you prefer. This is the new order, the new Russia, and now we have a new motive, the oldest of them all – money, real money. Big money. It's really not much different from ideology. It's just the accounting that's changed."

Silva waited.

"You're already rich, Silva," the fat Russian intoned. "You don't need money, but I know why you want to do it. To prove – to whom I wonder? – that you can. And, of course, there's the inexorable fact that you just love mayhem, and you're really good at it."

Antón closed his eyes and scowled. He fidgeted, adjusting his bulk in his chair. He poured a drop of vodka into his glass and uttered a tiny chuckle.

Silva grimaced and fought to control his breathing. He was used to Antón, but still –

Antón contorted his face, exercising and stretching his cheek and jaw muscles, and then said curtly, "The committee has given final approval. The initial payment of ten million euros is in your account in Mexico City. The rest will be paid on completion. Congratulations."

Silva removed his sunglasses and blinked his lens-tinted blue eyes. He'd worked for Antón for twenty-nine of his forty-seven years, first as a deep undercover officer of the KGB, infiltrating the mujahadeen in Afghanistan as a teenager where he became the legendary Ali al-Saif, killer of Russians, then for the SVR inciting Hezbollah to violence in Lebanon and Israel and solidifying his reputation as an extraordinary terrorist and killer of infidels and crusaders, and now he performed as an assassin for a private syndicate of Russian entrepreneurs and politicians, none of whom knew who he was. The only person on earth who knew his true identity was Antón Cosmovitch Valisnikov.

The plan to attack the Bohemian Grove now approved by Antón's Russian overlords, on the shelf for more than two decades, had been taken down from time to time, dusted off, modified and refined, then put back in mothballs to collect more dust. During the long wait, in addition to his assigned duties as a recruiter and trainer of terrorists, Silva had made certain preparations, just in case. Far from the locus of his actions in the Middle East, he'd become a Mexican citizen, acquired an American green card, purchased property in Sonoma County, established links in Ciudad del Este, Buenos Aires and Beirut, and waited. Over the years he'd come to understand that his plan to attack the Bohemian Grove would never be accepted at face value. There had to be a special reason beyond ideology to slaughter a large number of prominent Americans, and suffer the consequences. Something of tangible value had to be gained beyond the sheer thrill of doing it.

That special something had presented itself in the person of Boris Borisovitch Demetriov, the newly elected president of Belarus. The Russian businessmen who employed Antón had offered a billion dollars to Boris Boris, as he was affectionately known, for the rights to build a new natural gas pipeline from Russia to Minsk, the capitol of Belarus. Against the advice of his brother and closest advisor, Dmitri Borisovitch Demetriov, Boris had rejected the generous Russian bribe, and instead had indicated his willingness to accept a bribe for twice as much, two billion dollars, from a consortium of five American oil companies to build a natural gas pipeline from Rotterdam through the Netherlands, Germany and Poland to Minsk.

The insult pushed all the right Muscovite buttons. Outraged, the Russian cartel thought first to match – even increase – the American bribe, but then they decided they were pissed off enough to kill Boris and make Dmitri the president of Belarus. Fuck you, Boris. Let's blow up his car, they said. Well, Antón argued, for one thing you want to get the Americans, too, the slimy bastards, and that would mean blowing up a lot of cars in many different places. Besides, Russian fingerprints would be all over the wreckage. But what if the targets just happened to be in one location at the same time – all five American CEOs were members of the Bohemian Club – and what if the killing were done by people whom the Americans hated and feared – jihadi terrorist suicide bombers. Antón dragged out Silva's old plan and suggested that they disguise the assassination of Boris Demetriov and his American benefactors as a terrorist attack on the Bohemian Grove. The stupid Americans would be in such a politically correct tizzy over all the dead Muslims who killed themselves that they'd never suspect a fine Russian hand. The Americans would blame ISIS, perhaps al-Qaida, or even the Taliban, yet the right people would get the right message.

Naturally, the Russians asked: Where do you find Islamic suicide bombers capable of infiltrating Northern California? South America, Antón replied. In the last forty years Argentina, Peru, Uruguay, and Paraguay have experienced significant immigration from the Middle East, and that has accelerated with the wars in Iraq and Syria. From a pool of a million Spanish-speaking South American Muslims, many with ties to Hezbollah and Hamas, you can easily find fifteen fanatical suicide bombers. Put these swarthy young men with mustaches in the right clothes and they look exactly like Mexican migrant farm workers, like thousands of others in Sonoma County during the summer. And, as Spanish speakers, they would be invisible.

"Thanks to Boris, the pieces of the jigsaw puzzle finally came together," Antón said to Silva. "Boris has become enough of a nuisance to make himself a target. The political conditions are right because, as I'm sure you've noticed, the Americans are fabulously dim-witted with no clue as to how to deal with holy warriors, and the opportunity to make huge sums of money is staring us in the face."

"And Boris?"

"He'll be there at your precious Bohemian Grove. He's scheduled to speak on the first Monday of the encampment. They call them 'Lakeside Talks.' It's often the president of some godforsaken country, like Boris, or Henry Kissinger, people like that. The Bohemians made themselves a nice little lake back in the woods, and that's where they have their shrine, a huge owl."

Antón poured himself an inch of vodka, knocked it back and scrutinized the man he'd brought to Moscow from Aleppo so long ago.

"For heaven's sake, man, aren't you pleased? You can move ahead. I'd expect at least a smile, but you sit there like a rock."

"I can hardly contain myself," Silva said between clenched teeth.

"You certainly hide it well behind that Mexican mask."

Lowering his voice a few decibels, Silva declared, "We can throw a party, Antón. We can invite all the jihadis in this crazy place, and maybe we should invite the Mossad who set up shop right down the street. And all the old Nazis in this country, too. Why not them? And every smuggler within a hundred kilometers. Why don't we hold a press conference? I don't have time to celebrate because now there are logistics."

"Logistics," Antón said and smiled. "Now I know you're pleased."

Silva leaned across the table and said, "I have to move fifteen young men, most of whom have never traveled anywhere since they were babies, from Paraguay to California in less than three days, and I'm not taking them across the desert into Arizona."

Antón smiled. "Don't you think I've taken care of that? Have a little faith. After all, we've been planning this for a long time. Our good friend Pedro has done his job."

Silva took a long look at Antón and said, "Fútbol?"

"Yes. I've arranged for Las Pumas de Paraguay to play in youth soccer tournaments in Henderson, Nevada, and San Diego, California. It's all arranged exactly according to your plan, Silva. Your fifteen young South Americans comprise a very wealthy youth fútbol team that flies to tournaments in a chartered plane. I have fifteen Paraguayan passports and American visas issued in proper Spanish names, and since my Gulfstream doesn't have the range, a Boeing Business Jet is waiting to take you non-stop from Ciudad del Este to Las Vegas. Will that do? It's costing me four hundred thousand Yankee dollars."

Antón sipped his vodka and went on, "Pedro will meet you and your fútbol team in Las Vegas and take you to California. All the items you require and requested have been obtained; all details have been worked out according to your meticulous specifications, but I should ask – is there anything else?"

Silva finally cracked a smile and laughed. "You're astounding, Antón. Money talks, hey?" He reached for the vodka, pouring himself two fingers.

"It's not like the old days," Antón said wistfully, but then added with a sly smile, "Things are much more, shall we say, fluid, but it's still us against them in a most amusing game. It's the Cold War with another name. But keep in mind. We want you to liquidate Boris Boris, and we really don't care how."

Silva raised his glass, "Well then, old friend, to the Bohemian Grove. They won't know what hit them."

Antón lifted his glass and they clinked.

"That's the idea," declared the fat Russian.

10

Silva wasn't dozing, merely resting. There was no way he could fall asleep and let the stewards go near the boys unattended. To comply with American aviation regulations that required flight attendants, Antón had arranged for stewards because women would have been impossible. Nevertheless, the two gay Americans confused his boys and made them nervous, so he'd confined his fifteen mindwarped soldiers of God to the rear of the luxurious plane and kept the stewards up front in the forward cabin.

As far as the stewards were concerned, Mario Silva was a rich Mexican with an address in San Francisco and a nicely tailored Italian suit, enough to convince them he was an old queen who got off by sponsoring youth soccer teams, bringing them to the USA, and, as he hinted, abusing their trust.

The problem was his boys didn't act like boys. Wearing their neatly pressed soccer jerseys, they didn't horse around or play loud music or touch the catered meals. They slept or sat quietly for hours, contemplating their imminent arrival in Paradise.

For all but Numbers One and Three, the Palestinian Moachim brothers now called Rodrigo and Hernán, Silva's jihadis were experiencing their first flight. The Moachims had flown from Beirut to Buenos Aires at ages ten and twelve after one of their older brothers died fighting the Israelis and another perished in the Lebanese civil war. Palestine was not an abstraction for Numbers One and Three. They were true believers, and for Silva this was a godsend. Honor-bound by ancient tradition, they were filled with a passion for revenge.

"Mr. Silva?"

He opened his eyes and looked at the flight attendant, the blond one.

"We'll be landing in Las Vegas in ten minutes," the steward informed him. "A customs and immigration officer will come on board."

"Thank you. I'll tell the boys."

"I'll have to check their seats and safety belts before we land."

"All right."

Silva escorted the steward down the aisle and announced loudly in Spanish, "Attention, chicos! Fasten your seatbelts and put your seats in an upright position."

As the young men did as they were told, the steward made a perfunctory inspection and retreated to the forward cabin. Silva took a seat and fastened his seatbelt, saying to his charges, "Let me see your passports and customs forms."

As soon as the steward was out of earshot, Silva said quietly, "This will be the most dangerous moment. An American official will come aboard this plane to check your passports and bags. He's not looking for you. He's looking for smugglers, so you have nothing to worry about. He can probably speak Spanish. So speak Spanish! Answer his questions, and don't say anything else."

"What questions will he ask us?" Carlos, Number Four, wanted to know.

"We've been over this, but all right," Silva said patiently. "Where are you from? The answer is Ciudad del Este. Where are you going? The answer is Henderson, Nevada, and San Diego, California. Okay? You're a fútbol team. Who are you?"

"Las Pumas de Paraguay," they chorused together.

"Carlos, who is the goalie?"

"Andrés, Number Five."

"That's right."

"Luís, where are you from?"

"Ciudad del Este."

"Very good. Excellent."

"Are all Americans like the men on this plane?" asked Rodrigo, Number One, his face twisted with disgust.

"Why?"

"Son maricones." They're fags.

"You won't meet many Americans in Paradise," Silva replied with a broad smile. "Of that you can be sure."

The plane touched down at McCarran and began to taxi toward the small customs shed near the general aviation terminal. It was four o'clock on Saturday morning, Pacific Daylight Time.

.   .   .   .   .

The night had not been kind to Customs and Border Patrol Officer Leonard Briggs. He'd skipped his Gamblers Anonymous meeting, lost three hundred dollars playing video poker at the Rio, and when he got to work his first assignment was a charter from South America. His bad mood turned alarmingly foul.

Passenger manifest in hand, he climbed into the big Boeing where the flight crew was waiting with their flight documentation.

"Paraguay?" Briggs said, looking at his manifest for the first time. "Who the fuck charters a BBJ from Paraguay?"

"A soccer team," answered the captain.

"Pros?"

"No, amateurs. Very rich amateurs."

"Oh, shit," Briggs growled. "Just what I need. Anything strange or unusual happen on the flight? Any drugs? Anyone light up any reefer?"

"This was the quietest flight we've ever had," said the blond flight attendant. "They didn't talk, didn't eat – nothing."

"They must be nervous," Briggs said.

"I suppose so."

"Okay," Briggs said, smacking the manifest on his knee. "Pull all the luggage and lay it out on the tarmac. Yours, too, and don't give me any reason to bring in the dogs."

The captain called the baggage crew, and Briggs pushed into the main cabin.

The smiling man waiting inside was six feet tall, black-haired, brown-eyed, and elegantly dressed. Silva handed Briggs a Mexican passport and an American green card.

"You look familiar," Briggs said.

"Of course," Silva said with a wide smile. "I've come through here many times before. I love Las Vegas."

The conventional description of Ali al-Saif was familiar to every immigration official at every airport in the world: Syrian by birth, light-complected, 47 years old, slender, five foot ten with bushy eyebrows, almond shaped black eyes, thin nose, and a famous limp, a souvenir of his sojourn in Afghanistan with the mujahadeen. Yet Mexico's history of conquest and migration often produced a visual effect similar to that of the formidable gene pool of the Middle East, and to all appearances Mario Silva was exactly what his passport said, a distinguished, middle-aged Mexican with a straight Aryan nose, prominent high cheekbones, and slightly mongolian eyes.

"From Paraguay today, Mr. Silva?"

"Yes. Ciudad del Este."

"We don't get many charters from there."

"I don't suppose you do. These are a bunch of lucky kids. National champions," Silva said proudly. "Las Pumas de Paraguay. The Paraguay Panthers."

"Are you their coach?"

"I'm their sponsor."

"Where's the coach?"

"He's already here. He's waiting for us in the terminal."

"And where do you reside in the United States?" Mario Silva's green card wasn't tagged, the name not on any watch list.

At that moment of supreme narcissism, Silva admired his ability to throttle back his heartbeat and stitch up his bowels.

He replied with a smile, "San Francisco."

"Anything to declare?"

"No, sir."

The boys were sitting quietly behind Silva and watching Briggs' every move.

"A soccer team, hey? They all have their passports and visas?"

"Yes, sir. They do."

"Any minors? Any under eighteen?"

"No, the youngest is eighteen, the oldest twenty-three."

Silva turned and gestured toward the fifteen stocky young men in soccer jerseys strung out behind him.

"They're playing in tournaments in Henderson and San Diego. This is their authorization."

He produced a genuine letter from the Department of Cultural Exchange issued at the American embassy in Asunción.

Briggs read the letter, glanced out a window and saw the luggage and flight crew waiting on the tarmac. Two large net bags of soccer balls rested on the ground next to the suitcases. Was there cocaine in those balls? Should he tear the plane apart, pull all the panels and rip the seats? He wanted to. He knew what a chartered Boeing Business Jet cost, and big time smugglers could afford it. But why such a big plane? There would have to be a ton of dope for it to make sense. And why a soccer team? None of the names had been on any watch list, and he knew what was in those bags: dirty underwear, or if he was lucky, clean underwear.

"Okay. Let's see the first one."

"Rodrigo," Silva said to the first lad in line. "*Papeles.*"

Number One handed over his passport with an American tourist visa good for one month. He stared hard at the official, his eyes brimming with hate. Silva caught his breath, thinking Number One's loathing of infidels could spill over right there and then.

Briggs didn't see it, or if he did, he misread it. A good Catholic, he looked at Rodrigo, smiled at his crucifix, and stamped the passport.

"Welcome to America, Rodrigo."

· · · · ·

Silva trusted few people. One was Antón, and another was Pedro Lopez, a sixty-five year-old Cuban who lived in Miami. Pedro, like

Silva, had been recruited into the KGB as a young man by Antón, and his sources included construction and demolition companies owned by Russian mafias in Brooklyn. Pedro could purchase explosives and weapons without connecting any transaction to Mario Silva.

Since Silva had never run an operation in North America, over the years Pedro had supplied him with nothing more than documents, communication devices and other minor electronics, yet he hadn't balked when Silva had asked for three vehicles, eight Uzis, two thousand rounds of ammunition, 125 pounds of C4 plastic explosive, detonators, an electronic bug sniffer, and night-vision goggles with details for specific makes and models, price is no obstacle and no questions asked. Antón had given his heartfelt authorization and supplied the funds, and Pedro had flown to California to get a feel for the lay of the land.

"I won't bullshit you," Silva had told him as they stood in the vineyard in June. "It's going to be a risky operation. My Paraguayans will wreak havoc, you can be sure, but they might be as dangerous to us as to our targets. They aren't real soldiers – they pray more than they drill – but to our advantage, they will present a catastrophically overwhelming force, and our opponents will not be U.S. Marines. Your job is to make sure that you and I escape after the attack. Succeed, and you walk away with five million euros. That's five million reasons to do it, Pedro, and only one reason not to. You may die, but, as the French say, *alors, tant pis*, that's too fucking bad. This is a suicide mission for the jihadis, not for us."

"Anything else I should know?" Pedro asked.

"Yes. You should become acquainted with Islam. My boys are hotwired to distrust non-believers, infidels."

"You want me to become a Muslim?"

"No, but show some respect or they may turn on you."

·   ·   ·   ·   ·

When Silva and his jihadi soccer players entered the small general aviation terminal, Pedro was waiting in a bus driver's uniform, holding a soccer ball and a hand-printed cardboard sign that read, "Las Pumas de Paraguay."

Las Vegas never sleeps, the flow of high-rollers in private jets never stops, and people swirled all around them. The bright lights and noise came as a shock to the boys.

With a light tap on Pedro's shoulders, Silva said, "Get them out of here fast. Speak Spanish to them and English to me."

He took the ball from Pedro, bounced it to Number One and said, "Follow this man and don't talk. His name is Pedro and he is our friend. I'll see you on the bus in a few minutes."

Silva watched his small army of youthful terrorists march through the terminal and disappear through revolving glass doors. He walked to the other end of the terminal, stopped in front of a bank of lockers, thought for a minute to remember the code, punched a number into one of the lockers and withdrew a small suitcase. In a stall in the men's room he checked the contents: a laptop, two passports, fifty thousand dollars in hundreds, a small Glock and sound suppressor, a radio sniffer designed to find bugs, and six cheap, disposable mobile phones purchased by Pedro in Miami with no GPS trackers. Satisfied, he put the sniffer and one of the phones in his pocket, walked out of the terminal with the suitcase and called Pedro.

"Where's the damn bus?"

Pedro was waiting outside the conventional charter coach, his anxious eyes full of questions. Silva calmly turned on the bug-sniffer and walked around the bus, then almost ruined his expensive suit by crawling under the vehicle and inspecting it thoroughly.

"So these are your South American martyrs, hey?" Pedro asked when Silva was under the bus. "They look like zombies."

"You're very astute, amigo. They are for sure the walking dead." Silva finished his inspection and stood up, smiling and brushing himself off. "Is everything in order?"

"Yes."

"The other vehicles are in place?"

"In Santa Rosa, yes."

"And everything else?"

"It's all there, Silva. At least, it was yesterday. I can't be in two places at once."

Silva opened the suitcase, took out the laptop, turned it on and established a wireless internet connection to the airport system. A moment later he was watching a live camera feed from a Santa Rosa garage, an image of a flatbed truck with benches and canvas roof and sides, and a blue Ford Explorer.

He turned off the computer. "Let's go."

They boarded the bus. Pedro took the driver's seat and drove out of the parking lot onto Russell Boulevard. With no concept of what they were seeing, the fifteen young South American Muslims stared through the windows at the glow of Las Vegas.

Silva moved slowly down the corridor, a smile here, a kind word there.

"You all did very, very well on the plane and in the airport," he said in Spanish. "You can be proud of yourselves because we have now achieved our first strategic objective. We are in America!"

The boys were too mesmerized by the lights to cheer. Lives they would never live blinked in neon signs they couldn't read. They had landed in Hell, home of the Great Satan, and it was garish and strange and incredibly beautiful.

"Remember your discipline," Silva continued. "You may pray, but you must pray silently or in Spanish. Only Spanish! Praise be to Allah, blessèd be his name. Relax and get some sleep. It's going to be a long bus ride."

Silva shunted to the front of the bus and took a seat directly behind Pedro, asking, "Have you talked to our fat friend?"

"Sí, señor, and if you want to make sure, you can ask him yourself. He's right behind us."

Pedro had spotted the Lincoln Town Car as soon as the bus turned onto Tropicana Boulevard. He handed Silva an iPhone.

"Antón?" Silva said into the phone.

"Yes, my boy?" Antón's voice oozed out of the phone.

"You really shouldn't be here," Silva said, annoyed.

"I just want to know if there are any loose ends that need

adjusting, that's all. The stewards and flight crew? Will they be a problem?"

"No, I don't think so."

"You're sure?"

"Yes, I'm sure. We're fine. Please go away."

"Don't worry. I'm going to see our friends in Los Angeles."

"Yes. Do that."

The Lincoln swung around the bus and zoomed west.

.　.　.　.　.

"Mikhail," Antón said in Russian, "don't drive so fast. Don't attract the police."

"You promise speak me English, Antón Cosmovitch."

"Slow down!" Antón insisted, and continued in adamant Russian, "We don't have diplomatic passports anymore, and we're not in a hurry to get to Los Angeles."

Mikhail eased off the gas, took the onramp to the I-15 and settled in at almost legal speed.

"Okay, okay. You want me call girls in El Aaaay?" Mikhail loved to say L.A.; it sounded so American, so chill. Unfortunately for him, nobody in Los Angeles seemed to speak English. It was all Spanish or Russian, at least at Antón's house in Echo Park and the places he went.

Mikhail held up a phone and asked again, "Girls?"

"No girls."

"Boys then?"

"No boys either. This is business, Mikhail. Don't be a pain in the ass."

"How you say in English? Pen in the az? What means?"

"Just drive, Mikhail, and not too fast. I'm going to take a nap."

.　.　.　.　.

Boris Borisovitch Demetriov, the president of Belarus, a powerfully-built man six feet two inches tall with a glistening Elvis Presley pompadour, stood up and stretched, working his jaw muscles and flexing his abs. Once a hopeful Soviet Olympic weightlifter, he opened his arms wide to the sky and pulled his shoulders back, feeling great. He wished he could embrace everything he saw – the lush patio in the Presidential Suite of the Beverly Hills Hotel, the palm trees, the bikinis – and take it home with him. God, he loved California. It was fucking paradise. So many wonderful people to meet, beautiful, rich, powerful people with brains who posed no threat, who barely knew who he was. The sun was always shining, the sea refreshing and somehow reassuring. He liked it even better than Marseille. He would happily stay in Los Angeles for another month, but they told him the Bohemian Forest or whatever it was was even better. Wasn't Bohemia somewhere in Germany or maybe what used to be Czechoslovakia? Geography was not Boris's strong point. They told him he had to fly to Saint Rose, which meant being cooped up again with the two goons from the American Secret Service, but they wouldn't be with him on the grounds of the Bohemian Forest. As he understood it, he would be one of many presidents. No aides, no assistants, no bullshit, or rather a much better quality of bullshit, the kind that comes after a few shots of vodka. Or scotch. They told him most rich Americans drank scotch. Hmmm. What did that mean?

As he contemplated the American soul and its alcoholic preferences, his brother, Dmitri Borisovitch Demetriov, Minister of the Interior of the Republic of Belarus, as tall as Boris but slender and balding, entered the patio through a sliding glass door and handed Boris a phone.

"Antón Cosmovitch is calling, Comrade Boris."

"We're not comrades anymore, idiot. Address me as Mr. President."

"Of course. Go fuck yourself, Mr. President."

Boris took the phone and said, "Antón, my friend, I was just thinking about you."

"I wish that were true, Boris, but I know you. You don't think about anything except your dick. Nevertheless, I would like one more opportunity to persuade you to change your mind. You can't trust the Americans."

"I don't trust them, but I trust their money."

"You're a fool. Boris. They'll fuck you, and you know it."

"Only if I dress up in a dress, which I am told they do at this Bohemia Woods."

"They'll make you kiss their ass and lick their balls."

"For two billion, Antón, I'll suck their dicks, and so would you."

"Is that a no?"

"Go to hell, Antón. They already made a down payment."

"Boris, my friend," a note of desperation crept into Antón's voice. "Will you at least have breakfast with me?"

"No, Antón, not now. Maybe tonight."

"I know a place that would interest you."

"Tonight then, fat man. Tonight we can have a few drinks, for old time's sake."

11

Paul was asleep in the next room when Teddy woke up before dawn on Saturday morning. As much as he wanted to know Paul's thoughts, he let his partner sleep. After all, as far as Paul was concerned, they were on a dead-end detail. They would put in their seventeen days, write their report, and watch it disappear into the bureaucracy because nobody gave a shit. The people who could solve the inter-agency communications problem – the Attorney-General and the Secretary of Homeland Security – were stumbling around drunk and deranged inside the Bohemian Grove.

Teddy believed that years after Nine Eleven and Katrina, the government still didn't get it, and probably never would because the federal government was a collection of fiefdoms, each dedicated to promoting its agenda and increasing its power. He could tell the Pirates horror stories that would make them sell everything they owned and move to Costa Rica, but what would be the point? He had only twenty more years before he retired and moved to Costa Rica himself.

He wandered into the kitchen, started a pot of coffee, took a shower, and left a text on Paul's phone with instructions for the day.

Half an hour later, after a quick stop at Burger King just as daylight was beginning to paint Sonoma County in summer yellows and browns, Teddy was piloting the old red Suburban up Old Man Richardson's dirt road, juggling a thermos of coffee and a map marked up with details on every property that bordered the Grove.

It was going to be a gorgeous and hot summer day in the

redwoods. The last of the ocean mist was burning off, exposing tangles of manzanita and scrub oak. Teddy opened the windows and breathed the rich odors of the ancient forest.

The dogs started barking before he stopped, three big Rottweilers snarling behind a Cyclone fence next to Richardson's decrepit old house, hardly more than a shack. Teddy tossed three Burger King Whopper patties over the fence to the dogs, then crouched down and made friendly cooing noises to the suddenly happy beasts.

The front door opened and Teddy could see the glint of a gun barrel behind a tattered screen door.

A deep voice growled, "You're tresspassin'."

Teddy stood up but made no move toward the door. "Bernard K. Richardson?" he asked.

"Who're you?"

"Ted Swan, FBI. I'd like to talk to you, sir."

"FBI?"

"That's right."

There was a long, nervous pause before Richardson said, "You wasn't at Waco, was you, Mr. FBI man?"

"No, sir."

"Ruby Ridge?"

"I wasn't there, either."

"You gone arrest me?"

"No, sir. I just want to talk," Teddy said as courteously as he could. "I brought a thermos of coffee. Do you like fresh coffee?"

"Never touch it."

"I never met a Marine didn't like a cuppa joe," Teddy said, "especially a man who lied about his age to serve his country and came home with a Silver Star and a Purple Heart."

"Doctor over to the VA said don't drink it no more. How'd you know I was in the service?"

"Second Platoon, Company B, Second Battalion, Twenty-Seventh Marines, Fifth Marine Division," Teddy recited. "You lost your arm at Iwo Jima, Mr. Richardson."

A shaft of sunlight broke through the redwoods and struck the screen door, revealing the shadows of a dark interior, a life buried in the woods for seventy years.

"That was a long time ago," Richardson growled. "Is that what you want to talk about?"

"No, sir. I want to talk about the Bohemian Grove."

Another long pause. "You didn't come about the VA?"

"No, sir. The Bohemian Grove."

"What about it?"

"Could you step outside, Mr. Richardson, and put down the shotgun."

"No."

Sweat trickled down Teddy's back, and he felt the weight of his service Glock 19 pressing against his hip. He didn't want a confrontation, and he certainly didn't want a cranky old man to start shooting.

"That's okay," he said. "That's okay, we can talk through the screen door. What I'd like to know, sir, is how often have you seen Butler Rhodes drive up your road?"

"That son of a bitch is up here all the time. Last night he was up and down here twice."

"You sure it was him?"

"I seen a red truck two times. God damn. I know Butler. Me and him is in the same veteran's post. He lost his damn war."

"I have a red truck," Teddy said. "Were you drinkin' last night, Mr. Richardson?"

"That ain't none of your God damn business."

"Do you know where Butler goes when he comes through here?"

"Up there in the woods some damn place. He's on my property, that's all I know."

"How about the other properties around here. Does he go in there, too?"

"You mean over to the Mexican?"

"Is that your neighbor?" Teddy asked.

"Yeah, the Mexican," Richardson replied. "Owns the vineyard, and that's one sad bunch a' grapes, I can tell you, only I ain't seen him for about a month, the Mexican."

"I want you to take a good look at my truck, Mr. Richardson, because I may be coming back, and I'd like your permission."

Teddy unscrewed the thermos cap, poured himself a cup of coffee and waited.

The screen door cracked open and the snout of a double-barreled 12-gauge poked out, pointed at the ground. Barney Richardson stepped through the door, at 90 still a huge, strapping man with long white hair and a massive white beard, but missing his left arm. The left sleeve of his plaid wool shirt was neatly pinned up at the elbow.

"Wha'd you give my dogs?"

"Hamburger."

"Got any more?"

"No, that's all I brought with me, but I can bring more next time."

Richardson looked Teddy up and down and said, "You don't look like no FBI man."

Teddy held out his badge and ID and said, "My job is to help protect the Bohemian Grove, and I'm going around to all the Grove's neighbors just to tell you folks that we're here."

"Them Boheems ain't nothin' but a bunch of rich queers runnin' around the woods. What do you want to protect them for? You a queer, too?"

"I just want your permission to drive on your road, Mr. Richardson. That's all, and if I don't get it, I'll have to get a federal warrant and come back with a whole lot of cops and agents, and they'll probably take away your dogs. You don't want that, do you?"

"Would you do that?"

"I surely don't want to, sir. I only want your permission to be on your property without a problem."

"When're you comin' back?"

"Probably tonight. I don't want you calling the sheriff again."

Richardson cracked the shotgun, a gesture of good will, and said, "Ah, he don't never do nothin' anyway. I s'pose it's all right, but you bring somethin' for the dogs like you done."

"You bet, Mr. Richardson. Thank you. Now, your neighbor, you know where I can find him?"

"Like I say, I ain't seen him for some time. He has a house over to Monte Rio somewheres, down by the river."

"Mario Silva. That's his name, I believe," Teddy stated.

"I dunno what his fuckin' name is. All them fuckin' Mexicans got names that ain't American. And this one, he's a rich fuckin' Mexican from Frisco. He's probly queer, too, like the rest of 'em."

Smiling as he backed away, Teddy said, "Thank you, sir. I appreciate your cooperation, Mr. Richardson, and I'll be sure to bring back something tasty for your dogs."

Teddy got back into his truck and drove up the hill to the next ridge where he could see Mario Silva's vineyard and the road and fence around the Bohemian Grove.

He stopped the truck and walked down the hill through the trees and into the vineyard. A log cabin was on the south side away from the road, the windows shuttered and the door heavily secured with a chain. Teddy walked around it, figuring it was a bunkhouse for migrant workers who usually arrived in the wine country for the crush in September. As he walked back toward his truck, he picked one pale green grape and ate it.

It was sour.

.   .   .   .   .

The two-bedroom apartment in Guerneville Paul shared with Teddy Swan was furnished like a bargain motel suite with a kitchen, a little nicer than his apartment in Michigan but not much. Paul wandered into the kitchen, found a half full pot of coffee and poured himself a cup. A Starbuck's bag and a few spilled grounds decorated the counter, thanks to Teddy. He picked up the bag, neatly folded the top, leaned it tidily against the wall and swept the grounds into the sink.

Looking out the kitchen window, he saw a few pale, hardy trees poking branches toward a blue sky, and another low-rise apartment building across the street. The day looked bright and shiny, but nothing was going to cheer him up this morning.

He lay down on the couch in the living room, hands behind his head, and stared moodily at the ceiling. It was seven o'clock on Saturday morning, and on Saturday mornings in Detroit he had a regular, informal meeting with his Arabic tutor, Achmed, at a little café in Greektown, ostensibly to work on his pronunciation but really just to chat. The more he listened to Achmed, an assistant professor of Middle Eastern studies at the University of Detroit, the more he learned about Islam and the Muslim world, and the less he understood. In his life he'd known evangelical Christians, church-oriented Mormons, and devout Jewish Hasidim, but he'd never encountered people quite so wrapped up in religion as fundamentalist Muslims. It was clear that extremists in the Muslim community were a tiny minority, but the only way to separate them out was to learn their language. Yet, even if he mastered Arabic and came to grips with the culture, how would that help him prevent a terrorist attack?

He knew the answer, of course, and it came down to the long, slow process of detailed police work, developing informants and cultivating relationships that might generate useful intelligence. There was nothing glamorous about that, but he was willing to try. After two years in Detroit, just as he was just beginning to get a feel for the lives of Middle Eastern Muslims living in America, the Bureau pulled his chain and bam! The Grove detail.

Sitting in Jeremy's radio room yesterday had been mind-numbingly tedious, and he certainly wasn't looking forward to more of it today and then for the next two weeks. It was almost too much to absorb: the Grove, the Pirates, Teddy. Where was Teddy, anyway?

A moment later his phone rang, and when he answered, Teddy sang out, "Did you see my text?"

"Yes, but how am I supposed to get there? You made me an appointment at the sheriff's department in Santa Rosa, but..."

Teddy interrupted with: "Did you find the car?"

"What car?"

"Your ride is in the parking lot, Paulie. The keys are under the front door mat."

Paul opened the front door and saw a six-year-old black Mustang

GT convertible with a foot high wing on the trunk and dual chrome exhaust pipes the size of garbage cans. Shaking his head, Paul walked over to the car, asking Teddy, "What the hell is this thing?"

"Federal impound," Teddy said. "Used in a bank robbery. Some genius bank robber used his own inconspicuous car."

"Yeah, well, I want to be inconspicuous myself. I want a Honda," Paul said into his phone, shaking his head.

"Sorry," Teddy said. "This is what we got. They probably put a government radio in it, but don't use it. Use the phone. Jeremy's always listening, y'know."

Paul flipped open the glove box and exposed a Motorola.

"Okay. Where are you?" he asked Teddy.

"On my way to Albert's house on the river. This morning I think you should see the people who will back us up if the bad guys pay a visit to the Grove. You have an appointment at nine with the sheriff in Santa Rosa – he's a piece of work, I tell ya. Make nice, you know, bad guy, good guy. You're the good guy. I'm the bad guy." Teddy quickly told him about his encounter with the sheriff at Butler's. "And when you finish with the sheriff, you can go back to Jeremy's."

Paul found the car keys and asked, "How do I get to the freeway?"

．　　．　　．　　．

"FBI," Paul said to the female deputy behind the front desk at the Sonoma County Sheriff's Department headquarters in Santa Rosa. "I'm here to see Sheriff Hix."

"He's not in."

"I have an appointment."

"I'm sorry. He had to cancel all his appointments this morning."

"Can you tell me where he is?"

She smiled, saying, "You must be the only law enforcement officer in the county who doesn't know where Amory Hix is." She turned and gestured toward a TV mounted on the wall.

On the screen a grinning reporter was framed by a crackling bonfire. Deputies were hauling bags of processed marijuana out of a barn and hurling them into the flames.

"...five suspects have been arrested here at Buckminster Vintners, and according to Sheriff Hix, the high quality pot has a street value of four point two million..."

. . . . .

"You aren't going to believe it. The sheriff cancelled my appointment," Paul said on the phone to Teddy as he followed the deputy's directions up U.S. 101 to Healdsburg.

"Oh, yes I would," Teddy answered with a laugh. "Jeremy has a TV and we've been watching the sheriff do his thing. It's hilarious. Don't spoil his big day, Paulie. Make friends."

Paul drove through Healdsburg, a gentrified little upscale gem about fifteen miles up the Russian River from Monte Rio, then east of town through acres and acres of vineyards. He took a right at a sign for Buckminster Vintners and drove another mile. To his left, beyond the endless rows of vines, he caught glimpses of willows, and when the road curved closer to the river, he could see reeds in the sluggish dark green water and gravel beaches on the far bank.

He smelled the smoke before he saw it drifting over a low hill on his right. He passed through an open gate with another sign for Buckminster Vintners, drove over the hill and saw a TV truck, a van from the Press-Democrat newspaper in Santa Rosa, and Sheriff Amory Hix and seven deputies in surgical masks pulling armfulls of marijuana out of a barn and throwing them onto a burning pile.

Hix, his deputies, the TV crew and press corps were all stoned out of their minds, laughing and shouting gibberish, and Paul knew he would be too if stayed there more than thirty seconds.

Immensely pleased with himself and having a grand old time, the extremely tall Sheriff stood downwind from the fire, taking the full blast of gaseous tetrahydracanabinol right in the face.

"Sheriff Hix?"

"I already made my statement to the media," declared the sheriff. "You're late."

"FBI," Paul said, waving his creds.

"Oh, shit," the sheriff cursed, throwing up his hands. "Is this about last night?"

"No, sir," Paul replied, remembering to make nice. "I'm here to talk about the Bohemian Grove."

"What about it?"

"Do you have a plan to evacuate the Grove, Sheriff?"

The sheriff didn't want to look bad in front of his deputies again, so he took one more hit from the cloud of smoke and staggered out of the breeze.

"Sure. We have a plan. We have a plan for everything."

"We were thinking about having an exercise," Paul said. "We want to have a fire drill."

"Are you out of your mind?" Hix squawked. "At the Bohemian Grove?"

"Sheriff, what if I told you that such a drill was starting right now! What would you say to that?"

The sheriff was stoned all right, but not so stoned he couldn't see that if there were a fire drill right now, he was in big trouble. Two thousand very pissed off Bohemians would descend into his jurisdiction in total chaos and confusion.

The sheriff pulled his cellphone out of his pants pocket, dropped it, and mumbled as he bent over to pick it up, "I gotta call the fire department."

"Don't bother," Paul said. "There isn't any drill, but I think having one is a good idea."

"Oh, thank God. I got a four-point-two-million dollar pot bust going on right here. I don't need to worry about the God damned Bohemian Grove."

"I'd like to know, Sheriff, how many people in your department speak Arabic?"

"What? Arabic?"

"Yes. Arabic."

"How the fuck do I know? Probably none. Maybe, let's see, no, Marjeet is from Pakistan, I think." He turned and shouted to one of his deputies, "Hey, Arnie! We got anyone in the department speaks Arabic?"

"Nope," said one of the deputies. "We got Veetnamese, Mexican, Chinese, and Rosso and Martinelli speak Eye-talian. No Arab."

"How many Muslims are in your county?" Paul asked the sheriff.

"I have no fucking idea. Some, I suppose."

"Two thousand one hundred and thirty five."

"Well, thank you for your amazing FBI intelligence report," the sheriff snarled. "I'm sure I'll find that information extremely useful someday."

"Sheriff," Paul said, realizing he was a little woozy from the smoke. "For your sake I hope that day isn't today."

.   .   .   .   .

Driving slowly through the outskirts of Santa Rosa, concentrating on his motor functions because he was stoned, Paul paid no attention to the chartered bus with blackened windows that he followed for a mile. The bus turned into a small, isolated industrial park, and Paul was well down the road when Pedro opened an automatic door with a remote and drove the bus inside a spacious garage.

"Okay," Silva said to his boys, "Time to stretch your legs and change clothes."

The bus ride had been as uneventful as the flight. The freeways had put most of the boys to sleep, and they filed yawning out of the bus and stood around on the concrete floor of the garage.

An old Dodge flatbed and new Ford Explorer were waiting exactly as Pedro had left them. An array of migrant workers' clothing filled the back of the flatbed: Mexican guayabera shirts and t-shirts with sports and music logos, well-worn jeans, straw cowboy hats, dirty baseball caps, huaraches, cowboy boots, and a stack of brand new prayer rugs.

"Find things that fit, get comfortable," Silva said. "And then we shall pray to Allah, blessèd be his name, for a safe journey the rest of the way."

"Is it far?" asked Number One.

"No, but you'll be exposed in the back of the truck. People will see you. If they wave, wave back. Smile, and please, remember to speak only Spanish, even among yourselves."

"Do we still have to wear these crosses?"

"Yes. You're Mexicans now, and just as Catholic as Paraguayans."

While the boys changed, Pedro ran the bug sniffer over the waiting trucks, and Silva inspected the contents of the SUV: 125 450-gram bricks of C4 plastic explosive, detonators, night-goggles, Uzis and ammunition, all packed into boxes marked Black and Decker. Every specification had been met; every detail correct.

"You did a great job, Pedro. It's perfect."

"Thank you. With enough money, anything is possible."

"Indeed. When you were here, did you go over the route?" Silva asked.

"No. I didn't go anywhere near the Grove. No need to show my face over there."

"All right," Silva said quietly. "I'll drive the flatbed and you stay behind me, just in case one of them gets crazy and decides to jump and run."

"Do you think that could happen?"

"No, but if it does, you have to let him go. You can't leave the Explorer, not with this cargo."

Pedro stowed the soccer gear in the Explorer, and the boys looked splendid in their farm workers' clothes.

"You may wash and purify yourselves," Silva said, holding up gallon jugs of water. "God is great. And then we shall pray."

The boys ritualistically performed their ablutions and spread their new prayer rugs on the hard concrete. They knelt and bowed their heads toward Mecca as Silva began the prayer, "The martyr has seven special favors from Allah."

12

The cozy smell of frying bacon wafted through Butler and Maggie's house, invaded the bedroom, and started Jojo whining and pawing at the door. Butler crawled out of bed and let the dog race down the hall toward the kitchen.

Jojo barked and begged, and Maggie hollered, "Butler! Get your sorry ass in here. Amory Hix is on TV."

Butler could hear the TV blaring in the kitchen. Sweet Jesus, he was hungover, and not only from too much beer. He'd had enough of his old nemesis, the sheriff, and didn't need to see him on TV in his kitchen. He stumbled into the bathroom, thoughts swirling through his head like gnats: the Grove; Jeremy and his damned radios; Amory Hix's startled expression when Teddy said, "FBI." That had been priceless, but he almost went to jail last night – for nothing. And why did that old fart Barney Richardson care who drove up his road? Why did Amory Hix hold a grudge forever? He tried to think about the owl he had to finish but his mind saw only lights in his eyes and the muzzle of Amory's pistol. He should drive up to Richardson's jalopy of a house, give the old vet a gallon of gin and make peace. Then he should go over to Amory's house in Santa Rosa at three in the morning and hit him with a searchlight and an FBI SWAT team. Tit for tat, bro. Even Steven.

"Butler, come get your breakfast."

He finished in the bathroom, walked into the kitchen and stared bleary-eyed at the TV. The Santa Rosa station had gone to commercial, and some fool was telling him how white his teeth could be. He turned it off and sat down at the table.

"Amory made a big pot bust at Buckminster Vintners this morning," Maggie said as she handed Butler a plate of scrambled eggs. "I guess since he couldn't haul you away last night, he took it out on them. Your eggs are getting cold."

"Buckminster Vintners?" Butler mumbled. "Don't you know those people?"

"Yeah," Maggie said. "They're clients, or they were."

A graphic designer with an office in Santa Rosa, many of Maggie's clients were vintners and wineries, and some bought sculptures from Butler as well.

"Did you know they were growing dope?" Butler inquired, blinking, still trying to wake up. The kitchen was a little blurry. The stainless-steel pots and pans suspended against the wall were dazzling in the morning sunlight.

"I had no idea," she said. "I never went out there to Healdsburg. Those guys were techies from San Francisco with too much money and no taste, but they paid for a logo and labels. The TV had Amory standing next to a huge bonfire of burning pot, and he looked pretty stoned." She giggled and twirled her finger next to her temple.

"Too bad the cameras weren't here last night," Butler quipped. "Did you know Amory couldn't play basketball for shit when he was a kid? He'd just elbow people out of the way and knock them on their ass, and he still couldn't hit a shot. He was the tallest kid in school and couldn't make the team."

"Butler, I've heard those stories a million times. What I want to know is: Are you going to keep out of Barney Richardson's woods?"

"That's a negatory," Butler declared, putting an exclamation point on it with a slice of crispy bacon. "No."

"No? What do you mean 'no'?"

"I mean, I shoot a lot of pictures in those woods, Maggie. That's how I got the owl."

"You're incorrigible," Maggie pronounced in her best schoolmarm voice.

"I hope so. Anyway, I know how to make peace with that old man.

A half-gallon of gin will do the trick. He's all right, a little cantankerous, that's all, and he ain't nothin' compared to all these cops and the FBI, all this crap. I'm tired of Jeremy and his radio bullshit."

"You blame Jeremy?"

"If it wasn't for him and his radios, the FBI wouldn't care about us."

Maggie scrunched up her face, shook her head and wagged her finger, "Butler, Jeremy doesn't send you into Richardson's woods. You do that all by yourself. Why don't you forget about all this Bohemian Grove nonsense and come to the city today with Susan and me? Albert, too. We're going to have lunch with my mom and then maybe go to the movies."

Maggie took off her apron and Butler noticed she was wearing a fashionable tight denim skirt, lacey jacket and high-heeled sandals. All dressed up with her makeup on, she'd made him scrambled eggs, rye toast, cherrywood-smoked bacon from Pickett's, fresh orange juice and coffee. Some things in life were too good to be true.

"Give us a kiss," he said.

"No! You'll mess up my face."

"So what?"

She bent over and imprinted his forehead with pink lipstick. "Come to the city with us," she said. "We can have fun."

"I'll pass on the shopping trip."

"Did I mention shopping?"

"No, but that's what it is. Say hi to mom. I'm staying here. I gotta finish the owl."

Butler reached for his phone and called Jeremy in his radio shack.

"Yo, Butler. Good morning to you, sir," Jeremy answered, sounding a lot more relaxed than yesterday.

"You seen those FBI guys this morning?" Butler asked.

"Yes, indeed," Jeremy laughed. "Special Agent Paul is sitting here right now with Phillip and me, and I think he's stoned out of his mind. He was out there with Amory Hix burning pot. See Amory on TV?"

"I missed it," Butler said. "How many Bohos so far?"

"Let's see. Twelve hundred and seventy-nine. Is that right, Phillip? He's nodding," Jeremy lowered his voice and said, "Special Agent Paul mumbled something about Special Agent Teddy heading for Albert's. He wants to go out on the river."

"Really! He wants to join the Pirates? We'll see about that."

Butler hung up and dialed Albert who was in bed with Susan, dreamily enjoying post-coital bliss. Butler could hear the river trickling below their bedroom window and the joyous shouts of tourists in rented water craft.

"I think that FBI guy Teddy Swan is about to show up at your house," Butler said.

Albert sat upright and bellowed, "So?"

"He wants to go out on the river."

Holding the phone, Albert crawled out of bed and walked out on his deck overlooking the river thirty feet below. The sluggish summer stream was dappled dark green, and his small floating dock bobbed gently in the current. A big, blue rowboat lay upside down on blocks at the foot of the dock. On the far bank, through a tangle of willows, he could see a few houses on stilts and part of the fourteenth green of the Northwood golf course.

A party of tourists drifted by in bright yellow rafts.

"What does he think he wants to do, out on the river?" Albert asked Butler over the phone.

"I dunno. Take a look at the Grove from the water, I suppose."

To his left more willows and a stand of eucalyptus obscured Albert's view of Joanna's house and garden, and to his right he looked into the neglected back yard of his absent neighbor, Mario Silva, and Silva's rotted, unused dock. On the far side of Silva's property, concealed by trees, was the Bohemian Beach, a small stretch of imported white sand that allowed Bohos to frolic by the river. Behind the beach, the far reaches of the Grove extended back into the forest.

Annoyed, Albert hissed into the phone, "Butler, if you guys want to go out in the boat and fuck around with the Bohos, go ahead, but I'm not going with you."

"You pussy, Albert."

"They're my neighbors, man," Albert exclaimed, exasperated. "I don't want to provoke them. Besides, remember the Pirates' rule: we don't go into the Grove."

"But the Bohemian Beach is not in the Grove," Butler declared. "By federal law the banks of a navigable river shall be accessible to the public from the water up to the mean high water mark. That means the Bohemian Beach is accessible to me and you."

"Would you like to test that theory in court?" Albert demanded, his voice rising.

"You're damn right I would!" Butler spat into the phone. "Because they know it's true. Half the Bohos are lawyers. All those politicians are fucking lawyers."

"You're crazy, Butler," Albert said, staring at his phone. "Sometimes you are a child."

While Butler argued with Albert on the phone, Maggie sat across the kitchen table listening and becoming increasingly irritated.

"Let's take a walk on their beach," Butler suggested to Albert. He was grinning at Maggie who was looking at him, appalled.

"No," Albert said. "Not me."

"Let me talk to Susan," Maggie demanded and grabbed the phone away from Butler. "Albert!" she snapped. "Put Susan on."

Albert walked back inside and handed the phone to his wife.

Susan sat up in bed and said, "Maggie?"

"Susan, these guys are looking for nothing but trouble. It's ten-thirty. Are you ready to get out of here and go to San Francisco?"

"Give me half an hour."

. . . . .

The elegant, brown-shingled, craftsman-style houses on Albert and Susan's side of the little street, grandly named River Boulevard, were directly on the river. The homes across the street abutted the Bohemian Grove whose redwoods extended into their back yards. Towering eucalyptus and willows filled the spaces between the houses, and vines covered the garages that faced the street, melding the buildings into the forest.

As Maggie drove her Toyota Prius down the quiet street, she and Butler saw Teddy's Suburban parked in front of Albert's garage.

Susan answered the door, saying, "We have company."

Like Maggie, Susan was dressed for the city in heels and a linen pants suit tailored for her robust figure.

"One of them," Butler asked, "or both?"

"Just one, the white Bob Marley."

Teddy was outside on the deck overlooking the river, leaning back against the railing, a mug of coffee in his hand. Albert, in sunglasses, straw hat and shorts that revealed the football scars on his right knee, reclined on a chaise lounge shaded by a Pernod umbrella over a redwood table.

"Butler! Maggie!" Albert was feeling effusive. "Welcome to the Monte Rio field office of the FBI."

"Hello again," Maggie said to Teddy. "Thanks for last night. I don't know what would have happened if you hadn't been there."

"I think you'd be bailing your husband out of jail this morning," Teddy said with a big smile.

"Yes," Albert said. "Teddy was just telling us about that."

"Butler, I don't know what it is between you and Amory Hix," Susan said.

"It goes way back," Butler told her. "We grew up on the same block in Santa Rosa."

Susan cocked an eyebrow and waited for a story, but Butler lit a cigarette and stared at the river.

"I can tell you on the way to San Francisco, if you really want to know," Maggie said to Susan as they waved good-bye. "Are you ready? My mom is going to buy us lunch."

Albert watched the ladies pass through the house and out the front door, then said to Butler, "They're going shopping, so say g'bye to a grand, at least."

"No shit," Butler said, and then to Teddy, "What's up, man?"

Teddy peered into Mario Silva's back yard and said, "It's very interesting, Albert, that your neighbor, Mario Silva, is also Barney

Richardson's neighbor over on the south side of the Grove."

"I can't say Susan and I really know Silva," Albert said. "He's very quiet and he's hardly ever here."

Teddy asked, "Where is he when he isn't here?"

Albert shrugged. "I don't know, really. This is his second home, like a lot of houses around here. He lives in San Francisco, but he's originally from Mexico City, I think. He drops in for a weekend now and then, and he always shows up in September with a bunch of migrant farm workers to harvest his grapes. He was here maybe two months ago? I'm not sure."

"Does he ask you to look after his house when he's gone?" Teddy asked.

"Nope," Albert answered, shaking his head. "To tell you the truth, I've never been inside his house."

Teddy's phone rang and he answered, saying, "Okay...okay...now? You can hear them? Okay. Text me their names. Okay. Okay. Yeah. Got it. Thanks."

He put the phone back in his shirt pocket, said, "That was Jeremy," and they all gazed at the river for a few minutes. Tourists paddled canoes and inflatable rafts up and down the stream and laughter drifted above the spray. The morning sun was bright, the big trees beautiful, the tourists on the river healthy and energetic and it seemed as though Norman Rockwell had descended upon Sonoma County and painted the landscape with his all-American brush.

Teddy broke the spell by saying, "You could launch a fleet of inflatable boats here, go upstream a hundred yards to their private beach and walk right into the Grove."

Butler sagely shook his head and said, "Well, you could land on the Bohemian Beach, overpower the guards, if there are any, then trek a half mile through the woods to the campsites, evade the electronic surveillance that's back up in there, do your thing, then come back to the beach, and whoops! The guy you left behind with your boats is dead, and the boats are gone because someone across the river and called the cops. I tell ya, Teddy, a lot of things could go wrong."

"Unless you don't plan to come out," Teddy said.

"A suicide attack?" Butler said. "To attack the Grove requires guerrilla tactics, commando stuff, but you can't train idiots and suicide bombers are idiots, driven by faith, not by brains. You don't invest that much time and trouble in suicide bombers. Soldiers, even mercenaries, will take risks, but they want to live and fight another day. The kind of soldier who could get in also wants to get out. No, man. Nobody is stupid enough to attack from the river."

"What if it's an assassination?" Teddy said. "What if the bad guys know who is on the beach, and that's their target."

"What will that prove?" Butler asked. "That somebody can land on their beach and their fancy dock?" Butler waved his arms in the direction of the busy river. "People do it all the time, and they're sent on their way. As you can see with all these summer vacationers, this river is a very wet public highway."

"Well," Teddy said. "I think that if we land on their beach, that will be very instructive for Grove security."

"Well damn," Butler said with a laugh. "Yesterday you told us to stop fucking around with the Bohemians, and now you want to crash their party! We could all end up in jail, including you, Special Agent Swan. Why the fuck not? Let's do it."

"Holy shit!" Albert said loudly, his head swiveling furiously between Butler and the FBI agent. "That's the damnedest thing I ever heard of. You lunatics are two peas in a pod! You know that?"

"Listen, Albert," Teddy said. "Right now Jeremy is tracking some Bohemian guys from their campsite down to the beach. He can do that because the Blue Blazers are talking about it in the clear over their radios, and I want Bohemian security to know that. Look across the river, there, in the willows at the edge of the golf course. Do you see them?"

Teddy stretched out his arm and pointed at the tangle of willows at the edge of the golf course across the river.

"Yeah, I see 'em," Butler said. "Two guys."

"That's Paul and Phillip," Teddy said. "With a video camera and Jeremy's fiber optic parabolic microphone. They're listening to the guys on the Bohemian Beach."

Albert grabbed a pair of binoculars off the table, focused the lenses on the trees and started to laugh. "That's pretty cool," he said. "I wonder what they can hear."

At that moment the front door slammed. High heels clicked on the polished hardwood floor, and raucous female laughter erupted from the house.

"We changed our minds," Maggie shouted from the corridor.

Arms around each other, faces gleaming with mirth, the two women paraded onto the deck.

"We wanted to see what you were up to, you wild and crazy guys," Maggie declared. "We want to witness the debacle."

"And it's mimosa time," Susan announced and headed for the kitchen. A moment later the sound of a juicer joined the shushing of the river and the wind in the trees.

"Hi," Maggie said to Butler as she sat down next to him on a chaise lounge.

"You're stoned," Butler whispered in her ear.

Maggie reached around his neck and pulled him closer, saying, "Mom called and bailed on lunch, so we decided not to drive."

"Good thinkin'."

"Kiss me, you fool."

Butler bent over her and initiated a long, slow Hollywood kiss. Susan walked onto the deck with a pitcher of orange juice, a bottle of Mumms and five crystal flutes on a tray. She stopped to observe Butler and Maggie madly making out, then set the tray on the table and burst into song, belting out *Don't Cry for Me, Argentina*!

Maggie and Butler came up for air, and Maggie jumped to her feet, danced a little soft shoe and sang *Voulez-vous Coucher avec Moi.*

Susan poured mimosas and handed one to Teddy. "Got to get the day started right if you're going to save the world, G-Man! Hey! I have an idea. Let's do Teddy's hair!"

Butler winked at Teddy and said, "Tutti frutti, pal. That's Italian for loony bin."

Susan leaned toward Teddy and asked in all seriousness, "Are you a rastaman? Are the dreads for real, I mean, from religious conviction?"

"I was supposed to get a haircut this week, but it didn't happen," Teddy said.

"Noooo," Maggie cried. "It's cute."

Susan chugged a mimosa and poured herself another. Maggie sipped hers and grinned at Teddy. "What do you think, Susan? Braids or a pony tail?"

Butler announced, "Teddy wants to go out on the river in Albert's boat. Isn't that right, Teddy? He wants to play Navy SEAL and shake 'em up on the Bohemian Beach."

Teddy stared at the drink in his hand, then looked up at his hosts, his new friends, four people whose lives he was deliberately disrupting, four people who, it seemed to him, lived reasonably contented and independent lives that were not beholden to any institution or organization. If they wanted to drink champagne and orange juice and get silly on Saturday morning, that was their business, and he was envious of their liberation, but he had a job to do. He set his mimosa untouched on the table.

"Let's skip the boat and go through Silva's back yard," Butler said. "Over the fence and there you are, on the beach. Nothin' to it."

Teddy looked down into Mario Silva's back yard, once a well kept garden but now an overgrown patch of weeds. The big back porch had no furniture, and all the windows were shuttered.

"Hmm," he said.

"I wanna go in the boat," Susan declared. "I'll bring the champagne."

"Me, too," Maggie said, and began singing *Goodnight Irene*. After a few bars Susan joined in, then Albert, and finally Teddy. Butler gazed at the river and drank a little mimosa.

"This calls for appropriate attire," Albert said. "They don't call us the Pirates for nothing. Ho ho ho!"

"Oooo," Susan exclaimed. "Teddy looks like Johnny Depp as Jack Sparrow, don't you think, Maggie? I've got just the thing."

"The Big Bag of Stuff?"

Susan cackled and ran to the closet. A moment later she

reappeared with a huge white linen bag with a golden draw string.

Maggie looked into the Big Bag of Stuff and came out with a pirate's three cornered hat and a pair of shears. She grinned.

Teddy cocked his head and looked askew at the rowdy, ribald women, then at Albert, who twiddled his thumbs, and at Butler who returned his gaze with the look of a wolf in wolf's clothing.

. . . . .

As the Russian flowed past the Bohemian Grove and the houses along River Boulevard, the river in summer was a benign and charming stream barely a hundred feet wide and no more than eight feet deep. Canoes, bicycle paddleboats, rowboats, inner tubes and rafts drifted downstream at a lazy three knots. Turtles basked on rocks and hawks circled overhead. In the middle of the day the summer steelhead lurked elsewhere, in the deep pools and eddies downstream at Duncan Mills, waiting for dusk and its bounty of bugs on the surface.

A hundred yards upstream from Albert and Susan's, a swath of fresh, white, Monterey County sand lay on the small Bohemian Beach, and a floating dock protruded about twenty feet into the river then angled downstream. A small boathouse served as a temporary bar, and a young Mexican-American valet in a red vest stood ready to attend the four Bohemians lounging on the beach in comfortable rattan chairs.

Directly across the river, at the edge of the public golf course, and never noticed by the Bohos, Paul scanned the Bohemian Beach through the long-distance lens on Albert's video camera and saw four men in their fifties and sixties – all visibly fit, with perfect silver hair on their heads and chests, expensive sunglasses and prominent watches on their naked arms. These were big shots, boss men, captains of their ships, well-tanned specimens with hairy chests exposed to the sun.

Phillip was fiddling with Jeremy's enhanced parabolic microphone, aiming it at the beach and fine-tuning the electronics.

"Are you getting this?" Paul asked.

"I'm trying to," Phillip replied anxiously.

Paul looked at the river and glanced at his watch – Teddy was a few minutes late – then peered again at the Bohemian Beach.

"I got 'em," Phillip said. "Here," and he handed Paul a set of earphones.

Paul was astounded to hear the men on the beach so clearly. Their conversation had them sitting on the edges of their chairs and gesticulating for emphasis. They were shouting in every way except with their voices.

One guy, the oldest one, said, "Boris Boris is a wild man, a real bear, and he has a history of indiscretion. I think we should cancel his invitation."

"Bill," said the one with red hair, "you're a shit disturber."

"Roger," Bill answered the redhead. "You met him in Berlin. What do you think?"

"He definitely can be a handful," Roger replied, "but his brother Dmitri does his best to keep him in line."

"Will the brother be here?" asked Bill.

"Probably," Roger said. "They're always together."

"What is Boris going to say in his talk?" Bill asked.

"Who knows?" Roger answered. "I told him we wanted to hear about security for the pipeline, but he'll probably want to talk about how much he hates Putin and the rest of the Russians."

"That's just dandy," Bill said, scowling at the others. "We don't need that kind of bullshit."

"Are you saying it was a mistake to invite him here?" Roger asked.

"Yes," Bill said, a little piqued. "He's going to embarrass us."

"Well, it's too late now," Roger declared, growing impatient. "Telling him not to come could jeopardize the deal. You're nuts."

"Just think it over," Bill said. "Nothing jeopardizes the deal if Boris wants his money. We could tell him to fuck a donkey in Tijuana and he'd do it. Roger, I refuse to be embarrassed here at the Grove! I won't stand for it! Remember, I live here, not in New York or Texas. I go to the city club every week. I tell you I won't stand for it."

"Let's wait and see what kind of shape he's in when he arrives,"

Roger offered. "He has the Secret Service with him, doesn't he?"

"Yes. For what it's worth."

A security Blue Blazer was escorting a fifth Bohemian down the stairs to the beach. Paul immediately recognized John O'Shea, the Chief of Grove Security. The man with him, a stockier version of the guys on the beach, was dressed in pleated slacks and tasseled loafers with no socks with a sweater draped over his shoulders, its arms wrapped around his neck. Like the others, he hid his eyes behind sunglasses.

The men on the beach looked up from their conversation and watched the guys coming down the stairs.

"Isn't that John O'Shea with A.J.?" said the dark-haired younger guy. "I wonder why the chief of security wants to come down here?"

The redhead offered, "He probably wants to talk about Boris."

The security chief and his companion crossed the beach, and stood in front of the four guys in beach chairs.

Paul looked at his phone and said, "That's A.J. Hoff, CEO of Northern Star Energy."

A.J. Hoff said, "Bill, Mr. O'Shea tells me you want to cancel our invitation to Boris Demetriov. God damn! If I'm paying four hundred million dollars to the fucking president of Belarus, I'm gonna drink with him! And if he shoots off his mouth at the lake, so what! Bill, you pussy, stop whining and worrying about what other people think. You're worse than the fucking demonstrators yesterday. Shoulda run over the bastards. I told my driver that, and he mouthed off, so I stiffed him."

"You're one crude son of a bitch, A.J.," Bill snorted.

"Oh, get off your high horse. You want to do this deal as much as the rest of us. We're lucky the Chinese didn't offer this prick three billion. Boris is coming tomorrow, end of discussion."

"Hear hear," chorused Tom, Donald and Roger.

"Listen," A.J. said, trying to be conciliatory. "We can scope out his lakeside talk once he gets here. We already know Boris doesn't speak English so we'll have to use a Russian translator. If Boris really isn't up to it, the lecture can be cancelled without too much loss of face. It wouldn't be the first time something like that has happened."

At that moment Albert's blue rowboat appeared from behind the trees. Wearing a black, piratical do rag, a black eye patch and waders that came up to his chest, Albert knelt in the bow paddling furiously, aiming for the Bohemian dock.

Dressed in red satin dance-hall dresses and elaborate Victorian hats with wide brims and willowy feathers, Maggie and Susan sat together on the middle bench. Susan daintily poured champagne into Maggie's plastic cup. Manning the stern and paddling more cautiously than Albert, Butler wore a complete and authentic Captain Hook costume, including the hook, three cornered hat, eye patch, frock coat with outsized cuffs, frilly shirt, knee breeches, stockings, buckled shoes, and plastic saber.

The red-vested valet was the first to notice the pirate boat heading straight for the beach. He bolted onto the dock, waving his arms, wondering what he was supposed to do. Captain Hook? This looked like a Bohemian prank – the Bohos were always dressing up in costumes for some kind of jinks, high or low. He could never get it straight.

The Bohos on the beach watched, at first with alarm, then with amusement, and finally with alarm again as the scene unfolded.

John O'Shea ran onto the dock and began waving his arms frantically.

"Excuse me!" he yelled at the boat that was now ten feet from the dock. "This is private property. You can't land here."

As the boat slid up to the dock, Albert reached out and grabbed a cleat.

Watching through the video camera, Paul thought O'Shea was going to step on Albert's hand.

Butler eased the rear of the boat against the dock and held on.

Eyes popping, O'Shea yelled, "Excuse me, excuse me, but I must ask you to leave."

Butler hopped nimbly onto the dock, swept off his three-cornered hat and bowed deeply.

"You can't land here!" O'Shea exclaimed, balling his fists and looking like he was going to explode.

Butler struck a fencing pose with his saber and waved it in O'Shea's face. "This, good sir," he said with exaggerated pomposity, "is a free country! And I bid you greetings from the Russian River Society of Pirates and Thieves!"

"Ta da!" Maggie exclaimed with a peal of laughter.

Butler stuck the point of his polystyrene saber into the dock, leaned on it and declared, "The Russian is a navigable river, and by federal law the banks of a navigable river shall be accessible to the public up to the mean high water mark."

He waved the sword in the direction of the Bohos on the beach, indicating quite clearly what he meant. "If you wish to dispute that, call the Coast Guard. They know the law."

From the front of the boat, Albert employed his basso profundo to maximum effect with a magnificent laugh that froze the men on the beach. Susan suddenly stood up and the boat wobbled violently. She held out two hands, one clutching a bottle of champagne, and the valet rushed forward, took the bottle but missed her free hand. With a shriek she fell backwards into the river with a resounding splash.

From the water she shouted to the valet, "Thank you for saving the Mumm's, young man. You're a true gentleman."

"How's the water?" Albert inquired.

"Chilly – but refreshing."

Albert in his waders slipped out of the boat into the waist-deep water and lifted his wife onto the dock where she sat, feet dangling in the water. She laughed and reached for the champagne. Maggie stood up and the boat rocked again, but she managed to step onto the dock without going into the river. Albert began striding with long, slow-motion steps through the water toward the beach.

Completely flustered, O'Shea turned to the valet and shouted, "Do something!"

On the far side of the river, Phillip and Paul couldn't contain themselves anymore and doubled over with laughter. They both sat down on the ground and laughed uncontrollably.

Albert waded out of the river, walked up to the recoiling Bohos and said, "Good morning, gentlemen. Greetings from the Russian River Society of Pirates and Thieves. We know the Bohemian Club appreciates a little theater, so relax and enjoy our little play."

At that moment Teddy appeared out of the woods behind the boathouse. Special Agent Theodore Swan of the FBI danced onto the beach in a goofy jester's cockscomb hat, red, green and blue checkered jerkin, bombasted hose, yellow stockings and long pointy shoes with bells at the tips.

"Gentlemen," the jester said to the Bohos, "Agent Swan of the FBI at your service. A security exercise, if you please."

Trembling with rage, O'Shea scrambled off the dock and screamed at Teddy, "Swan! You're trespassing! I'll have you arrested!"

"I don't think so," Teddy said calmly. "The sheriff seems to be incapacitated right now."

Embarrassed, distraught and frustrated, O'Shea wanted to rip the braided hair out of Teddy's head. "What the hell is this?" he screamed.

"It appears to be a breach of your security," Teddy said. "You might want to review your radio procedures, Mr. O'Shea. Whenever one of your members comes down to the beach, his location is reported over your Blue Blazer radio system, and anyone can listen. As for trespassing, perhaps you should speak to your attorneys. And look across the river and maybe you'll see the telescope and parabolic microphone, or maybe you won't. You certainly haven't yet."

Teddy took his creds from his hat, flashed his gold badge at the Bohos, and read from Jeremy's text on his phone. Pointing to each of the Bohemians one by one he said, "Mr. Bill Anthony, CEO of Shield Oil, Mr. Donald Matthews, chairman of Texas Pipe and Drill, Mr. Roger Blake, president of Valdez Alaska, Mr. Tom Bunderson, chairman of Petrotech, and Mr. A.J. Hoff, CEO of Northern Star Energy. All of you are from Ye Olde Owls camp, and I thank you." He put the phone back in his hat.

Susan stood up on the dock, shook her wet dress, smiled at the men on the beach and asked. "Would you gentlemen care for some champagne?"

The Bohos were too shocked to reply.

"Gentlemen," Butler said with another sweeping bow. "It's been a pleasure."

"We're going to Pickett's for lunch," Maggie announced. "You're all invited."

And with that, Albert and Susan and Butler and Maggie and FBI Special Agent Teddy Swan boarded the big blue rowboat and paddled away downstream, leaving John O'Shea feeling like toxic waste, the Bohos astonished and amused, and the Mexican valet in fear of losing his job for laughing.

.   .   .   .   .

Phillip and Paul watched the debacle across the river, recorded as much as they could, then walked across the golf course, packed their gear into Paul's Mustang and drove back to Jeremy's.

Phillip was feeling extreme angst on behalf of Albert and Butler, who, he was certain, would be sued or otherwise punished in retaliation by the Bohos on the beach.

"Don't worry about them," Paul said. "The Bureau can protect them. What I want to know is: Who the fuck is Boris Boris?"

Phillip said, "Boris Demetriov, the president of Belarus."

"Where the fuck is that?"

"It used to be called White Russia, then Byelorussia, then Belarus," Phillip said, and the high school math teacher gave Paul the FBI agent a quick lesson in the history and geopolitics of the former Soviet Republics of eastern Europe.

"You know what's happening in Ukraine," Phillip said.

"More or less," Paul answered indifferently. "So, you say these American oil companies want to build a natural gas pipeline and the Russians don't like it. How do you know this?"

Phillip rolled his eyes and replied, "I read *The Wall Street Journal*."

13

The laughter under the fig tree at Pickett's punctuated the festive Italian accordion music tootling from Susan's iPhone and tiny Bose speakers. Bottles of champagne and platters of cold cuts and rotisserie chickens covered the red and white checkered and lacquered tablecloth.

It was ninety-eight degrees Fahrenheit at noon.

Tourists and truckloads of migrant farm workers inched along River Road in sweltering weekend traffic, and Pickett's parking lot was full of minivans and SUVs. Techie daytrippers from San Francisco carried sandwiches and drinks from the store to the extra tables the General had set up near the fig tree, and everyone stopped complaining about the prices when they took the first bite.

The commedia dell'arte was free.

Maggie and Susan had exchanged their soaking wet dresses for shorts, t-shirts, sandals and sun hats, and were entertaining themselves and the bemused tourists with Punch and Judy hand puppets from the Big Bag of Stuff.

"Oh, Punch," Maggie said as her Judy wagged her head. "I'm so glad you escaped from the evil Bohemians and didn't drown."

"Wawawawawa," Susan squawked, and her Punch opened his jaws, grabbed Maggie's Judy in his mouth and shook her like the rag doll she was.

"Oh Punch, you're such a manly man!"

The puppets were interrupted by Teddy the jester and Albert in his black do-rag fencing with chicken bones like fifth graders in the cafeteria.

"Take that, you scallywag," Teddy said, lunging forward.

"Ho ho ho!" Albert retorted with a counterthrust. "They don't teach you this at the FBI Academy, do they? Take that!"

"Oh, Punch," Judy exclaimed, "which one is the Bohemian?"

"Wawawawawa. I'm pretty sure it's not the African. Wawawawawa."

Butler, still dressed as Captain Hook, regaled the tables and the parking lot with an intoxicated outburst.

"Welcome to Monte Rio!" he bellowed. "Home of Pirates and Thieves. This morning, we were Pirates, but now…now we're thieves because we have to steal back the truth! We're surrounded by lies!"

"Lies! Lies!" cried Judy.

"Wawawawawa," shouted Punch.

"Almost everything I was taught all my life that I should believe is a lie," Butler ranted. "Religion is a lie, government is a lie, and ordinary people, bless your hearts, are pretty much full of lies right up to their eyeballs. They don't know what to believe because they are surrounded by so many lies they can't tell the difference, and so they believe what's easy, what everyone around them believes. And what is a lie? Here's a clue: the louder they shout that it's the truth, the more certain you can be that it's a lie. Ha!"

"You're just a grumpy old man, Butler," Albert said. "Look on the bright side."

"The bright side? The bright side? Bobby Dylan told us the truth fifty years ago, but nobody listened. Ha! Nothin' has changed. We still have a crappy government that's run like the marketing department of a smarmy oil company. What a nightmare. And do you know who's responsible? I'll tell you. The Bohemians! The Bohos run the show and surround us with lies that make them richer than Midas and keep the rest of us fat and stupid."

"Bad Bohos, bad Bohos," scolded Judy.

A young woman at one of the tables stood up and cried, "What are Bohos? I don't know what any of this means."

"I told you this place was a little bit nuts," said the young man sitting with her. "The food is terrific, though, isn't it? Just like the reviews said."

"But we showed them, didn't we?" Butler declared with a sly grin. "Aye, me hearties, we plundered and pillaged and sent the dread Bohemians scurrying back to their caves in the woods. No quarter! No mercy! Aye, aye, arrrrgh!"

"Oh, can it, Butler! You ain't that much of a pirate," Maggie shouted. "And Teddy looks more like Jack Sparrow than you look like Captain Hook."

"I still want to do his hair," Susan said. "Do you want to do his hair, Punch?"

Punch dived into Susan's Big Bag of Stuff and came up with a huge pair of cardboard scissors.

"Wawawawawa! Chop chop."

Butler raved, "The only real pirates on the Russian River are the capitalist warmongers in the Grove!"

"Oh, shut up, Butler. Don't spoil the party with a load of bullshit," Albert declared and grabbed Butler and put him in a headlock. Butler skipped free and ran around the tree, shouting, "When you strip away the lies, you're left with existential absurdity and nothing else. That's all there is and people can't stand that. Shouting out the truth to strangers is like pissing into the wind. It's not comfortable, it's not polite, it's not...it's not..."

He sat down at the table and lit a Camel.

"Are you finished?" Maggie inquired, then said to the tourists, "Excuse him, folks, he's just Butler."

"What is that music?" another woman asked Susan. "It sounds familiar."

"The soundtrack from *The Godfather*."

"Of course."

A rumble and cloud of dust preceded Deputy Alice who zoomed into the parking lot on her Harley with her wife Betty in a sidecar. Wearing motorcycle boots, jeans, and a black Oakland Raiders t-shirt, Alice stopped next to Albert's Lamborghini and kicked up her heels when she saw the costume party under the fig tree.

"Oh!" Betty exclaimed, taking off her helmet to reveal short, spiked, green hair. "Punch and Judy. And Pirates. What fun! Alice, you didn't tell me this was dress up."

"Hell's bells, I didn't know Susan would be here."

Squealing with mischievous delight, Susan grabbed Betty by the hand, dragged her over to the Big Bag of Stuff and started pulling out hats and costumes. Betty picked a few items, scampered over to Albert's truck and emerged a minute later as Tinker Bell. The short, green tunic matched her hair, and the wings, wand, and the bag of fairy dust fit her mood.

Alice sat down at the table, frowned at the champagne and asked Butler, "Got any beer?"

"Hear about last night?" Butler asked, fishing around the overloaded table for some beer.

"Oh, yeah," she said. "Last night at your place and this morning in Healdsburg. Things are always poppin' here in River City when Amory Hix is around."

Giggling, Betty showered everyone at the table with fairy dust.

Glowering at the silver sparkles all over her Raiders t-shirt, Alice demanded, "What the hell is this?"

"Gris gris," Albert answered. "Betty thinks it's fairy dust, but I know it's Mardi Gras voodoo gris gris. Tinker Bell was originally from New Orleans. Didn't you know that, Alice? It's true. Susan! Change the music! Let's have Dr. John!"

A moment later the powerful little speakers were rocking to a New Orleans second line beat and *Iko Iko*. Alice was happily clapping her hands.

Butler pushed around some champagne bottles and said, "I know there's some Beck's in here someplace."

Teddy's head was spinning. Who were these people? What was he doing here? Was he going to get snockered on champagne and play dress-up all day? He began to feel guilty because he was having so much fun. It was hard to concentrate on protecting the world when his motley jerkin was covered with bits of silver glitter and his ears were full of speeches about existential absurdity. What the fuck was that?

Betty sat down between Teddy and Alice and pouted. "No one believes in fairies anymore. The world is a cynical place."

"Cheer up, sweetie," Alice said. "Let's dance."

Alice and Betty were dancing cheek to cheek to *Mama Roux* when Paul drove noisily into the parking lot in the tricked-out Mustang, his exhaust rumbling like Texas.

Alice stopped dancing, accepted a bottle of Beck's from Butler, popped it open by setting the lip of the bottle cap on the edge of the table and slamming it with the heel of her hand, and watched Paul walk over to the fig tree.

"Nice car," she said to Paul. "Wanna race?"

"Paul, have you met Deputy Alice? She's the local constable," Butler said. "Alice, meet Paul Kruger, Teddy's partner in crime-busting."

Alice laughed and said, "At least you look like a Fed, except for the car."

"Pleased to meet you, too."

Butler leaned over to Albert and mumbled, "I never would've believed in a million years that we would party with all these cops."

"Is this a party?" Albert said straight-faced. "I thought this was lunch."

Dr. John wailed and let the good times roll. A passel of tourists vacated one of the tables and another sat down. Two limousines and a Rolls-Royce crossed the bridge, and the sun smiled on Monte Rio.

"We invited the Bohos who were on the beach to lunch," Maggie said to Paul, "but I guess they decided not to come. Hi, I'm Maggie Rhodes, Butler's wife."

"Hi," Paul said. "Paul Kruger." Then he said to Teddy, "Carter McGee wants us in Santa Rosa."

"So the shit has hit the fan," Teddy declared, pulling off his jerkin and jester's hat.

"Yup."

A few minutes later Paul and Teddy drove off to prepare for their meeting in Santa Rosa, and Butler repaired the microphone in the fig tree, re-attaching the wires Teddy had disconnected the day before.

Betty returned Tinker Bell to the Big Bag of Stuff, and she and Alice zipped away toward the ocean and Jenner-by-the-Sea. With a crowd of tourists waiting for the table, Susan and Albert quickly packed the Big Bag of Stuff into the Lamborghini.

"Come hang out, you guys," Susan said to Maggie and Butler, as she climbed into the truck. "We can watch the Giants on TV and drink more champagne."

"I gotta work on the owl," Butler said.

"I'll come," Maggie said. "Butler, you can drive the Prius home."

· · · · ·

A few minutes later, standing alone under the fig tree, the keys to Maggie's car in his hand, Butler watched Mario Silva's flatbed truck drive into Pickett's parking lot, the back jammed full of Mexican farm workers.

Feeling friendly and not in all that much of a hurry to get to his studio, Butler checked out the Mexicans, all hard, solemn-looking young men, most of whom were dressed in clean, white peasant blouses, jeans and huaraches, a few in t-shirts and boots. He saw crosses dangling from a few necks.

Butler smiled and said, "*Buenas tardes.*"

Several of the men nodded and grunted in reply. "*Buenas,*" said one, a wispily bearded face under a straw cowboy hat.

"*Hace mucho calor,*" Butler said politely. It's hot.

"*Sí, sí, mucho calor,*" said another, yes, yes, it's very hot, waving his hat in front of his face.

· · · · ·

Silva sat in the driver's seat of the old Dodge flatbed and swore. Damn! Where was Pedro? As he approached the Monte Rio bridge, Pedro should have been right behind him in the Explorer, but the Ford had become separated in the heavy traffic.

Violating his own rules, Silva began cursing madly under his breath in Arabic as he pulled into Pickett's parking lot. He called Pedro on a disposable phone.

"Where in bloody hell are you?"

"I got cut off and lost sight of you," Pedro replied nervously. "So I pulled over."

"Stay where you are," Silva ordered. "I'll come back and find you."

Glancing in the rearview mirror he saw a guy he dimly recognized as one of the locals starting to talk to the boys in the back.

. . . . .

The driver's door swung open and Mario Silva stepped out of the cab, looked at his phone and then put it in his shirt pocket. He smiled at Butler.

"Hey, Señor Silva," Butler said. "Long time no see."

As far as Butler knew, Silva was Albert's part-time neighbor, a businessman from San Francisco and gentleman farmer. Surrounded by big trees and cut off from most of the daylight, his vineyard had never prospered, but Silva had done his best to plant new vines several years ago and was preparing to harvest his crop in September.

Silva paused a moment, letting his memory bank kick in as he registered the droopy mustache, the fancy cowboy boots and the ruby studs in the man's ears. Finally, he said, "Butler! Hello. Hi, how are ya."

Frowning, Silva was standing next to his truck and peering down the highway.

"Lose somebody?" Butler asked. "One of your guys fall out?"

Silva made himself laugh. "No, no," he said. "My foreman. I think he got caught in traffic. I think he's lost."

"How's the vineyard?" Butler asked.

Silva glanced up at his farmhands and replied, "We have to thin the crop. Lots to do. We're going to repair the bunkhouse."

"These guys gonna work for you?" Butler gestured toward the boys.

"Well, let's hope so."

"Can I buy your guys a beer?" Butler offered. "*Amigos. ¿Quieren una cerveza?*"

From the back of the truck the boys were staring bug-eyed at Butler with his seven ear studs, the women in shorts at the picnic tables, all these naked Americans, these infidels. Their eyes were bulging, verging on sensory overload, and Silva had to summon every iota of self-control to defuse the situation.

He hesitated, glancing up at his jihadis before saying, "Thanks, Butler. No, no beer. Maybe Coke or Pepsi or whatever the General has."

"You got it."

Butler went into the store, now busy with customers, and grabbed two six-packs of Mexican cantaloupe flavored soft drinks. Waiting in line at the cash register, he heard a fragment of conversation coming from the fig tree and repeated by the small speaker behind General Pickett who was standing at the counter.

"*Asif! Ana astshaan.*"

"*Por Diós, habla español.*"

"Did you hear that?" an astonished Butler asked the general as he laid his purchase on the counter.

"Hear what?" asked the General.

"From the speakers."

"I'm too busy to pay attention, Butler."

"Some kind of weird language. Say, General, you ever hear of Mexican farm workers who didn't drink beer?"

"I don't see too many farm workers in here, Butler. That'll be twelve-seventy."

Coming out of the store, Butler saw Silva's truck rumbling out of the parking lot and heading back down River Road toward Guerneville. As they receded into the distance, the young men in back looked hot and thirsty.

"Well, I'll be a son of a gun," Butler said to himself. "What am I going to do with twelve bottles of cantaloupe juice?"

He sat down at the picnic table, opened a bottle of *fresca de melón*, and thought about how loony it really was, this goofy little town in the middle of the woods.

Mexicans farm workers who didn't drink beer. He'd never heard of such a thing.

14

A hot and lazy Saturday afternoon on River Boulevard. The Russian River gurgled, a leaf blower churned somewhere up the block, and Sly and the Family Stone teased the galaxy through Albert and Susan's formidable sound system. It was one hundred and three degrees and steaming.

An empty bottle of Mumm's teetered upside down in a silver ice bucket. A fat joint in a Route 66 ashtray had been reduced to a stubby roach. In the heat of the afternoon, Albert, Susan and Maggie were in the final throes of a sweaty ménage-à-trois. Albert was on his knees fucking Maggie, slapping her ass and increasing his rhythm to a manic pace as he was about to come, and Susan, sitting on Maggie's face and leaning over to kiss Albert, was writhing in orgasm and shrieking, "Oh god, oh god, oh god."

When Albert began to spurt, he pulled his thick cock out of Maggie, and, roaring, "Sweet Jesus!" splashed a fountain of semen across Susan's chest. They all collapsed in a groaning, sticky heap.

Sly Stone merrily crooned. Albert laughed his joyous big laugh and the women giggled.

"It's hot," Maggie said, trying to catch her breath. "It's like a sauna in here."

"Albert," Susan puffed, "you really have to fix the air-conditioning."

"The guy can't come 'til Monday," he answered through his laugh. "He's Jewish. He doesn't work on the sabbath, and neither do I."

"You're supposed to be Buddhist," Maggie answered breathlessly.

"I don't think they have a sabbath."

"Well, Buddhists say the fewest stupid things," Albert philosophized, "so they win by default."

They lay panting and sweating until their heartbeats returned to normal.

"I need a shower," Maggie mumbled, eyes closed. "It's hot."

"What's for dinner?" Albert asked dreamily.

"Let me up," Maggie squealed. "I really want to jump in the shower."

Susan and Albert rolled over and Maggie disappeared into the bathroom. A moment later the shower began to hiss. Susan moved over to cuddle sweetly with Albert.

Albert deeply appreciated the fact that he had somehow arrived in paradise without the inconvenience of dying. Susan was a metasexual peach with a voracious appetite and a willingness to share, and she loved him. Here in their house they weren't black or white or Jewish or Buddhist, just Albert and Susan, and Maggie was their friend. It was almost too good to be true.

"You okay?" Susan asked.

"I'm fine. You?"

"Wow," she said. "What a day."

"It would've been a lot different if you'd gone to San Francisco," Albert said.

"We can still go," Susan exclaimed, sitting up with a big smile. "We can go to the new oyster bar for dinner."

"Nah," Albert shook his head. "We don't have to go that far. We can go to Marshall over on the coast. They have the best oysters Rockefeller."

"That's an idea. That's a very good idea. Now you're talkin'."

"Should we invite the FBI?" Albert asked.

Maggie came out of the bathroom with a huge towel and asked, "Invite the FBI to what?"

"Dinner in Marshall," Susan said.

"I think he's cute, that Teddy. Let's."

"He's too skinny," Susan said. "I like the other one."

"I still want to do Teddy's hair," Maggie said.

"C'mon, Albert. Let's everybody go."

The ladies both looked at Albert and laughed. They knew Albert should never smoke pot in the middle of the day, especially the killer Indica that Susan got from her rich, marijuana-dispensary-owning real estate clients. Albert wasn't going anywhere soon. He was dead asleep.

.   .   .   .   .

Silva knew driving away from Pickett's was unneighborly, but he couldn't risk more conversation between Butler and his boys. Being rude was a small price to pay for security. As he backtracked along River Road searching for Pedro in the Explorer, he recited little mantras to keep himself steady. No plan is perfect. Something always goes wrong. It was plain bad luck running into Butler, whom he hardly knew, and he never would have guessed the guy spoke Spanish. He couldn't blame Pedro for getting lost. They'd gone over the route from Santa Rosa but hadn't taken heavy traffic into consideration. Keep calm, Silva told himself. Keep your wits. This is a minor setback, not a disaster.

He found the Explorer parked next to Jiffy Quick with a very nervous Pedro behind the wheel. A cargo of machine guns and plastic explosive would make anyone a little anxious.

"So sorry," stammered the Cuban. "I thought it was better to stop than overshoot. All this traffic!"

"No problem," Silva said, keeping his temper under control. "Follow me. If the old man with one arm comes out of his house, don't stop. He's my neighbor and I'll talk to him later."

The little caravan moved out, and Silva thought: Thirty-six hours to go, thirty-six hours to keep his jihadis focused on Paradise with prayer and purification, thirty-six hours until payday.

Silva drove the flatbed across the Monte Rio bridge and along the Bohemian Highway to Richardson's Road. As he drove up, climbing the steep hill in low gear, the rough surface jostled the boys in the back and the dogs barked ferociously. Pedro, following in the Explorer, noticed that the bouncing and barking produced no more than frozen stares from the young seekers of glorious death. The dogs didn't frighten them. Nothing frightened them except Silva.

The trucks crawled up and over the ridge, following the track through the woods past the spot where Butler usually parked his pickup, continued down to the graded Bohemian Grove perimeter road and turned into a lane that ran along the edge of the vineyard. Silva pulled up to the log bunkhouse and stopped.

He stood absolutely still outside the truck, listening to the steady buzz of insects, the rustle of the breeze, the drone of a distant aircraft. No nearby motor intruded on the tranquility of the countryside. No one had taken interest in their arrival.

He unlocked the bunkhouse door, quickly swept the one big room with the sniffer, and ushered the boys inside.

"Keep watch," he said to Pedro, who nodded. "Make sure no one followed. We'll unload the Explorer later, after dark."

Bunk beds and plastic chairs filled one end of the room, and the other contained a kitchen table and chairs that concealed a staircase that led down to a subterranean storeroom. Silva pushed the table out of the way, descended into the basement, and returned with two boxes of gloves and pruning tools. He gathered his jihadis around him.

"My brothers," he said to his martyrs, "we are now less than a kilometer from our target, and the security people there will notice our trucks within a few minutes, if they haven't already. For the next few hours you will be farm workers, working on the vines closest to the cabin and farthest from the road. It is of vital importance that you speak only Spanish in the vineyard. If you have any questions about the vines, ask Davíd, Number Six, who, as you know, has done this work before. Keep in mind that Pedro and I will be very strict as long as we're here. There will be no lapse in discipline."

He handed out gloves and shears, led them into the sunshine and set each to work trimming fruit away from a vine. Then he returned to the basement, retrieved two bottles of wine and carried them out to the road.

A Hummer came along in a few minutes, its CD player playing Tower of Power's *What Is Hip*. Silva stood in the middle of the road and waved and the Hummer stopped. The blue blazered driver turned down the music.

"Good afternoon, gentlemen," Silva said, smiling effusively and stepping around to the passenger's side. "It's a beautiful day. I'm Mario Silva, and this is my vineyard."

The Blue Blazer in the passenger's seat stuck his arm out the window to shake hands. "Yes, yes, Mr. Silva, I remember you," he said. "What're you growing here, chardonnay?"

"Pinot noir, actually, and my manager is angry because he thinks I've neglected the crop. I tell him, I do it the old-fashioned way. I don't irrigate, I make the grapes work for their water, but him, he's a scientist, he wants me to dig a well and build a trellis. Now, it is so hot, I have to drop crop, you know, cut away some of the fruit, because it is so hot. What can I say?"

"How long are your men going to be here, Mr. Silva?" the driver asked.

"Two or three days. A little pruning, and maybe some work on the bunkhouse. I'll come back with another crew in September for the harvest. And gentlemen, please, this is from last year's vintage."

He handed the bottles through the window.

"Hey, thanks!"

"You're more than welcome. Enjoy." He displayed a big, toothy Mexican smile and repeated, "Enjoy."

"Well, good luck," the Blue Blazers chimed together.

"Thanks."

The Hummer continued along the road toward the South Gate. Silva waved and walked back to the cabin.

"I'm going to walk up the hill and see my neighbor, Mr. Richardson," he said to Pedro, "and make sure he's not going to bother us."

. . . . .

"Mr. Richardson? Hello! Mr. Richardson?"

The dogs were making so much noise, Silva wondered if the old man could hear him.

"Mr. Richardson?" he shouted.

The door opened a crack.

"Who's there? You're trespassin'."

"Mr. Richardson, it's Mario Silva, your neighbor from the vineyard."

"Who?"

"Silva, Mario Silva, your neighbor. I brought you something, Mr. Richardson, a gift."

"A what?"

"A bottle of Beefeater gin. I want to be a good neighbor."

The door opened a little wider.

"Was that you in them trucks?"

"Yes, that was me and my foreman, Pedro. We brought some farm hands, and they'll be staying in my bunkhouse for a couple of days."

"Mexicans?"

"Yes, Mexicans, just like last year. They won't bother you. They'll be working in the vineyard. Pruning, mostly."

Silva could see him now, the bushy white beard, one sleeve pinned up to his shoulder, the other holding a double-barreled shotgun.

"Be quiet now! Shush!" the old man yelled at his dogs who stopped barking and began to whine. Then he said, "Them grapes are sour."

Silva smiled. "It's only July," he said. "They'll get sweeter as they ripen. Here." He extended his offering, a half-gallon bottle of gin.

"What's that?" the old man growled.

"A gift. Something to keep you warm when the fog rolls in."

"My doctor told me not to drink hard liquor no more."

"Well, then," Silva said, taking a step forward, "you can give it to your doctor."

Richardson chewed on his lower lip, grunted, set down the shotgun and pushed the door open. Silva handed him the bottle, and the old codger cradled it under his good arm, saying, "You make sure them Mexicans don't go wanderin' off'n your property, or that federal FBI will come back."

Silva quickly looked away so Richardson wouldn't see him swallow hard. "Oh, really?" he said, sounding as casual as possible as he turned back. "When were they here?"

"This mornin'," Richardson said, suddenly effusive. "Damndest federal I ever seen, got hair looks like snakes. Knew all about me, and you, too, and he says that him and Butler Rhodes was gonna be in these woods on account of the Boheems."

Butler again, Silva thought. And the FBI.

"You don't say."

"Said they was goin' to locate all the Boheem's neighbors, so I s'pose they'll be talkin' to you."

"Thank you, Mr. Richardson. Thanks for letting me know."

"You wouldn't have none of them illegal aliens over there, would'ja? We got so many illegals in the county 'cause all them welfare bums don't want to do no work. You can see 'em all just standin' around over to Santa Rosa. Just standin' around, doin' nothin'."

"You said FBI, didn't you, Mr. Richardson? FBI, not the immigration people, la migra, ICE."

"All them federals is the same to me, but this one, he says he was from the FBI, and he shows me some fancy badge, and he give the dogs somethin' to eat."

"That sounds like an excellent idea. A smart man would do that," Silva said. "I'll bring them something myself when I come back." Silva winked and smiled, adding, "Don't forget to give that bottle to your doctor."

As he walked away, he glanced back and saw Richardson unscrewing the top of the jug.

·   ·   ·   ·   ·

At the bunkhouse he told Pedro that the FBI had been questioning all the Grove's neighbors. "No one has ever talked to the neighbors about

Grove security before," he said. "This is a new development. I'm not sure what it means."

"Do you think they know something?" Pedro said, sounding alarmed.

"No. If they did, the FBI would already be here."

"We can take the boys back to Santa Rosa and stash them in the garage," Pedro said.

Silva seemed to consider this possibility, but he shook his head and said, "No, moving would be terribly upsetting and expose them to even more people. The last thing we want to show is fear or anxiety. I don't think our risk is significantly increased by the FBI talking to the Grove's neighbors."

"I think it is exactly that, Silva," Pedro said emphatically. "The FBI was here. I don't like it. What would the FBI think if they saw this. Look at them," Pedro said, gesturing toward the jihadis sweating in the vineyard.

Surrounded by four-foot-tall grape vines lush with fat leaves and heavy clusters of small, green grapes, most of the boys were sitting or kneeling in the dirt, exhausted by the heat. Others were absently eating grapes or staring into space. The only one energetically hacking away at a vine with his shears was Davíd, Number Six, an Argentinean-Lebanese.

Pedro pointed at the faux vineyard workers and said, "I don't know the first thing about grapes, but even I can see they have no idea what they're doing."

"Number Six! Davíd!" Silva shouted in Spanish.

The young man stood up with a pair of pruning shears in his gloved hands and walked over to Silva and Pedro.

"Sí, señor."

"Number Six," Silva said. "You worked in a vineyard in Argentina. You know this work, and you must help the others."

"I've tried, señor, believe me, but their minds are not on the grapes. We are all – I must include myself, señor – we are all praying and trying to purify ourselves. And Rodrigo is saying these grapes will be used to make wine, that this is the devil's work."

"Rodrigo! Number One! Come here."

"Sí, señor."

"All of you, come here."

The heroes-to-be gathered around Silva and listened as he spoke to Rodrigo.

"Number One, do you believe in your mission?"

"Sí, señor, of course."

"Do you pray to Allah for success?"

"Constantly."

"Then you should know that these grapes will never be turned into wine – never. After we accomplish our mission, this vineyard will be abandoned, but in the meantime, working with the vines is absolutely essential to your success. You must remember your lessons and all I have taught you, and behave as if your enemies are watching every minute."

"But, Señor Silva, no one is here."

Silva placed his hands on his hips, looked up at the high, white sky, then back at Rodrigo.

"Look around," he commanded, "and tell me what you see."

"The vineyard and the trees, señor," Rodrigo said. "Many trees."

"The devil is more clever than you can imagine," Silva declared. "There are cameras in those trees, Number One. Cameras! Pointed at you! You were told that during training. Do you remember?"

"Yes, señor."

"They must see only what we want them to see. Our enemies are watching, right now, this minute. You must look upon this task of pruning the vines as an act of purification and humility. You must prove yourself worthy."

The Bohemian Hummer drove by a football field away, adding a visceral emphasis to Silva's exhortation. A small cloud of dust hovered in the air after the SUV had passed.

"Do you understand me, Number One?"

"Yes, Señor Silva."

Silva leaned close to Rodrigo and said, "Then work as if the success of your mission depended on it, and may Allah, blessèd be his name, look upon your work as an act of purification and humility."

As Rodrigo walked away, Silva said to Pedro, "This is hopeless. Let them stay out here until the Hummer passes again, but if they're going to pray, they might as well be inside."

15

It was one hundred and five degrees when Teddy drove his ratty old truck into a parking lot next to an anonymous, glass-walled building on the outskirts of Santa Rosa, the seat of Sonoma County some twenty miles east of Monte Rio. He parked next to a fleet of huge, black SUVs, each with a splendid array of antennas on the roof.

Teddy took a deep breath and set his shoulders. Having stopped at their apartment in Guerneville, both he and Paul were dressed to federal standards in cheap, dark suits, skinny ties and shiny oxfords, with concealed automatic pistols tucked into shoulder holsters. The long sleeves of Teddy's suit covered most of his tattoos, but his dreads framed his face with righteous defiance.

Teddy's phone rang. "Yeah...yeah," he said. "We're here. Okay. Yeah."

Already sweating, both Teddy and Paul donned silvered sunglasses and got out of the truck.

The glass doors opened and into the parking lot stepped a perfectly neat and trim African-American in federal dress, FBI Special Agent in Charge Carter McGee, their boss.

Without a greeting, McGee demanded, "Do you have the recordings?"

"Yes, sir," Teddy replied.

"And the video?"

"Yes," said Paul, handing over two memory sticks as they passed through the lobby and stepped into the elevator.

McGee smiled, stroked his tidy little goatee and said, pointing toward the ceiling, "They're all pissed at you, Swan. The Secret Service is up there, and the NSA, DSS, and Homeland Security, plus that asshole from the Grove, O'Shea, and the Sheriff, and they all want a piece of you. More than anything else, I think they want to give you a haircut."

"Why?" Teddy asked. "Is it 1969 all over again?"

Still smiling, McGee said, "You're upsetting everybody's applecart."

"That's too fucking bad," Teddy snarled. "Their apples are rotten."

"And what about these Russian River Pirates?" Carter McGee asked, no longer smiling. "Jeremy Steadman and the rest of them?"

"They're certainly no threat to the Bohemians," Paul replied. "That's a joke."

"They have as good a chance of finding bad guys as the NSA," Teddy declared.

"You're Feds," Carter McGee said. "So you gotta play ball. You're lucky. The Secret Service is on your side."

Paul snorted and the elevator slowly rose to the second floor.

"Agent Swan," Carter McGee asked with a sly chuckle. "Did you really dress up as a court jester?"

"Sho' 'nuff, boss. Paul has it all on video."

The elevator door opened and the three FBI agents walked down a short corridor and into a cramped conference room where a meeting of the local Counter-Terrorism Joint Task Force was in progress.

A red-faced John O'Shea, still wearing his blue blazer, was standing up and pounding his fist on the flimsy table. At least a half-dozen men and one woman were seated around a conference table littered with phones, tablets, notepads and bottles of water, most of which bounced and rattled with each blow delivered by O'Shea.

The chief of the Santa Rosa Police was seated next to O'Shea, and next to him was a female colonel from the Army National Guard, then a jackbooted captain from the California Highway Patrol, and several anonymous dark suits with ear buds, denizens of the black room at the Grove. Amory Hix, the lanky Sonoma County sheriff, sulked at the far end of the table.

Before Carter could introduce his agents, O'Shea jutted his chin aggressively toward Teddy and shouted, "Swan! You and your gang of clowns trespassed on Bohemian Club property and terrified five of our members. Good lord!" He threw his hands up and looked around the table and asked his colleagues, "Do you condone this kind of behavior?"

A brief period of clucking and shaking of heads ended when Carter McGee declared, "Yes. Yes, indeed, if it produces results."

This affirmation was met with a collective gasp except for Teddy and Paul, who slapped hands, which drew more frowns.

"Sit down, Mr. O'Shea," said Carter McGee. "Please sit down."

Fuming, O'Shea sat and glared at Teddy and Paul who sat down across the table from him. Carter McGee remained standing, saying, "I appreciate that you're upset, Mr. O'Shea, but we're here to assess our joint security procedures surrounding the Bohemian Grove. In the next twenty-four hours we have the President of Belarus due to arrive, and you and your people are broadcasting that confidential information to the world."

"Wha..what!?" O'Shea sputtered. "What are you talking about?"

Carter McGee leaned forward, saying, "Mr. O'Shea, when FBI Special Agent Swan arrived on your beach this morning, he already knew the identity of the five Bohemians who were there, and he knew that they were discussing the arrival of Boris Demetriov tomorrow."

"What are you talking about? What is this?"

"It is exactly what I told you this morning," Teddy said. "It was a test of your security. You failed. We have video and audio, Mr. O'Shea."

O'Shea sneered and stammered, "You..."

"Mr. O'Shea," Carter McGee barked sharply, and with a nod to one of the nameless, earbudded men in the room, he continued, "I have a report from the NSA installation inside the Grove. With the most sophisticated, high-tech, classified equipment available, the NSA is able to listen to all of us. I repeat: All. Of. Us. This is not completely unexpected, because plucking electronic communications out of the air is the specialty of the National Security Agency."

Carter McGee dropped a large photographic print on the table, a portrait of Jeremy Steadman in all his Birkenstock glory.

"However, without any classified equipment, and without a multi-billion dollar government agency to assist him, Jeremy Steadman — I'm sure you all know his name by now — is able to do the exact same thing. If Jeremy can do it, anyone can. Terrorists can."

Carter McGee dropped similar portraits of Phillip, Albert and Butler on the table, leaned forward on his knuckles, looked at each individual at the table and said, "Now the point of all this is that these Russian River Pirates are not a threat. We don't know who the threat might be, or where it might come from, but it's not going to come from Butler Rhodes, Jeremy Steadman, Albert Flowers or Phillip Mercier. Get that through your heads. If there is a threat out there, these are the people who have the best chance of finding it. Now, the Bureau doesn't like eavesdropping any more than the rest of you, but whether we like it or not, Jeremy Steadman and the Pirates have demonstrated how careless we are. If we make it possible for them to listen to us, then the blame is on us, not them."

From the end of the table, Amory Hix spoke up. "Butler Rhodes was a sniper in Vietnam," he announced. "And he's built a shooter's blind somewhere in the woods overlooking the Bohemian Grove. I'd say that's a threat."

"We know you think that way, Amory, and that's why we've been talking to him," Teddy responded coolly at first, but then he raised his voice. "All he shoots up there is a camera, and he's as much a threat to the Bohemians as the guys at Buckminster Vintners, which is absolutely zero. Nada, Sheriff, zilch!"

Still stoned from his morning adventure, Amory Hix tried to stand. Shaking his fist, he caught his long legs in his neighbor's folding chair and fell back heavily in his seat. Several people shouted at once, the police chief and the highway patrolman yelled at the sheriff, Amory barked at Teddy, and Carter McGee hollered at everyone. The room teetered on the edge of total chaos until a tall, athletic gentleman in a beautifully tailored Saville Row suit and a clear plastic ear bud stood up slowly with a look of extreme distaste on his handsome Latin face.

They all looked at this man who suddenly dominated the assembly by calmly staring everybody down. The shouting stopped. The room quieted.

"For those of you who don't know me," he said. "I'm Raul Rodriguez from the Secret Service."

Rodriguez looked around the room, made eye contact with every individual, and said, "This is not going to turn into a petty dispute between a couple of federal agents and the local authorities. This is a Joint Task Force and we are going to work together."

He looked around the room and made sure he had everyone's full attention.

"Each of you has an agenda that you now must put aside," Rodriguez said in a voice that trembled with barely controlled fury. "Every year during the Bohemian Grove encampment we have visits from one or more heads of state. Kings, presidents, and prime ministers have all come through here, and this year it will be Boris Demetriov, the president of Belarus. His arrival is supposed to be confidential, but because of the Pirates we know this information has been broadcast. From now on, the safety of Boris Demetriov takes precedence over anything else."

He pointed at Amory Hix and said, "Sheriff, we'll need your manpower to secure the airport and the county roads. We have Boris Demetriov scheduled to come in tomorrow afternoon, and after him, we will have Saudi royals on Wednesday. A pair of Saudi princes are already here, and next week we'll have British royals. They all need to get in and out with as little fanfare as possible. We will be busy."

He pointed at O'Shea and said, "Do not mention Boris Demetriov by name under any circumstances on your communication systems. From now on he is 'Caviar.' Got that?"

"Caviar," O'Shea said.

Paul whispered to Teddy, "How long before Jeremy has that?"

Rodriguez pointed at Teddy and Paul and said, "You have your Pirates listen for any Russian language communications. You might hear Boris or his people, or you might come across someone interested in him. The Russians really don't like Boris, and they pose a real threat to him, but I want to make sure they don't try anything here. Not on my watch. You got that?"

"We're on it," Paul said. "We're going back to Monte Rio now."

· · · · ·

At the top of Starrett's Hill in Monte Rio, Jeremy stood up from his radio console, walked outside to check on the sweltering heat wave, looked around and immediately spotted the black SUV parked in the shadows across the street.

Spooks, clumsy spooks. The windows were blacked out, and three small antennas protruded from the roof.

"Well, fuck me," Jeremy said to himself. "This tears it."

Jeremy was pissed. He stormed into the house.

"The thrill is gone," he said to Phillip who was very stoned and lying on Jeremy's couch, ignoring the babble from the radios and listening to Miles Davis through headphones.

"Phillip, can you hear me?"

"What?"

"It ain't fun anymore!"

"What?"

Jeremy grabbed his phone and called Teddy who was back in the apartment in Guerneville, changing clothes.

Without preamble Jeremy announced, "We quit."

"Say what?" Teddy replied.

"You heard me."

"I'm on my way," Teddy said. "I'll be there in fifteen minutes. Don't do anything crazy."

When Teddy drove his Suburban into the driveway, Jeremy was sitting outside in an aluminum lawn chair, smoking a pipe and reading a magazine. Miles Davis pumped his magic through the outdoor speakers.

"You're not listening to the Bohos," Teddy said. "Don't you want to know the next time one of the Olde Owls goes to the beach?"

"Why should I care?" Jeremy dropped the magazine into his lap and looked spitefully at Teddy. "I can't do anything about it."

"What if I paid you?" Teddy said. "How much would you need?"

Jeremy puffed on his pipe, looked up at the trees and sky and said, "What do you mean, pay me?"

"You should be compensated for your time and trouble." Teddy said. "Hell, man, you deserve to be paid."

"Pay me how?" Jeremy spat. "With some kind of government contract and vouchers and purchase orders and billing and social security numbers and all that crap?"

"Is that a problem?"

"Probably. It depends on how much money we're talking about."

"You tell me."

"Okay," Jeremy said without hesitation. "Day rate as an electronics consultant to the Federal Bureau of Investigation, twenty-five hundred per day for seventeen days, plus fifteen hundred a day for my assistant, Phillip. That's a total of sixty-eight thousand minimum for the both of us. Plus overtime plus expenses."

Teddy laughed and said, "You have it all figured out."

"You asked. That's the answer."

"I can clear that. The paperwork takes a few days," Teddy declared. "Let's go inside."

"There's something else."

"And that is?"

Jeremy tilted the brim of his hat toward the black SUV. "Explain to me why the NSA is across the street."

"What?" Teddy jerked around and his jaw dropped. "Jesus. I don't know how I missed them when I drove in. God damn Sam."

Teddy crossed the street and knocked on the driver's blackened window. After a few seconds the window lowered three inches. Teddy held up his badge.

"Swan, FBI. Got some ID?"

A National Security Agency credential flipped open for a second and snapped shut. Teddy saw two guys with sunglasses and ear buds, one in the driver's seat and one in the back with enough electronics to decipher the universe.

"We know all about you, Swan," the driver said. "We knew you'd be here."

"What do you want with Jeremy Steadman? You're gonna spook him."

"Is that a joke?"

"No! Son of a bitch! If there are any bad guys within a hundred miles of this place, Jeremy has as good a chance of detecting them as you do, maybe better. I'm having a hell of a time just keeping headphones on him, and you're making it that much more difficult."

When the driver didn't respond, Teddy lost his cool and began to yell, "Why don't you get the hell out of here and leave him alone? What the fuck is the matter with you?"

"Up yours, Swan," the driver snarled and showed Teddy a middle finger. He shut the window and drove away down the hill.

"Fucking morons," Teddy swore, kicking dust as he walked back across the street.

Jeremy puffed on his pipe and noticed it was out. "You swear on your gold badge, Agent Swan," he said sternly. "You swear the federal government will pay Phillip and me our day rate, and you won't cheat us or bullshit us in any way. You swear!"

"Okay, I swear."

"Don't take advantage of us, Mr. FBI."

"Russians," Teddy told him. "Find me some Russians."

"Russians?" Jeremy said, puzzled, scrunching up his nose. "What is this, the Cold War redux?"

"Just humor me, Jeremy," Teddy said. "Find some Russians. We're looking for Boris Demetriov and guys who might want to take him down. Remember Boris?"

"Yeah, the president of Belarus," Jeremy said. "That's like being king of the moon. Big fucking deal."

Inside, Phillip remained on the couch, headphones on, eyes closed, grooving to Miles.

"Wake, up, Phillip! Back to work!" Jeremy yelled.

Phillip slowly opened his eyes, lifted a headphone off one ear and said, "What?" He saw Teddy and said, "Hello."

"Get it together, Phillip," Jeremy hissed. "Chop chop."

"Why? This is ridiculous. I'm gonna drive up to Mendocino and go surfing."

"Marika?" Jeremy said. "That crazy surfer chick again?"

"Yeah, that crazy surfer chick. She's a lot more interesting than all these rich pukes protected by the government." Phillip sat up and stretched. "A lot more interesting. I don't know how you can stand it, Teddy. It's sickitating, playing nanny to all these zillionaires."

"That's what you think, is it?" Teddy asked.

"Yeah," Phillip answered. "It's all bullshit."

"Would you still think the same thing if I said I was gonna pay you?" Teddy asked.

Phillip blinked several times and said, "What are you talking about?"

Teddy said, "How does fifteen hundred a day sound to you?"

"Wow!"

"I thought so."

Jeremy unplugged Miles and said to Phillip, "Why don't you take a cold shower and clear out your fuzzy head. You ain't going surfing, not today. We're going hunting for some Russians."

Jeremy sat down and put on a headset. "Okay," he said to Teddy. "These computer-controlled receivers can automatically search hundreds of frequencies, so it's already set up to search all the local VHF and UHF frequencies. I can program it to flag a bunch of Russian-sounding words along with words like 'Boho' and 'Grove.' We'll go for taxi and limo dispatch, ambulance companies, stuff like that."

"Russians?" Phillip said, puzzled. "Russians?"

16

Four hundred miles south, in a Beverly Hills Hotel room adjoining the presidential suite, Steve Hofer and Martin Broom, the two Secret Service agents assigned to Boris Demetriov, were playing Texas hold 'em with the Belarusian president's four bodyguards.

The Belarusians were winning. Yuri, the only one who could speak English, had just pushed two hundred dollars in tens and twenties into the pot.

"All in," he declared, trying but failing to hold a poker face. He broke into a smile.

"Think you got somethin'?" Broom said.

The door popped open and Dmitri Demetriov, the president's tall, balding brother, came into the room saying in Russian that Boris was heading to the Polo Lounge for dinner. Yuri translated, adding, "Boris wants to be discreet so you guys have a reservation a few tables away."

"Right now?" Hofer asked.

"Yes. Dress appropriately, but," Yuri paused, fingering his heavy, gold necklace, "let's finish the hand first."

"I fold," the two Americans announced simultaneously.

Laughing, Yuri gathered in the pot. All the bodyguards pocketed their cash and left the room with Dmitri.

"Shit fire," Hofer said. "We can't hide in the god damned Polo Lounge. We have to sit around like spooks with ear buds."

"That's what we are, pal. Straighten your tie. Let's go."

Five minutes later the two agents walked into the hotel's famous restaurant that was filling up with glitterati. Pink tablecloths, dark green booths, polished flatware, forty- dollar hamburgers, starlets with fabulous cleavage, but no Boris.

"Do you have a reservation for Boris Demetriov?" Broom asked the maitre d'.

"Yes, of course. For breakfast every morning."

"We've been fucked," Hofer said.

· · · · ·

The anonymous Mercedes limo followed by a smaller BMW emerged from a hotel service entrance onto Sunset Boulevard and inched north through the evening traffic. In the rear of the limo, to the great amusement of the Demetriov brothers, Antón poured French vodka and regaled his guests with stories of his many adventures. "But there is nothing like the next exploit, is there. The strange perfume, the touch of new flesh, the taste of the next drink. It's what keeps us alive."

"Antón Cosmovitch, you are a pimp," Boris declared with a bark. "You were a pimp for the KGB, and you're still a pimp for Vladimir Putin."

"I provide," Antón replied agreeably, nodding his head.

"So do the Americans," Boris said. "And they're very generous."

"I understand," Antón said. "Business is business, but that doesn't prevent us from enjoying ourselves, does it?"

Boris laughed. "Antón, don't be cute. You still want to persuade me not to do this deal with the Americans, but you shall fail. Don't you understand that if I let your Russian masters control my natural gas supply, that things will be exactly as they are now – and I will continue to have Russian overlords? That's unacceptable, to me and to my people."

"Boris, you pretend to be a White Russian, a Belarusian," Antón said with cosmic patience, "but you're as Russian as Vladimir himself. And you don't need the money. What can you buy with two billion dollars that you can't buy with one?"

Boris grabbed the bottle of Grey Goose and chugged, turned to

Antón with a twinkle in his eye and answered, "Russian angst. Russian frustration. Russian defeat. That's what I can buy, and I love it!"

Antón sighed. "That's our way of life," he confessed. "We get that for free."

Mikhail piloted the Mercedes up Sunset Boulevard through Beverly Hills and Hollywood all the way to Alvarado Street where the signs were in Spanish, convincing Mikhail once and for all that few people in Los Angeles actually spoke English. When the boulevard veered away at the base of the hills, Mikhail continued straight ahead, and they began the steep climb into Echo Park.

A vast grid of lights spread out beneath them. In the back seat Antón lowered the window to admire the steep ravines and quirky, eccentric feel of a neighborhood afflicted by a century of sustained decadence and benign neglect. After several dips and turns, Mikhail arrived at the gated entrance to a slightly rundown 1930s mansion with whitewashed Greek columns. A guard opened the gates and waved the limo and BMW onto the curving drive that led to the house. Faded yellow lights illuminated the broad porch, and music seeped through the walls.

Antón gestured grandly and said to his guests, "Do you remember this place from the old days?"

"I don't think about the old days," Boris snorted.

"I'm not suggesting we reminisce," Antón said. "I merely wondered if you recall coming to this house some years ago. It was well-stocked then, and still is."

"I like the beach," Boris declared. "The women are already mostly naked."

"I remember this place," Dmitri said. "Boris, this is where we used to take LSD and watch Jodorovski movies. *El Topo*."

Antón chuckled and uttered, "Yes, yes."

"Is it still yours?" Dmitri asked Antón.

"Oh, yes. The entire staff is Russian."

Mikhail turned around in the front seat and said in fractured English, "In all thiz Loz Angeleez, thiz best partay."

"Mikhail, open the fucking door," Antón commanded.

"Da! Da!"

Mikhail bounced out of the car and pulled open Boris's door. The president of Belarus stepped into the velvet Southern California night and took a deep breath, relishing the air gloriously scented with jasmine.

"Ahhhhh!" he exhaled noisily. "Caleeforneeah."

While Boris strolled around the grounds, inside the car Antón said quietly to Dmitri, "They'll take your cell phones when you first go into the Grove. You'll have to come out to the Service Center to make the call."

"Will that be a problem?"

"I shouldn't think so. Use this."

Antón handed Dmitri a white disposable phone, and Dmitri put it in his jacket pocket.

"And this man," Dmitri said, "you say he'll be wearing their security uniform, a blue jacket. How will I know him?"

"His name is Silva, and he speaks Russian like a Moscow native."

"All right."

The front door of the mansion flew open, and two young women in low cut black cocktail dresses skipped down the steps to the car. The blond immediately attached herself to Boris, encircling his arm with both of hers and pushing her breasts against him. The brunette waited for Dmitri to exit the car and greeted him with kisses on both cheeks. The Demetriov brothers and their escorts disappeared up the steps and inside the house.

Antón could hear a band playing primitive rock and roll. Mikhail circled the car, closing the doors bang bang bang bang, snapping his fingers and shuffling his feet on the pavement as he gyrated to the music.

"Let's partaaaaaaay!" Mikhail sang, tossing his driver's cap into the front seat and handing the keys to a valet.

"Mikhail," Antón said severely, "you watch too much TV."

"Best way learn English. Let's partaaaaaaay!"

Antón knocked on the driver's window of the BMW. "Comrades," he said to Yuri and the rest of the bodyguards, "Relax. It's going to be a long night."

.　.　.　.　.

The sky in the west was sunset red as Silva drove the Explorer down River Boulevard and stopped in front of the house he'd owned for fifteen years. In the fading light the street was quiet, virtually unchanged in the two months he'd been gone. American flags hung limp in front of several homes, still flying from the Fourth of July. The lights were on next door at Albert and Susan's, and on the other side the Bohemian Grove loomed dark and mysterious. He took a deep breath, smelling the trees and the river just behind the houses. What Silva didn't smell was any hint of suspicion or undue curiosity from his neighbors.

He keyed a remote to open the garage door, drove inside, turned off the truck and closed the door behind him. The house was booby-trapped to incinerate any intruder who got beyond the garage. He punched numbers into a box on the garage wall, turning off the sensors and disarming the explosives and incendiaries, then unlocked the inner door and went upstairs, turning on lights.

The furnishings were sparse but comfortable, a few books in several languages, a big Apple desktop, and a sewing machine. This was his country sanctuary, his dacha, his place of repose, and he would miss it. The house was destined to be destroyed, and all that would remain would be subtle traces of Ali al-Saif. Eventually the Americans would discover that Ali had lived among them for thirty years. They would learn that Mario Silva was indeed Ali al-Saif, and they would track him to Mexico and then Paraguay and perhaps Argentina where they would investigate certain mosques. In Silva's estimation, they would only succeed at making more enemies. They would never trace him to Moscow.

He walked through the house, pausing to put a kettle on the stove to make tea, then went out the back door to the porch. To his surprise, his neighbor, huge, friendly Albert Flowers, was a few yards away, leaning against the rail on his brightly lit deck, a cold drink in his hand.

"Hey!" Albert said loudly, not quite shouting. "Hey! Mario!"
Silva waved.
"Hey! Good to see you, Mario. Glad you're back."

"Hello, Albert. It's been a while, yes."

"Mexico again?"

"No. South America this time. Brazil. I love the music."

"That's cool, yeah, that's very cool, Brazil. Wow," Albert exclaimed in a good-natured, friendly way. "You'll probably hear some music from our neighbors. The Bohos are back, too."

"Ah, yes, the Bohemian Club." Silva gazed at the vast darkness to his right. "That's what I hear."

"Too bad you weren't here this morning," Albert said with a big smile. "You missed all the fun."

"Oh, really? What happened?" Silva inquired politely.

Animated, Albert pranced around his deck, gesturing madly as he spoke. "We got in my old rowboat and paddled right up the river to the Bohemian Beach and landed on their dock where a bunch of Bohos were getting suntans. Haha! It was pretty funny. We dressed up like pirates and everything, including these two guys from the FBI."

"The FBI?" Silva asked, a brain jerk response.

"Yeah, no shit, the FBI, only these guys don't exactly fit the stereotype. Well, one of them does. Anyway, they're trying to improve Grove security, so we dressed up and showed the Bohemians how easy it is to get in there. I tell you, Mario, it was hilarious."

"I bet it was, yes, pretty funny. Old man Richardson told me the FBI was over at his place," Silva said. "They were talking to all the Grove's neighbors."

"Well, it's gotta be these same guys, Teddy Swan and Paul, I forget his last name," Albert said.

"Sorry I missed them. Maybe next time."

"Say, Mario," Albert said brightly. "We're about to go out to dinner. Care to join us?"

The invitation hung in the air like a suspended sentence.

"Love to, love to, thanks, but I'll have to take a rain check," Silva said smoothly. "I have a crew over at the vineyard, and I have to get back."

"How's the vineyard going?" Albert asked.

"It's burning up with all this heat. I've neglected it."

Silva's phone rang. He looked at it and said to Albert., "Sorry. Excuse me, but I have to take this. My foreman... Yes? Sí. Pedro? ¿Qué pasó?"

Silva went back into his house, listening to Pedro as he turned off the lights and boiling kettle. In the garage he reset the alarms and pocketed the cell phone that would allow him to detonate the explosives from anywhere. As a diversion he was going to blow up the house during the attack.

Outwardly calm, his mind was suddenly racing toward panic. One of the boys had gone missing.

"I'll be right there. Don't use that phone again."

.   .   .   .   .

Heart pounding, breath coming in short whistles, Silva drove slowly toward the bunkhouse, trying not to stir up a cloud of dust and too preoccupied to notice that Barney Richardson's dogs were silent.

One of the kids had run away. How could this happen? Where could he go? Where did he think he could go? How long before the authorities react? What could the kid tell them? His name, Silva, and that was enough. How could Pedro screw up so badly? He stopped next to the bunkhouse.

Pedro opened the door and came out, frightened and nervous.

"Did you find him?" Silva asked as he got out of the truck.

"He came back."

Silva's heart slowed, but he flashed murderous eyes at Pedro and fired queries like bullets. "Did he see anyone, talk to anyone? Did anyone see him?"

Ashamed, Pedro refused to look him in the eye.

"I don't think so. He says no."

"Who was it?"

"The youngest one, I think he's Number Three."

"That's Hernán. Tell me what happened."

"They were all asleep, and he woke up and said he wanted to go outside to take a crap. He refused to use the toilet. I turned my back for one second and he was gone, bolted into the woods. I couldn't leave the others, so I called you, and a few minutes later he turned up, feeling ashamed."

"And the others?"

"They're waking up."

"Where is he?"

The other boys were lying or sitting on their bunks, rubbing their eyes. Hernán was bound hand and foot in the basement, drenched in sweat and urine. A murmur of revulsion swept over the boys as Pedro roughly hustled Hernán, still bound, into the middle of the room and dumped him on the floor.

"What's happening?" asked Rodrigo, Hernán's brother.

"Hernán tried to run away," answered Léon.

"No. I don't believe you. He's – he wants to die a martyr, praise be to Allah."

"I'm afraid it may be true. We shall see," Silva said harshly. "Number Three, look at me. Look at me."

Hernán struggled to his knees and looked up at Silva, terror in his eyes.

"How far did you go?"

"I don't know. Not far."

"Did you see or talk to anyone?"

"No."

"Number Three, what were you thinking?"

"I don't know. I was afraid."

"Afraid of what?"

"The pain."

Another tremor passed through the boys.

Silva struck a pose with his hands on his hips and said, "There will be no pain. There is only pain if you fail in your mission, and there is no pain in Paradise."

Rodrigo could no longer hold his silence, and he said desperately, "Your word is our law, Silva, but he's my baby brother. He had no intention of jeopardizing the mission."

"This is serious," Silva said. "Give me a gun."

Hernán began to pray quietly, with dignity.

Pedro handed him the Beretta.

"Silencer," he said and held out his hand like a surgeon.

While he waited for the sound suppressor, Silva composed himself and spoke in Arabic.

"Have you made your peace with God?" he asked Hernán.

A nod.

"Do you accept my authority to do this?"

Another nod. "I am guilty," Hernán said.

Silva took the silencer and looked at it, then at the boys, one by one.

"This is a critical mission," he said. "You all know that discipline among us must be ruthless, because a failure by one can destroy us all. For that reason, by my authority – " Silva laid the weapon on the floor and arranged himself on his knees in an attitude of prayer. "– I believe in the infinite mercy of Allah, praised be his name. This boy shall die a martyr, and not by my hand."

Bedlam, shouts of joy, backslapping and kissing. Hernán wept. Rodrigo snatched up the gun and was about to fire it through the roof as an expression of happiness when Silva tackled him and took away the gun.

These fucking peasants, Silva thought. They think they are going to die for God, but the truth is they're all going to hell for me.

"Calm down," he said. "We've accomplished nothing yet."

. . . . .

Silva carried an ornate box upstairs from the basement and set it on the table.

"Young men," he said in Arabic to his startled charges. "From now on, here in this cabin you may speak any way you wish. You will remember who you are and who your ancestors were. I caution you that outside, in the vineyard, you must speak Spanish, but you will not be outside very much before tomorrow night. I have gifts for you."

He opened the box and presented each martyr-to-be with a gilded copy of the Holy Quran and a plastic jug of pure water.

"You may eat or fast, as you wish, and of course, you will pray and purify yourselves. Soon you will be in Paradise, but before then you will consign many, many infidels to eternal torture. Death to the Zionists and the Crusaders!"

While the boys prayed, Silva went outside where Pedro was watching the lights of the Bohemian Hummer pass by.

"They've increased the patrols to every ten minutes," Pedro said. "I don't like it."

"I'm not worried," Silva replied. "Let's unpack the truck and get everything inside."

While the boys knelt on their rugs, heads deeply bowed in prayer, Silva and Pedro rapidly carried Black and Decker boxes into the concealed basement room.

"Munitions of terror," Pedro said off-handedly as they unpacked Uzis, sound-suppressors, ammunition, bricks of plastic explosive and detonators.

Silva opened a box of Uzis and took one out. "The real weapons are the boys, the human bombs. They create terror because they're willing to die, and their enemies are not."

Silva inspected the gun, sighting down the barrel and operating the mechanism several times.

"To tell you the truth," Pedro said. "I don't understand suicide bombers. The whole idea doesn't make sense to me."

Silva sat down on a box of C4 and gazed pensively at the Cuban. "They are true believers, Pedro. Islam is a very pure religion, a simple religion, and it shines like a beacon at the end of a very dark tunnel. In Islam, all of life is pointed toward the very single purpose of getting you, the believer, to Paradise when your life on earth is finished. If you live your life correctly, you'll make it. In its most fundamental form, Islam is absolutely evangelical. It tolerates no deviation from the strictest belief. Infidels become Muslims or die. Period. And if you kill infidels, especially infidels who have in any way harmed or threatened Islam, you get a ticket to Paradise. If you are martyred in the process, you are blessed, and your family is blessed. This may explain the religious part of suicide bomber psychology, but certainly doesn't explain all of it. There are political and social aspects, too. Often, the martyr is motivated, not by hatred of his enemy, but love of his family. He helps them get to Paradise as well as himself, and he also probably exacts revenge for some past wrong."

"Still," Pedro said earnestly. "They're young and desperate and poor, but the world is full of poor people who never think of blowing themselves up."

Silva casually opened a few more boxes and examined their contents. From one he took a telescopic reflex suppressor, a metal tube about ten inches long, and screwed it onto the barrel of the small machine pistol.

"Don't make assumptions. They're not all poor," Silva said. "Some come from families that are quite well-off, families that can afford tuition at a madrassa. But you are a man of the West, Pedro. You may be an ex-Communist, as I am, but you still see conflicts in society as occurring between classes. In the Middle East, in Islam, this is not always the case. The conflict is between those who believe and those who do not, or those who believe differently. It was that way in the seventh century, and for the true believers, the fanatics, the extremists, that hasn't changed. If you want to understand suicide bombers, you have to think in a seventh century fashion, a way that rejects all science, all reason, all forms of tolerance, and arrives in a state of perfect, intractable purity."

"That's fucking crazy."

"That's right, at least to a Western way of thinking, but on Monday these kids are going to be heroes. Their videos are going to be on TV and on the Internet. On Monday morning the United States is going to wake up and be told that a huge Muslim threat now exists in South America. People will say what happened in the Bohemian Grove was funded by ISIS, or Al Qaida or the Muslim Brotherhood. It doesn't matter. This will be perceived as a second Nine-Eleven, and even when the Americans eventually do put the pieces together and figure it out, it still won't matter. Heroes like these martyrs will be heroes forever in the Ummah, the world-wide community of Islam. At least seven radical groups will claim it was their doing, and to some extent they'll be right because we exploited them all to recruit our boys. These kids believe that on Monday they will be sitting in Paradise watching their families watch their videos."

"And what will it mean to you, Silva?"

He didn't answer right away. His jihadis would never know they were dupes – a means to an end. They would die as martyrs, absolutely convinced of the justice of their cause. Still, Silva wasn't so cynical that he couldn't admire the purity and strength of their faith. They were true believers who were convinced that if the world believed as one, it would be as one, and peace would reign. They believed in an ideal world that had never existed and would never exist, a world that rejected science and reason and replaced human intelligence with simplistic faith. This belief had once carried the Islam of Mohammad halfway round the world.

He, too, had once believed that if the world believed as one, it would be one. He had believed in Marx and Lenin and the righteousness of the people. He had believed that once the entire planet converted to Communism, all the ills of the world would end. It didn't work out that way. Battered by corruption and abuse of power, his faith in the Party and the ideology had finally been shattered in Afghanistan.

Faith, he had learned the hard way, was nothing more than fervent hope.

Silva had much more than hope, and no intention of ending his life in the Bohemian Grove. He would drive the Bohemian Hummer into the camps, his jihadis would kill Boris Demetriov, and he would escape amidst the confusion of bullets and exploding human bombs. At that moment Mario Silva would vanish, and when investigators found their way to the vineyard, the ruins of the house on River Boulevard and his apartment in San Francisco, Ali al-Saif would be a shadow hero once again. When his fifteen South Americans were celebrated as martyrs in Damascus and Beirut, he would be in Moscow with a new name and a new face.

As he spoke he looked into more boxes, found a magazine and

bullets for the Uzi, and loaded the magazine and fit it into the gun as if he were checking his order from the grocery store. Pedro watched him with the eye of a man who was proud of his work and the goods he supplied.

Finally, Silva said, "I've become a mercenary, Pedro, a PMC, a private military company. I am the face of war in the twenty-first century." He fixed a level glance on the Cuban. "And no one will ever know my name. Including you."

And with a sudden phhhhst from the Uzi he unzipped Pedro from his sternum to his third eye. The smell of fresh blood and gunpowder suddenly filled the basement room.

"Sorry, amigo," he said. "I forgot to mention sexual repression. You see, by denying basic human sexuality, religious fanaticism turns people into bloodthirsty homicidal maniacs. I'm surprised you didn't know that, but after all, you were only an infidel. I am an apostate."

17

Three miles away in Butler's studio, the owl was finished, a metal predator for a Boho, a bauble for his garden in Pacific Heights. Butler opened a bottle of *fresca de melón*, chugged half, and wiped the sweat from his brow. Not bad, he thought, not bad at all. The bird had a spark, a ferocious desire to live that shined through the steel. Too bad for the squirrel. Too bad for all of us, Butler reasoned, because in the end we're all squirrels and even the owl gets eaten.

Long shadows streaked across Maggie's Farm. Silhouetted against the sky, the spinning windmills mined a steady breeze from the Pacific. Saturday night was in a hurry, rushing in with big gusts to sweep away the lingering remnants of the day.

Jeremy had called and gleefully delivered the news that he and Phillip were now on the federal payroll. Good for them, Butler thought. Teddy was still at Jeremy's, cracking the whip and recording the arrival of more Bohos and their distinguished guests. Butler knew that sooner or later Teddy would call, or suddenly show up and want to go back into the woods.

Susan's Mercedes roadster came up the long driveway and crunched to a stop in front of the studio. Maggie wobbled out of the driver's seat.

"Hi, Butler."

"Hey, babe."

"I'm a little tipsy," she said. "Albert and Susan want to go to Marshall for dinner, and they want to invite Teddy and Paul, too."

"Did you guys drink more champagne?"

"Uh-huh."

"You shouldn't be driving, Maggie. You're gonna get popped."

"You do it all the time."

Butler's phone rang.

"Aren'tcha gonna get that?" Maggie asked.

Butler read the display. It was Teddy. He said, "No."

The phone rang and rang and finally stopped.

"Albert and Susan want to take the FBI guys to dinner," Maggie said, walking haphazardly toward the door to the house. "Don't you think that would be fun?"

"No," Butler said. "I've had enough FBI, Maggie, okay? Let's give it a rest. They're gonna be here for two more weeks, same as the Bohos."

"Okay," Maggie yawned. "I think I'll take a little nap."

Butler watched her stumble into the house, thinking she wasn't going to make it to dinner or anywhere else. Jojo ran out of the house, madly wagging his tail. The screen door banged. The wind died and the windmills stopped spinning. Saturday night had arrived.

. . . . .

Within a few minutes Maggie fell asleep in front of the TV, and Butler decided it was time to make peace with Barney Richardson. He changed into his camouflage fatigues, tossed a gallon of cheap supermarket gin into his truck and drove up the highway and into the woods, making as much noise as possible to rouse the dogs and bring the old man out of his house.

No barking, no yelping, only forest sounds, a light wind in the trees. As Butler's truck approached Richardson's house, his headlights picked out motionless Rottweilers sprawled around the pen as if they were dead. One beast lifted his head and whined, then lay his heavy snout back on the ground and panted in silence. Butler had seen this before. The crazy old man got shitfaced, laced the dogs' water dishes with gin, and they all stayed drunk and stupid until the liquor ran out.

Sleep well, old man. Dream of being eighteen again, a boy with two arms charging the beach at Iwo Jima.

He left the jug on the doorstep and drove up the hill. No one followed, no Teddy, no black SUV. He checked the gear in his backpack, selecting only the camera, and jogged through the trees, light on his feet, taking it easy.

Running, he thought about Maggie, about his life. He had a damned good life. He didn't kiss anybody's ass. He made things people wanted with his own hands. How many people did that anymore? He hadn't made too many people miserable over the years. He just made fifty-one of them dead.

He knew he'd never get over it, and even if he did, the world wouldn't let him. He never knew their names but never forgot their faces. The woman with the AK and bandoliers. The old man in the boat who smoked Salems like Ho Chi Minh. The renegade American with a peace symbol on his headband. The kids bothered him the most, the young Viet Cong soldiers who all looked fifteen. Now Teddy Swan shows up and waves old military records in his face.

Once, years ago, a security company called him from Virginia. A silky voice with a genteel, upper-class, southern accent politely inquired, "Would you be interested in working in Iraq?"

"Doing what?" Butler had replied. "I'm a welder now, a sculptor. Do you want me to weld?"

The voice wouldn't tell him over the phone what his duties might be, but the man did say they'd pay him one hundred eighty thousand dollars a year. Would he like to come to Virginia and talk about it? Could they send him a ticket? No thanks, he said, but they sent him a ticket anyway, and he incinerated it with his welding torch. They never called back.

He arrived at Fat Freddie in a cloudy mood and quickly hoisted himself up to his blind, surprising a squirrel that bounded away as he crawled on hands and knees onto the platform. Taking a deep breath, he lay on his back and looked straight up at the massive trunk and graceful branches rising another hundred fifty feet.

Fat Freddie was a thousand years old. In the eleventh century, when Fat Freddie was a seedling, the world was a brutal, savage place where the few ruled the many with mystic fiction and fear. Religious wars were popular. Oppression was in fashion.

Nothing much had changed. After a thousand years, religious wars were still popular, and a handful of men still held sway over the billions, determining the fate of the multitude and profiting from their wars. Today, here in America, that meant the Bohos.

The Bohos ruled the land. If America went to war, they made the bullets and the profits. How many Bohemians invested in security companies that hired people with his special skills to work in Iraq?

Long ago Butler had decided he would never again fire a rifle with intent to kill. Twice a year he went to the range and fired the Sharps dead-eye, without a scope, and he could hit a playing card at 600 yards. From time to time he thought about hauling the Sharps up to his blind. Could he hit a target the size of a pumpkin at 900 yards with a sniper's rifle manufactured in 1859? Could he pick off the security guards that were back in the trees behind the fence? The Sharps was good enough, but was he? He didn't really want to know. It might be fun, though, to blast off the Sharps and see how Grove security reacted to that big sound. Blam! They'd go nuts. He laughed out loud.

Teddy Swan would want to throw him in jail for having such ideas.

He cleared his mind, banishing all thoughts. He took his breath in measured beats. Finally, calm and still, he rolled over and gazed at the moonlit panorama of the Grove, the perimeter road, and Mario Silva's vineyard. Two hawks were riding the currents above the trees, and he watched them drifting on their marvelous wings and looking down on the forest. He pulled the camera from his backpack, but when he found the hawks again they'd dropped below the tree line and he couldn't get a good shot.

Scanning the vineyard through the camera lens, he spotted a Ford Explorer SUV and the flatbed truck he'd seen at Pickett's parked next to Silva's bunkhouse. Light filtered through slits in the shutters. Silva's Mexicans were in there, the farm workers he'd seen in the truck. He didn't hear a generator, so he guessed they had lanterns of some kind.

Migrant workers usually made a campfire and hung around outside, often playing music and always drinking lots of beer. He saw no fire and heard no music, and he thought that rather strange.

The Bohemian Hummer appeared and trundled down the road, blasting Bob Seger and the Silver Bullet Band into the night. As the security vehicle passed the vineyard and disappeared around the bend toward the South Gate, a dozen men suddenly stood up among the vines and moved into the road.

Butler punched off four quick shots with the Nikon, capturing Silva's Mexicans in huaraches and battered boots, jeans, soccer jerseys and tattered cowboy hats. One carried a book. Mario Silva stood in the middle of the road pointing at the fence, gesturing this way and that, then turned and led his band of laborers back into the vineyard.

Butler guessed that Silva had marched his new vineyard hands out to the road to tell them to keep the hell away from that fence. He probably had not tried to explain the Bohemian Grove, but he surely told them about the armed guards. Stay away from the fence. Okay, jefe. Sí, señor.

Pondering Silva and his farmhands, he thought their being out there in the middle of the night was strange, and even more curious was their hiding from the Grove security patrol. Then he reasoned that the Mexicans were illegals, naturally adverse to anyone who resembled authority. Silva wasn't the only vintner in Sonoma County who hired illegals. Truckloads of Mexicans rambled up and down the county highways every day, and Butler figured it was none of his business. Then he remembered the weird language he'd heard through General Pickett's speaker; it must have been an Indian language, Nahuatl or some such, although the Mexicans looked like mestizos, not Indians. These were very weird Mexicans who didn't play music, didn't sing sad songs about lost love and narcotics smugglers, and didn't drink cases and cases of cerveza.

Ten minutes later, the Hummer returned, playing no music for a change, and this time Silva was standing by the side of the road, waving. The Hummer stopped, Silva gestured toward his workers standing back among the vines, and they waved. As the Hummer moved on, Butler snapped two images of the Mexicans huddled in the middle of the vineyard, thinking it was all very peculiar. When the car curved out of sight, Silva led his men back to the bunkhouse, went inside and shut the door.

Butler had a strong urge to slide down to the forest floor and sneak over to Silva's bunkhouse, but he resisted, thinking that would be an outrageous invasion of privacy. Silva and his Mexicans were none of his business.

Almost as if he were reading Butler's thoughts, Silva suddenly opened the door and stood in the backlight looking directly at Fat Freddie, a quarter-mile distant. Butler popped off one shot with the long lens before the door closed.

He watched the Hummer pass by once more but didn't bother turning on the radio to listen to the guards. Thinking about Mexicans and beer had made him thirsty, so he stuffed his camera in his backpack, descended to the forest floor and made his way home.

. . . . .

Susan's Mercedes was still parked by the windmills, the lights were off in the house, and Maggie was still asleep in front of the TV. It was ten o'clock, time for the news, but Butler didn't want news. The world was going to hell whether he learned about it this very minute or not. He turned off the TV, puttered around the kitchen, made a salami sandwich, sat down to eat it, and checked his phone messages. Teddy, Jeremy and Albert had all called more than once, but the only message he listened to was from the man who'd commissioned the owl.

"I think I'll be up your way tomorrow, Mr. Rhodes, and I'd like to come by and see the bird."

Up your way? You mean you might just happen to be at the Bohemian Grove. Butler didn't call back. The owl was done and if the guy showed up, he could cart it away.

Munching his sandwich, he considered watching a movie or picking up a book and calling it a night. He had three histories and two novels on his "Read before you die" shelf, and he snatched up *The Western Way of War: Infantry Battle in Classical Greece* by Victor Davis Hanson, recommended by Albert. No thanks, no war today. He hefted a slim volume, *The Grifters* by Jim Thompson, one of his favorite writers, but he had too much energy to surrender his mind to a master maniac. Besides, he was still thirsty, so he changed into a riverboat gambler's long black coat, gold embroidered vest, ruffled white shirt, and black string tie.

Just before he left, he went to the back of his studio, pulled the Sharps out of its cabinet, put it in the rack behind the seat in his pickup, and headed for town.

18

Occupying most of a large sofa in the drawing room, Antón contemplated the magnificent view of Los Angeles that spread like a golden haze below Echo Park. Antón didn't share Boris's infatuation with Southern California. The weather was too mild and forgiving, and the palette of earth tones and neon eluded his taste for darker, more brooding colors. He preferred places where violent human emotions were displayed raw, not fabricated for mass consumption. Ciudad del Este was such a place, and he'd lied to Silva about how much he detested Paraguay. Deception was his profession, after all, and if a lie served him better than the truth, then he lied. The assassination of Boris Demetriov had been approved three months before he'd informed Silva because he'd wanted to keep his former protégée on edge. It seemed to have worked. After twenty-four years, Silva was in position to wreak havoc on the Bohemian Grove. His suicide bombers were in place, and all that was lacking was Boris Demetriov's presence beneath the big trees.

Why wait an extra day?

"Mikhail!"

"Yes, comrade Cosmo."

"Where is Boris?"

"Still upstairs."

"And Dmitri?"

"In the kitchen on the phone."

"Call the pilots and have them get my Gulfstream ready. Tell them to file a flight plan to Santa Rosa. And don't drink any more. You have to drive to Burbank."

. . . . .

Upstairs, Boris pulled his dick out of the dark-haired Russian girl and stared at it, frowning.

"Did you come?" she asked in Russian.

"No."

"What's the matter?"

"I don't know."

"You want to fuck me in the ass?"

"No."

"You want a different girl? I'll call Tanya."

"No. I want a drink."

A few minutes later a somewhat disheveled Boris Demetriov came downstairs and sank into a big easy chair in front of the big picture window. A waiter brought him a small carafe of vodka and a glass and laid it on a coffee table.

"Had enough?" asked Antón.

"I'm bored with Russian girls. This is California," Boris replied, sweeping his arms toward the panoramic view. "I want blond surfer girls."

Antón smiled, and Boris was too self-absorbed to notice the viperish glint in the fat man's eyes.

"That can be arranged," Antón said. "You should have all the women you want before you go to the Bohemian Grove. They don't allow women during the summer encampment."

"So I've been told."

"Don't be concerned, my friend. The Bohemians can be quite accommodating."

"You've been there?"

"Yes, with Gorbachev many years ago, but a place like that doesn't change much."

"What do they do all day, all those men?" Boris asked.

"They drink," Antón replied. "They drink seriously, and they do what men do when they drink. They sing. They tell stories. They play cards and other games, and they eat. Mostly, they drink. The Bohemians also have incessant theater and music as diversions, and it's rather amusing, actually. One is never bored, I can assure you of that."

"Scotch," Boris declaimed. "Rich Americans drink scotch."

Antón agreed. "Indeed they do," he said, "but I'm sure they'll have anything you want."

With a sneer Boris said, "And some things I don't want, like the Secret Service."

Antón swiveled his large head to and fro and remarked with a chuckle, "I don't see them here."

With a gesture of disgust, Boris said, "They'll be waiting at the Beverly Hills Hotel, and they'll be unhappy and want to lecture me."

Antón sighed. "You are a president, Boris, incredible as that may seem," he said, "and such a lofty status always comes with velvet shackles. At the Bohemian Grove you'll have the privilege of feeling the shackles loosened a little. You'll be impressed, and I know you're a man not easily impressed."

Boris roused himself to his feet, shuffled around the large room, hands in pockets, and stared out the window.

"They want me to make a speech," he said, hunching and shrugging his shoulders. "They want me to convince them that I can protect their pipeline, but I'm no good at speeches."

"I don't mean to be presumptuous," Antón said, "but perhaps I can help. I can write a speech for you, in English, and your man Yuri can deliver it while you stand to the side and smile."

Boris seemed to consider this proposition, but he said, "It would be easier to cancel the trip. 'The president has been called away on urgent business.'"

Antón raised a bushy eyebrow. "Blond surfer girls?"

"What's more urgent than that?" Boris laughed.

"As I recall," Antón said casually, "the Bohemians are quite adept at taking care of their sexual needs, and they patronize a number of luxurious brothels near the Grove. Some members keep their mistresses nearby. They certainly don't endure privation of any sort."

Boris poured himself a shot of vodka, knocked it back, and said thoughtfully, "When I was upstairs, I finally remembered this place, this house. I remembered the chandelier in the bedroom. I remember seeing it as a cascade of diamonds or something like that."

"Thirty years ago you took LSD in that room, Boris. I knew you'd remember eventually."

"Who exactly owns this house?" asked the president of Belarus.

"I do," Antón answered. "The deed is in my name."

"Would you sell it to me?"

"Why? Are you tired of Beverly Hills?"

"It's just a thought."

Quick as a cobra, Antón said, "Here's another whimsical thought. Why don't you fly to the Bohemian Grove in my plane? It's far more discreet than yours, and it would be a marvelous trick to play on the Secret Service."

Boris laughed. "You devil. You astonishing, fat devil."

"It's only a ninety minute flight." Antón looked at his watch. "You could be sitting around a campfire at the Bohemian Grove by midnight. And since nobody expects it, it's far more secure than your plane with its flags and presidential markings."

Boris protested, "I don't have my things, my clothes."

"Have them sent later," Antón suggested. "Besides, you can get anything you need – and I emphasize anything – at the Grove."

Boris giggled. The Secret Service would have a fit. He knew the Service was already at the Grove – that had been made quite clear in the invitation presented to him in Berlin by the red-headed Bohemian, Roger Blake – at least he would rid himself of the two idiots who shadowed him around Beverly Hills.

"Perhaps we can write the speech on the plane," Antón suggested.

"Fuck the speech. Bring some girls. Let's go. Dmitri! Yuri!"

·   ·   ·   ·   ·

Paul drove the Mustang into Jeremy's driveway and Jeremy came outside to see what he wanted.

"Just checking on the Russians," Paul told him. "Or I should say, the White Russians. Boris slipped away from the Secret Service in Los Angeles this evening and nobody knows where he is," Paul explained. "We need to find him. The Secret Service is really pissed."

"We have a lot of radio traffic right now," Jeremy said. "You know about the sheriff, right?"

"No," Paul said, shaking his head. "What about the sheriff?"

Jeremy opened the screen door and ushered Paul inside. Phillip was standing up at the radio console, dancing and shouting and raising his fist like he'd just won the lottery. An avalanche of noise was coming from the speakers, a harsh jumble of expletives, edgy dispatchers and grumpy cops.

Bedlam was erupting in the Sonoma County Sheriff's Department.

First, two of the men arrested by Amory Hix that morning at Buckminster Vintners claimed through their attorneys that the sheriff had busted them because they had refused his demand for a shakedown. The attorneys called a press conference and on live TV revealed videos of the sheriff asking for fifty thousand dollars from each of their clients. It didn't take long before these two videos and a video of Sheriff Hix stumbling around a smoky vineyard stoned out of his mind went viral on the Internet.

TV trucks from San Francisco and Sacramento surrounded Hix's house in Santa Rosa, and Jeremy could listen to them, too. The sheriff had gone incommunicado inside his house and refused to speak to anyone. Reporters were camped out on his front lawn. All the Sonoma County Sheriff's Department's mobile units around Santa Rosa were pulled off their beats and directed to the sheriff's house to help the Santa Rosa police control the growing crowds. All over the county deputies pulled their cars off the road and sat listening to their radios, talking on cell phones, checking the Internet and laying odds on the sheriff's resignation. Law enforcement all over the county collapsed.

Phillip was stoked, dancing and squirming in his seat. "What a riot!" he shouted. "What a hoot!"

Jeremy turned on the TV, adding a replay of the attorneys' press conference to the cacophony in the little house. The sheriff's department babbled from one set of speakers in the radio console; another pair was tuned to the Santa Rosa police; and a third set scanned the Highway Patrol.

"I don't care about the sheriff," Paul declared. "Russians, Jeremy. Russians! This is just more bullshit that makes Bohemian Grove security impossible. Fuck!"

As Jeremy began re-programming the radios to search for Paul's Russians, Phillip groaned and complained to Paul, "Dude, you're a killjoy."

"Hey!" Paul rebuked him sharply. "You're being paid good money. Do your job."

Phillip rolled his eyes. Paul shrugged. He believed searching for Russians was a waste of federal time and money, but rather than stand over Jeremy and Phillip and making them nervous, he pushed through the screen door and went outside to commune with the stars and the crickets. He sat quietly in a lawn chair and contemplated the serenity of the Russian River valley at night. He began to wonder what craziness Teddy Swan might get him into next.

He heard the grinding sound of an old Volkswagen air-cooled engine, and a Karmann Ghia of uncertain vintage pulled into his driveway. A cute young woman got out, her tight jeans and short top exposing a large swath of tattooed midriff. She could have been Asian or Mexican or Persian, Paul couldn't tell. Her short hair was henna red, and she had assorted body piercings and more tattoos peeking out from under her clothes.

Paul didn't know what to think, so he stared and said, "Can I help you?"

"I'm looking for Phillip Mercier. Is he here?"

"And who might you be?"

"Marika."

"I'll see if Mr. Mercier is available. Just a moment, please."

Paul went inside, shut the door behind him, and hollered, "Hey, Phillip! There's a girl outside looking for you."

Phillip lifted his earphones and asked, "What?"

Paul jerked his thumb toward the door and said, "Marika."

"Oh, shit."

Jeremy looked up and asked Phillip, "Did you tell her you were here?"

"Yes."

"She isn't one of your students, is she?" Jeremy asked with a leer. "You bad boy."

Phillip confessed, "She used to be."

"You're a government contract worker now, Phillip," Jeremy lectured. "I need you here and you have to earn your fifteen hundred a day."

Phillip jerked off his headset, glanced at a likewise grinning Paul, banged through the screen door and went outside.

"Marika!"

"Hi, baby."

"What are you doing here?"

She put her arms around him and kissed him, creating an instant conflict between his head and his gonads.

"Aren't you glad to see me?" she asked. "Since when do high school math teachers work on Saturday night in the middle of summer?"

"I, shit, see, I got this new job, and, shit..."

She silenced him with another kiss, this time grinding her pelvis into his and curling her leg around his knee.

"Oh, Jesus," he panted. "Oh, God."

She dragged him into her little car.

"Let's go to your house," she said, unzipping his fly.

.　.　.　.　.

"I like your airplane even better than your house," Boris said to Antón as the Gulfstream g550 taxied toward the runway at the Bob Hope Airport in Burbank. "What do you think, Dmitri? Should we get one?"

"Why don't we get seven, Comrade President," said Boris's brother, his voice dripping with sarcasm. "One for every day of the week."

"We certainly can afford them," Boris continued blithely, "thanks to the generosity of the Americans. Feel the leather on these seats. This is nicer than the Beverly Hills Hotel."

The engine whine suddenly shifted in pitch, a sound Antón always found thrilling, and the plane began to accelerate. Moments later they were airborne and climbing toward 30,000 feet.

"Antón Cosmovitch," Boris bellowed, "you douche bag, why did you leave the girls in Los Angeles?"

"It's a short flight. I thought we might write your speech."

"I'm not going to give these people the benefit of my wisdom. Or yours. To hell with the speech."

"As you wish, Boris," Antón said. "The Bohemians will be too intoxicated to notice, anyway."

Yuri stood up and stretched, saying, "Boris, we have to let our hosts know we're coming. Should I call them now?"

"He's right, dear brother," Dmitri said. "They're going to be surprised as it is."

"What are they called, our hosts?" Boris asked. "It's a club within a club, right?"

"Ye Olde Owls," Yuri said in English, translating the name into Russian which provoked a round of guffaws.

"Birds? Old birds?"

"We also need transport," Yuri continued patiently. "Antón, do you have Internet on this plane?"

"We have everything on this plane. Internet, phones, television, whatever you need. Mikhail can show you."

"I need to dial this number," Yuri said, and he gave Mikhail a mobile phone number.

·　·　·　·　·

At ten o'clock in the evening Secret Service Agent Raul Rodriguez finished his sixteen hour day shepherding distinguished guests around the Bohemian Grove and retired to his beautiful, redwood-paneled corner room on the third floor of the Main Lodge, relaxing with a shot of fine single-malt scotch. The TV news was on, a live camera panning over white Sheriff's Department police vehicles surrounding Amory Hix's house in Santa Rosa. The media was doing everything possible to advertise the absence of law enforcement throughout the county, but Rodriguez was determined not to think about the sheriff and the problems he was creating until five the next morning. He turned off the TV and booted up a computer to play poker on line.

His phone rang. He didn't recognize the number on the display, but anyone who had his number deserved a response.

"Rodriguez," he answered.

"Mr. Agent Raul Rodriguez, Secret Service?"

"Yes."

"I am Yuri Mikhailovitch Ustov, personal representative of Boris Borisovitch Demetriov."

"Yes, Yuri. I know who you are," Rodriguez said, setting down his scotch and scrambling to attention. "We met at the briefing in San Francisco last month. Tell me, please, Yuri, where is President Demetriov? Is he all right? We've been looking for him for hours."

"Oh, yes, he is perfectly fine. He is now, we are – Boris and his brother Dmitri and me – we are now on an airplane flying to Santa Rosa."

Rodriguez blinked, stunned. All he could say was, "Now?"

"Yes. We are going to land in one hour and five minutes. Is that right? Yes, they tell me that's right."

Rodriguez was already tying his skinny black tie. He stammered, "That's fine, Yuri. We'll meet you at the airport."

"Oh, no, not necessary. Boris says don't bother. I would like to speak to Mr. Roger Blake at Olde Owls camp, please, and tell him we will soon arrive."

"Of course, Yuri. Roger Blake, certainly, we can help you there," Rodriguez said, stalling for a second while his mind raced forward, trying to get a handle on the situation. "Like we told you in San Francisco, no phones are allowed inside the Grove, so our security people will go to Ye Olde Owls camp and inform Mr. Blake that you are arriving. That can take a few minutes. Can you leave a number where he can call you back from the Service Center?"

"Sure." Yuri gave Rodriguez the number of the phone on the plane.

Rodriguez finally got a grip on his voice and said sternly, "Yuri, the Secret Service will provide transportation from the Santa Rosa airport to the Grove, for the president's safety."

"No, no. Not necessary. Thank you. Good-bye." Yuri ended the call.

"Oh, fuck," Rodriguez swore, and within seconds his ear piece and mic were in place and he was calmly issuing orders to the duty officer, Agent Walter Smith.

"First, tell Grove security to send someone up to Ye Olde Owls to tell Roger Blake his guest is going to arrive at his camp in less than two hours, ready or not," Rodriguez said. "And get three class one vehicles ready to go to the Santa Rosa airport in five minutes. Put on our best drivers. This is going to be a fast ride."

Next, he called the black room and gave the NSA the phone number on the plane. "I want to know everything there is to know about that plane, who owns it, who filed the flight plan, what the connection is to Boris, and any other calls made on that phone. You know the drill. I want it all and I want it in ten minutes. Call me back on this cell."

The laconic answer from the black room came back, "We'll see what we can do, Agent Rodriguez."

19

On board the plane, an impatient Yuri searched the Internet for limousines in Santa Rosa, California, and came up with Zinfandel Limousines, 24 hr. Executive Jet Service Our Specialty. He dialed.

A sleepy female voice answered, "Zin Limo."

"Hello? Santa Rosa?"

"Yes?"

"I need limousine at Santa Rosa airport in one hour. Can you do?"

"Hang on a minute. Let me try him on the radio."

Darlene MacIntyre, Bobby's wife, cradled the phone against one ear, padded over to the ancient two-way Motorola in the corner of the den and keyed the mic.

"Hey, Bobby?"

"I hear you, Darlene."

"Can you pick up at the airport in an hour?"

"Sure, why not? Where're they going?"

"Sir?" Darlene spoke into the phone. "What is your party's destination?"

"Bohemian Club."

"Bohemian Grove?"

"Yes, Bohemian Grove."

"Bobby? They're Bohos."

"Okay."

"And sir, what's your party's name?"

"Ustov. Yuri Ustov. Three persons."

"Bobby, your party's name is Yuri Ustov. Got that?"

"Ustov. Got it."

"Sir, what type of aircraft?"

"Private jet."

"Yes, but the aircraft type, sir. What kind of airplane?"

Darlene heard an exchange in a foreign language and then, "Gulfstream g550."

"All right, Mr. Ustov, the fare will be one hundred and twenty-five dollars."

"That's fine. Thank you. One hour. Good-bye."

"Bobby, it's a Gulfstream g550 and they're Bohos so I quoted them one twenty-five."

"Good girl. Now go back to sleep and turn off the phone. This is the last call I'm taking tonight. I got my regular at two."

. . . . .

"Here's your Russians," Jeremy said to Paul. "I got a hit on this limo dispatch."

They listened to Darlene's radio conversation with Bobby.

"Phillip knows that limo driver," Jeremy said. "His name is Bobby MacIntyre."

"That's Boris Demetriov, sure as shit," Paul said. "I'd better call Rodriguez."

Rodriguez answered from the front passenger's seat in his black GMC urban assault vehicle, one of three government trucks barreling out the Main Gate, red lights flashing, on route through Saturday night traffic to the Santa Rosa airport, eighteen miles away over busy, two-lane country roads.

"Jeremy got a hit," Paul said into his phone. "A Yuri Ustov called for a Zinfandel Limousine to meet him at the airport. The driver's name is Bobby MacIntyre. Is this Yuri your guy?"

"Absolutely. Yes. Spot on," Rodriguez declared. "Thank you, thank you. We'll run his plate. I sure as hell didn't hear about this from the black room. Hey!" Paul heard Rodriguez shout before he hung up. "Step on it!"

Bobby MacIntyre had had plenty of time to fill up his Lincoln with gas, restock the bar in the passenger compartment, and smoke a joint before he got to the Charles M. Schultz-Sonoma County Airport in Santa Rosa.

Starting on Friday morning, he'd made fourteen trips from the airport to the Bohemian Grove, and managed to squeeze in two weddings and one quinceañera. Pretty good weekend, and it wasn't over yet. After he delivered Mr. Ustov and his party to the Grove, he had a regular Saturday night call at two a.m. at the 101 Casino in Petaluma, a high-rolling Chinese poker player who went to The Oaks in Emeryville near Oakland, a two-hundred-fifty dollar ride.

Bobby knew the security guard at the airport who opened the gate and let him drive onto the tarmac.

"Plane's due in three minutes," the guard told him.

Bobby got out of his car and gazed at the private jets lined up as far as he could see. Dozens, maybe hundreds, he thought. Jeez, and they cost what? Five, ten million apiece, maybe more, twenty mil, and what's that? A billion dollars worth of rich men's toys? Two billion? Three? Bohos had been passengers in his car almost non-stop for two days, and they were good customers, good tippers except for that one jerk, A.J. Hoff. They'd run into the demonstration, and that was just bad luck. He wouldn't forget that guy, but one crappy load out of fourteen wasn't too bad.

The Gulfstream landed, lights blinking, engines whining, and rolled along the runway like a giant mosquito. Bobby checked his waybill where he'd scribbled the name, "Ustov."

The plane taxied close to the hanger and stopped near the Lincoln parked with the doors open. The engines began to wind down, and an airstair opened in the fuselage and dropped to the tarmac.

The first guy down was a stocky prize-fighter type with a thick neck, wide-collared open shirt, heavy gold chain, pleated slacks and Gucci loafers. Bobby thought: This classless thug doesn't look like a

Boho. The first man reached the bottom of the stairs, and two more came out of the plane, both tall and well-built, one almost bald and the other with movie-star hair, both with gold chains and expensive, bad suits. The one with the hair was drunk and had to be helped down the stairs by the other one. The name "Ustov" echoed in Bobby's head, and his mind clicked: Russian mafia. Holy shit.

Yuri walked over to Bobby and said, "Zinfandel Limousine?"

"Yes. Mr. Ustov?"

"That's me," said the prize fighter. "I am Yuri Ustov. We are three persons."

"That's fine, Mr. Ustov. To the Bohemian Grove, right?"

Boris and Dmitri crawled into the back of the limo, and Yuri got in with them and shut the door.

"No luggage?" Bobby said.

"No luggage."

"Okay, let's rock and roll."

As he got in the car, Bobby caught a glimpse of a huge man in a white suit standing in the door of the plane. Then he disappeared, and the stairs began to revolve back up into the airframe.

Bobby got into the driver's seat and lowered the smoked glass partition.

"Gentlemen," he explained to the rear compartment, "there is complementary champagne and a full bar with ice back there. I'm sorry, but you have to use plastic cups. Can't have any broken glass on the upholstery. It's about thirty minutes to the Grove, so....."

"Got vodka?" Boris growled, using half his English vocabulary.

"Yes, sir."

All the Russians laughed. The gold chains were dazzling, and Bobby closed the partition.

He drove out of the airport and started to boogie down North Laughlin Road. Like everybody else, Bobby knew there were no county deputies on patrol, so he cranked the Lincoln up to eighty-five and was rolling like a bandit, and suddenly he was startled to see flashing red lights behind him. Damn! Cops! Shit! The SUV in the mirrors had to be the Highway Patrol. He pulled over to the shoulder and stopped, and was immediately blinded by extreme white light pouring through all his windows at once. His door was pulled open.

"Step out of the car, please."

He couldn't see anything except the lights, and he put his hands up to shield his eyes. Someone asked him, "Mr. Robert MacIntyre?"

"Yes."

"Okay. Step out of the car, please."

The lights were lowered and Bobby saw a half dozen civilians in dark suits and fancy headsets surrounding his Lincoln. One guy was crouched by the back door, talking through the open window to his passengers.

The guy with the hair was passed out and leaning on the prizefighter.

"Hello, Yuri."

"Hello, Agent Rodriguez."

"Do you know this guy?" Dmitri asked Yuri in Russian.

"We had a briefing in San Francisco last month. He's Secret Service. He speaks Russian."

"Ah, Secred Serbice," Dmitri exclaimed in fractured English.

"I see Boris is taking a nap," said Rodriguez in perfect Russian. "You must be Dmitri Demetriov."

Dmitri extended an arm over and around Boris and shook hands with Rodriguez.

"Mr. Demetriov, sir," Rodriguez said in his most diplomatic manner, "We are responsible for your brother's security as long as he's in this country, and I insist that you ride with us. I insist."

"We have to go with them," Yuri said to Dmitri. "I don't think we have a choice."

"We would prefer that what happened in Los Angeles stays in Los Angeles," Rodriguez said a little more sternly. "I won't hold it against you because you're here now, and that's fine, but you will accompany me to the Grove. There will not be a debate."

"Boris, wake up," Dmitri said, prodding his brother. "Wake up."

Boris growled, "Fuck you, let me sleep."

"Wake up! The Secret Service wants to talk to you."

"Go fuck a goat and let me sleep!"

"Yuri," Rodriguez said sharply. "Get him out of this car and into our vehicle. If you don't, we will."

"Come on, Boris."

Boris began to thrash and strike out, smacking Yuri in the face, but Dmitri managed a hammer lock and they pushed him out of the car and onto the ground, face down.

Boris puked and passed out. Yuri found a bottle of water and a box of tissues in the car and gently cleaned his president's face and made him sit up. Bits of gravel stuck to Boris's cheeks. Together, Dmitri and Yuri half-carried the besotted man to the middle SUV and shoved him into the back seat and got in after him. Rodriguez got into the front passenger's seat.

Bobby stood next to his car, watching the spectacle. "Hey!" he shouted, jumping in front of the trucks so they couldn't move. "Do I get paid?"

Rodriguez lowered his window and said, "You didn't go anywhere."

In the seat behind him, Yuri yelled, "Open the window! Open the window!"

When it lowered, he pulled a wad of cash from his pockets and gave Bobby three hundred-dollar bills.

"All right," Bobby said with a big smile. "You're a class act, Mr. Ustov. Call me any time. Who is that guy, the drunk guy?"

"The president of Belarus."

"Jesus," Bobby swore. "I thought you guys were mafia."

With a twinkle in his eye, Yuri said, "Same thing."

. . . . .

At the airport the Gulfstream taxied down a long row of jets and parked. In the main cabin Antón pondered the universe – he considered the vastness of everything as a mere extension of himself – while Mikhail cleaned up the mess left behind by Boris.

"Can we go back to Los Angeles now, Comrade Boss?" Mikhail

asked as he threw away a wad of paper towels.

"No, my boy. We're going to stay here on the plane and await the results of our Machiavellian machinations."

"Can I go into the town?"

"No."

"Can I call the limo driver and have him bring...."

"No."

"You are a hard master, Antón Cosmovitch."

"Do I not love you, Mikhail?"

"You say you do, but you lie about everything."

"Do I not take care of you, always?"

Antón raised himself to his feet and knocked on the cockpit door. The door opened and the pilot, full-breasted and voluptuous, took Mikhail by the hand, and pulled him into the cockpit.

"Well, don't I?"

The door shut with a loud click. Antón looked at his watch, retrieved a disposable phone from his briefcase, and called Silva.

·   ·   ·   ·   ·

Two battery-operated lanterns illuminated the interior of the bunkhouse. Kneeling on their new prayer rugs, most of the boys recited special prayers for martyrs along with every other prayer they could remember. Several combed their hair, ritually bathed with bottled water and offered prayers for their purification. Tomorrow they would make their videos.

They had twenty-four hours before the attack, twenty-four hours to pray and reconcile their short lives with their fate. None had ever known a woman or the thrill of discovering a new idea. Their lives had been imbued with hatred and a lust for revenge against people they'd never met. Like young, stupid soldiers since time immemorial, all that awaited them was violent death.

For Silva, their ardor was a tonic. Downstairs in the basement, he'd laid out the suicide vests, and was pushing half-inch ball bearings and detonators into the soft, putty-like plastique. Manipulating the pliant explosive with his fingers was deeply sensual, mixing arousal with the potential for great violence.

Silva personally sewed vests for all his martyrs, taking their measurements with great care and marking down the numbers like an old-world tailor. He preferred first quality denim, sturdy but pliant and bleached white as a symbol of purity. In the Middle East, where suicide vests had to be designed for concealment from explosive-sniffing dogs and metal detectors, he often used a volatile, acetone-based explosive to fool the dogs, and improvised detonators that occasionally failed. In Monte Rio he had no such restrictions. Pedro had provided C4, a high-quality, military grade plastic explosive, and proper detonators powered by nine-volt batteries.

He'd taken the boys' measurements in Paraguay months before, added a centimeter here and there to allow for growth, and used the sewing machine in his house on River Boulevard to fashion fifteen sleeveless vests with eight prominent vertical pockets sewn outside, four in front and four in back.

He was stuffing each pocket with a one pound brick of C4 embedded with a dozen ball bearings and a detonator. The detonators were connected by a wiring harness to a covered toggle switch powered by a nine volt battery. All the martyr had to do was flip up the cover and push on the switch. The exploding C4 would expel the half-inch ball bearings with bullet-like speed, killing or maiming anyone within twenty yards. The martyr would die instantly, his torso essentially vaporized, but, because of the shaped charges, his legs and head were sometimes undamaged. In one instance in Tel Aviv, the legs were found still standing.

Pedro's corpse lay behind the boxes of munitions, and Silva was talking quietly to the dead man as he assembled the vests.

"The world has entered a dark age, Pedro. Minds are closing everywhere, and faith has triumphed over reason because reason has yielded to greed and decadence. I'm a perfect example, more perfect than the Bohemians who are excellent examples themselves. I learned my lesson in Afghanistan.

"In Afghanistan, you see, the Russians never understood the power of the poppy. I tried to tell them, but they never listened. I was an Arabic speaking communist *agent provocateur* sent by the Russians to stir up the mujahadeen. The first time I led a mujahadeen patrol into a Russian ambush, the Russian soldiers were so stoned they couldn't fight. The result was a great victory for the rebels, and I was hailed as a hero by the mujahadeen. That's when they started calling me Ali al-Saif, Ali the Sword. Ha! My sword was a hypodermic needle. It happened again and again, and I knew the Soviet cause was hopeless. I almost went over to the other side, and perhaps I did, for a while, but I made a great discovery about myself, something the fat man had known all along."

At that moment one of his disposable phones interrupted his soliloquy.

Only one person had that number, the keeper of his secrets, and Antón would call only to tell him the operation was aborted. He glared at the phone, reluctant to answer and prepared to become enraged. He snapped it open with a sharp, "Da?"

"We're here in Santa Rosa," Antón said in English, his voice as smooth as the finest vodka. "Our friend is on his way from the airport as we speak. You can proceed tonight if you wish."

Silva's scalp suddenly tingled, as if a jolt of electricity had passed through his body. He began to tremble.

"Tonight? You mean – I see," he stammered.

"You sound surprised."

"I am."

"I don't mean to upset your schedule," Antón said, "but the opportunity was there, so I took it. It's entirely up to you, and you'll hear from our associate soon, perhaps within the hour. You can tell him whether it's tonight or tomorrow after you assess the situation. Either way is fine with me."

What Antón had sensed many years before in the young man from Aleppo was a ruthless passion for orchestrated violence. Silva was a finely-honed psychopath, and the Russian knew what Silva would say before he heard it.

"Tonight is good," Silva whispered. "Tonight is very good."

"You have your own exit plan, I presume?" the fat man asked.

"Don't concern yourself with that, Antón."

Silva ended the call. A feral smile pulled back his lips and exposed his teeth. He held his hands in front of him and willed them not to shake, telling himself that many people were going to die tonight, but not him. Not him.

20

On Saturday night the population of Monte Rio doubled. The rasp of finely-tuned motorcycles cut through the night, laying down a bass line for the tricked out Japanese hotrods whining in harmony along River Road. Headlights streamed across the bridge in both directions, guiding hip chicks and cool cats from all over to the saloons. Raucous laughter drifted up from the municipal beach, and flashlights on night canoes dotted the black river. No Sonoma County deputies were watching the traffic, and that didn't seem to make much difference.

In The Pink Elephant Marty the bartender and all the patrons in the crowded saloon were watching the Sheriff Hix saga on the TV behind the bar. Reporters on Amory's lawn and in his driveway were milling around, interviewing one another.

"He's gonna quit," Marty declared to all the drinkers at the bar. "I don't see he has a choice."

The Elephant was jammed, the crowd sweaty close. When the band took the stage and hit the first rowdy notes of *Sweet Home Alabama*, people jumped to their feet, forgot about the sheriff and flat out rocked.

"I like this joint," Teddy said.

"Well, I'm just glad as hell," Marty yelled as he poured a half dozen shots of Jack for customers stacked three deep. "So you'd better spend some real money for that prime stool on Saturday night."

Teddy laid a twenty on the bar. "Do we speak the same language?"

Marty leaned over and whispered into Teddy's ear, "I know you're a fed."

Teddy tilted his dreadlocks close and asked, "Who else knows?"

"Butler and Albert and them guys, but you already know that."

"Yeah. Who else?"

Marty looked around and spotted Deputy Alice and Betty on the dance floor. Alice at that moment stopped dancing to answer her phone. After listening for a few seconds, she rushed out the door, Betty in tow.

"Deputy Alice, she knows," Marty said. "I dunno. I didn't tell nobody."

Teddy raised an eyebrow.

"Maybe my old lady, but she ain't here. I think people know, though, man. They just know."

"Okay," Teddy said. "I'm not here to bust anybody. I'm not DEA, all right?"

"You packin' heat, Mr. po-liceman?"

"Always. And call me Ted."

Teddy sipped his beer, took out his phone and called Butler who didn't answer. Sooner or later Butler would show up in the bar, and Teddy would try to cajole the guy into showing him where he went in the woods. If it didn't happen tonight, he had plenty of time.

There were worse things than spending two weeks on the balmy Russian River. The world didn't look too bad from little Monte Rio, Teddy thought, probably because you couldn't see very much of it. He'd worked in small towns before, interesting towns full of eccentrics, freaks and artists, but Monte Rio was different. In six weeks not a single local citizen had blinked at his dreads or tattoos. That had never happened before, not anywhere. It got him thinking maybe he could live in Monte Rio. Hell, he didn't live anywhere, really. He had an apartment in Fresno with nothing in it he could call his own. He was thirty-seven years old, and all he had was his job as resident freak of the FBI, pay grade GS-13. He was a certified and approved, licensed-to-kill terrorist hunter. Hot damn.

Women liked that, if he told them, for about three days. Usually, he didn't have to tell. They either went for the look, or they didn't. Marcie didn't. His ex-wife Marcie was remarried and living in

Baltimore, two blocks from where they'd both grown up in Hampden. Her new husband had no tattoos and came home every day.

Sorry, Marcie, but this isn't a nine-to-five gig. Terrorists never take a day off. Teddy was certain another Timothy McVeigh was out there somewhere, but he wasn't quite so certain that he should devote every minute of every day to searching for that elusive phantom. Or Paul's Arabs, or the Secret Service's Russians, or any other damn fool thing.

Jesus Christ, Teddy wondered, was Monte Rio a psychic magnet that attracted crazy people from all over, or was it a mystical force that made them crazy once they got here?

What was he going to accomplish here in Monte Rio in the next two weeks? He and Paul and the Pirates had already proved that Bohemian Grove communications security was all fucked up, but so what? Nothing would change.

He wanted to get drunk, stoned, and crazy like everyone else in the Pink Elephant, but he knew that when he was crawling on the floor with every cell in his body soaked with alcohol and drugs, the bad guys would come out of nowhere. The bad guys who didn't exist. Christ, he was facing another fifteen days on edge with nothing to do but prepare for a paranoid delusion.

That was his life, and as thin and one-dimensional as it seemed, it was all he had. After Monte Rio, he was assigned to a golf championship in Ohio for a week, then a week undercover at a gun and ammo convention in Dallas, then a week of meetings in Fresno followed by a week of meetings in New York to prepare for the World Series. If he lived in Monte Rio, he'd never be here. He'd be like Albert and Susan's neighbor, the guy – what's his name? Silva. He'd be like Mario Silva.

.   .   .   .

Butler was so pre-occupied with Silva's strange Mexicans that, when he pulled his vintage pickup into downtown Monte Rio, he was almost run down by three huge black SUVs, red and blue lights flashing like Christmas, that roared onto the Old Bohemian Highway like a runaway train, zoomed across the bridge to River Road and turned east.

Butler made sure no more deadly speeding trucks were coming before he parked and walked a block to the Pink Elephant. Usually deserted except for a few smokers, downtown was jammed. People spilled out of The Pink Elephant and into the street, more animated than usual with everybody talking excitedly.

When he saw the pimply-faced teenage son of one of his old girlfriends, he asked, "Hey Eddie, what's goin' on?"

Grinning, the kid said, "No cops, dude. Don't you watch TV? The sheriff shot himself."

"He what?!"

"Blew himself away."

"Amory?" Butler exclaimed. "Holy shit."

Inside the Pink Elephant, the rowdy band had to compete with the TV where a female reporter in front of a hospital emergency entrance was saying, "...and word from Santa Rosa Memorial Hospital is that Sheriff Amory Hix is still alive but in critical condition. From Santa Rosa Memorial Hospital, this is Carolyne Rose, and it's back to you in the KFTY TV 50 studios, Ron."

Someone in the back shouted, "Fuck the sheriff! Put on the ball game!"

Marty the mixologist shouted back, "Go next door!"

There was no next door.

Butler pushed up to the bar and said, "Jesus, Amory Hix shoots himself and fucks that up, too. What's that all about?"

Marty the bartender crossed his eyes, stuck out his tongue, squeezed his eyes shut, and put his finger to the side of his head. The barflies laughed. The band played on.

Butler squeezed over next to Teddy who sat restlessly on his stool watching the TV, thinking: This bullshit with the sheriff is really nuts. This is exactly the kind of distraction we don't need.

Teddy texted Paul at Jeremy's and asked, You watching this?

It's crazier than you think, Paul replied. Boris just landed & the Secret Service has gone bananas. Come up here & listen.

OK, Teddy texted back, and said to Butler, "Jeremy found the Russians."

The band broke into a long, loud guitar riff, and Butler hollered, "What?"

Teddy shouted, "It's too fucking loud in here. Let's go outside."

With a wave to Marty, Teddy and Butler pushed through the crowd and through the door until the decibel level dropped to audible.

"Jeremy found the Russians," Teddy repeated when they reached the street where people were discussing the sheriff and happily smoking weed.

"What Russians?" Butler asked, a little baffled.

"The guy the Bohos on the beach were talking about, Boris Demetriov. Remember him?" Teddy explained. "Jeremy was looking for him and I guess he found him."

"You got Russians," Butler said, lighting a Camel. "I got Mexicans. Weird Mexicans."

"Mexicans?" Teddy echoed. "What Mexicans?"

"I went back into the woods tonight, up Richardson's Road, and that guy Silva was out there in his vineyard with a crew of migrant Mexican farm workers. That was a little strange, to be out there at night."

"Mario Silva?" Teddy said, his interest piqued. "The guy with the house next door to Albert? I was just thinkin' about him," Teddy said. "I haven't met him yet."

"Yeah, that guy, Mario Silva," Butler nodded. "I saw him this afternoon at Pickett's after lunch, after you guys left. That was weird, too. He had all these Mexicans in the back of his truck, so I said I'd buy 'em a beer, but Silva said no beer. You ever hear of Mexican farm workers who didn't drink beer? Not me."

"I don't know much about Mexicans," Teddy said. "I'm from Baltimore."

"Yeah, well, when I was inside the store, I could hear them talking," Butler went on. "They were right next to the microphone in the fig tree, y'know, and they were talking in some weird language, and Silva told them to speak Spanish. Isn't that peculiar? I think maybe they're Indians, like Mexican Indians, like maybe they speak Nahuatl."

"What's Nahuatl?" Teddy asked.

"It's a Native American language," Butler replied. "It's what the Aztecs spoke,"

"Aztecs? In that vineyard next to the Grove?" Teddy asked.

"Yeah," Butler affirmed, vigorously nodding his head. "Silva has a bunkhouse he uses every year for migrant farm workers. I think maybe we should take a look."

They were approaching Teddy's truck and he was fishing in his pockets for the keys. "This is all very interesting, Butler," he said. "But I gotta go up to Jeremy's and check out his Russians."

"Them Russkies always get people's attention," Butler commented. "Mexicans? Never."

They reached Teddy's truck and got in.

Butler tried to explain why Silva's vineyard workers were strange. "The Mexicans who come here as migrants work hard all day, back-breaking stoop labor, and at night they hang around a campfire with guitars and cases and cases of beer. Cerveza. That's their way, they drink beer and sing long, sad ballads about narcotrafico. These guys didn't do that."

"How do you know this, Butler?"

"'Cause I hang out, man, and I speak a little Spanish, and I like *tacos al carbón*."

"Well," Teddy said, pulling into Jeremy's and parking next to Paul's Mustang, "we can check out your Mexicans after all this other crazy shit is sorted out."

"Whatever, man," Butler said.

As they stepped on to Jeremy's porch, a flare of radio static and a burble of cop talk burst through the screen door.

Jeremy and Paul were listening to the Secret Service drivers as they raced back from the Santa Rosa airport with Boris Demetriov, his brother and his bodyguard.

"What's happening?" Teddy asked.

"Fun and games," Jeremy said with a huge, toothy smile. "The

Secret Service is stuck on River Road. They're on this set of speakers. There's been an accident. The Highway Patrol is on this other set."

Paul added, "I think a logger lost his load."

.   .   .   .   .

A gigantic redwood log blocked both directions of River Road just inside Guerneville, and traffic was backing up behind the keeled-over truck. Sirens and flashing red and blue lights were not going to budge a log six feet in diameter and thirty feet long. The big Freightliner cab lay on its side, and the dazed driver was sitting on the ground talking to a squatting California Highway Patrolman. The lights atop the CHP Ford Explosion were flashing red, spookily illuminating the scene. More cars were backing up on the far side of the overturned logging truck, some turning around, and more flashing lights and sirens from an approaching fire truck added to the confusion.

Rodriguez couldn't believe this was happening right in his path. His driver was lost and confused; Boris was passed out in the back seat; Yuri had a pistol out and was twisting and turning, looking for an ambush, and Rodriguez thought he was going to start shooting the civilians who were gathering to gawk at the wreck.

Yuri screamed, "This is fucked up! This is fucked up!" and then broke off a long stream of Russian profanities.

Arms wrapped tightly around his brother Boris, Dmitri was thinking: Not now! Not now! This can't be Silva now, can it? Holy Saint Cyril, it isn't supposed to happen this way.

"Get us out of here!" Dmitri shouted in Russian.

"Baba gugu," Boris said in universal drunken baby talk.

"Don't worry," Rodriguez said unconvincingly in Russian. "It's just an accident."

"Fuhguddyzitvolikigrrrr," Boris announced.

"This is all fucked up!" Yuri reminded everyone in the SUV, aiming his pistol at a little kid standing by the side of the road.

Thinking that Yuri believed he had diplomatic immunity no matter what he did, Rodriguez shouted, "Don't shoot! Don't shoot!"

"These cocksuckers!" Yuri screamed. "They're after Boris. I'll save you, my president!"

"Find an alternate route," Rodriguez shouted at the driver, punching up the navigation system. "We're in fucking Guerneville. There has to be a way around this. Wait a minute!"

Rodriguez jerked open his door, jumped out of the SUV and ran over to the CHP cop who was talking to the derailed truck driver. Flashing his Secret Service credentials, Rodriguez declared breathlessly, "Secret Service. I need your help."

"Wha...wha...wha..." uttered the startled highway patrolman. The driver of the logging truck was on his knees, eyes red and bleary.

Rodriguez insisted, "I need to get around this mess, right now."

"Um, okay, um, turn around, go back to, um, Redwood Court, and, um..."

Rodriguez grabbed him by the arm and said, "You're coming with me."

Rodriguez dragged the highway patrolman into the front passenger seat of the middle SUV. Using their sirens as prods to move the other cars out of the way, the three huge, intimidating government trucks with blacked-out windows made U-turns.

Officer Oliver Maybeck, CHP, counted three computer screens and seven very bright LED displays on the dash. He was squeezed between two guys in dark suits with ear buds who smelled of gun oil, sweat, and cheap cologne. Three more guys were in the back, shouting and babbling in a foreign language.

Lights flashing, sirens blaring, engines screaming, tires smoking, the trucks blasted through the night, the truck with Boris, Rodriguez and Officer Maybeck now in the lead.

"Just give the driver directions," Rodriguez said to the cop, and to the driver, "Go go go!"

"Turn left!" Maybeck yelled, and the truck lurched to the left, followed by the other trucks, and roared down a darkened lane through the trees.

"Turn left again, here!"

They raced down a quiet street of cottages and bungalows, running parallel to the highway. An ambulance with flashing lights passed them going the other way.

"Left again."

They reeled around the corner and the highway was in front of them, the main street through town. The road was clear to the right.

"Thanks, officer," Rodriguez said, and reached over and opened the door for him.

Officer Maybeck tumbled out of the SUV and watched the trio of federal vehicles roar west through the middle of Guerneville. He'd been with them no more than three minutes, just long enough to go around the block. With shaking hands, he patted his empty pockets for cigarettes, so mind-blown he forgot he quit. To his left a quarter-mile away he could see the giant log, the turned over Freightliner cab, two fire trucks and backed-up traffic. Coming partially to his senses, he fumbled for his radio.

Forgetting protocol, he said into his hand-held radio, "This is Maybeck. I've been kidnapped by the Secret Service."

.　.　.　.　.

Up at Jeremy's everybody cracked up.

"Unit ninety-seven, are you still at the scene of the accident?"

"What? No. I've been kidnapped. I was kidnapped, but now I'm...I'm walking back."

"The paramedics are on the scene, Unit ninety-seven, and they can't find you. You say you were what?"

"Never mind. You'll never believe me anyway. I'm back at the accident now. Here's the Fire Chief. I'd better talk to him. Ninety-seven, out."

The radios danced, the speakers sang, and Jeremy was grinning ear to ear.

"Is it always like this on Saturday night around here?" Teddy asked.

"Actually," Jeremy said, "this is pretty quiet. Usually the Sheriff's Department stirs things up, traffic stops that turn nasty and things like that, routine domestic violence and neighborhood shootings. This America, Teddy. Everybody has guns."

"And we only get this federal excitement when the Bohos are here," Butler said. "Well, the DEA is always here because nobody told them that cannabis is mostly legal in California. Otherwise, we get wine country tourists, Russian River fishermen, and Mexicans. They mix it up pretty good on Saturday night."

"You say Mexicans, but not like your Mexicans," Teddy said.

"No, regular Mexicans," Butler said.

"What are you jabbering about, Mexicans?" Jeremy asked.

"You ever meet any Mexicans who didn't drink beer?" Butler asked Jeremy.

"Sure," Jeremy said. "All the time. The ones who don't drink beer usually drink tequila. I work with lots of Mexicans at the supermarket."

"Those are our Mexicans," Butler said. "Mexican-Americans and Mexicans who've been here a long time are the same as anybody else, but migrant farm workers, Mexicans from deep Mexico, those are rural people, country people. You know what I mean? They're different."

"So what?" Jeremy said. "There are thousands of migrants in Sonoma County. They work the vineyards and pick olives and grapes and apples, and then they go down to Salinas and pick lettuce, and artichokes in Watsonville...."

"And they drink beer," Butler said.

"So?"

"These guys didn't."

"Jesus, Butler, maybe they're Jehovah's Witnesses," Jeremy argued, eyes bulging. "There's lots of Mexican evangelicals. They have a whole bunch of Spanish language, born-again Christian churches in Santa Rosa, and those folks don't drink."

"Could be, could be," Butler conceded. "It's just an anomaly, one of those little quirks in the universe that doesn't quite make sense. Like a white FBI guy with dreadlocks."

"Butler," Jeremy said, "you know damned well that when the

Bohos are here nothing makes sense. That's why we started doing this in the first place. What did you call this place today? A loony bin."

"Well, I got pictures of these Mexicans tonight. Wanna see?"

"Hang on," Jeremy said.

He turned up a speaker and they heard, "Cola Five, this is Cola One. Caviar is approaching the Main Gate."

"It's Boris Boris time," Jeremy said.

21

At midnight the blue-blazered messenger delivered the message to Roger Blake in the tent he shared with A.J. Hoff, and Blake's response was heard by all encamped members of Ye Olde Owls.

"The son of a bitch is coming now?"

Pandemonium, commotion, blithering fuss, grumbling and drunken belching. Owls emerged from their tents and gathered around the campfire, a few in their pajamas, others in silk smoking jackets, most still in jeans and plaid shirts. Maurice, the white-jacketed, African-French camp chef and valet, silently offered a tray with shots of Cognac and glasses of port.

"He's going to be here in less than an hour," Roger explained. "We have to be hospitable and make him welcome. It's really not an inconvenience."

"Bullshit," snorted Bill Anthony. "It may not be an inconvenience for you, Roger, but it is for others."

"Stick it, Bill," Roger said, heating up.

"This is just downright rude," Bill insisted, his angry tone matching Roger's.

Wading into the middle of this dispute, A.J. Hoff said, "Bill, I don't think Boris learned his manners at your boarding school. It appears he makes his own rules."

"Well, I have to go down to the Service Center and call him," Roger said, gesturing toward the waiting messenger and his golf cart. "There's really nothing to do. His tent is ready, and we have everything we need."

Blake climbed into the golf cart with the messenger, and they puttered down the path past the other camps in Southland. A party was in full swing in Dogtown, and he waved at a few friends.

"Hey, Roger, why don't you guys come on down," shouted one of the Dogs, a California state senator. "It's a margarita party."

"Maybe in an hour or so, thanks. We have a guest coming in."

"The Cossack? We heard about him. Is he bringing his horse?"

"He's a White Russian, a Belarusian, and that's different."

"Well, he's certainly welcome here, whatever he is. Hope he likes tequila."

"Thanks, I'll tell him."

. . . . .

A topless Bohemian tram was waiting at the Service Center for late-arriving guests.

"You here for Ye Olde Owls?" Roger asked.

"That's what they tell me," the driver answered, pointing at his radio.

The Secret Service night duty officer, Agent Walter Smith, met Roger at the service center front desk and handed Blake a conventional landline phone, saying, "You're going to speak to Yuri Ustov, Mr. Demetriov's bodyguard. He speaks English."

"That's fine," Roger said. "I know Yuri."

White dialed. The phone rang on Antón's plane.

"Mr. Yuri Ustov?"

"Not here," answered Mikhail. "Wrong nummer."

Confused, Roger shook his head and said to the Secret Service agent, "What the hell? Somebody said it was a wrong number."

"I'll call Rodriguez," said White, dialing his boss in the truck. "He'll straighten this out."

Rodriguez cut off White's explanation by saying, "Don't worry about it. We're at the Main Gate."

. . . . .

The headlights of the SUVs flashed through the windows as the trucks stopped in front of the Service Center, and Roger went outside to welcome his guests, the president of Belarus and his party.

Agent Smith tapped Roger on the shoulder and handed him three numbered canvas bags that bore the Bohemian Club's owl logo. "Here," he said. "For the phones."

"Right. Thanks."

In the lead truck Rodriguez turned around to face the Belarussians.

"Gentlemen, our only concern is your safety, and that's only a problem if you leave the Grove."

Rodriguez watched Yuri and Dmitri pull Boris out of the truck. The bodyguard threw one of the president's arms over his powerful shoulders and grappled with Boris's waist to hold him up.

"It won't be a problem tonight, that's obvious," Dmitri said.

"Mr. Demetriov? Mr. President?" Blake said tentatively, glancing from Boris to Yuri. "Ah, Roger Blake here, ah, I tried to call you, sir, on the plane, but, ah..."

"Mr. Blake," Yuri said with a big smile, almost dropping Boris to shake hands. "I am Yuri, Yuri Ustov, perhaps you remember from Berlin, and Boris, well, Boris is, what you say, DUI, drunk under influence, yes. DUI. Where do we go, please?"

Dmitri rushed forward to help prop up his bother, and Roger indicated the waiting tram.

"This way, please. This way."

Rodriguez took the three numbered canvass bags from a confused Roger Blake and followed the Belarusians to the tram.

"I need your weapons and your phones, all your phones," Rodriguez said in Russian. "If you want to make a call, you can come here to the Service Center to use your mobiles."

Yuri gave up two phones and a Ruger automatic pistol.

"And the other one," Rodriguez said.

Rolling his eyes, Yuri produced a second pistol from an ankle holster.

"The holsters, too."

"Do you want to search me?" Yuri demanded.

"Yes," Rodriguez answered without hesitation. He promptly climbed into the open tram and patted down all three Russians, retrieving another phone and a pistol from Dmitri, a third pistol from Yuri, and one phone and smudges of vomit from Boris. He missed a tiny Beretta Pico .38 Yuri had hidden in his underpants.

"This is outrageous," Dmitri protested as he watched the precious white phone he needed to call Silva drop into a bag. "I'm going to complain to the State Department."

"That's easy," Rodriguez said, walking away with the bags. "You'll find the Undersecretary of State in Cave Man camp. I'm sure he'll be interested in your complaint. Welcome to the Bohemian Grove."

As Rodriguez started to walk away, Dmitri cried out, "Wait! I have to make a call."

"Yes? Now? Okay."

Rodriguez fished around in Dmitri's bag and extracted a heavy, black phone.

"Not that one," Dmitri said. "The white one."

Dmitri took the phone and found the one number stored in memory. He dialed, smiled at Rodriguez and turned away.

"Hello?" Silva answered in Russian.

"Silva?" Dmitri said.

"Yes."

"Yes. Hello," Dmitri said, trying to cover his mouth. "We've arrived at the Bohemian Grove, and I wanted to let you know they are taking our phones. We'll be in the camp in a few minutes, and then I'll be out of reach."

"I understand. Should I come tonight?" Silva inquired.

"Yes. Study hard," Dmitri said and hung up. "My son," he said to Rodriguez.

Rodriguez held out the bag and accepted the phone. He turned and as the tram began to move, he said to Roger Blake, "They're all yours. Good luck."

.　.　.　.　.

The National Security Agency technicians in the black room who rotated eight hour shifts were named Madera, Drake, and Belinski, and their tasks included monitoring cell phone traffic during the encampment, a job made easy by the SIM card in each phone. They didn't trace or listen to every call on every phone, only those of special interest, and for decades the NSA had denied to representatives of the Bohemian Club that they ever touched any of the phones. It was a gentlemen's agreement that they would never, under any circumstances, touch a member's phone. Guests, especially foreign guests, were simply never mentioned. When Saudi royals arrived, for example, Drake pulled the SIM cards from their phones, copied them, and put them back.

When Rodriguez knocked on the door of the black room, the night shift operator, Daniel Belinski, let him in, asking, "You want the intel on the Gulfstream?"

"Yes."

Belinski pushed a button on his keyboard and displayed a photograph of Antón sitting at a desk with a view of the Kremlin through the window behind him.

"The plane is owned by a Russian national, Antón Cosmovitch Valisnikov, former KGB, Sixth Directorate, Division of Industrial Security; former SRV, also for industrial security; now employed by the Moscow Petroleum Consortium as their head of security. He flew into Los Angeles two days ago from Mexico City in the Gulfstream. The day before that he was in Foz do Igaçu, Brazil. He owns a house in Los Angeles and another in Marseille, France. CIA has a lot on him if you're interested, but it's all old stuff."

"Only the highlights."

"He's not on any watch list, but he's been suspected of almost anything you can think of: connections to at least three Russian mafias, selling old Soviet munitions to third-world countries, illegal export of oil and natural gas, but he's never been charged with anything, anywhere. He's a Cold War relic, now a private citizen but very well connected. He once worked for Gorbachev. They don't keep active tabs on him anymore."

"That's enough. Why was he in Brazil?"

"You got me," said the spook. "Who knows?"

"Give me what you have on calls to and from that plane."

"Okay," Belinski said, punching up a different screen. "Working from the most recent, there was one call to the plane from the Service Center."

"Yes," Rodriguez said. "That was Roger Blake."

"One call was made from the plane to you."

"Yes, that was Yuri."

"One call made to Zinfandel Limousines in Santa Rosa."

"Yuri again."

"And one call made from the plane to a number with a Miami area code."

"Okay. Now check this out," Rodriguez said, producing the white phone from Dmitri's bag. "A call was just made on this phone, and I want to know whom he called."

"Whom?" Belinski's lips burbled with the 'm' and he smirked.

"Don't be a wiseass."

Belinski pried open the back of the phone, took out the SIM card, and plugged it into the chip drive connected to his computer.

"Okay," he said, fingering his keyboard. "There's only one number in memory, and someone called that number, area code 305, that's Miami. Let's see. That's the same Miami number that was called from the plane."

"The same number?"

"Yes, both this number and the number of this white phone are pre-paid, so there's no record of who bought it, only where and when...and that was...in Miami, six weeks ago. I'd say the two Miami phones with sequential numbers were purchased together. These are cheap phones with no GPS trackers."

"Can you find out where the other phone was when it was answered?"

"I have to go through the wire room in San Francisco to do that."

"Do it," Rodriguez said, trying to process the information. "Two phone numbers in Miami. Someone on the plane called Miami, and Dmitri called the same Miami number ten minutes ago from another phone with a Miami number."

"Two phones with sequential numbers," Belinski reminded him.

"Interesting," Rodriguez said, looking into the bags of Russian phones and weapons. "Look at these phones."

Belinski examined the phones, saying, "All high-end, first-class phones. This one, let's see, this one is pretty fancy, probably encrypted. This is a top-of-the-line, Russian- made government phone. Want me to check it out?"

"Not yet. It probably has tamper-proof devices, anyway. No, it's the cheap white one that's of special interest right now. Find out what you can about those calls."

"I have a tech in the wire room who can do it. It'll take a few minutes, maybe half an hour. They're busy in Frisco."

"Okay. You let me know ASAP."

. . . . .

The tram arrived at Ye Olde Owls, and all the Owls stood up and raised their glasses to greet their guests. Boris, suddenly awake and energized by the smell of wood smoke, jumped to his feet, spread his arms wide, and exclaimed in loud and clear Russian, "Let's eat!"

Roger Blake, sitting next to Yuri on the tram, said quizzically, "What's going on?"

"He sobers up fast sometimes," Yuri said, squeezing past Roger to run after his president. "He's hungry."

"Oh, we can take care of that."

Boris stepped off the tram and marched toward the roaring campfire, hands extended to warm himself, a huge smile on his rough face, teeth gleaming like the world's most expensive cosmetic dentistry, hair flowing back in a hairdo that would have looked right on Elvis. He wore a gauche gold chain and looked like he'd slept in his clothes, or worse, but despite all these shortcoming the president of

Belarus radiated a fabulous charm.

He stepped up to the nearest Owl, Bill Anthony, took his hand and pumped it up and down, grinning and babbling cheerfully in Russian. "Preevyet! Preevyet! I am Boris Borisovitch Demetriov. I love that you have a big campfire. It reminds me so much of home. I build a big fire outside the presidential mansion every night. It's so nice. And look at all these wonderful big trees. Yuri, tell these assholes that I'm starving, and I don't want any prissy fag food. You understand?"

Yuri scurried behind Boris, providing a running English interpretation, "Hello, hello, he is Boris Demetriov. He likes your fire, says it reminds him of home. And the trees, he likes the trees. Hello, I am Yuri, Yuri Ustov. He is very hungry, the president says."

"Maurice! Get this man something to eat," shouted A.J. Hoff to the camp chef.

Boris moved on to the next man, a very confused Rob Hamilton, at 82 the oldest Owl, who was in his pajamas. "Preevyet! Preevyet! What a wonderful thing this is. Hello, hello. Yuri! Don't these guys know how to dress?"

"Who is this man?" Rob cried. "Why is he in our camp?"

"He's our guest," Bill said. "The president of Belarus."

"Bella who?"

Dmitri and Roger Blake got off the tram, and Boris finally recognized Roger.

"Roger! Roger Blake! Hello, hello. So this is the Bohemian Forest you told me about in Berlin. Are you sure we're in California? Where's the beach?"

Yuri expounded, "Boris says he's so happy to be here, Mr. Blake."

"Hello, hello. I am Boris Demetriov. Dmitri! This is my brother, Dmitri Borisovitch Demetriov, the Minister of the Interior of the Republic of Belarus. Say hello, Dmitri, to all these fine gentlemen. Which of these pricks are giving me my money? Yuri! Find out who the moneybags are. I want to kiss them. I'm sure they would like that, they all look like effeminate queers, except that one."

He pointed rudely toward A.J. Hoff. "That one looks like a man. Tell him I need a drink."

"Boris, slow down," Yuri said. "I can't keep up."

"Food! Drink! Now!" Boris bellowed. "Hello, hello," he said to A.J. Hoff.

Maurice in his chef's whites rushed out of the lodge and presented Boris with a with a steaming bowl of cassoulet. Boris bent over and sniffed.

"Cassoulet," he said, pronouncing the French word correctly. He smiled and shook his head. "I hate the fucking French."

"He doesn't like French food," Yuri interpreted.

"This is different," Maurice said. "New Orleans style with chili peppers."

"I don't think he wants it," Yuri said.

"Would he like some venison, do you think?" Maurice asked.

"Venison?" Yuri asked Boris. "Deer meat?"

"Oh, yes, definitely," Boris said, vigorously nodding his head.

"That's a splendid idea," said A.J. Hoff. "Rig the spit. I like this guy already."

Maurice ran into the lodge to retrieve a side of freshly butchered deer loin.

"A.J. Hoff, camp captain," Hoff said, stepping up to welcome the guest and shake his hand.

"He's the chief camper," Yuri said. "A.J. Hoff. He's one of your investors."

"Well, tell him to get me a drink," Boris said.

"He's thirsty," Yuri said in English.

"What does he want?" A.J. Hoff asked.

"What would you like, Boris?"

"Beer! I want beer. Anything but scotch."

"He wants a beer."

"Get him a beer."

When Maurice reappeared with a bottle of Beck's and the pink flesh of the trespassing deer over his shoulder, Boris said, "Yuri, tell them maybe they're not all assholes. Who shot this buck?"

Yuri said, "He wants to know who shot the deer?"

"One of the guards," said A.J. Hoff.

When Yuri translated, Boris laughed and said, "At home you would lie and say you did it. But I like your honesty. Yuri, ask him if he shoots."

"Boris would like to know, Mr. Hoff, if you are a sportsman? Do you shoot?"

"Tell him tomorrow we'll go to the skeet range and he can try my new Perazzi 12 gauge."

Several Owls assembled an electric spit, skewered the venison, and the smell of roasting meat quickly enveloped the camp.

Boris smiled and drank his beer. Maurice beamed. The Owls noisily congratulated themselves on their wisdom for securing the venison. The scene was so uproarious that Bohos from nearby camps began drifting in to see what the fuss was about. When one of the Dogs arrived with a bottle of tequila, Boris pointed and demanded, "What's that?"

"Tequila."

"Let's have some of that."

The bottle made its way to Boris who tilted it and began to chug.

"Hoo hoo hoo hoo," went the Owls.

"Woof woof woof woof woof woof," went the Dogs.

Dmitri took a seat on one of the stone benches around the campfire and looked at his watch. It was just after one o'clock in the morning. The Bohemians crowded around Boris, passing bottles from mouth to mouth, the campfire illuminating their faces with a satanic glow. The president! All his life Dmitri had watched his brother make a spectacle of himself, but this would be the last time.

A whirlwind is coming, Dmitri thought. Fuck you, Boris.

22

Over on River Boulevard, Albert was too restless to do anything except pace around his deck. The first Saturday night at the Grove was always prime peccadillo night, and after looking forward to the Bohemian encampment all year, Albert had expected to be in Guerneville or Rio Nido by now, following a Boho to a secret trysting place and having a few laughs. Landing on the Bohemian Beach had been entertaining, but being forbidden by the FBI from chasing Bohos to their secret rendezvous spots was gnawing away at his mischievous nature.

He watched the sheriff's saga on TV, and spoke on the phone with Jeremy who delivered a blow by blow description of the Secret Service chasing down Bobby MacIntyre. There was just too much going on for him to stay home. After considerable fidgeting, he told Susan he was going to Jeremy's.

Peeved, Susan whined, "Albert, you promised."

"Well, maybe I did, but so what?"

"Don't go running around getting into trouble, Albert. Please. Haven't you had enough excitement for one day?"

"God is on our side," Albert proclaimed. "And the FBI."

"Damn it," Susan pleaded, reaching out to hold him. "Those guys are crazy, they're all crazy, the FBI, Butler, Jeremy, all of 'em."

Albert took a freshly dry-cleaned, bright yellow Samoan shirt from his closet, put it on and said, "Well, sweetheart, crazy is never boring. I'll see you later."

· · · · ·

Albert found the rowdy party mood he was looking for at Jeremy's. As he got out of his truck, he heard The Band crooning through the outdoor speakers, *Up on Cripple Creek*. Phillip and his girlfriend were ensconced on a lawn chair, smoking pot in a bong and making out. Inside, Jeremy had put earphones with Mickey Mouse ears on Teddy, and both Jeremy and FBI Agent Swan were laughing like madmen. Jeremy's eyes were linebacker bright with glee.

Butler was sitting on the couch in his Maverick costume, cleaning his antique rifle.

"What are you doing with that thing?" Albert asked, pointing at the Sharps.

"Basic maintenance. It's an old gun. Needs lots of tender, loving care."

"Now?"

"Why not?"

"You gonna shoot somebody?"

"Nope, but I might want to scare 'em a little bit."

"You sure looked dressed the part, Mr. gamblin' man," Teddy said to Butler, taking off his earphones. "Is it always a costume party when you're around?"

"Pretty much, yeah," Butler said, as he assembled his ramrod and oiled a piece of cloth. "What good is life if it ain't fun?"

Paul was on the phone with Carter McGee, explaining how Jeremy was able to track the Secret Service as they corralled Bobby MacIntyre. Bobby had left his microphone on in his limo the whole time Rodriguez was kidnapping Boris, and then Bobby had obliged his eavesdroppers further by describing the entire incident to Darlene, his wife, over the air.

Paul said to Carter McGee, "So now Boris is in the Grove, drunk out of his mind, and there were no bad guys at the airport or on the highway, no terrorists, no Russian commandos, no bad guys at all, just a lot of Secret Service paranoia."

"The Secret Service is always a little edgy," said Carter McGee. "They have to be. Perhaps they could be more discreet, but that's not their style."

"Well," Paul said. "Boris might leave the Grove again tonight. Who knows?"

Carter McGee replied, "If he does, I'm sure Raul Rodriguez will be right with him."

"Maybe, maybe not. Don't forget they lost him in L.A.," Paul reminded his boss. "In any case, Boris or no Boris, this local sheriff demanding bribes is going to be a Bureau headache. Do you want us to look into it?"

"That can wait until Monday," Carter McGee answered. "Fuck the sheriff. What else?"

"Teddy!" Paul hollered. "We got the sheriff and Boris covered. Carter wants to know what else?"

"Butler here has discovered some weird Mexicans," Teddy replied.

"Weird? Whaddaya mean, weird?" Paul asked.

From the couch Butler answered, "They don't drink beer."

"Oh, for chrissake. Is that it? That's what's weird?" Paul said.

Teddy shrugged and frowned.

"And they speak some foreign language that isn't Spanish," Butler added.

"What's that?" Carter McGee asked Paul over the phone. "I didn't hear."

"We'll check it out," Paul told his boss, "some unusual Mexicans, but it can probably wait until tomorrow morning."

"Okay," said Carter McGee, hanging up. "Keep me posted."

"The hell with you people, big, bad Eff Bee Eye," Butler declared, standing up and sighting down the clean, empty barrel. "Maybe I should talk to the Secret Service and tell them about the Mexicans. They sound like guys who know how to get shit done."

"You don't think we can get anything done?" Teddy asked, a little miffed. "If we did things the Secret Service way, we'd be all over your Mexicans."

"So why aren't you?" Butler demanded.

"Let's just say there are trivial issues like the Constitution, probable cause, warrants, stuff like that," Teddy answered. "If we busted in there, it would be like last night when the sheriff showed up at your house with no warrant. And even if I wanted to, I can't go poking my nose into people's business just because you, Butler Q. Citizen, think they're weird. Everybody thinks somebody is weird. I'm sure there are people who think you're weird, and I know damned well plenty of people think I'm too weird for words."

"Aren't you even curious?"

"What I'm curious about, Butler," Teddy said earnestly, "is where you go in the woods to see all these things you think are so strange. That's what I want to know."

"Fat Freddie," Butler said.

"Say what?" Teddy responded, furrowing his brow.

"That's where I go, to a tree named Fat Freddie. Don't you remember the Fabulous Furry Freak Brothers? The comic book from the Sixties? No, you're too young."

"Fat Freddie!" Albert roared. "Fat Freddie! That's fuckin' great!"

"Yeah? Fat Freddie?" Teddy said, wrinkling his nose. "And then what? You just hang around this tree?"

"I go up about a hundred fifty feet. I built a blind," Butler said.

"A sniper's blind," Teddy offered.

"No, man, a photographer's perch," Butler exclaimed, starting to show his irritation. "I got the photo of the owl up there. I shoot a lot of wildlife. With a camera, not with this," Butler said, raising the Sharps. "I took some shots tonight with my Nikon. The camera's in my truck."

"Go get it," Jeremy said. "We'll take a look."

"Albert," Teddy asked, "did you know about this?"

Shaking his head, Albert said slowly, "I had no idea, and I can't believe Butler is telling us his deepest, darkest secret. I'm flabbergasted."

"Jeremy?"

"This is all news to me."

Butler laughed. "I figure you'd pester me until I told you, Mr. FBI, so I'm telling you. It's no big deal, really, as secrets go. It's just that, y'know, I never told anyone because the tree is on Old Man Richardson's property."

Teddy asked, "How far is your blind from Silva's bunkhouse?"

"A quarter of a mile, a little less. Four hundred yards."

"I don't want to knock on the Mexicans' door, but I wouldn't mind looking at them from four hundred yards away," Teddy said. "That's perfectly legal. What do you think, Paulie?"

"Yeah," Paul agreed, "but I wouldn't mind knocking on their door, either."

Butler waved them off. "They're gonna be asleep, man. It's late."

"But you said they were outside tonight," Teddy protested.

"Yeah, but that was two, three hours ago. Migrants work early in the morning, when it's not too hot."

"I wanna see Fat Freddie," Albert insisted. "Yeah!"

"It's only a tree, man," Butler declared, shaking his head. "Ronnie Reagan said, 'If you've seen one redwood, you've seen 'em all.' Fat Freddie is just a tree like all the other damn trees."

"Ha!" Albert snorted. "I know you got more respect than that, Butler."

Butler winked and Jeremy said, "Get the memory card out of the camera. We'll take a look."

Butler pushed open the screen door and went outside. Phillip and Marika were gone, and Butler wondered if Phillip would get paid if he went AWOL. Now that the FBI finally wanted to see his photos, Butler wondered if he could get paid for the images on the memory card. Hmmm. He laughed at himself, musing about ways to take money from the government. Was it government by the people, of the people, and for the people, i.e. for Butler Q. Citizen, as Teddy called him, or was it government for the Bohos? Did it make any difference? What the hell. He grabbed the camera bag out of his truck and took it inside where he pulled the memory card from the Nikon and handed it to Jeremy.

"Let's see these pictures on the big monitor," Butler suggested.

A moment later they were looking at a grainy, slightly fuzzy image of Silva and his field hands in the vineyard. Huddled around the vineyard owner, the Mexicans were wearing white soccer jerseys with big numbers. Silva appeared to be pointing at something far away, beyond the vineyard. All the soccer players were looking in that direction.

Jeremy clicked through several photos of Silva and the soccer jerseys, then three shots of the Blue Blazer Hummer passing by, then back to the first group photo.

"Look," Butler said, "Go back. When the Hummer passes by, they all drop down out of sight. Silva, too."

"They're undocumented illegals," Teddy said. "They think the Blue Blazers are cops, or some kind of authority."

"That's what I figured," Butler said.

"What are they doing out there? Playing ball at midnight?" Paul asked.

One of the young men was holding a soccer ball under his arm, casually pressing it against his body.

"Why not?" Teddy replied. "So what?"

"In a vineyard?" Paul asked, scratching his head. "That's nuts."

"Can you do anything about this picture?" Butler asked. "Sharpen it up a little?"

"Sure," Jeremy replied, punching buttons. The picture magnified but became grainier and less sharply defined.

"They look like Mexican soccer players to me," Jeremy said. "Just like hundreds you might see in Santa Rosa every weekend. Soccer is easy to play, all you need is a ball. One of them is holding a book. I wonder what it is."

"The rules of soccer?" Butler quipped.

"Soccer doesn't have rules," Albert declared. "Soccer has laws. And the Brits call it football."

"Can you blow it up some more?" Teddy asked.

"Sure. Let's see."

The high-resolution, low-light image jumped in size, then jumped again, becoming fuzzier and grainier each time.

"Center on the book," Teddy said. "Can you tell what it is? Can you read the cover?"

"No," Jeremy replied. "The title is in a foreign script, maybe, I dunno what. Hebrew maybe? Arabic?"

"Arabic?" Paul, who was looking at his phone, jerked his head around. "Arabic?"

"It's not real clear," Jeremy said. "It's grainy."

Paul looked, blinked, and said, "It's clear enough. That book is the Holy Quran."

"The what?" Butler asked

"The Koran."

"You sure?" Teddy asked.

"Yes," Paul said succinctly, and repeated, "That's what it is, the Quran. After two years in Dearborn, Michigan, studying Arabic, I'm damned if I can't recognize that."

They all looked at one another and blinked and sucked air through their teeth.

"Damn," Teddy said. "Damn."

"The Quran simply means Islam," Paul said. "It's a religious text, like the Bible. It doesn't mean terrorism."

"Damn," Teddy said again.

"When I was in Pickett's this afternoon," Butler said, "and Silva and his farm workers in the truck were under the fig tree, I heard something through the general's speaker system that I thought at the time was maybe Nahuatl, or some other native American language, but maybe it was Arabic. All I know for sure is that Silva told the guys in the truck in Spanish to speak Spanish. Why would he do that?"

"Because they have something to hide," Paul said. "They're Muslims, Arabic-speaking Muslims who also speak Spanish."

"So what if they are?" Jeremy said. "So what? Is that a federal crime?"

"Maybe. We don't know yet, but we're gonna find out," Paul answered.

"Holy shit," Butler said. "Mexican Muslims? Do they have Muslims in Mexico?"

"How do I know?" Jeremy said, "Why not? They got everything else."

"We gotta check this out," Paul said. "Damn. That's what we're here for. At least that's why I'm here. We gotta check them out."

"Check them out how?" Teddy said. "Bang on the door and shout 'FBI' as loud as we can and see what happens?"

Paul looked at Teddy and asked, "What do you have in the truck?"

"Regular government issue," Teddy replied. "Benelli tacticals and HKs, two each, windbreakers, hats, commo gear, all the usual shit."

Jeremy and Albert blinked and looked one another, neither comprehending the weapons lingo.

Butler understood. The Benellis were high-performance, anti-riot shotguns, and the HKs were Heckler-Koch automatic assault rifles, in a word, machineguns.

"What!?" Butler squawked. "You've been carrying HKs and scatter guns around here all this time? What the fuck!?"

"Yeah," Teddy said. "It's my job. I'm a federal cop."

"Jee-zus," Butler said.

"I don't really expect to use them," Teddy said, trying to sound reasonable. "Any more than you intend to use that Sharps."

"But you have them," Butler said.

"Yessir, I do, but I don't want to threaten a bunch of Mexicans with them, either. Who knows what might happen if the Bureau shows up at their bunkhouse door? It isn't like the Bohemian Beach." Teddy turned to Paul and said, "I should call Carter McGee. Jesus Christ, he thought you guys might turn something up, and it looks like you did."

Teddy reached for his phone, but Paul held up his hands in a gesture that said 'Wait.' "Hold on, hold on, just a minute. We don't need to take heavy artillery up there, but if you call Carter McGee, he'll do much worse," Paul went on. "He'll call in the fucking Marines and we'll have a giant mess on our hands. Let's just go up there quietly and check it out, then call Carter McGee if we have to. You know the deal, Teddy, like I learned in the Navy. It's much better to beg for forgiveness than ask for permission."

"I dunno, man," Teddy said, taking out his phone. "You never know what pile of shit is waiting for you to step in it."

"Hey! Hey! Hey! Wait a minute, wait a minute," Albert sputtered, waving his arms around and signaling time-out. "We don't need to take an army over there to Silva's. That's crazy. Now, listen to me. I can do it. Silva knows me. I'm his neighbor. If I knock on his door, he won't freak out. I can talk to him and find out what's goin' on."

Teddy and Paul both turned to look at the big former offensive tackle from Stanford, both thinking Albert was fearsome enough to scare the shit out of any migrant farm worker, Muslim or not.

"Sounds good to me," Paul said. "That works."

"Whaddaya think, Butler?" Teddy asked.

"I think if Albert wants to knock on Silva's bunkhouse door, I can watch him from my blind," Butler answered. "What's the worst that can happen? A buncha guys wake up mad in the middle of the night because they gotta go to work early in the mornin'. No big deal."

"We hope it's no big deal," Paul said. "But just in case, I'll go with him. We don't really know who is in there."

"Yeah, yeah," Albert said, nodding enthusiastically. "All we have to do is knock and we'll find out."

"Maybe you're right," Teddy said, eyeballing the Pirates. "But we don't want any vigilante bullshit."

There was a moment of awkward silence that was interrupted by radio static and routine checks by the Blue Blazers. Jeremy fiddled with his receivers and for a moment they listened to the AWACS plane thirty thousand feet up talk to the tower at Travis Air Force Base ninety miles away.

Butler gathered his rifle and ramrod, and Teddy put on his hat. They all looked at one another, uncertain what emotions to reveal, if any.

Finally, Jeremy said, "If you're going back up in the woods, and be four hundred yards apart, you'll need radios. I have just the thing in the greenhouse. Cobras."

"Right on," Teddy said. "Sounds better than phones."

Just then they all heard a Volkswagen engine, and a moment later Phillip pushed through the screen door into the radio room. His face was red, his clothes were wrinkled and his baseball cap was pulled down tight over his forehead.

Butler stepped over to the door and watched the Karmann Ghia drive away. "Where's she going?" he asked Phillip.

"Her sister's in Santa Rosa," Phillip said. "She's pissed off, and I'm an asshole."

"Aren't we all, my son?" Butler said. "Aren't we all?"

"Phillip!" Jeremy exclaimed. "The prodigal has returned. Hallelujah. Sit down and go to work, boy. Things are gonna pick up around here."

Jeremy vacated his ergonomic chair and handed Phillip a set of earphones and a sanitary wipe.

"What's happening?" Phillip asked, sitting down.

"I'll explain later," Jeremy said. "Right now I gotta fix up these guys with some country radios."

"We're going to check out Butler's farm workers and see if they're Mexican or not," Paul said.

"What else could they be?" Phillip asked.

"We don't know," Teddy answered. "Take a look at the pictures."

As Jeremy hustled out to the green house, Phillip gazed at Butler's photo of the migrant farm workers in the vineyard at midnight, the image blown up to reveal the book held by one of the soccer players.

"That book is the Islamic Quran, the Recitation," Phillip said, his voice full of excited surprise. "The word of Allah as delivered to the Prophet Mohammed by the angel Gabriel. No one carries that holy text around lightly," Phillip said to the FBI agents. "You get a book like that in a madrassa, a Muslim religious school."

"That's right," Paul said, nodding. "That's exactly what it is."

"How do you know that?" Teddy asked Phillip.

"We had sensitivity training at school. We covered all kinds of groups and extremists, including Muslim jihadis, gun-crazy militias, violent gangs, even cops." Phillip flashed his eyes at Teddy and Paul and declared, "This is your worst nightmare."

"We hope not," Teddy said.

Phillip pointed at Butler's Sharps and said, "If these guys are crazies, and they have modern weapons, that antique won't do you much good."

"Don't worry about it, Phillip," Teddy said. "You're going to stay here and help Jeremy keep track of what's going on." Then he asked Butler, "You have ammo for that thing?"

Butler nodded. "Back at the house, in the studio."

Jeremy returned with a pile of small, Cobra radios, belt-clips and slim, light-weight headsets.

"Let's all try channel one-one-oh-six," he said, fitting a Cobra headset over his big skull. "And remember, they'll hear you in the black room. These radios are not secure."

"So what? They don't need to be," Teddy said viciously. "Those assholes in the Never Say Anything club won't know what or who they're listening to."

"Yeah," Paul said. "They are the nightmare, worse than the Secret Service."

Butler grinned, put on and adjusted his headset, plugged it into the radio and clipped the radio to his belt, saying, "No wonder the government is all fucked up. You feds all hate each other. It's a non-stop playground fight with you kiddies."

Teddy grinned. Paul shrugged. Albert laughed.

Jeremy said, "Let's do a radio check," and they all fiddled with their gear until they could send and receive on channel one-one-oh-six.

Albert was into it, saying, "One, two, three, four, one, two, three, four," into his microphone.

"It works, it works," Butler said. "Relax."

"Do you think you'll go into the vineyard?" Jeremy asked.

"You have to, to get to the bunkhouse," Butler replied.

"Then you'll probably run into the Blue Blazer Hummer patrol," Jeremy warned.

"If they show up, we'll talk to them," Paul said, "and let them know what we're doing."

"All right," Teddy said when they all had their communications coordinated. "Mount up. Let's go."

"Oh, man," Butler said. "You seen too many movies."

· · · · ·

Raul Rodriguez fielded calls from the Department of State, the Belarusian Embassy in Washington and their consulate in Los Angeles, and assured all the anxious officials that Boris Demetriov and his party were safely inside the Bohemian Grove. Yes, Boris was drunk, and no, there was no "international incident." Boris was sobering up in Ye Olde Owls camp and making a lot of new friends. The Owls loved him.

For the second time that night, Rodriguez shut down the computer in his office and prepared to turn in. He had one more detail to chase down, the Miami phone calls, and he dialed the black room.

"Belinski," said the bland voice in his phone.

"Did you hear from the wire room in San Francisco?" Rodriguez could hear Belinski yawn.

"Oh, yeah. I was just going to call you."

"And?" Rodriguez said impatiently.

"Both calls to that Miami number were generated by the other Miami number and answered locally. Both phones were using tower 1768C, right here in the Grove. Both those Miami numbers are either in the Grove, or very close, maybe Monte Rio, somewhere right around here."

"That's what I wanted to know. Put tags on those phone numbers, and let me know if those phones are used again."

"Okay," Belinski said. "I'll let them know in Frisco."

"Thanks," Rodriguez said.

He had to talk to Dmitri, and it couldn't wait until morning.

· · · · ·

It didn't take long for Boris to adopt the grandest of Bohemian customs. The Belarusian president and his five benefactors, A.J. Hoff, Roger Blake, Bill Anthony, Donald Matthews, and Tom Bunderson stood together at the foot of an ancient Sequoia Sempervirens a fair distance away from the campfire and ceremoniously peed on the tree.

"Yuri," Boris said as all the men zipped their flies and returned to the campfire. "Ask about the girls."

Yuri was exhausted. Boris was like that pink rabbit on American TV, the one who never stopped. The president burned alcohol like gasoline and kept his motor running until he smashed into a wall and collapsed. He'd done that once tonight, but Yuri had seen him cycle from sobriety to inebriation and back four times in one night. The man was insatiable. In Yuri's opinion, his chemistry was not normal. Boris was a freak.

He said, "Boris, they really want you to stay in the camp."

"Who is 'they'?"

"The Secret Service. Rodriguez. He doesn't want you to leave."

"Fuck the Secret Service. Ask Hoff about the girls."

"Boris..."

"Stop whining. Ask him."

Yuri reluctantly looked at A.J. Hoff and said, "He's horny. He wants girls."

Hoff grinned and scratched his hairy chest. "We can do that," he said. "But we prefer to make arrangements in advance..."

Yuri interrupted by reiterating, "He doesn't like to wait. He prefers blond American girls, natural blonds with big bosoms, not implants. He hates implants."

Roger Blake, sitting on the stone bench with his legs crossed tightly and a cardigan thrown across his shoulders in the posture of a well-bred boarding school alumnus, tried unsuccessfully to control his rebelling facial muscles. He twitched. He looked at his elegant watch and said, "How about an hour from now? I can take him in my Range Rover."

"Roger," A.J. Hoff said with genuine affection, "you're an angel."

"Yes, a four hundred-million-dollar angel. Don't translate that, Yuri. Please."

"What are they saying?" Boris asked as Blake walked off in the direction of the service center.

Yuri replied, "Blake is going to call the brothel, I think."

"Good," Boris said. "Here's what we're going to do, Yuri. We're going to let them take us to their whorehouse, and from there we'll go directly to the airport and get on Antón Cosmovitch's plane and go back to Los Angeles."

"Boris! Mr. President! Mother of God! You don't like it here? This is a fabulous place."

"I wanted to meet these men, Yuri. And I did. Fine. I've looked them in the eye, A.J. Hoff, Roger Blake, all of them, and pissed with them on their holy tree. Fine. If they want to talk to me about details, such as where to deposit the rest of the money, we can talk in Los Angeles. No. I've seen their Bohemian Glade, and I don't want to talk to them here. This is their fucking sacred tribal ground. No."

"What about Dmitri?"

"We'll leave him here. He can make the speech. He's the Minister of the Interior. Who gives a ram's ass?"

Boris laughed, and seeing Boris laugh, A.J. Hoff laughed and all the Owls nearby laughed.

.   .   .   .   .

Rodriguez wasn't laughing when he arrived at the Ye Olde Owls campground, where the evening festivities were winding down. Maurice was collecting empty glasses and placing them on a tray. Hands and face shining with grease, Boris busily gnawed on a meaty bone. Most of the Owls were retired to their tents. Quiet clarinet music and wood smoke drifted over the camp.

Discreetly, Rodriguez walked up to Roger Blake and asked what was going on.

"We're taking Boris to Mary's."

"Oh, shit," Rodriguez groaned. "Just Boris?"

"Yuri will go with him."

"Where's Dmitri?"

"In his tent."

A few of the Owls had retired, calling it a night. Most of the venison remained on the spit, and the Texan Donald Matthews was telling a small group of Owls about the pirates on the Bohemian

Beach.

"Makes you wonder about Grove security," he said.

Rodriguez knocked on the sturdy door of the tent assigned to Dmitri and Boris.

"Dmitri Borisovitch," Rodriguez said in perfect Russian. "I'd like to speak to you, if I may."

Dmitri came to the door dressed in a silk dressing gown, borrowed from one of the Owls, and smoking a pipe.

"Yes?" Dmitri said as he opened the screen door.

"That phone call you made, to your son, from the white phone?"

"Yes?"

"Where is he, your son?"

Frowning, Dmitri replied, "Why do you ask?"

"It's a question of national security, your national security," Rodriguez said, and then added succinctly, "That call was local."

Anger flashed in Dmitri's eyes. "Are you telling me you traced my call? Outrageous, that's just bloody outrageous. That's a violation of protocol. You can't do that."

Rodriguez sneered, "Do you want to complain to the State Department?"

His face exploding with anger, Dmitri hissed, "Yes."

"Do you want to file your complaint before or after Boris visits one of the local whorehouses?"

The shock on Dmitri's face caught Rodriguez by surprise. The president's brother pushed the Secret Service agent aside and raced out of the tent, shouting, "Boris! Boris! Where are you going? What are you doing?"

23

They took two trucks, Teddy and Butler in the Suburban, Albert and Paul in the Lamborghini, and they stopped at Maggie's Farm to pick up ammunition for the Sharps.

"You sure you want to do this?" Teddy asked Butler as they drove up the long driveway.

"No, I'm not sure at all," Butler answered before they got out of the truck, "but I'm not gonna let you fuck it up. The Sharps makes a hell of a noise." He gestured with his thumb at the locked rear compartment of the Suburban. "If we have to scare someone, let's do it that way and not with machineguns."

"Good thinkin'," Teddy agreed. "But Paul and I will back up Albert with shotguns, just in case."

"Well," Butler said with a raised eyebrow, "that's the local way of saying hello. You've met Barney Richardson."

"Oh yeah, he's a one-armed cowboy if I ever met one," Teddy said. "He's not very fond of you, Butler."

"He hates the idea that we lost in Vietnam," Butler explained. "He felt betrayed. He'll never get over it, but he's had PTSD since 1945, so I don't blame him."

The lights were on in the house, and Maggie was waiting outside the garden door.

"Hi, babe." Butler grinned, a roguish look in his eye.

"What are you guys doing? It's almost two in the morning."

"Hunting," Butler answered.

"What? You're kidding. Hunting for what?"

"Spooks," Butler said. "The place is crawling with them."

"Hi, Teddy," Maggie said.

"Hi, Maggie."

"I still want to do your hair."

"Tomorrow," Teddy said. "You can do it tomorrow."

"You promise?"

"Sure."

She peered at the Lamborghini truck in the driveway and waved. Albert and Paul waved back. Then she turned back to her husband, shook her finger and spat, "Whaddaya mean, spooks? Butler, are you going back up into Richardson's woods?"

"A brilliant deduction, dear lady," Butler acknowledged, bowing deeply. "Yes, and I'm taking these federal po-lice with me, so I'm not worried about Ol' Barney. He's probably still stone drunk and passed out. And you know the sheriff is incapacitated."

"So what's up there? It isn't spooks. You guys," Maggie pointed at Teddy, swung around and pointed at Paul, "you guys are the spooks. So what is it?"

"Weird Mexicans," Butler replied. "Look, I'll explain in the morning. We gotta get this show on the road."

"Wait a minute," Maggie insisted. "Weird Mexicans? Narcotraficos? Smugglers? Cartel gangsters? What's going on here, Butler? Whatever it is, it isn't any of your business. Let these cops go up there on their own. You and Albert don't need to get involved."

Butler leaned toward Teddy and said, "Her father is a retired San Francisco police captain."

"Dirty Harry?"

"Something like that."

"She's tough," Teddy said, nodding his head.

"Yeah."

Butler thought, shit, Maggie is right, but Teddy and Paul and Albert were headed up to Silva's bunkhouse because of him and his photographs. He couldn't bail out now.

He said, "Ah, shit, Maggie..."

Albert and Paul had the Lambo's doors open and were about to get out and join the discussion when Maggie bit her lip, performed an abrupt about face, went back into the house and slammed the door.

"She doesn't like guns," Butler said. "Any guns. Ever."

He led Teddy into the studio, snapped on the lights, and woke up Jojo from his spot in the corner. The dog wandered over and sleepily nuzzled Teddy's thigh. Butler turned on the sound system and Carlos Santana added his magic to the night. *Oye como va.*

Butler unlocked his gun cabinet and took out a box of ten replica Sharps linen cartridges. Heavy in his hand, he shook the box like maracas.

"The Sharps is really loud," Butler said. "It's enough to wake up everyone in Sonoma County."

"Got any blanks?" Teddy asked.

"Nah," Butler said, turning off the lights and the music. "Nobody makes 'em any more. All I have is live rounds. Finding any ammunition is hard enough, and it's damned expensive."

"Aw right," Teddy said. "Let's rock and roll."

While Teddy and Butler were in the studio, Paul sat in Albert's truck looking with amazement at the twenty-year-old Lamborghini's frayed Italian luxury. The seats had several tears and the stitching in the leather dash was coming loose, but all the metric instrumentation was illuminated bright orange.

"Is this really a Lambo?" Paul asked, boggled.

"Yes," Albert answered, adding, "And by the way, my shirts aren't Hawaiian. They're Samoan. Samoan people tend to be bigger than Hawaiians."

Albert lowered his window, stuck out his head and hollered, "Goddammit, Butler, get your ass moving!"

"Shit, Albert, don't be too anxious," Butler replied, coming out of the studio. "Remember last year."

"Well, we don't get to chase the Bohos around this year, so this is as close as we're gonna get. Let's go, let's go."

"Hang on a minute, big guy," Teddy said. "We're not gonna let you go up there naked."

Teddy unlocked the back of the Suburban, spun the combination lock on the hidden compartment, took out two sinister, black Benelli anti-personnel shotguns, and handed one to Paul along with a box of twelve gauge shells.

"Don't I get one?" Albert asked, almost rhetorically.

"No, Albert," Paul said. "You'd pull the trigger and dislocate your shoulder."

When they were in the Suburban, Butler said to Teddy, "You realize that going over to Silva's bunkhouse and getting in these people's faces is stupid and dangerous. No matter what happens, somebody isn't going to like it, and you'll get called a lot of nasty names. You and Paul - the FBI - will be accused of racial profiling."

"So what?" Teddy said. "It's for a good cause."

"What's that?"

"We have to protect the Bohos," Teddy replied with a grin, starting his truck, turning around and heading down the driveway. "Otherwise, the world will end."

Butler laughed, and Teddy laughed even louder. Maggie, watching from inside the screen door, didn't laugh at all.

.   .   .   .   .

To Silva, the conversation with Dmitri was a private adhan, the Muslim call to prayer, and he intended to heed the summons. Boris, not unexpectedly, had done the unexpected and arrived early. The clock was ticking. On behalf of the Russians he was going to strike a blow not only against Boris and all the treacherous leaders of the former Soviet republics, but he would deliver an insult to Islam while attacking the main enemy, the Americans. This was his chance to bring all his enemies to their knees at once.

A life of resolving conflict with violence had come to this, his greatest action, an assassination disguised as a terrorist attack. His jihadis were ready, emotionally primed by their journey. The most innocent of dupes, they were faithful shuhadâ whose eagerness to die was about to be monstrously betrayed, their belief in Paradise turned against them.

He made one more thorough inspection of the suicide vests, carefully checking the circuitry on each one, then he picked up his hand drawn map of the Grove, an Uzi and a single magazine and went upstairs.

Battery-powered lanterns in the corners of the single room cast sharp shadows on the walls of the bunkhouse. The boys were praying zealously, the susurration of their prayers the sound of Silva's childhood. No matter how far he strayed from the faith of his Sunni forefathers, nor how meaningless and destructive he believed that faith to be, the rhythmic murmur of men deep in conversation with their god was always soothing, a counterpoint to the sounds that would come soon enough: violent explosions and screams of agony and death. This was the overture; that was the symphony, and the crescendo would be Boris begging for his life.

On their knees, heads deeply bowed, the young supplicants for martyrdom faced Mecca, some reading verses from the Holy Quran, others reciting martyr's prayers with their foreheads pressed into the soft bristles of their prayer rugs. Brandishing the Israeli assault weapon, Silva carefully stepped around them to the front of the improvised mosque, and pinned the map of the Grove to the wall.

There was no way to break it to them gently. He jammed the magazine into the Uzi, making a loud click that broke the spell. Some of the boys looked up.

"Praise be to Allah, our schedule has been advanced twenty-four hours," he said in sharp Arabic, bringing the boys to attention. "The hour of jihad has come. It is time. We are not going to wait for tomorrow night. It is the will of Allah that we carry out our mission tonight. Now!"

It took a moment for the significance of his words to penetrate the trance of their prayers. One by one they stopped praying and looked at him. In a few seconds he saw every imaginable emotion in their faces: fear, joy, rapture, astonishment. They didn't have twenty-four hours to live; they had less than one hour before they blew open the doors of Paradise. The air was suddenly thick with heavy breathing.

"You've trained for weeks and prepared for this moment your

entire lives," Silva said. "Prepare yourselves one final time, and remember your discipline. You are soldiers of God. Death to the Crusaders."

He expected them to repeat his call, "Death to the Crusaders!" but instead, after a long, tense pause, he heard a single high-pitched voice: "We haven't made our videos."

Videos! Twenty-first century martyrs, twenty-first century children. If they didn't make their videos, they would feel unfulfilled, their families would feel cheated, and, more importantly, Silva knew, if his martyrs felt disgruntled when their minds needed to be clear and blank, there would be nothing but trouble.

Silva swore under his breath in four languages and said, "All right, but you have to keep it short. Each of you, say your name, your true name, your family name, the name of your city in the new world and place of origin in the Old. Say one, brief martyr's prayer, and all honor will come to your families. Remember, Allah, praised be his name, has no need of videos. He sees your hearts and knows you are pure."

He offered a short, fearsome prayer for their success, condemning their enemies and all infidels to fire and perdition, then went into the basement to gather a video camera and lights. When he returned upstairs, the boys were burbling with excitement, shouting slogans and raising fists of defiance to disguise their terror.

While he was setting up the camera and lights, Silva suddenly heard motors in the woods and saw a glimmer of light through the shutters. The light came from vehicles three or four hundred meters away, lights from the forest on the hill opposite the Grove where there should be no lights.

"Be silent," he ordered the boys, and opened the door to listen.

"What is it?" asked Number Fifteen.

"Shhh."

Outside, headlights flickered in the woods, and when the lights went dark, he heard distant voices. The old man? Maybe. The FBI? Not their style. If the FBI or Secret Service had the slightest suspicion of his operation, they would come crashing through the vineyard with dozens of men, dogs, and helicopters. No, this was local, a nuisance he had to deal with. He guessed teenagers, who sometimes drove into the woods for sex and liquor parties.

Then the headlights came on again, and a car motor, and a vehicle descended the hill to the perimeter road and approached the vineyard. It wasn't the Grove security Hummer. Silva activated motion sensors in the lane from the perimeter road to the bunkhouse, sent the boys into the basement with a command to be silent, pulled the shutters aside an inch and looked out.

. . . . .

As the Pirates and the FBI passed Old Man Richardson's dark house, Butler noticed that the gallon jug he'd left on the doorstep was gone. The dogs were still passed out.

"What's with the dogs?" Teddy asked.

"Gin," Butler said. "Richardson feeds his Rottweilers gin, and they're all gonna die of cirrhosis."

"Jeez. What's the world coming to?"

Butler directed Teddy to drive past his usual parking spot, and the Suburban led the Lamborghini deep into the woods, following Richardson's Road through the trees, up and over the ridge.

"I come out here at night and run," Butler explained. "I leave the truck back there and run a couple of hundred yards through the trees, so if anybody follows me, like you did, they still won't find Fat Freddie. Stop here."

Teddy stopped the truck, turned off the motor and lights, and Albert shut down his SUV. They were on a gentle down slope, and when the headlights went out, the redwoods blocked most of the light from the half moon. All they could see were the dark outlines of the nearest huge trees.

The four men huddled in the dark woods, looking like science fiction Martians under their radio headsets.

"Fat Freddie," Butler announced, and pushed the button on his remote.

They heard the winch and looked up. The rope and sling came down, almost hitting Albert — hey! — Butler grabbed a knot on the rope, slipped into the sling and pushed the button. He went up twenty feet and stopped, gently rocking back and forth three feet from Fat Freddie's enormous trunk.

"That's very cool, Butler," Teddy said through his microphone. "How long have you been doing this?"

"About ten years."

"Where the hell are we?" Paul asked.

"A quarter mile from Silva's bunkhouse," Butler answered.

Looking up again, the three men on the ground each pondered an ascent to a hundred fifty feet. A fall would be fatal. Butler lowered himself to the ground and said, "If you follow Richardson's Road on down the hill, in about two hundred yards you'll come to the Grove perimeter road, and just a little ways up the road is the vineyard and a lane that leads to the bunkhouse. You can drive right up to it. I can see it all from the blind. They drove a couple trucks up there this afternoon, a flatbed and an Explorer SUV, and they're parked at the side of the bunkhouse."

"What are we waitin' for?" Albert panted. "Let's go. Let's go!"

"What are you going to say to him, if Silva comes to the door?" Paul asked.

"Well, I've been thinkin' about that," Albert said. "I was on my deck today, and Mario Silva came out of his house onto his deck, and we were talking, just shootin' the shit, 'cause I haven't seen him in a long time, and he got a phone call he said was from his foreman at the vineyard, and he rushed away in a big hurry. So I'll ask him about that. Is everything okay? Maybe there was medical emergency. Who knows?"

"Sounds reasonable," Paul said.

"Horseshit," Butler said, "Nothing sounds reasonable at three o'clock in the morning, Are you kidding? They're gonna be pissed."

"We'll be right behind you, Albert," Teddy said.

"I can take care of myself," Albert snarled. "Let's go."

"Don'tcha just love it, Albert?" Butler said. "Last year, you were chasing down a Boho and the Feds protected him. This year, it's just a buncha Mexicans, and the Feds are on your side."

"Fuck you, Butler," Albert snapped. "Let's go."

"Good luck," Butler said. The winch churned and Butler rose until he was lost among the massive branches of thousand-year-old Fat Freddie.

24

The platform was eight feet wide and ten deep, built of redwood planks and supported by two huge branches. Small branches and redwood needles blanketed the surface.

Butler lay on his stomach in the shooter's prone position, holding the rifle and sighting down the long barrel which rested on a sandbag. Then he put the Sharps aside and looked through his camera and 400 millimeter lens at Mario Silva's bunkhouse.

A faint breeze gusted through the high branches.

Lights flickered around the edges of the imperfect shutters over the windows.

He heard the engine whine from Albert's truck and saw a flash of red tail lights and the headlight beams cutting through the trees below him.

"Hey hey," he said through his Cobra microphone. "Can you hear me?"

"Loud and clear," Teddy said.

"It's all workin'," Jeremy said from five miles away. "Shut up."

. . . . .

The Lambo bounced down the hill, its old, off-road suspension pushed to the limit.

Bouncing in his seat but keeping both hands on the wheel, Albert said, "Did you know that Ferruccio Lamborghini made tractors for farmers and he started building sports cars because he was pissed off at his neighbor, Enzo Ferrari."

"Really?" Paul said. "They were neighbors?"

"You're just a fountain of information," Teddy scoffed. "Your neighbor, Mario Silva, did he say where he'd been?"

"Yeah, Brazil."

"What business is he in?" Teddy asked

"I really don't know," Albert answered. "Maybe real estate in San Francisco."

They arrived at the perimeter road and paused.

"Jeremy?" Teddy said into his mic.

"Yeah?"

"Is a Hummer near by?"

"Yes. Give him a minute."

And ninety seconds later headlights bounced along the road and then the Blue Blazer patrol pulled into view, the loudspeakers quiet.

"Flash your lights," Paul said to Albert. "Let him know we're here."

Albert did, and the Hummer stopped. Paul and Teddy got out of the car, leaving the shotguns behind. Albert watched them show their badges and identification cards, and then they waved and the Hummer went on its way. The two FBI agents got back into Albert's dirty yellow truck.

"The South Gate to the Grove is just down the road," Teddy said. "There's a guard shack down there and a few guys. They invited us to stop by for coffee."

"Did you tell them what we're doing here?" Albert asked.

"Sure," Paul replied. "They know Silva has guys in there. They've seen 'em."

"Okay," Albert said. "Let's go."

Teddy spoke into his mic, "Butler, can you see us?"

"No. I see your headlights. I saw the Hummer."

Albert turned onto the perimeter road, travelled a short distance, and turned into the smooth lane of double tire tracks that led to the bunkhouse. They could see lights behind the shuttered windows. As Albert drove up the lane with minimum speed and maximum caution, a chain of floodlights suddenly illuminated the lane, the bunkhouse, and the entire vineyard. Albert stopped behind the Ford Explorer and left his headlights on, Hollywood style.

"This is weird," Albert said.

"There's lights on inside there," Paul said. "If you don't want to knock on the door, I will."

"No, that's okay," Albert said nervously, taking off his headset and opening the truck door.

Both Teddy and Paul pumped shells into the chambers of their shotguns: ka-thunk! ka-chunk! sending a shiver down Albert's spine.

Teddy said into his mic, "Butler, you see us yet?"

"Yep," Butler answered, looking through his camera. "I see Albert getting out of the car, walking to the door."

An exterior flood lamp over the bunkhouse door blazed to life, the door swung open and Mario Silva, wrapped in a gray flannel bathrobe, stepped out and closed the door behind him.

The lights flared in the viewfinder of his night vision camera, so Butler put down the Nikon and picked up the Sharps. Four hundred yards away and one hundred fifty feet below him, the lights were so bright that the mustachioed Mario Silva was a clearly distinguished sliver of living flesh inside the slotted front sight of the antique weapon. He moved the rifle an inch and Albert's fat, dark brown head was in the slot. Butler smiled and put the tiniest bit of pressure on the trigger. It had been a lifetime since anyone he might want to shoot was in his sights, but he had decided a long time ago not to kill Albert. He couldn't kill them all, Albert, Maggie and Susan, so, he thought, he might as well live and let live. Besides, there was no cartridge in the chamber.

"Albert! What a surprise!" Silva said loudly, grinning from ear to ear. "What in the world are you doing out here?"

Almost blinded by the lights, Albert shaded his eyes and mumbled, "Um, ah, just wanted to see if you were all right, Mario. You left in such a hurry this evening."

"Well, thanks, that's very kind of you to be concerned, but everything is okay now."

"Glad to hear it," Albert said.

There was an awkward moment of silence. Silva put his hand up to deflect the bright headlights of the Lamborghini. He asked, "Who are these guys with you, Albert?"

"The FBI," Albert replied. "They're here checking on the Grove perimeter security, and I'm their guide. Me and Butler Rhodes."

"The FBI?" Silva said, trying to see the shadowy figures sitting inside Albert's car. "I heard they were checking on all the Grove's neighbors."

"Yeah," Albert said, grinning sheepishly and taking a step backward, saying, "Sorry to bother you, Mario, see you soon, over on River Road. Sorry."

He stumbled and almost fell over himself trying to get back into his truck.

"Holy smokes," he said when he was in the driver's seat. "That's really spooky. Damn. I sure didn't expect him to come out like that, all friendly like. And all these lights! Jeez."

"Butler," Teddy said into his mic. "What do you see?"

"Just the guy, Silva. And now Albert's truck, backing up. Silva is going back inside. All the lights are still on. A lot of bright illumination."

Albert glanced nervously from the FBI agents to the bunkhouse to the vineyard and back, and suddenly all the lights went dark.

"Butler," Teddy said. "What's happening?"

"Not much. The lights in the bunkhouse are still on," Butler replied.

Albert quickly backed his truck all the way to the Grove perimeter road, then drove the short distance to Richardson's Road, turned around, shut the car down, and sat in the driver's seat, furiously drumming on the steering wheel. Next to him, Paul fiddled with his shotgun. Teddy sat in the back and tried to stretch his neck and shoulder muscles. The tension mounted with every heartbeat.

Paul declared, "We still don't know who or what is in that building."

"I didn't ask," Albert said. "Should I go back?"

Paul and Teddy looked at one another for a long moment before

Teddy answered, "No, his driveway is rigged with motion sensors, so who knows what else he might have. Let's wait and see."

"Wait for what?" Albert squawked. "Oh, man, we could be here all night."

"They have to come out of there sometime," Paul said.

"Yeah," Albert said, looking at his watch. "At dawn, to work in the vineyard, about three hours from now. Shit."

"Think we could get a warrant?" Paul asked.

"Not a chance in hell," Teddy snapped. "All we'd get is a reprimand for annoying some judge."

"Listen up," they all heard Jeremy say in their earpieces. "The Blue Blazers are coming back."

They saw the headlights first, then the Hummer coming out of the trees to their left at a steady five miles per hour.

"Flash your lights," Paul said, getting out of the car, wearing his headset but leaving his shotgun. "Maybe I can talk to these guys."

Albert reached over to keep the Benelli from falling out and was surprised the barrel was cool to his touch. Teddy got out of the back seat and into the front, holding both shotguns between his knees, and watched Paul stop the Hummer, climb in, and drive away around the bend to their right.

The noise from the receding Hummer was dampened by the trees. The redwoods that towered over the Lamborghini blotted out what moonlight there was, and the forest was dark. Albert opened the windows and they could smell the rich, damp, primeval forest floor. A gentle breeze whistled through the lowest branches. Nothing else moved.

·   ·   ·   ·   ·

The Blue Blazers in the Grove security Hummer were vintage jazz aficionados, and the ancient redwood forest reverberated with the mellow tones of Cal Tjader. Tony, the new guy, motored along the perimeter road under the towering redwood canopy at a stately five miles an hour, the headlights bouncing off tree trunks and forest ferns and catching the eyes of the odd raccoon.

Jim, the veteran Blue Blazer in the passenger's seat, gestured with both hands to encompass the dense woods on their right, telling the new guy, "All this property, this entire hill, belongs to an old fart named Richardson. The Bohemians have been trying to buy it for years, but he won't sell."

"Maybe I wouldn't either," Tony said. "Maybe he just doesn't want to move."

Jim raised his eyebrows and said, "They offered him twenty-four million dollars for eighteen acres."

"Hmmm," Tony replied. "Maybe he doesn't need it."

Then they saw Albert's lights flash.

"It's those FBI guys again," Jim said, turning down the music.

Paul was standing in the middle of the road and Tony stopped.

"Hey, fellas," Paul said, speaking through the open passenger's window, his yellow FBI windbreaker flapping in the slight breeze as he bent down and displayed his creds. "FBI. Mind if I ride along?"

The guys in the Hummer looked at each other, shrugged their shoulders, and Jim grinned and said, "Sure. Why not?"

Jim turned up the music and said, "We play music to scare the deer away."

The door locks clicked open and Paul climbed in back, leaned over the back of the front seat and said in a friendly way, "My name is Paul. Who are you guys?"

"I'm Tony," said the driver. "This is Jim."

Jim scooted around to face Paul and said, "We heard you guys were around, the FBI." Then his face broke into a wide smile and he said, "Our boss got fired today because of you."

Surprised, Paul asked, "O'Shea?"

"Yeah," Jim said enthusiastically. "He was a real asshole, so thank you."

Feeling bad – he really didn't want to cost anyone his job – Paul said thoughtfully, "So O'Shea is gone."

"Yeah," Jim said, nodding his head. "We heard that something happened on the beach down by the river this afternoon, and O'Shea got called to FBI headquarters in Santa Rosa. When he got back to the Grove, he was fired."

"So we're thinkin'," the driver said, "maybe you can tell us what happened."

"That was a Counter-Terrorism Joint Task Force meeting in Santa Rosa," Paul said confidentially, as if he were revealing a state secret.

"Were you there?"

"Yeah," Paul conceded. "I was there."

Paul realized that since his first unpleasant encounter with O'Shea yesterday at the main gate, there had been a sea change inside Grove security. If he played his cards right, he would have an opportunity to get inside their operation and see how it worked and how it failed.

"It was a classified meeting," Paul said, "but I can tell you that your Grove security has a lot of holes in it, and it seems Mr. O'Shea paid the price." Still leaning over the back of the front seat, Paul pointed to the radio microphone hanging on the dash. "Your radios, for example, have a high-end Motorola encryption system but you don't use it. You talk in the clear, and anyone can listen."

"We could have told you that," Jim said. "But who wants to listen to us?"

They came to Silva's vineyard, and at the far end of the rows of vines Paul could see faint lights still on in the bunkhouse windows. The half moon sparkled on the five acre plot cleared of redwoods long ago. Paul gazed at the orderly rows of vines, each leafy, fruit-laden vine about four feet tall and tethered to a stake.

"This vineyard belongs to our neighbor, Mario Silva," Jim said. "Nice guy. Gives us a few bottles of wine every year."

"Did you know Silva has Mexican migrants in his bunkhouse now?" Paul asked.

"Yeah, the day shift mentioned them," Tony said. "They saw them this afternoon."

"Have you seen them?" Paul asked.

"Nah, not tonight," Jim answered. "They'll come out at daybreak."

Rolling along, the big Hummer was reduced to Lilliputian proportions by the giant trees. Looking up at the canopy hundreds of feet above his head, Paul was awestruck. He almost forgot about the Bohos and the Pirates and Silva's Mexicans and surrendered himself to the wonder of the redwoods.

He jerked his mind back to the task at hand and asked, "So, how long have you guys worked security at the Grove?".

"I'm new," Tony said. "I just started, but Jim here..."

"I've been working the Grove for five years."

"Year round?"

"No, just for the encampment, like most guys. I drive an armored truck in Santa Rosa," Jim said.

"And I'm a fire fighter in Cloverdale," Tony added. "Small time, small town."

Running alongside the road was a fence that looked at first like a vine-covered hedge, but when the road drew close, Paul could see Cyclone mesh topped with razor-wire. In places he could glimpse a much smaller barrier inside the fence, log railings set on three-foot high posts, running parallel to the fence, an elegant trip wire that reminded members and Grove staff not to approach the perimeter and all its electronic devices.

The Hummer followed the fence to a metal gate and a rustic wood cabin inside the fence. Tony activated the gate with a remote, drove through, closed the gate and parked next to another white Hummer.

Cameras on the roof of the cabin were aimed at the road, and the hedge and vine-bearing fence marched off in both directions away from the gate. On the far side of the small parking lot Paul could see dense, redwood forest and a well-lit, asphalt path that led through the trees and up and over a hill.

A big guy in a blue blazer stood outside the cabin door, smoking a cigar, warily eying Paul, the stranger.

"This is George Porter, the South Gate night shift manager," Jim said, and to the big guy, "Hey, George. This is Special Agent Paul Kruger. He's with the FBI."

They shook hands and George chuckled and said, "Welcome, welcome. Come on in, Special Agent Kruger."

Paul followed George through an outer office and lounge where several Blue Blazers sat around a card table playing dominoes and into the cabin's main room where two walls were covered with banks of flat-screen monitors. A half-dozen Blue Blazers sat at computers and watched the screens. To Paul, the set-up looked like the security room in a big casino.

"This is the smaller, South Gate version of the Screening Room in the Command Post of the Main Administration Building which is about a mile and a half north of here, over the hill," George said, gesturing in a northerly direction. "That's where the Secret Service is, and the communications center for the Grove."

"And the Black Room?"

"The NSA?" George said. "Yeah, them, too."

"Do any of those federal agents ever come down here?" Paul asked.

"No. Never."

Paul quickly scanned the monitors. Virtually all the screens displayed images of trees, here and there a hedge, a fence, a small wooden structure, a guard in a blue blazer, and still more trees.

Unimpressed, Paul said, "You have a lot of cameras."

"One hundred fifty-two around an eight mile perimeter," George said. "And here at the South Gate we monitor forty-eight. The cameras are all on the perimeter, not inside the camps or anywhere in the Grove. Our job is not to intrude on the privacy of our members."

"And what is your job, as you see it?" Paul asked.

"Down here at the South Gate, our job is to patrol the southern perimeter and keep deer out of the Grove."

"That's it?"

"There isn't anything else to do except watch the monitors, and there's never anything to see. We have cameras every hundred and fifty yards along the perimeter, and almost as many motion detectors and heat sensors, but there ain't nothin' here but these God damn trees, and deer which can jump over the fence. We're half a mile from the nearest Southland camps, and members almost never come down here. There's nothing for them to do here."

The monitors glowed green with images from the high-end night-vision video cameras arrayed around the long, wooded perimeter of the Grove. The half moon provided enough light to enable the enhancement technology, but most of the cameras were pointed at the fence and not the actual perimeter. Paul tried to follow a Hummer making a circuit in the dark, but the coverage was spotty and whenever the truck's headlights struck a camera, the monitor flared and whited out.

"Can you see Silva's vineyard on your monitors?" Paul asked.

"No, " George answered. "Just the road. Doesn't matter because you can't see much of anything, no matter what. Nothing that moves ever appears on the monitors except our vehicles and the deer. And with so many cameras, some are always out of whack and need maintenance and repair. They're mostly a pain in the ass."

Smiling agreeably, Paul asked, "Ever had an intruder?"

George paused to think a moment, then answered, "One, years ago, on the east side. It was just a drunk."

"That's it?" Paul responded, a little incredulous. "One?"

"We get kids once in a while, teenagers from Santa Rosa who don't know where they are," George said. "The locals know better than to mess with us. Once in a while some Russian River tourist flies a drone into the Grove, and we bring those babies down real quick. No big deal."

"So you're not really concerned with trespassers," Paul said. "And all this fancy, high-tech security isn't designed to, say, repel a posse of armed invaders. It's just to make the Bohemians feel good."

"You got it," George said.

Paul asked, "Do you keep any weapons here?"

Laughing, George answered, "I guess you could say that," and he showed Paul a small arsenal of deer rifles, a couple of nice shotguns, and a genuine Stinger, a hand-held, rocket-propelled, anti-aircraft missile.

"You expecting an air raid?" Paul asked.

"You gotta be kiddin'," George laughed. "We got this 'cause one of the Bohos owns the company that makes the fuel for these things. We're not expecting an air raid or any other kind of raid, Special Agent, because there's nothin' to expect."

Paul pulled out his phone and texted Teddy: Defense readiness state: Zero.

"When's the next patrol?" he asked George.

"A few minutes," George said. "I'm driving."

.   .   .   .   .

In the Lamborghini Teddy read Paul's text and said to Albert, "You don't have to hang around here in the woods, Albert. You did a very brave thing tonight, but why don't you call it a night."

"I think you're right," Albert said sleepily. The adrenaline rush he had felt walking up to Silva's bunkhouse door had now deserted his nervous system, and he was crashing. He hoped he could make it home.

"There's no reason for me to hang around here. Butler!" he said into his headset.

"Yeah?" Butler answered from his perch in Fat Freddie.

"What do you see?" Albert asked.

"Not much. The forest. A couple foxes in the vineyard."

"Wanna go home?"

"No, dude. I think I'll stay up here a while."

Looking at Teddy, Albert said into his microphone, "These guys are gonna be here all night."

"That's okay," Butler said.

"All right, dude. Adios."

Albert started the Lambo and headed back up Richardson's Road toward Fat Freddie and Teddy's Suburban.

He said to Teddy. "Butler likes it out here, anyway. I don't mind chasing Bohos around, but I don't feel the same way about Mexicans. Live and let live, I always say."

"If they are Mexicans," Teddy said.

"What else could they be?"

"Who knows?" Teddy replied as they arrived at his Suburban. "See ya 'round, Albert. We only got fifteen days of this left."

Teddy climbed into his truck and settled in to wait. Albert

continued on past Old Man Richardson's house. The dogs were awake, but too hungover to bark. They whined instead as the peculiar yellow Italian truck rolled past, but Albert was too sleepy and stoned to notice.

He fell asleep at the wheel before he reached the Old Bohemian Highway and almost crashed into a tree, but his front bumper scraped a rock and he woke up in time and stopped. He snorted, pulled out a handkerchief, blew his nose, and decided it was foolish to drive. He turned off the Lambo, folded his arms over the big steering wheel and went back to sleep.

25

Up on Starrett's Hill, the clock on Jeremy's wall ticked over slowly. The half moon passed over the Russian River valley at a country pace and headed for the Pacific Ocean. Life in Monte Rio slowed to a crawl and even most of the campers in the Bohemian Grove gave up their parties and games and went to sleep.

"Listen to this," Jeremy said to Phillip. "It's the Blue Blazers at the Main Gate."

Phillip plugged his headphones into Jeremy's receiver and heard, "Cola One, this is Cola Five. We have Caviar at the Main Gate. Destination Mary's."

"Roger that, Cola Five. The Secret Service wants you to hold Caviar at the gate."

"Roger that, Cola One."

"Caviar," Jeremy said to Phillip, "is our friend, Boris Boris."

"Him again," Phillip smirked.

"You better tell Butler and those guys," Jeremy said, tapping the Cobra radio still attached to his belt. "The FBI is very interested in Boris."

. . . . .

The Blue Blazer at the Main Gate politely went around to the driver's side window of the Range Rover and said to Roger Blake, "Security wants you to wait for the Secret Service, Mr. Blake."

Yuri leaned over Blake's shoulder from the back seat and shouted,

"Open the fucking gate! Let us out of here!"

"I'm sorry, sir, but..."

Yuri interrupted him by pulling out the Beretta Pico tucked into his underpants which had escaped Rodriguez's search earlier in the evening. He wildly waved the little pistol out the window of the Range Rover.

"Open the gate! Now."

The Blue Blazer's eyes bulged at the sight of Yuri's gun.

"I will fucking shoot you if you don't open the fucking gate!" Yuri screamed.

Roger Blake cringed. Boris grinned. The guard stiffly moved to the gate controls.

As the metal gate slowly swung open, and Roger Blake drove through the opening, a huge black Secret Service SUV pulled up behind them, bright lights flooding Blake's English truck.

Yuri turned around, saw Rodriguez walking toward the Range Rover, and shouted to Roger Blake, "Don't stop. Go! Go! Go!"

And Roger took off down the hill. Rodriguez ran back to his truck and the Secret Service SUV blasted out the gate for the second time that night.

·   ·   ·   ·   ·

Mario Silva could not have survived thirty years of continuous warfare without preparing for contingencies, including nosy neighbors and shadowy national police. His first instinct had been to strike immediately and kill Albert and the two men in the truck, but he hadn't known who else was in the forest, and he didn't know how his boys, still downstairs making their videos, would react to sudden combat.

Why was the FBI here? Was it what Richardson had told him, that they were simply introducing themselves to all the neighbors of the Bohemian Grove? Nonsense, they didn't do that kind of thing at three in the morning. Like all police agencies, the FBI was stupid and predictable. If the FBI had suspicions about Silva and his migrant workers, if they had picked up any kind of evidence or had any meaningful reason at all to come to his bunkhouse door in the middle of the night, they would come themselves with papers and court orders and military ordnance, and not send a surrogate like his geeky, nerdy Monte Rio neighbor, Albert Flowers.

Albert had said, "Me and Butler Rhodes," and there was that guy again, that Butler with his droopy mustache and hand-tooled boots and jeweled studs in his ears. Albert might be a big stumbling fool, but Butler Rhodes was far more than what he seemed, and he was probably out there, somewhere. There was something unsettling about Butler. He was like a high-flying, circling falcon, a hawk coming out of the sun. He was old – at least seventy – but he had a sinewy, confident way of carrying himself. His bearing was, what? It was, it was... military! Yes, that was it. Butler was an old, blooded veteran, Silva could sense it, and that made Butler dangerous.

He was out there now with how many more FBI? What was going on here? His carefully crafted plan, years in the making, was unraveling. Everything had been moving along so smoothly when one of his boys ran away and he had to kill Pedro. Then Boris arrived early. Now Albert and the FBI were knocking on his door in the middle of the night. He was no longer certain that his boys could deal with the Blue Blazer's Hummer, as they had been trained to do, and then make it to the South Gate if they encountered interference. He needed to know what was going on around him, and he needed to know immediately.

His secure phone rang again. Now what?

. . . . .

Running as much as walking, Dmitri made it to the Administration Center in ten minutes, collected the white phone from his bag, and stepped outside to the parking lot to call Silva.

The lot was surrounded by tall hedges and filled with an amazing collection of expensive cars. The air smelled good, laden with deep forest scents and smoke from wood fires, and from somewhere in the distance he heard music, violins muffled by the slight breeze, a mournful tune at four in the morning.

A half dozen men were wandering around, dark shadows among the silent cars, talking on cell phones retrieved from the Service Center. Dmitri heard one say, "...but I'm telling you, we got the contract. It's in the bag. We configure the entire system, and they buy it as a package. Who says so? The Secretary of Defense says so."

Dmitri dialed. Silva answered, "Silva."

They spoke in Russian.

"This is Dmitri Demetriov calling again, Boris's brother."

"I know who you are, Dmitri."

"Boris has left the campground. He's going somewhere called Mary's."

Silva thought his heart might bounce out of his chest, but he said, "Mary's Massage Parlor and Escort Service, yes, I know it. In Guerneville. Is he coming back to the camp?"

"I don't know," Dmitri replied. "He's Boris. He might do anything. He might decide to visit San Francisco, or New York, for that matter. He's Boris."

"I understand," Silva said. "Thank you, Dmitri."

Silva broke the connection, took a deep breath, and went downstairs.

"We're almost finished making our videos," said Number Six in Arabic. "Two more."

"Take your time," Silva said. "I have to leave again. Stay here until I get back."

"There's a dead man back against the wall, the bus driver."

"Don't worry about him. He was an infidel, and he knew too much about us."

"Has he gone to hell?"

"Most certainly. You'll never see him in Paradise."

"I hope we're going there soon."

"Yes, if Allah is willing, but for now, be patient and wait until I get back. Pray and purify yourselves. Allah loves you. He is your guardian."

. . . . .

It was so quiet and peaceful up in Fat Freddie that Butler thought he might take a nap. The Mexicans wouldn't come out of the bunkhouse until dawn, and then they would do something really exciting like work in the vineyard. He thought if he was John Steinbeck he might tell a story about them, but he was Butler Rhodes and he was merely curious.

He didn't hear a generator making electricity. He bet it was hot and stuffy in that old cabin with no air-conditioning. And no beer. And probably no ice. Something was all out of whack here.

The bunkhouse door opened.

"Hold on," Butler said into his headset. "What's this?"

"What? What?" Jeremy and Teddy responded simultaneously.

"Silva is coming out and getting into the Ford Explorer. Now he's turning the truck around and heading down the driveway past the vineyard. Fast. He's in a hurry."

"What about the Mexicans?"

"Haven't seen 'em. Wait. There's one of 'em, in a white football jersey with a big number six."

"What's he doing?"

"Nothing. Standing in the door watching Silva drive away. Now he's gone back inside and shut the door. I can see Silva's headlights. He's coming up Richardson's Road."

"I see him," Teddy said from his Suburban near Fat Freddie where Albert had dropped him off.

Teddy ducked down under the dash as the bright blue Ford drove past, not knowing if the driver saw him or not.

"Now what?" he said into his headset. "What do you think, Paul?"

Paul was still in the guard shack at the South Gate.

"That means the Mexicans are in there alone," Paul said. "I'll stay with the Blue Blazers until they come out."

. . . . .

At four o'clock Belinski was nearing the end of his shift in the black room when the screen lit up with a face from the wire room in San Francisco.

"Yeah?" Belinski answered, yawning.

The nameless face in San Francisco said, "You asked us to put tags on a couple of Miami numbers."

"Yeah, that's right."

"One of those numbers just called the other from the same tower as the last time, 1768C, the one closest to you."

"Gotcha, thanks."

Belinski reached Rodriguez as the Secret Service agent sat in the back of the black government SUV racing along Highway 116 toward Guerneville.

"Your Miami phone numbers," Belinski said. "They just called one another again from our local tower 1768C."

At ninety miles per hour, as his driver chased Boris in the Range Rover, Rodriguez's mind tried to compute and assess what little information he had. There was a call just after Boris's arrival at the Grove and another just after his departure an hour and a half later. Dmitri Demetriov had one of those phones, and he was calling someone outside, but close by, who could be anyone, a boyfriend, a girlfriend, a Belarusian security detail. Or Dmitri could be a traitor to his brother and whoever he was talking to was an assassin, stalking Boris. That was a scenario Rodriguez considered a rather remote possibility, but he needed to know more.

"Can you tell me anything else about those phones?" Rodriguez asked Belinski.

"Sorry. We do what we can."

·   ·   ·   ·   ·

Deputy Alice believed she was the only Sonoma County officer on patrol in all of West County when she pulled into the 24-hour Jiffy Quick on Highway 116 between Monte Rio and Guerneville. Her radio was dead. Nothing was happening. The expected crime wave caused by the absence of sheriff's deputies never happened.

Most of her fellow deputies were in the Santa Rosa all-night Denny's reeling over Amory Hix's plight. After the broadcast of the bribery videos, the deputies knew there would be a ruthless FBI investigation, and they wanted to know who knew what about Amory's shenanigans.

A really good cop, Alice knew more than any of them, but she wasn't at the meeting in Santa Rosa; and if she were, she would have nothing to say. Instead, she was sitting in her Ford Crown Vic cruiser sipping sour Jiffy Quick coffee to stay awake when she heard the rollicking screamer and saw the bright headlights coming from the west.

The Range Rover flew down the highway right in front of her and lit up her radar gun at ninety-eight miles per hour. Holy smokes! Bohos in Ferraris and drunken teenagers never went that fast on this part of the narrow, windy River Road.

Alice hit lights and siren, but before she could pull onto the highway a big, black SUV with government plates whooshed past at the same manic velocity. No flashing lights or siren for that bad boy. She mashed the accelerator to the floor, and the clunky Police Interceptor pulled out and joined the high-speed train as the shrieking, red-and-blue-flashing caboose.

She grabbed her radio microphone—

.   .   .   .   .

— and Jeremy and Phillip heard, "This is Unit Forty-Two. I have reckless drivers heading east on Highway 116. Radar says ninety-eight. I have a gray Range Rover and a black GMC Yukon with exempt government plates."

Jeremy and Phillip looked at one another and said simultaneously, "That's Alice."

"Slow down, Alice," Jeremy prayed out loud. "You're chasing Caviar, fucking Boris Boris, and if he's going to crash and burn, don't go with him. Please."

. . . . .

Roger Blake concluded that hitting a redwood tree at one hundred miles per hour was far more dangerous than the tiny pistol flaunted by the crazy Belarusian bodyguard in his back seat, so he hit the brakes and the government truck behind him slowed as well. Alice killed her siren but left the red and blue flashing lights on as she heeded Jeremy's prayer and punched the brake pedal. All three cars slowed without mishap, and Roger could see Alice's lights behind the black SUV. The Range Rover's digital heads-up speedometer dropped rapidly - 90, 80, 60, 40 - while Roger's heartbeat seemed to speed up as they rounded a wide bend and entered Guerneville. They passed a disabled logging truck parked on the shoulder and Roger turned left, went a short block and turned right into a neighborhood of small hotels and seasonal resorts, closed restaurants and businesses, and several spas, two of which were lit up and busy at four-thirty in the morning, with Mary's massage parlor nestled discreetly between them.

Roger stopped in front of Mary's, Rodriguez pulled up behind him, and Alice right after that. Roger had his phone out and was calling Mary.

"We're in front," he said into his phone.

He turned around to speak to the Belarusians and saw that Boris had passed out and was snoring on Yuri's shoulder.

Rodriguez tapped on his window and Roger lowered it.

"Nice driving," said the Secret Service agent. "If you had killed Boris, I'd have a hell of a time explaining what was going on."

"He's drunk. He's out of it," Roger said, jerking his thumb toward the back seat.

Rodriguez leaned farther into the window and said in Russian, "Yuri, give me your phone."

"What phone? I don't have a phone."

"A phone with a Miami area code."

"I don't know what you're talking about. My phone is in a bag at the Grove."

"Someone in your party has a phone," Rodriguez said. "How about Boris?"

Yuri adjusted his position and wrapped a beefy, protective arm around Boris, saying, "He'll wake up in a minute. He always does."

"I can search you again, Yuri."

"Go ahead. You won't find a phone."

Rodriguez smiled and said to the bodyguard, still in Russian, "I feel like I've been chasing you all night."

Yuri grinned in return and answered, "It's true, you have. You're better at it than your colleagues in Los Angeles. But here," he said and gave Rodriguez his little Beretta. "You missed it the first time."

"Why don't we all go back to the Grove and go to sleep?" Rodriguez suggested in English as he stared at the tiny pistol in his hand. "Is that too much to ask?"

Alice left her motor running and lights flashing, got out of the car and was walking toward Rodriguez who was standing outside the Range Rover when she turned to watch a blue Ford Explorer cruise slowly by, the driver hidden by mirrored sunglasses and a straw cowboy hat as he checked out the police action on the other side of the street.

Alice looked Rodriguez up and down and said, "Mind if I ask what's going on?"

Rodriguez flashed his badge and ID and said, "Secret Service."

"I figured something federal," Alice said, pushing her cop hat back off her forehead and wiping her brow with a perfumed, silk handkerchief, a gift from Betty. "You know I clocked you at ninety-eight miles per hour. Somebody must be really horny to want to get to Mary's that fast."

Rodriguez smiled. Local cops usually didn't have the balls to give him smartass lip, and he was delighted.

"You got that right," he said to her, "but we're going to take him back now, only not quite so fast."

"Good," she said. "You never know who might be out on that

highway. We have plenty of drunks around here."

"Thanks, Officer," Rodriguez said. "I'm glad to see you're on the job considering what's happened in your department."

The blue Explorer came back down the street going very slowly the other way, and Alice checked him out again.

She turned her attention to Roger Blake and said, "I could ask you for your license and registration, but —"

At that moment Boris woke up, saw Alice's face a few inches from his own, and shrieked. What Boris thought he saw was the fat, round, acne-scarred face of a courtesan offered to him by the brothel. When he was finally out of breath from screaming, he burbled and gargled in twisted, Russian baby talk.

Roger Blake flinched, Yuri winced, and Alice took an awkward step backward and reached for her baton.

Rodriguez stepped in immediately, saying, "Diplomatic immunity, sheriff. Be cool. Be cool."

Mary's front door opened a crack and two pairs of eyes looked out, saw flashing police lights, and promptly slammed the door. All the lights in the building blacked out.

"If you're going back to the Grove," Alice said to Rodriguez, "I can give you an escort."

"That's okay, thanks," Rodriguez replied, grateful that Alice deliberately was not asking who the passengers in the Range Rover were. "But that's not necessary."

Alice bent over, peered into the Range Rover again, saw a couple of sloppy drunks in the back seat, laughed a gutsy belly laugh and sauntered back to her car.

Sitting behind the wheel of her cruiser, she watched the Explorer park at the end of the block. The driver shut down the lights but didn't get out of the car.

Rodriguez had a brief word with Roger Blake, then returned to his vehicle and both trucks turned around and headed back toward Monte Rio at sober speed. Alice watched the tail lights of the government SUV disappear around the corner, and a moment later, the blue

Explorer pulled into the street and followed. Alice thought that was curious, if not downright peculiar, so she followed the fleet of trucks, this time without police lights and siren, figuring the Explorer was driven by another Boho for his own salacious reasons. All these guys went to Mary's, then changed their minds.

"These people," she said. "Jeezus."

The Range Rover and the big Yukon presently crossed the Monte Rio Bridge and turned up hill toward the Main Gate of the Bohemian Grove. The blue Explorer, however, crossed the bridge but instead of following the Bohos, the driver continued straight on the Old Bohemian Highway, passed Butler and Maggie's place and then turned up Richardson's dusty road. Holy shit, Alice thought, whoever he is, he's gonna wake up those dogs and then Barney Richardson will be on the phone calling her! Oh boy, what countrified irony. She couldn't wait.

The blue truck drove past Richardson's old cabin and the dogs didn't make a peep. Her cop instinct told her something here didn't smell right, but Alice couldn't quite identify the offending odor. She followed without any lights and as quietly as she could, but she was pretty sure the driver of the Explorer knew she was behind him.

The blue truck and the following police car quickly cut through the redwoods, went up and over the hill and down toward the Bohemian Grove perimeter road, passing Albert's Lambo and Teddy's Suburban both of which appeared empty to Alice. The blue Explorer drove a short ways along the Grove perimeter road, then turned up the lane that ran alongside Mario Silva's vineyard.

From the foot of the lane Alice watched the Explorer come to a halt behind a big flatbed truck next to the old, log bunkhouse. Alice, an old-fashioned girl in many ways, determined that the driver had to be Mario Silva or someone who worked for him, and furthermore that Mario and his migrants had no business following Bohos and government trucks to Guerneville whorehouses at four-thirty in the morning, so she drove up the lane, stopped behind the Explorer, and put on her best stern cop attitude with her hat. As she got out of her police car, all the floodlights above the lane and the bunkhouse powered on in a sudden blaze, and Alice was momentarily blinded.

She never saw Mario Silva get out of the car with a silenced Uzi, but Butler did.

26

Butler lay on his perch looking through the big lens on his camera, watching a young four-point buck feast on Silva's grapes, when he saw headlights on Richardson's Road, still dark under the canopy of giant trees. Wherever Mario had gone, he was coming back. Butler called Teddy on the Cobra.

"Teddy, you see him?" Butler asked over the radio.

"Yes," Teddy said from his Suburban parked near the base of Fat Freddie.

"He see you?" Butler asked.

"I don't know. He went by fast. A cop is following him."

"Jeremy, you hear a cop?"

"No, not a peep."

"Paul?"

"I'm just getting in the Hummer at the South Gate. I don't see anything but trees."

Butler swung his camera around and watched the blue Explorer drive up the long driveway next to the vineyard. A white police car pulled up the lane and stopped right behind Mario's truck. Powerful floodlights suddenly came on all at once and the display on his camera whited out for a brief second before the software adjusted. The door of the police car opened and Deputy Alice stumbled out, both hands shading her eyes, clearly temporarily blinded.

Mario Silva got out his truck and Butler could not believe what he was seeing through the long lens. He pushed a button and switched the camera to full video.

Just as the first gray streaks of dawn spilled into the Russian River valley, Mario Silva brandished a weapon that looked like a small, black assault rifle with a silver sound suppressor screwed onto the barrel. Butler saw the muzzle flash and saw Alice jerk as a half-dozen bullets drove into her body like hot rivets. Still convulsing, she crumpled to the ground.

No one heard her, but her last words were, "Tinker Bell—"

.   .   .   .   .

Butler scrambled for the Sharps, not sure if he could get a shot off, or if he really wanted to, but before he could open the ammunition box, and before he could sort out the ethics of being judge, jury and executioner, Alice lay still and Mario Silva jerked open the door and disappeared into the bunkhouse.

"Yo!" Butler said into the Cobra mic. "Listen up! Silva just shot Deputy Alice. She's dead. He unloaded a full magazine into her. I got it all on video."

"A magazine? Say what?" Jeremy squawked. He jumped up from his silver console and began gesticulating wildly all over the small room. Phillip, alarmed, stopped listening to the Air Force air traffic controller at Travis AFB and switched to the Cobra frequency.

"Alice?" Jeremy asked. "Our Alice? Somebody shot... Alice?"

"Mario Silva," Butler answered, his heart racing, trying to be clear. "In front of his bunkhouse. She drove up behind him and the son of a bitch just blew her away, cold," Butler declared, shocked. "I can't fuckin' believe it."

"I saw them drive by, both cars," Teddy said. "He shot her? Damn. What the — ?" He jumped out of the Suburban, raced to the rear, pulled open the back, hastily grabbed a bullet-proof vest and yellow FBI windbreaker, scrambled into both garments, then jammed a magazine into one of the HKs.

"Where is he? Where is he?" Teddy asked frantically into his headset.

"He went back inside the bunkhouse," Butler answered.

"Why would he shoot Alice?" Jeremy wondered. "Alice?"

"Shit," Paul said, squirming next to George in the Blue Blazer Hummer, "We have to go in. Right now. Teddy, call Carter McGee. I'll be in front of the vineyard in two minutes." He turned to George, saying calmly, "Step on it!" and the big truck lurched ahead.

Special Agent Paul Kruger pulled out his service Glock, chambered a round and clicked off the safety.

.   .   .   .   .

In the black room on the second floor in the rear of the Bohemian Grove Main Administration Building, night shift National Security Agency duty officer Daniel Belinski was fuming because his relief never showed up. Fucking Andy Drake was AWOL and he was stuck on the board. It had happened before.

It had been a quiet night, a routine shift of long, boring frequency checks, long, boring satellite fly-by's, and long, boring phone calls he had to record. Rodriguez and his goons had been chasing around like maniacs all night, trying to keep up with Boris the Belarusian. Good luck with that. Wouldn't Rodriguez love to know that Boris was tagged: his shoes, his watch, his phone, even his Ruger pistol was tagged, and so was everyone in his party. Ha! Fuck the Secret Service. They were almost as big a pain in the ass as the FBI, especially that freak Teddy Swan.

It was a quarter to five in the morning and Belinski was drinking his sixth cup of coffee and thinking about a hit of crystal meth, just to stay awake. There was plenty of that in Monte Rio. All these fancy agents were sitting in the middle of one of the biggest industrial scale meth operations in California, and they didn't have a clue. Stupid shits. At least that Sheriff had had enough sense to try and make some real money out of all the crap around here. He was an idiot, but an idiot with imagination.

Against the rules, Belinski was watching an old Al Pacino movie on Netflix and barely looking at the monitors and displays when the automatic scanners locked on to Cobra channel one-one-oh-six, usually used by construction crews, and he heard multiple voices transmitting on the same channel.

Listening, momentarily fascinated and paralyzed, a million questions jumped out at him.

Silva? Who was Silva?

Alice? Who was Alice?

"... the son of a bitch just blew her away, cold. I can't fuckin' believe it..."

"What the —? What is this?" Belinski blinked and asked aloud. "What? Who?"

Then one of the voices said, "Teddy, call Carter McGee," and he knew he was listening to the FBI, but not on one of their approved frequencies. He guessed it was that rogue Teddy Swan who'd been up at Jeremy's earlier in the day, making friends with the Pirates. For some reason beyond Belinski's comprehension, the FBI, instead of shutting them down, was in love with the Pirates and went out of their way to protect them. What bullshit!

Whoever they were, the crew transmitting on Cobra channel one-one-oh-six was very close. The direction finders were beginning to zero in, first on Jeremy Steadman's installation up on the Starrett's Hill, then on the South Gate.

This was really unusual because Jeremy never transmitted. Never! But he was transmitting now on the Cobra, talking in the clear! Why would he do that? And the other transmitters on Cobra channel one-one-oh-six had to be the rest of the Pirates. His suspicions about them had been right all along: those bastards were up to something.

Clearly, there was gunplay, someone was shooting someone, close to the Grove, too close, near the southern perimeter road and the South Gate. Belinski's suspicious, paranoid mind churned through a few possibilities: It was the Pirates. It was the FBI. It was a deal gone wrong in a meth lab. It was another dirty sheriff. It was some tequila-crazed, homesick Mexican farm workers. It was some lunatic old hippie murdering his common-law wife. Whatever it was, it was pretty exciting, better than Netflix, that was for sure.

He called Rodriguez.

. . . . .

Outside the bunkhouse, an alarming number of things beyond Silva's control were going wrong, including the arrival of daylight which deprived his designated martyrs the cover of darkness. Yet inside the hot and stuffy old log cabin the situation was even worse.

Returning from Guerneville —he knew he was gone too long— Silva found eight of his martyrs-to-be wearing their suicide vests under their soccer jerseys, ready to embark on their mission, but six of the jihadis knelt on their prayer rugs or lay on their bunks, dazed, zombie-like, their lethal vests scattered around the big room. One of the boys, Hernán, the youngest, whose life Silva had spared, was in the bathroom, naked to the waist and puking. The trap door to the basement was open and the smell of Pedro's rapidly decomposing body was starting to drift upstairs.

He expected another urgent call from Dmitri, telling him Boris was back in Ye Olde Owls camp, but there was no way he could wait for a call. He had to unleash his terrorists now. Butler, he believed, was still out there, and he had seen Albert's yellow truck and the red Suburban in the woods. That meant the FBI, and whoever was in the red truck, even innocent teenagers having a sex and liquor party, posed an immediate threat. And the dead policewoman would be missed before long.

He went downstairs, quickly delivered a last, cynical salute to Pedro, checked the explosive charges destined to destroy the bunkhouse and their phone connection, grabbed a box of Uzis and magazines and a football jersey for himself.

The training in Paraguay had not included preparations for combat. The boys thought they were soldiers, but they were not. They were suicide bombers trained to stop the Hummer, kill the guards, storm the South Gate, and attack the defenseless Southland region of the Bohemian Grove. And nothing else.

Silva spent one intense moment indulging in ferocious self-recrimination for his shortsightedness, calling himself dirty names in several languages. Scoundrel! Fool! Fucking idiot! — but right now his only viable options were to send his charges on the mission they were trained for, or abandon them entirely, detonate the explosive charges in the basement and in the walls, and escape with his life. Compassion never entered into Silva's calculations. The boys were doomed.

Boris was another matter. If he survived, the Russians would be furious. If he could manage to assassinate Boris, the Russians might let him live and even keep the money. But Boris or no Boris, this was not his suicide mission.

He had deeply miscalculated, he knew that now. In an attempt to eliminate Boris and his five American benefactors all at once, he had over-reached. He had conflated an old plan with too many new exigencies. Too ambitious, too complicated, too inflexible, his plan was destined for failure. Stupid, stupid, stupid. And instead of a tightly controlled situation, with multiple exit paths and alternate tactics, there was now a huge unknown outside his door, and multiple elements beyond his control.

He didn't take long to make a decision. He took the Uzis upstairs and gave them to the six oldest jihadis, numbers one through six.

"Those of you who are ready, you have to go now," he said. "We can't delay any more. Remember your training. Attack the Hummer. Kill the guards. Then we move on through the South Gate to the camps. For the rest of you, follow us to Paradise, or stay in this cabin and go to Hell!"

Like his house on River Boulevard, the log bunkhouse was rigged for demolition to be triggered by phone. All he had to do was call one number and both buildings would explode like Hollywood sets. They didn't know it, but any boys who stayed behind would be incinerated along with their Qurans and prayer rugs, football jerseys, and prayer beads.

. . . . .

Butler had the Sharps loaded and the door to the bunkhouse in his sights when it opened and a big red number twenty on a white jersey appeared and quickly dashed into the vineyard, followed by a string of Mexicans in white football jerseys with big red numbers, some perhaps with weapons, and they all vanished into the vineyard.

Butler's mind flashed back to dawn breaking over the Mekong Delta, an image of Viet Cong troopers with Kalashnikovs moving in a line along the edge of a rice paddy, his last shoot. He felt sick. Human beings in his field of fire was not something he ever wanted to see again, but here they were.

He had no reason to start killing the Mexicans, but he sure as hell could let them know he was there, so he squeezed the trigger and put a round into one of the big floodlights on the roof of the bunkhouse. The Sharps erupted with a monstrously violent report, and it seemed as though the entire ravine between Richardson's hill and the Bohemian Grove reverberated with the crack of the antique rifle.

. . . . .

"I heard that," Teddy said from his Suburban.

"So did I," said Paul, from the Hummer.

"Heard what?" Jeremy asked.

"The Sharps," Teddy said. "Like Butler said, it's loud. Very loud."

Over the hill, near the Old Bohemian Highway, in the trees off to the side of Richardson's Road, the shot woke up Albert who wondered, at first, if what he heard was a sonic boom. Then he remembered the Sharps from the Fourth of July and he wondered why Butler was shooting and what he might be shooting at. Just as the first light of day began to filter through the redwoods, he plunked the Cobra head-set back over his ears, started the Lambo, turned around and headed up the hill toward Fat Freddie.

"Hey!" Albert said into his mic. "What's happenin'?" but he heard no response.

. . . . .

Crouching out of sight in the vineyard, Silva heard the shot and recognized the sound – he'd heard that rifle in Afghanistan but hadn't known what it was, an old Enfield perhaps, certainly not a modern weapon. The Pashtun had vast arsenals of vintage guns.

He saw the light shatter on the bunkhouse roof and knew the shooter was somewhere in the trees, either on Richardson's side of the ravine or in the Grove itself.

"It's getting light enough to see," Butler said into his mic, "and all these guys came out of the bunkhouse, Mexicans wearing white football jerseys with big red numbers. I think some of 'em had guns. They went into the vineyard and ducked down. I can't see 'em. It's like they're trying to hide," he explained.

He watched the Hummer enter his field of fire.

. . . . .

"Slow down," Paul said from the passenger's seat to George who was driving. "Let's not run into an ambush."

George slowed to a crawl as the Blue Blazer truck approached Silva's vineyard. For once, the loudspeakers on the roof were silent.

"Look out," Paul cried. "There's someone in the road."

George stopped. Two young men in white football jerseys with red numbers stood in the middle of the road, holding black Uzis and blinking in the glare of the headlights.

"They have guns!" Paul shouted. "Back up! Get away from them!"

"What's going on?" George cried, terrified, jamming the Hummer into reverse. "What's happening?"

"Just do it! Back up! They killed a cop!" Paul had his Glock out and was trying to find the switch to open the Hummer window.

"God damn it!" he swore.

"Shit," George muttered as Number Two and Number Six walked toward the Hummer, then with a loud whine the car started to speed up in reverse and the two Mexicans broke into a run, chasing it.

With the truck accelerating backwards, Paul found the window switch, pushed it, and the window started to come down, but before he could stick his pistol through the opening and start shooting, George crashed the rear of the Hummer into a tree, tossing himself around inside like a man-sized balloon. Paul, wearing his seatbelt like a sensible federal agent, saw the driver's side window shatter as Number Two unloaded his Uzi with a terrible racket, and three seconds later George was dead, his blood and brains splattered around the interior of the Hummer.

Miraculously unhit, Paul, his mind turning to white heat, leaned across the prostrate George and emptied his Glock wildly in the direction of the Mexican from three feet away and missed with all nine shots. Number Two raised his Uzi again to shoot Paul but his magazine was empty and he had another but didn't know how to insert it into the gun.

"Teddy!" Paul shouted into his mic.

Holding the HK with both hands, the yellow FBI windbreaker flapping in the wind behind him, Teddy ran down the hill and onto the perimeter road where he could see the two Mexicans in football jerseys chasing the receding Hummer a hundred yards away.

"I see them. I'm coming!"

"Butler!" Teddy hollered. "Butler! Do you see them?"

Number Two dropped his weapon and managed to pull open the driver's door and pull George's body halfway out of the truck, as he was trained to do. Wild-eyed, he began screaming at Paul in a mixture of Spanish and Arabic and was astonished when Paul, who was shooting his pistol at him, shouted back in Arabic.

Number Six tried to shoot into the Hummer, but he left the safety on, and when the Uzi refused to fire, he began to curse and look around crazily for help. More football jerseys popped up in the vineyard and began jogging toward the road.

"Butler!" Teddy shouted.

"Shut up."

Three hundred fifty yards, a slight wind from the west, and a two hundred fifty foot drop. Standing next to the Hummer, Number Two's face loomed through the barrel sight as if it were thirty feet away, a young man's face. In the early morning light Butler saw a wispy mustache and blazing eyes, a face he'd seen in the back of Silva's truck. Somehow, in a frozen instant, he had to do what he never wanted to do again. He didn't have time to think and sort it all out. He knew the consequences. He kept Number Two squarely in his sights and squeezed the trigger.

The Sharps erupted with another monstrously violent report. Without looking up, Butler cocked open the breech, and started to reload.

As Number Two started pulling George's body from the passenger's seat, Butler's bullet passed right through the soft C4 in the front of his vest and into his chest where it lodged in his spine. The heavy bullet didn't kill him, but it knocked him to the ground where he rolled over onto his back next to George's body.

Number Six saw Number Two fall and ran around the car, shouting, "Faud! Faud!"

Number Six saw his friend Faud blink, fatally wounded. Faud's fingers twitched.

"God is great," mumbled Faud. "God is great."

Number Six knew what was coming. The jihadis had been trained for only one thing.

"God is great," chorused Number Six, and he reached for the toggle switch on his belt. Paradise was waiting. He was blessed. His family was blessed. God was waiting to grant him all the delights and privileges of the blessed.

Inside the Hummer Paul heard them and he, too, knew what was coming. He tried to open the car door, but it was stuck. Oh shit, he thought. If this is what it's all about, then maybe God isn't so great. This is fucked.

Number Two found the toggle switch on his belt and pushed it simultaneously with Number Six.

Both vests detonated. With a tremendous whump, sixteen pounds of C4 from two jihadis demolished the Hummer, instantly killing Paul and both terrorists and raining body parts and burning debris on the Bohemian Grove perimeter road. A cloud of smoke rose from the burning remnants of the Hummer, and the flames cast an eerie illumination over the ancient redwood forest.

"Holy shit!" Butler exclaimed. "They're suicide bombers! They have vests under those jerseys."

"Aaahhhhhhhhh!" Teddy groaned into his mic. "Those sons-of-bitches killed Paulie. They killed my partner! What the fuck is this?!"

"It's an attack on the Grove," Butler answered. "I think they want to kill some Bohos."

Enraged, Teddy ran along the road toward the burning Hummer until Butler stopped him with a sharp, "Get down, Teddy! Get on the ground and into the trees!. There's more of 'em in the vineyard."

Teddy veered off the road and dived behind a redwood across from the vineyard just as a hail of bullets sliced into the tree above him, showering him with shredded redwood bark.

"Jesus fucking Christ," Teddy muttered under his breath.

Teddy had never seen anything like the scene along the Bohemian Grove perimeter road. The Hummer was burning. Black smoke and the smell of blood drifted on the morning breeze. Anger began to rise in his throat like bile. The impossible was happening. The war on terror had come home, not to New York, not to Detroit, not to Florida, but to the beautiful Russian River valley in Northern California. His mind was spinning. Someone was shooting a machinegun at him; Paul was dead; Alice was dead; one of the Blue Blazers was dead; at least two suicide bombers were dead; the Bohemian Grove was under attack, and the only man effectively defending the Bohos was a guy who hated their guts, Butler Rhodes.

Then he saw Albert's yellow truck come bouncing noisily down the hill.

. . . . .

Silva saw a man in a bright yellow windbreaker with big blue letters FBI running along the road and knew his operation was in dire jeopardy. His only goal now was to escape, and his jihadis would have to be his first diversion.

A burst from his Uzi sent the FBI agent sprawling into the trees between the perimeter road and the fence, where he cowered behind a huge redwood. He had to keep this hero pinned behind the tree while his jihadis stormed the South Gate.

"Go! Go! Go!" he shouted, first in Spanish, then in Arabic, while he crawled toward the blue Explorer. "Stay down! Head for the South

Gate! God is great!"

Number Four either didn't hear or didn't understand. He stood up. "What's happening?" he cried. "Where are they? I can't see anything! Ali! Ali! What should I do?"

With daylight increasing every second, Butler easily picked out the white jersey with the red Number Four against the dark vines and darker trees. Against his will and against his earnest wishes for a world without mayhem, he martyred another soldier of God with a head shot.

Three more jihadis with Uzis rose up, firing wildly into the trees in all directions. Butler picked off Number Eight, and the others immediately dropped back below the vines.

By the fourth booming shot, Silva saw the Sharps' muzzle flash and knew Butler was high up in the trees on Richardson's hill. A sniper.

27

"McGee," said Special Agent in Charge Carter McGee sleepily from his bedroom in Santa Rosa. He blinked and frowned at the phone in his hand as if it were a hot grenade.

"Swan here."

"Yes, Teddy. What is it?"

"We have terrorists at the South Gate to the Bohemian Grove and—

"Oh my —"

"— we need back up. They killed a cop and...and—"

"Yes, Teddy?"

"— they killed Agent Kruger. They killed Paul."'

"Oh my God."

"Yeah. We're looking at suicide bombers with vests and assault weapons. Four are down but I don't know how many are left. Somehow a local, Mario Silva, is involved. You need to check him out."

"Mario Silva, okay. Where exactly are you, right now, Teddy?"

Teddy looked up at the wide-spreading lower branches of the redwood tree above him. A four inch long bright yellow banana slug slimed over an exposed root near his foot. He thought of Butler's rant earlier in the day, 'All that's left is existential absurdity,' but he said to Carter McGee, "I'm behind a fucking redwood tree about two hundred yards west of the South Gate to the Bohemian Grove. I'm across the Bohemian Grove perimeter road from Mario Silva's fucking pinot noir vineyard. You can find my phone with GPS, Carter. The truck, too. All the Bureau commo gear is in there. We're using Cobras."

"We?" Carter McGee asked. "Whaddaya mean, 'We,' Agent Swan?"

"Me and the Pirates."

"Oh, shit. Civilians."

"You were right about them, Carter, the Pirates. They found the bad guys."

"If you say so," acknowledged Carter McGee. "Now what?"

"We need backup," Teddy insisted.

Rushing around his bedroom getting dressed, Carter McGee said, "The local sheriff's department is a mess right now, and most of the Bureau extras have gone back to Fresno and San Francisco. The best I can do is a SWAT team and maybe a bomb squad from the Santa Rosa Police. Realistically, it might take a couple of hours."

"Jesus Christ, Carter, we don't have a couple hours," Teddy replied. "I doubt if we have a couple of minutes."

. . . . .

Boris and Yuri were asleep in the guest tent while Dmitri paced nervously around the smoldering campfire in the center of Ye Olde Owls camp, watched closely by Raul Rodriguez who sat with Roger Blake on the stone bench surrounding the camp's hearth. The spit and roasted venison were gone. A Blue Blazer golf cart was parked nearby.

Dawn was breaking on Sunday morning in the Bohemian Grove, the third day of the encampment. Maurice, the chef in impeccable kitchen whites, stepped outside the pantry for a morning smoke before breakfast.

"Bonjour, Monsieur Blake," Maurice said, and he nodded at the Secret Service agent in mirrored sunglasses sitting with Roger Blake on the bench.

"Messieurs," Maurice said, and offered Rodriguez and Roger Blake each a cup of coffee. Real china, real silver, real coffee, real cream, real Cognac, real Maurice smile.

The crisp morning air, tinged with salt from the Pacific and smoke from dozens of wood fires, was delicious. Rodriguez looked around and couldn't believe the serenity and wondrousness of the place. This truly was paradise, a fantasyland created by the world's richest men for their pleasure. What could be better? It wasn't complicated or weird or sinister in any way. It was just a redwood funhouse, with a really good wine cellar.

Rodriguez heard music, a dawn saxophone solo from a nearby camp. It was Sunday morning and someone was playing *Amazing Grace*. Good lord, it was beautiful.

A few men emerged yawning from their tents. Two, in running gear, took off jauntily down the path toward the South Gate.

Then they all heard the booming, echoing crack of the first rifle shot and perked up.

"What was that?" Roger Blake asked.

"Sounded like artillery," Rodriguez said.

Then they heard automatic small arms fire in the far distance, and the Sharps two more times, then an explosion, then machineguns again. Rat-a-tat-tat-tat-tat-tat.

Rodriguez heard the distant gunfire and instantly knew that on this beautiful July morning one of his Bohemian nightmares had suddenly come true. He just didn't know which one yet. Armed intruders? A lone wolf crazy? Anarchist wackos?

Somewhere close by, just over the hill, a firefight was taking place, and his instinct was to rush toward the sound and confront whatever he found. Alas, his duty, much to his irritation, was to babysit the esteemed guest of the United States of America, Boris Demetriov, the asshole president of Belarus, and keep him out of harm's way.

Damn. Rodriguez took off his sunglasses, rubbed his eyes with his palms and shook his head, thinking, Oh damn.

In the next few seconds a flood of ideas and facts raced through his mind. The Grove's first line of defense, the Sonoma County Sheriff's Department, had been crippled by the flame out of Amory Hix. Most of the deputies were in Santa Rosa, at least an hour away. The next, inner line of defense, the Blue Blazers, were not and never had been capable of defending the Grove against a determined assault. Now they, like the Sheriff's Department, had been decapitated by the firing of John O'Shea.

Only the FBI and the Pirates were left.

Rodriguez had known about the Pirates for months. It was Daniel Belinski in the black room who had discovered the Russian River Society of Pirates and Thieves and tracked them ever since. When a wealthy individual – Albert – started buying every piece of exotic radio equipment available in Silicon Valley, and then a known radio geek, Albert's friend – Jeremy – set up that gear as a massive radio interception station in Monte Rio right on top of the Bohemian Grove, these activities did not escape the diligent attention of Daniel Belinski of the National Security Agency.

Although the naturally suspicious and paranoid Belinski wasn't so sure the Pirates were harmless, Rodriguez was in agreement with the FBI's Carter McGee that Jeremy, Phillip, Butler and Albert were of great value. The Pirates had already proved that Grove communications were compromised, and with their stunt on the Bohemian Beach they had effectively demonstrated that the Grove's ability to protect itself was inadequate.

Ting-a-ling-a-ling.

Now, almost as startling as the gunfire, with cell phones prohibited in the Grove, the ringing in Rodriguez's jacket pocket was as loud as the timpani in an overture.

Ting-a-ling-a-ling.

Roger Blake jumped up, agitated. Yawning and scratching, more men emerged from their tents, and Dmitri began jerking spasmodically, almost as if he were shot, hit by a stray round, but with all of Boris's comings and goings and the expected arrival momentarily of a suicide squad bent on slaughtering everything that moved, he was perilously close to losing his mind.

Dmitri Demetriov heard more gunfire and didn't know what to do. Any minute now a platoon of suicide bombers was going to burst into the Grove and create unspeakable chaos. The bombers would enter the camps, the tents, and destroy themselves and dozens of these rich Americans. A man he knew only by the code name Silva was supposed to come to Ye Olde Owls camp in a Bohemian security vehicle. Silva and his minions were supposed to kill Boris, and he and Silva would drive away in the Bohemian car.

Then the Russians would make him, Dmitri Demetriov, president of Belarus.

Ting-a-ling-a-ling.

Rodriguez extracted the phone from his pocket, saw that the call originated in the black room, and answered, "Yes?"

"I think we have armed men near the South Gate," said Belinski. "There's been a shooting. The Pirates are involved. They're talking on Cobras and I'm listening."

"Good Lord," Rodriguez exclaimed. "I hear gunfire!"

Then Rodriguez noticed Dmitri taking off down the path, running toward the Administration Building and his phone. Somehow, Rodriguez wasn't sure how, he suspected that all these odd occurrences were connected.

"Can you jam those phones, those Miami phone numbers, just those numbers?" Rodriguez asked Belinski.

"Yeah, sure."

"Then do it," Rodriguez said. "Do it now!"

.   .   .   .   .

Careening down Richardson's Road, Albert heard more gunfire but had no idea what it meant. Rushing past Teddy's Suburban, he hit the horn, eliciting no response from the empty truck, and arrived at the bottom of the hill, wheels churning, engine screaming, transmission whining and horn blaring.

As soon as he turned onto the perimeter road, he saw the burning Hummer. Smoldering body parts were strewn about the road and vineyard. Albert wasn't expecting to come upon a battlefield in the middle of the redwood forest, and he certainly wasn't expecting the sudden appearance of Teddy Swan, who popped out from behind a tree on his left, waving frantically and shouting into his headset mic. Albert abruptly realized that while he had slept in his truck, his headset had become disconnected from the Cobra radio attached to his belt, and he began to swear, "Oh shit oh shit oh shit," as he hit the brakes and scrunched to a stop next to Teddy's tree, opposite the vineyard.

Bullets stitched the passenger side of the Lamborghini — thunkthunkthunkthunk thunkthunkthunk — as Albert dove out the driver's side and scrambled behind the tree alongside Teddy.

"Oh shit oh shit oh shit," Albert repeated, eyes bulging and face dripping with sweat.

"Easy, Albert," Teddy said. "Just stay here. You're all right."

"Who...who's shooting at us?" Albert asked breathlessly.

"Mario Silva," Teddy replied.

"My neighbor? Holy Jesus. Why?"

"He has suicide bombers trying to get into the Grove, and we're in their way," Teddy answered. "We got Mexicans in football jerseys with suicide vests. They killed Deputy Alice and my partner and at least one Blue Blazer."

Albert frowned and growled, "They what? What? Suicide bombers? Oh, no. Alice? Our Alice?"

"Yeah, Alice."

"And Paul? Oh, shit. Paul?"

"Yeah."

"These are Silva's Mexicans?"

"I don't know who they are, Albert. I haven't had a chance to ask 'em."

More bullets slammed into the Lambo and the tree, making both Albert and Teddy duck and wince.

"I thought you went home," Teddy said, almost as an aside.

"I didn't make it. I fell asleep," Albert explained, peeking around the tree. "You ever done this before?" he asked, pointing at the HK Teddy was holding precariously. "Been in a firefight?"

"Nope," Teddy answered, and he peeked around the other side of the massive redwood.

"See anything?" Albert asked.

"Nope."

"You know," Albert said, blinking heavily several times, "My wife Susan wanted to take you out to dinner last night, but it never happened. So I'm thinkin', maybe we can do it tonight. You like oysters?"

. . . . .

From his perch in Fat Freddie, Butler watched Albert's truck screech to a halt opposite Silva's vineyard, and he flinched when a line of nine millimeter bullets raked the side of the dirty Lambo.

"Hey, Teddy," Butler spoke into his radio. "You okay?"

"Yeah man," Teddy said. "I got Albert here."

"Good," Butler said. "Don't let him do anything stupid. We don't need no heroes."

"Yeah man. No heroes."

"I think there's more hostiles in the bunkhouse and maybe two or three more in the vineyard," Butler said. "Including Silva."

Teddy crawled on his belly around the tree and scanned the neat rows of grape vines. The pinot noir vines were lush bushes, like small hedges, and a man could easily conceal himself behind one, but Teddy could see the edges of a white shirt halfway down the nearest row.

"I think I see one," Teddy said into his headset. "Oh yeah. Oh shit!"

Teddy heard shouts in a language he didn't understand, and then two football jerseys suddenly stood up in the vineyard and charged Teddy's tree, Number Five shooting wildly with an assault rifle and Number Seven running, head down, with no rifle, only a suicide vest laden with C4 under his jersey.

The sun was now completely above the eastern hills and the tops of the giant trees, illuminating the vineyard with the full light of day. Butler was looking into the sun but able to compensate. He saw Number Five fire his Uzi at Teddy's tree, and he saw Teddy shoot back from twenty-five yards. Unfortunately, Agent Swan had spent so little practice time on the range with the automatic HK that his whizzing bullets went over the heads of the two charging jihadis and fell harmlessly to earth a half-mile to the south.

From three hundred yards away Butler squeezed the trigger of the Sharps again and cut down Number Five, Andrés, an eighteen-year-old child of Buenos Aires whose grandparents fled Haifa for Argentina in 1947. Andrés fell into the road, his throat torn away, his lifeless hands inches away from the toggle switch which would detonate his vest. A prayer, unspoken, died on his lips.

Number Seven, Estebán, a native of Lima, Perú, whose parents lost their home to settlers in the West Bank in 1997, kept running toward Teddy and Albert's redwood refuge, screaming gibberish unintelligible in any language. Albert reacted like any good offensive lineman who witnessed an interception. He sprang to his feet and rushed, knees churning in high style, toward the bright red Number Seven, who, ironically, was wearing Albert's collegiate colors.

"Stop!" Teddy shouted. "Albert! Stop!"

"Allahuh akbar!" shrieked Estebán as the unfortunate Albert flattened him by driving the crown of his head into the Peruvian's chest.

Arms flailing, legs flopping, screaming like a voodoo priest, Estebán reached for the toggle switch on his belt, found it and pushed. Eight pounds of C4 wrapped around his torso detonated with an enormous concussion, transforming the intimately mingled Estebán and Albert into a violent mist of red debris, scorching the Lamborghini and gouging a chunk out of Teddy's tree.

.   .   .   .   .

"Oh Jesus," Butler said from his perch as he watched a cloud of dirty smoke from the suicide bomber's explosion drift toward the Bohemian Grove. "Teddy? You all right? I'm coming down," he said as he scrambled into his sling and started his descent from Fat Freddie.

"Oh shit," said Teddy, who was close to hyperventilating. "Oh shit, oh shit. I couldn't stop him. Fuck! I couldn't stop him."

"Listen," Butler said from his sling. "Watch out. Silva's still out there."

Killing human beings with his antique sniper's rifle was not what Butler had in mind earlier in the evening when he took a few photos of Silva's Mexicans. It was not what he had in mind when he took the rifle with him over to Jeremy's. And defending the Bohemian Grove from a shadowy group of suicidal maniacs was most definitely not what he had in mind Friday afternoon when he agreed to cooperate with the FBI. The Pirates had no business getting involved in a war, but here they were. Out of the blue, in less than thirty minutes, eight people were dead, a fucking bloodbath in his back yard. Machine guns! Good lord! And he'd used the Sharps, something he'd sworn never to do. No, sir, this was not what he had in mind, but it was what was in his face. Monte Rio was under attack.

It occurred to Butler that in his life he'd gone from decorated soldier to complete, anti-war pacifist, and in fifteen minutes the pendulum had swung back the other way. In the crash of thoughts careening around his skull, he suddenly had a better understanding of the Vietnamese peasants he'd made war upon so long ago. They were just like him, protecting their homes. The people of Iraq probably felt the same way. There were no simple answers, and in the end there would be no profound understanding, either. One thought emerged from all the others: The fucking Bohemian Grove had been a big, fat target just sitting there for more than a century, a symbol of greed and decadence, an icon of power and wealth, a slap in the face of democracy, fairness and equality, and for that Albert and Alice and Paul had died.

Who was Mario Silva, anyway? Butler wondered. What exactly was happening here? Who were these migrant farm workers in football jerseys and suicide vests? He knew he'd seen more men in the back of Silva's flatbed than came out of the bunkhouse, so where were they? Still in there?

"Teddy," Butler whispered into his headset as the winch lowered him toward the ground, the Sharps across his knees. "I'm coming down. You call the cavalry?"

"Yeah man, but don't expect them any time soon."

"Jeremy?" Butler said. "You listening?"

"Loud and clear."

"Any help on the horizon?"

"The Santa Rosa Police SWAT team and bomb quad are on their way to the Santa Rosa airport. ETA there twenty minutes, then thirty more minutes to the Grove."

"We're on our own, cowboy," Butler said.

. . . . .

Silva watched the last pair of divine soldiers in the vineyard make the painful journey to Paradise. The first, Andrés, was felled by the sniper in the trees, and then Esteban liquidated himself, taking Silva's neighbor Albert with him. You should have kept yourself to yourself, Albert, you nosy bastard.

The boys who remained in the bunkhouse were of no use to him now. As soon as he was a safe distance away, he intended to blow the plastic explosives in the basement, and his South Americans, like Pedro, would never tell their story. Likewise, he intended to destroy his house on River Boulevard with its computer and sewing machine. The FBI would search the wreckage and find the computer, of course, and perhaps even restore its memory, but the incriminating data led to his South American networks, Hezbollah and al-Qaeda, not the Russians, never the Russians.

He swiftly analyzed the situation, reckoned his assets and liabilities, and tried to guess what Boris's next move might be. Boris the unpredictable, Boris the bizarre. Was he still in the Bohemian Grove? Was Boris aware of the threat, and if he was, would he flee? Where would he go? Los Angeles? Minsk? Would he sniff out Antón's part in the scheme? Silva believed that if he could get to the Santa Rosa airport and Antón, he could escape and live to fight another day.

Silva took a deep breath and made a dash for the Explorer, expecting a shot from the sniper that never came. In a few seconds he was in the blue truck, breathing heavily, starting the motor and turning the truck around Alice's body and her police car, its driver's side door still wide open.

He gunned the truck engine and rushed down the lane toward the road and the tree that barricaded the FBI agent.

At the sound of a racing truck motor, the bunkhouse door opened and Number Twelve watched Silva drive away.

. . . . .

"Butler!" Teddy shouted into his headset. "He's coming this way! He's in his truck!"

"Shoot his tires!" Butler hollered back. "Stop him!"

When Teddy stepped out from behind the tree, the truck was a blue dragon thirty yards away and barreling right at him. Behind the driver's wheel, Mario Silva was a fleeting target in a straw cowboy hat and mirrored sunglasses.

Teddy pulled the trigger on the HK and chewed up some dirt in the road and then, as the truck abruptly turned left, stitched a full magazine of bullets into the slab side of the Explorer. As the truck spun its wheels and moved away from him in a cloud of dust, Teddy dropped the assault rifle, pulled out his service Glock pistol and blasted away at the receding SUV, shattering the rear window. As Teddy ran after it, shooting, the truck turned up Richardson's Road toward the spot where the Suburban was parked.

"Butler!" Teddy shouted again. "Butler!"

.   .   .   .   .

Silva ducked under the dash as the side of his truck absorbed a blast of bullets from the FBI agent behind the tree. He turned up Richardson's Road toward the empty red Suburban, guessing that the sniper was down out of the trees by now, but Butler was nowhere in sight. Silva grabbed his phone and speed-dialed the detonators in the bunkhouse and on River Road, thinking those explosions would distract any pursuers, but the phone refused to connect to the local tower. No signal. No nothing.

He had another disposable phone, in a bag on the floor of the truck.

On the steep, rough road the truck was slowing down while he groped for the second phone. The FBI shooter was still behind him and firing his pistol, demolishing the rear window. Silva growled like a frustrated bear, found the second phone, but before he could remember the number he wanted to call, the truck's velocity had dropped almost to zero. He looked up.

Butler suddenly stepped out from behind the Suburban and was standing in the middle of the road right in front of him, not more than ten yards away, holding his old rifle in a shooter's position and sighting right down the barrel at almost point blank range. Silva twisted the wheel to the right, stomped on the gas pedal and tried to hurtle the truck around the old hippie with the vintage rifle, but Butler held his ground and fired. Silva registered the muzzle flash and then the windshield exploded in front of him just as the front bumper of the truck caved in both of Butler's knees. The truck jumped up and over Butler, throwing him aside, then hit a tree and toppled over on its side, engine roaring, wheels spinning.

Butler lay in the road, groaning, moving his head, alive. Teddy ran to the truck, looked inside then reached in and turned off the engine.

The forest was suddenly silent. Then birds chirped. Then the distant sound of Old Man Richardson's howling dogs drifted down the hill.

Silva was dead, the top of his head missing. The interior of the Explorer was bathed in his blood. Flies began to buzz around Silva's warm corpse.

Teddy Swan took a moment to catch his breath. A few feet away, lying in the middle of the rough-hewn road on a bed of ancient, chevron-shaped redwood leaves, Butler was alive but grievously wounded.

"Jeremy," a shaken Teddy said into his headset. "Call the medics in Guerneville. Get an ambulance out here right away. Butler's hurt. Silva ran over him in his fucking truck."

"What happened to Silva?" Jeremy asked.

"He's dead," Teddy said. "Butler shot him."

"The bunkhouse," Butler said, drifting toward unconsciousness. "The bunkhouse."

28

The distant gunfire awakened Yuri just after dawn, and a moment later the bodyguard nudged Boris who stumbled sleepily into the bathroom.

"What do I hear?" asked the president of Belarus as he peed.

"Shooting," Yuri said from the door of the tent. "I hear Uzis and an HK, and explosions that sound like plastique."

"You recognize those guns by the way they sound?" Boris asked, pulling on a shirt and pair of pants.

"Yes."

"I'm impressed," Boris declared, and asked, "What does it mean?"

"This is America," Yuri replied. "Everybody has guns. It could mean anything."

At that moment a slightly disheveled Secret Service agent Raul Rodriguez walked up the path to the guest tent and announced in Russian, "President Demetriov, we have to get you out of here."

"But you spent so much time and energy to get me here and keep me here!"

"I'm sorry, but we have to go," Rodriguez said, opening the screen door.

"Where is my brother?" Boris asked "Where's Dmitri?"

With a smile, Rodriguez replied, "He's probably in the Administration Center trying to make a phone call, but his phone won't work."

"You disrupted the phones? Why?" Boris asked.

"To protect you, Mr. President. We need to get you out of here, right now. Let's go."

Rodriguez bowed courteously and gestured toward the waiting golf cart.

"But...but...but..."

"Now," Rodriguez insisted.

"We'd better go," said Yuri. "We were going to leave, anyway, remember?"

"Okay," Boris said, throwing an arm around Yuri's shoulders. "We were going to a party. Sure, let's go."

Boris and Yuri, both only half dressed, piled into the back of the cart and Rodriguez began driving along the asphalt path that led to the Main Administration Building and the waiting government armored SUVs.

Rodriguez wore an earbud and lapel microphone and was directing the defense of the South Gate while driving this lunatic head of state to safety.

"Agent White, Agent McAllister, assist the Blue Blazers at Cola Three and report back to me. Agent Short, meet me at the Main Service Desk. You'll be driving Caviar."

"Roger that."

"What exactly is happening?" Yuri asked.

"Armed intruders are trying to enter the Grove at the South Gate," Rodriguez said, waving at two of his agents on speedy bicycles heading the other way. "We're not sure how many there are or what their target is, but you have to leave now, for your safety."

"Armed intruders?" Yuri said. "Is that what that noise was?"

"Yes."

"Who are they? American crazies? Gun control crazies?" Yuri asked, unsure of the American politics surrounding weapon possession.

"We don't know who they are, not yet," Rodriguez said.

"Are you going to evacuate the entire camp?" Boris asked.

"We don't know that yet, either," Rodriguez said, knowing full well what a calamity that would be. "I hope not."

Men were wandering out of their camps, listening to the distant gunfire and wondering what was going on. The golf cart arrived at the Main Administration building where the Belarusians could collect their numbered bags with their phones and weapons.

A collection of black, government SUVs was lined up near the service entrance to the parking lot to whisk assorted dignitaries out of danger.

At that moment Dmitri, phone in hand but still in his English dressing gown, rushed up to his brother and beseeched him, "Boris, where are you going? Are you leaving again?"

"Who have you been talking to on your phone, Dmitri?" Rodriguez asked.

"Boris," Dmitri pleaded, ignoring the Secret Service agent, "Come back to the camp."

"He can't," Rodriguez said. "None of you can. You're coming with me."

"Why?" Dmitri wailed. "What's happening?"

Yuri answered, "They say the Grove is under attack."

Dmitri knew it was true and tried to look surprised. His face contorted beyond his control.

"Then give me my gun," he demanded of Rodriguez. "If we're under attack, I want to defend myself."

"Yes, yes," Yuri concurred.

A Bohemian tram pulled up to the Service Center. Accompanied by five men, two of whom were Secret Service, a pair of Saudi princes hustled through the Service Center without stopping for the usual courtesies accorded Boris, a head of state. The Saudis rushed to a black Yukon and were gone in seconds.

Taking advantage of the distraction, Boris took a step back, processing tiny bits of seemingly disparate information like a chess master assembling a delicate defense. Even with enough alcohol still in his bloodstream to waste an army of his enemies, Boris was a shrewd politician and a determined survivor.

"No," he said firmly. "No guns."

"Boss," Yuri said, "something is not right. If I don't have my guns, they could kill you."

"Somebody is trying to kill me, that's for sure," Boris declared, "and I think I know who."

"Do you think it's me?" Yuri asked.

Boris raised an eyebrow, as if he were inspecting his bodyguard with a fine German monocle, and said, "No."

Rodriguez opened the door of the government truck driven by Agent Short, his best driver.

Boris said to Rodriguez, "I have diplomatic immunity, right?"

"Yes."

"For anything?"

"Well, almost anything."

"Okay," Boris said. "Where are you taking me?"

"Agent Short will drive you to your presidential aircraft at Burbank Airport in Los Angeles," Rodriguez replied. "I have to stay here."

"Fine," Boris said, "but we have to make a stop on the way."

Then he whirled around and smashed his fist into his brother's face. "You dog, Dmitri," he sneered, and as Dmitri crumpled to the ground, Boris kicked him and then kicked him again. "You Russian dog."

.   .   .   .   .

Teddy duckwalked through the vineyard toward the bunkhouse, moving cautiously from vine to vine. When he was halfway there, the door opened and a half dozen young men filed out, some in football jerseys, others naked to the waist. They stood at the edge of the vineyard near the flatbed truck and Alice's police car, hands and arms akimbo, nervous and frightened.

"Hands up! Hands up!" Teddy shouted, brandishing one of the shotguns from the Suburban. When nothing happened, he tried Spanish he'd learned from TV. "Manos arriba! Manos arriba!"

Their hands went up. They understood Spanish. Maybe they were Mexicans, but that made no sense. Mexicans didn't become suicide bombers.

He knew he was within range if there was an explosive charge under one of those jerseys, but as long as he could see their hands they probably couldn't detonate. He didn't know how to tell them to take off any vests they might be wearing, and he wasn't sure if that was the right thing to do if he could talk to them. He had to keep them exactly where they were until help arrived, if it arrived.

"Jeremy," he said into his headset. "I got seven Mexicans here. What's happening?"

"The Santa Rosa SWAT and bomb squad are leaving the airport now on a Chinook."

"What about Butler's ambulance?"

"Medics are on their way. They're on the Old Bohemian Highway."

"This is fucked up," Teddy said. "This is all fucked up."

The first to arrive was Barney Richardson who woke up thinking the battle sounds came from another bad dream about the war. His dogs were howling, as hungover and bad-tempered as their master. Barney got dressed, grabbed his shotgun and stumbled down the hill. He didn't have to go very far before he came upon Butler lying in the road and the Explorer turned over on its side. His Mexican neighbor was inside, dead, shot all to hell. There was nothing he could do so he continued on down the hill to the vineyard.

Teddy saw him walking up the lane, the double-barreled twelve gauge L.C. Smith in his good arm and against his shoulder. Richardson stopped next to Deputy Alice's bullet-ridden body and stared at her.

"Jesus Christ," he said quietly. "Is that Alice?"

"Yes, sir," Teddy replied.

"Hey," Richardson said to Teddy Swan. "You're the federal fed my dogs, ain'tcha?"

"Yes, Barney," Teddy answered. "That's right."

"What the hell is going on here?" Richardson demanded. "Butler Rhodes is up there all fucked up, and that Mexican is in his truck with his head damn near blown off. We got illegal aliens here? You ain't the Migra, are you? Did they kill Alice?"

He waved his shotgun in the direction of the nervous and confused young men huddled near the bunkhouse door.

"FBI," Teddy said and repeated, "FBI. Put the shotgun down, Barney." He turned his weapon on the wannabe martyrs and snarled, "Manos arriba! Manos arriba!"

A pair of Blue Blazer Hummers appeared from the direction of the South Gate and stopped at the foot of the lane. Four men with shotguns assembled at the foot of the lane, unsure what to do since they were off the reservation.

Rodriguez finally arrived in a golf cart, drove past the Blue Blazers and up the lane to where Teddy Swan and Barney Richardson held a half dozen young men under armed guard.

"Is this all of them?" Rodriguez asked.

"I don't know," Teddy replied. "I haven't been inside."

Then they all heard the ambulance coming over the hill, siren shrieking, and then the helicopter roared overhead and within minutes the little ravine between the Bohemian Grove and Richardson's Hill was swarming with armed men in body armor and full military regalia.

The bomb squad went inside the bunkhouse, found the unexploded vests and the C4 embedded in the walls, and deactivated all the explosives. Ambulances carried Alice to the morgue and Butler to the hospital in Santa Rosa.

Rodriguez began the interrogation of the captured young men by asking, "¿Quien eres?" Who are you?

"*Las Pumas de Paraguay*," said the living martyr called Tomás. "*Jugamos a fútbol.*" We are the Wildcats of Paraguay. We play football!

.   .   .   .   .

From his plane at the airport in Santa Rosa, Antón had observed the swarm of police cars around the National Guard hangar and heard the helicopter take off. Silva had at least provoked a reaction, and it was time to depart the Russian River valley. Silva had his own exit scheme, and the fat Russian would learn the results soon enough.

He knocked on the door to the cockpit, and the pilot stuck her head out.

"Let's go," he said.

"Mexico City?"

"Yes."

The jet turbines began their shrill music, and just as the plane started to move, they heard the squeal of tires. A huge, black Yukon SUV was speeding toward them past rows of Gulfstreams and Lears.

Antón wasn't going to put up with any official nonsense, but the SUV stopped right in front of his plane, causing the pilot to hit the brakes. A rear door in the truck opened and a severely beaten but alive Dmitri Demetriov was pushed sprawling onto the asphalt. The door slammed and the SUV roared away.

Antón stared through the portholes of his jet at Dmitri and knew he had lost. Boris lived. Silva and his jihadis had failed. It was going to cost him millions. He frowned, calmly considered his options and lit a cigar.

"Get him," he said to Mikhail. "We'll take him with us. Perhaps we can sell him back to Boris."

EPILOGUE

Time stopped making sense. Butler didn't know how long he'd been in the hospital, two days or two weeks. Both his legs were in plaster casts and held up by traction. His chest was sore, and the doctors told him he'd broken some ribs and punctured a lung and he'd better not smoke anymore.

Maggie and Susan stayed in his room for days, sitting next to each other on a love seat, holding each other and crying on each other's shoulder until they were dehydrated. One day they left for Alice's funeral, and the next day they went to Albert's funeral, and afterward they came back and cried some more.

Betty, Alice's wife, came by with a flag presented to her by the Sheriff's Department at Alice's funeral. She gave the flag to Butler and had a good cry with Susan and Maggie.

Jeremy and Phillip wandered in at all hours. Jeremy had a recording of Albert's big laugh, and when he played it everybody in the room laughed with Albert, and then they cried some more. Nurses, doctors, and medical technicians came in and went about their business, and even Barney Richardson came by with a card signed by members of the local Veterans lodge.

Teddy Swan came and sat and answered the questions he could. He didn't have many answers.

None of the hostiles, as Butler called them, or bad guys, as Teddy called them, got into the Bohemian Grove. No Boho was injured or inconvenienced in any way. Except in the few camps near the South Gate, like Ye Olde Owls, most Bohemians slept through the incident and later were told wild tales about alleged intruders.

Who was Silva? Nobody knew for sure. Teddy told Butler that DNA analysis identified him as definitely not Mexican. He was mostly Middle Eastern, with European, African, and Jewish markers. He could have been anybody from anywhere.

In the bunkhouse the Santa Rosa bomb squad and FBI specialists from San Francisco managed to disarm the explosives in the walls and the unused suicide vests. The plastique was all high-quality C4 of American manufacture, but so far no one had been able to trace its provenance. The FBI also dismantled the explosive charges in Silva's house on River Boulevard and searched the property. They found American, Mexican, Panamanian, and Paraguayan passports, a little over a half million dollars in cash, and credit card accounts that led to extensive travels in South America. It was going to take months to unravel it all, but so far all indications pointed to radical imams and terrorist networks in South America.

Who were the Mexican migrant farm workers? Teddy said they made videos and left passports. They were from four different South American countries: Paraguay, Argentina, Peru and Venezuela, and they were all Muslims from families that had emigrated from the Middle East, from Lebanon, Palestine, Syria and Iraq. That didn't make a whole lot of sense, but in a thoroughly globalized world, what did make sense? Not much. Sonoma County Social Services had the survivors in a halfway house in Santa Rosa, holding them until Immigration and Customs decided what to do with them.

Paul Kruger's remains, carefully collected and identified by a forensic team, were shipped to his mother in Phoenix for military burial. He was thirty-four years old when he died in the line of duty. Teddy was going to accompany the coffin to Arizona.

George Gleason, the veteran Blue Blazer who died with Paul, was buried in Cloverdale with full military honors.

Butler was glad he didn't have to go to all the funerals. When he closed his eyes, he saw young men being blown apart by his bullets. Nothing was easy. Nothing would ever be quite right again.

When the hospital room got too crowded with visitors, Butler thanked everybody, hit the morphine button and pretended to go to sleep. It was easier to sort out loose ends that way.

Did the guy come pick up the owl? Maggie said yes, he left a check, and the owl was now in his garden in Pacific Heights.

Were the Bohemians still partying and carrying on? Naturally. Were Phillip and Jeremy still spying on the Bohos? No. Did they get paid by the FBI? Not yet.

Were Albert's affairs in order? No, they were a mess, but Susan was okay, financially if not emotionally. In Alice's case, however, everything was tidy and taken care of. Alice owned several apartment buildings in Santa Rosa and had put everything in a living trust fund for Betty.

Finally, Teddy brought in Carter McGee and Raul Rodriguez. Even Daniel Belinski came to the hospital and stood silently just inside the door.

"Did you know Amory Hix is in the next room?" Teddy asked.

"No. Really?" Butler smiled.

"It's true," Maggie said. "They say he may recover."

"Well," Butler declared. "Ain't life grand! Ain't it just grand?"

THE END